The Night Of Knives

Also by the same author

Trail of the Dead
The Blood Price
Invisible Armies

JON EVANS

The Night of Knives

HODDER &
STOUGHTON

First published in Great Britain in 2007 by Hodder & Stoughton
An Hachette Livre UK company

1

A CIP catalogue record for this title is available from the British Library

Hardback ISBN 978 0 34089608 2
Trade Paperback ISBN 978 0 340 89609 9

Typeset in Sabon by Hewer Text UK Ltd, Edinburgh
Printed and bound by Clays Ltd, St Ives Plc

Hodder & Stoughton policy is to use papers that are natural, renewable
and recyclable products and made from wood grown in sustainable
forests. The logging and manufacturing processes are expected to
conform to the environmental regulations of the country of origin.

Hodder & Stoughton Ltd
338 Euston Road
London NW1 3BH

www.hodder.co.uk

To Kate

I Congo

1

'I think something's wrong,' Susan says.

It takes some time for the words to trickle into Veronica's mind. She is too busy breathing to pay much attention to anything outside her body. Her lungs feel on fire, her feet are alive with blisters, her mind is lost in a fog of exhaustion. She doesn't even think to wonder why they have stopped until she registers the concern in Susan's voice.

Veronica lifts her head, looks around, tries to re-engage with the world. It seems like they have been trekking for ever in this damp heat, up this steep and muddy trail. They are still in deep jungle. Montane rainforest, technically, but it feels like jungle, in the most alien and forbidding sense of the word. There is a reason this is called the Impenetrable Forest. The vegetation here is so violently, densely fecund that even the greenery has greenery: roots and branches are covered by moss, vines hang on vines, the boulders that dot the trail look like verdant hillocks. Leaves and ferns glisten with water from recent rain. Birds chirp, monkeys hoot, water burbles, clouds of pure-white butterflies flutter through the damp air. Only a few shafts of light fall through the massive canopy trees into the dense thickets below.

Ahead of them a walkie-talkie emits a burst of static, followed by a half-dozen sentences in some African language. Their guide holds the walkie-talkie close to his ear. In his other hand he holds his panga, a viciously curved machete. He looks carved out of ebony, short and powerfully built. After a pause he pushes his radio's red Talk button and speaks in a slow and careful voice. Veronica can't remember his name. Something biblical.

'What happened?' she asks Susan. 'Why did we stop?'

The blonde British girl shrugs. 'I don't know. I think he saw something. On the ground.'

Veronica looks down and sees nothing but mud and underbrush. But then she is a city girl, while their guide has spent decades tracking gorillas through this rainforest – he can probably deduce volumes from a broken twig she wouldn't even notice. She had total faith in him when they departed park headquarters, he seemed so tough and self-assured. Now his voice sounds uncertain.

She looks around at the others. The Canadians, Derek and Jacob, are about ten feet away. Derek stands erect, breathing easily, his lean and muscled body already ready for further exertions. She can see the dragon tattoo coiled around his left bicep. Veronica has hardly admitted it to herself, much less anyone else, but Derek is the real reason she is here. Jacob is beside him, his pale, lanky, goateed form doubled over with hands on knees, gasping for air. Veronica feels sorry for him, but also grateful that she is not their foursome's weakest link. Susan looks like a model, willowy and fine boned, and Veronica expected her to wilt like a fragile flower; but it seems she's tough, too.

The rest of their gorilla group is far enough behind to be invisible, but Veronica can hear the rustling of the hanging vines and underbrush as they catch up. The Brits appear first, Tom and Judy, slow and portly and middle aged but surprisingly durable. They look like they're still enjoying themselves. Diane and Michael behind them do not. The two fiftysomething Americans are thin but not fit, and Diane in particular looks haggard. The Ugandan guards bring up the rear, two men in camouflage uniforms with scary-looking rifles slung over their shoulders.

'What's this, then? Elijah finally call for a tea break?' Tom asks, hoarse but cheerful. Elijah is their guide's name, Veronica

4

remembers. 'Why start now, just when we're having so much fun?'

'We don't know yet.' Susan too is British, but her clipped upper-class accent is entirely unlike Tom and Judy's broad syllables. 'He saw something on the ground.'

'Gorilla dung?' Judy asks, excited.

Susan frowns. 'I don't think so.'

'Then what?'

Elijah's walkie-talkie crackles with new life, and everyone goes quiet.

'What's the story, mate?' Tom asks, when the disembodied voice falls silent.

Elijah shakes his head. 'Silence, I beg you. Give me silence.'

His low singsong voice is hypnotic. They obey. Elijah turns in a slow circle, peering intently into the jungle, so dark and overgrown it feels almost more like a cave than a forest. The idea makes Veronica uneasy. She doesn't like confined spaces.

Veronica glances back at the guards in time to see them exchange a tense glance. A tendril of anxiety slithers into her gut and begins to tighten into an icy knot. Susan was right. Something is wrong.

Elijah completes his rotation, considers for a moment, and says quietly, 'We must turn back.'

It is Michael, outraged, who breaks the silence. 'What? No. We can't go back now.'

'You may return tomorrow.'

'No. Out of the question. We have to go to Kampala tomorrow, we've got a flight the next day. We are absolutely not going back now. We've already climbed an hour, we're already here. They can't be far away now. You said it would only be an hour.'

'Really, Michael, if he thinks it's better—' Diane begins, looking like she wishes she had never come to Africa.

He cuts her off. 'We paid four hundred dollars each, for a full hour with these gorillas, and we're going to stay here until we find them. You can bring these other folks back tomorrow. My wife and I need to see them *today*.'

Veronica winces. She hates being around Americans like Michael, the ugly tourists who give her country a bad name. Elijah is wholly responsible for their collective well-being, in this jungle literally on the edge of civilization, and Michael is berating him as he would a dishonest taxi driver. He reminds Veronica of her ex-husband Danton at his worst. She wants to shout at him but knows it wouldn't improve the situation.

Elijah doesn't answer directly. Instead he barks out something in an African language, and both guards unsling their rifles. Michael takes a step back, eyes wide, as if they might respond to his demands with gunfire.

Elijah says, 'We go back, all of us, now.'

'What's going on? Poachers?' Derek sounds icily calm.

'Yes, poachers,' Elijah agrees quickly. 'Now *go*.'

The group turns around and begins to retrace its steps, moving fast, any remaining reluctance snuffed out by the sight of readied weapons. They move through silence; the birds and monkeys have all ceased their chatter. Veronica is right behind the guards. She can see the tension in their muscles, and feel her heart thumping rapidly inside her ribcage. She tells herself that nothing will happen, this has nothing to do with her. Just poachers hunting gorillas, they won't come after tourists, and even if that were to happen, they have two armed guards with them, they'll be fine.

She jumps as the silence is broken by a loud *crack* from somewhere within the jungle. It sounds like the breaking of a sturdy branch. Veronica thinks she might have seen a camera flash. One of the guards twitches, slips on the mud and falls face first only a few feet ahead of her.

'Stop!' Elijah shouts. He sounds alarmed now. Frightened. 'Fall down! Fall down, all of you!'

None of them obeys. Veronica turns to stare at him, unsure that she even heard him correctly: *fall down*? Elijah's eyes are wide and he is waving his arm violently as if miming a falling tree. He grabs

Jacob by the shoulder and actually shoves him to the ground. Beside him, without further encouragement, Derek drops gracefully into a push-up position. Tom, Judy, Michael and Diane, closer to the guards, stand frozen in place.

Veronica turns back towards the fallen man. An awful notion has birthed in her mind. The world seems to be moving in slow motion. His uniform is now thickly stained by a dark liquid, and he is twitching erratically, like some kind of broken machine. The other guard seems to have disappeared into the jungle.

'Down!' Derek shouts. 'Everyone get down!'

The fallen guard's breath is fast and shallow, blood is seeping from his torso into the dark mud beneath him. Back at park headquarters, only an hour ago, Tom and Judy started talking to him, and he told them proudly he had five children. Veronica knows she should try to help him. She is the only person here with medical training. But she doesn't move.

Another hollow *crack* erupts from the jungle, louder and closer than the last, from where the other guard disappeared. It is followed quickly by two more, even louder, even closer. Veronica slowly starts to back away from the fallen guard, telling herself it's too late, she can't do anything for him. Then she sees movement in the greenery beyond him, less than ten feet away, and she freezes again.

A levelled rifle emerges from the jungle, held by a short and wiry man dressed in rubber boots, ragged khaki shorts and a black Tupac Shakur T-shirt. His face is marked with vertical scars. His gun is aimed directly at Veronica; she can look right down the dark eye of its barrel.

Foliage rustles like paper as other intruders advance through the shadowed jungle all around. The pungent scent of gunpowder fills the air. Veronica stares disbelievingly at the gunman before her, as if he might be a hallucination. She feels very cold.

2

The intruder stoops to take the fallen guard's rifle. He is so close Veronica could take a single step forward and touch his hand. She feels paralysed, barely able to breathe. He takes the weapon and stands straight again, waiting for something.

Veronica forces herself to move, to turn her head and look at the others. There are more intruders among them, she can't tell how many but the jungle seems alive with motion, there must be at least eight or ten. Most look similar to the man who stands an arm's length away from her, but two of them are much smaller, like children. All of them are armed. Banana-shaped ammunition clips protrude from their battered wood-and-iron rifles.

Two of those weapons are pointed at Elijah. He and the rest of the gorilla group seem to have turned into statues. The one exception is Derek, who as Veronica watches draws himself up slowly from his push-up position into a tense crouch. His eyes dart in all directions, as if looking for an avenue of escape, but one of the smaller intruders watches him carefully, keeps his weapon aimed straight at Derek's heart.

She hears a slithering sound behind her and turns to see two more intruders dragging the other guard out of the jungle by his legs. His limp arms trail behind him like loaves of bread. His face is masked with dripping blood and somehow distorted. Veronica can't make out exactly what happened to it and doesn't want to.

She knows she should be terrified, but she feels more horror than fear. She is not yet frightened for herself, not in her blood and bones. So far it is all too dreamlike, too strange, surreal and silent. It feels like everyone is playing a part, going through motions scripted for them long ago. Surely this performance will soon be over and everyone involved will go back to their regularly scheduled lives.

The guard lying before her stops breathing. It is nothing like a movie death scene, it is far more stark and simple.

One of the intruders speaks. She can't see his face – he is aiming his gun at Elijah, keeping his back to Veronica. The words are in an African language. Elijah hesitates. He looks thoughtful. Then he pushes the red Talk button on the walkie-talkie and begins to speak quickly. About ten words in he is silenced by a loud burst of gunfire like a whole string of firecrackers going off.

Veronica closes her eyes involuntarily against the bright flashes. When she opens them again Elijah lies dead or dying on the ground, his rag-doll body torn by a dozen wounds. It takes her a moment to understand. He was told to put down the walkie-talkie, or maybe to tell it reassuring lies, and instead he told park headquarters what was happening, and was killed for it.

The man who spoke to Elijah, and then murdered him, starts barking new orders. He sounds angry, thwarted. Veronica cries out with pain and dismay as the intruder standing above grabs her arm and half drags, half leads her to their leader. The rest of the gorilla group is similarly escorted, arranged into a rough line, then forced to kneel in the damp undergrowth.

None of them dares to resist. This doesn't feel unreal any more. It feels very real and very immediate. It feels like they are all about to die. Veronica doesn't know what to do, she can't think, she feels weak and sick, as if she has the flu. Her mind seems stuck in neutral, unable to move.

'We have money,' Michael says weakly. He pulls his money belt out and tugs open its zip with fumbling fingers. 'You can have it. American passports. Everything. You can have it all.'

The intruders' leader takes two quick steps towards him and kicks him in the stomach like a soccer player taking a free kick. Michael doubles over and makes gagging noises. Money spills from his hands. Diane begins to shriek, but tentatively, she is panting and can't get enough air into her lungs to really scream, and when the man who kicked her husband turns menacingly towards her, she chokes and falls silent.

There are men behind them now. Veronica feels strong hands on her arms, dragging them behind her back, pulling them together. Then she feels rope against her wrists. A bolt of panic surges through her. She will be utterly helpless, she has to do something – but there is nothing to be done. The rope tightens, is knotted. Hands fumble at her waistband. She fears she is going to be stripped and gang-raped right there, but she is soon released. The man goes on to Jacob beside her. He too looks sick with terror.

'It's going to be OK,' Derek murmurs to her. He manages to sound a little as if he means it, even though his arms too have just been bound behind him.

'*Silence*,' the leader hisses at him, pronouncing it the French way.

Derek nods, but it's a nod of acceptance, not submission. Veronica is glad she is beside him. He seems to radiate strength.

Soon they are all bound, and all connected by lengths of yellow rope tied to their belt loops, a poor man's chain gang. Veronica wriggles her hands and tries to straighten her arms, but the knot on her wrists is tight and secure, there is no escape. The position of her arms is uncomfortable and her shoulders have already begun to ache.

'*Allez*,' the leader says, and then in accented English, 'We go. We go fast.'

He begins to pull them to their feet. Veronica dares to look directly at him for the first time. He is big even for Africa, over six feet tall and broad shouldered. His cheeks are marked with vertical scars. What was once his right eye is now an empty crater of scar tissue. His face is drawn into a tight expression, as if he is in pain. Like the rest of his men, he carries a gun on his back and a panga dangling from his belt; unlike them, he also bears a looped-up whip that makes him look a little like a black Indiana Jones.

Once they are all on their feet, he and three of his men begin to lead their roped-together prisoners off the trail and into the underbrush. Derek is at the front of the chain, and Veronica second. The other four abductors follow, leaving the three dead men behind. One of the small men acts as navigator, guiding everyone else through the opaque jungle. He's maybe four foot six, but he has a goatee. It takes Veronica a moment to understand. Not a child. An adult pygmy. His features are finer than those of the larger men, his skin is lighter, and he marches barefoot through the jungle. The trail he leads them along, if it is a trail, is entirely invisible, but somehow they avoid the worst of the tangled vines and dense undergrowth, and the men in front rarely have to use their pangas.

Veronica remembers sitting in her Kampala office and reading Wikipedia articles about the Impenetrable Forest, just after she accepted Derek's invitation to come along on this weekend expedition. According to Wikipedia, pygmies used to live here, until the Ugandan government expelled them in favour of the jungle's more lucrative denizens, the gorillas. Now the pygmies are the lowest of Uganda's low, despised and dispossessed. She remembers how hearing Derek's voice made her a little dizzy and light headed, when he called and invited her to come. The memory is so vivid it is almost like she is actually back in Kampala.

She tries to drag herself back to the present, but her mind is buzzing like an insect trapped in a jar, constantly ricocheting in new directions, bouncing again and again off the sheer terrifying enormity of what just happened. Nobody speaks as they move westwards, along the ridge instead of up it. It isn't as physically difficult as climbing, but the muddy ground is slick and uneven, especially when they cross little streams, and keeping her balance is a real challenge with her arms tied behind her back. Veronica never appreciated before how much her arms contributed to walking. Her legs are already tired, and soon she is sweating and breathing hard again. The exertion clouds her mind, but in a strange way also makes it easier to think, absorbs some of the white-noise panic that at first drowned out any coherent thought.

They are travelling west, towards the Congo border. That makes awful sense. This national park is right on the Uganda–Congo frontier, and the eastern provinces of the Congo are among the few places on earth with no real government, home to a civil war that began almost a decade ago and still simmers despite the presence of UN peacekeepers. These men must have come from that land of lawless anarchy to capture white tourists. The thought gives Veronica hope. Even if rescue doesn't arrive, these men will want to ransom their victims, that is why they have been captured and not simply killed and looted. She is helpless, but at least she is valuable.

Ahead of her, Derek slips on mud; and as he turns to right himself, he twists his head and mutters to her, 'We need to slow down and mark the trail. Pass it on.'

He keeps walking, a little more slowly now. Veronica understands. It will take at least half an hour for a rescue party to get from park headquarters to where they were ambushed. Then their rescuers will have to follow this hidden pygmy route through dense jungle. That will take time and luck; they need to help with both.

She waits for a few moments; then she too feigns a slip and fall, a feint that nearly becomes the real thing, and uses her recovery to whisper the message to Jacob. She hopes he understood. She hardly needs to tell Jacob to slow down, his breath is already ragged, and the rope connecting their belts keeps tugging her back. She suspects Michael and Diane, farther back, are in worse condition yet.

The leader stops and turns to his captives, hand on the hilt of his panga. '*Vite*,' he says angrily. 'Fast. Fast.'

Veronica knows she shouldn't speed up, but sheer physical fear propels her. Derek alone ignores the angry exhortation, and she nearly bumps into him. The leader drops back, grabs Derek by the collar of his shirt and pulls him along for a little while. Derek has to scramble to keep his footing. He is released with a warning look. At first he continues at this faster pace; then, by degrees, he begins to slow down again. Veronica follows his lead.

After a while they are all told to stop. A man walks along the line of prisoners and pours a few swallows of water into the mouth of each from a big two-litre plastic bottle that once contained Coca-Cola. Then the march resumes. Her shoulders hurt, the rope is beginning to chafe her wrists, and she is helpless against the jungle's swarming, buzzing insects; her exposed skin is already mottled with itching bug bites.

Soon they reach a wide and shallow stream. The pygmy leads them straight into the water and then uphill, along the stream. Veronica winces. She has read about this kind of thing in books. The water will wash their tracks out of this muddy stream bed and make pursuit almost impossible – they won't even leave a scent to follow.

Derek manages to reach into his back pocket with his bound hands and unearth his wallet. He slips and falls into the water – and in doing so, tosses his wallet into the shallows at the edge of the stream. Veronica's heart lifts. If rescuers find it they will at least know to go upstream. Derek bounces up quickly from his contrived fall, and looks down to the ground as he keeps walking, ignoring their captors' leader's one-eyed glare.

A few minutes later, the other pygmy runs up alongside the chain of prisoners. This second pygmy holds Derek's dripping wallet. The one-eyed man takes it without even breaking stride, the second pygmy rushes back to his position at the back of the column, and Veronica groans aloud with dashed hope.

They crest the ridge, and soon afterwards turn back to the right, heading west again. The sun is now high above them. Its light is mostly swallowed up by the canopy trees, but the heat is growing intense. Behind her Jacob is lurching more than walking, wheezing with every breath.

The one-eyed leader rounds on them again. 'Fast! Fast!'

They speed up a little, but he still looks unhappy. Then, as they are traversing a particularly steep stretch, Jacob slips on something and falls. He slides far enough down the slope that Veronica and Susan, his neighbours in the human chain, are pulled to the ground, and Derek and Judy beyond nearly follow. Jacob lies gasping in a cluster of huge ferns until two of their captors pull him forcefully to his feet.

The one-eyed man considers Jacob for a moment, expressionless, then motions them all to continue. Jacob manages to stumble along farther. It is Diane who falls next, second to last in the chain. She lies weeping in the mud, doesn't even try to get up. The one-eyed man stalks over to her.

'Up,' he commands. 'Up!'

'I can't.' Diane looks up at her tormentor. Her face and bottle-blonde hair are smeared with mud and tears. Earlier Veronica thought she was maybe fifty. Now she looks older. 'Please, for God's sake, I just can't.'

'Let her go,' Michael says desperately. He too seems to have aged ten years in the last half-hour. 'You don't need her. Take me and let her go.'

The one-eyed man ignores him. He stoops towards Diane, grabs her bound wrists and lifts. Veronica winces. Diane screams with new agony as her shoulders are wrenched in their sockets. Somehow she manages to scramble to her feet.

'You see?' the leader says. His alien accent sounds half French, half African. 'Yes you can. Yes you will.'

For a second Veronica crazily imagines him as a power-of-positive-thinking public speaker, and almost giggles. Then he starts to pull Diane's shirt off her.

'No,' Michael says, his eyes wide. 'No, please, that's not necessary. We'll go fast. I promise.'

Again he is ignored. Diane's shirt is pulled over her head, and back along her bound arms, revealing a pale, wrinkled body and a white sports bra. The one-eyed man's hand drops to his belt and draws out his panga.

'No!' Michael starts forward – but another man, the one in the Tupac Shakur T-shirt, casually grabs Michael's arms from behind, holding him back, and then stoops, reaches between Michael's legs and squeezes his testicles hard. Michael gasps; his body contorts as if he has been shocked with a thousand volts. The man keeps squeezing and twisting, his face expressionless, a man doing an undesirable but necessary job. Michael drops to his knees, whimpering pathetically, writhing helplessly, lost in agony, his wife forgotten. His eyes are completely white; the pupils have rolled back into his head.

Veronica stares with horror as the one-eyed man severs Diane's bra with his machete. Diane's weeping intensifies into a kind of breathless ululation. He replaces his panga and unfurls his whip, made of some kind of thick leather cut into a helical shape, like a stretched-out phone cord. Another of his men takes a position in front of Diane, forces her down on to her knees and forehead, then lifts up her arms as far as they will go, exposing her back. The whip whistles through the air and smacks into Diane's upper back. The impact doesn't sound that forceful, but it wrenches a howl of amazed agony from Diane's throat, a cry more animal than human. Her whole body arches and writhes, instinctively and futilely seeking escape; her legs scrabble feebly at the ground as the whip pulls back and immediately strikes again, catching the scream in Diane's throat, reducing it to a series of choking whimpers.

Derek steps up behind Veronica, close enough to touch, and she starts with surprise. He murmurs, 'On the front of my belt there's a Leatherman. Try to get it and pass it back to me. Not now. We're being watched.'

Veronica turns and looks, sees the little leather pouch on Derek's belt, and the pygmy guide watching them carefully. She turns back in time to see Diane and Michael released. Michael crumples head first to the ground as if kowtowing. The one-eyed man coils up the whip, restores it to his belt loop, steps forward to the moaning, weeping heap that is Diane, grabs her by her hair and pulls her back upright. As she staggers to her feet Veronica momentarily sees that two red lines have been carved across her back. Both are already dripping blood along their length.

'Fast,' the leader warns her, 'or I give you more. Ten, twenty, fifty. Fast.'

Diane, sobbing for breath, does not respond, but the one-eyed man seems satisfied. He nudges Michael's face with his muddy rubber boot and commands, 'Up.'

Michael obeys with a moan. His lined face is wet with tears. The one-eyed man walks back up the chain of prisoners. He nods at Tom and Judy, as if with approval. He stops in front of Susan for a moment, grabs a handful of her blonde hair, carefully inspects her chiselled face. Susan is rigid with terror. After a moment the man smirks and moves on to Jacob.

'Fast,' he warns him.

'*Vite*,' Jacob agrees breathlessly. '*J'ai compris.*'

The one-eyed man raises his eyebrows. '*Tu parles français?*'

'*Un peu.*'

Veronica is next. She looks away as he approaches, but doesn't move. She tells herself, be nondescript, don't make him notice you, be the grey woman, the girl who isn't there. But when he reaches out to touch her face, she instinctively recoils, takes a step away. His expression darkens. He grabs a handful of her hair and twists so hard that she whimpers and tears fill her eyes. He pulls her head back savagely, traces the fingers of his other hand down her cheek. They feel like sandpaper. He is smiling. She sees to her horror that his incisors have been filed into sharp points, like a vampire's.

'*Les sauvages Congolaise,*' Derek says scornfully. '*Les bêtes d'Afrique. Vraiment, les Belges avaient raison.*'

Immediately Veronica is released. The man spins towards Derek, finishes the movement by punching him in the stomach. Derek falls backwards to the ground, groaning loudly, crumpling into a ball. The one-eyed man stoops, grabs Derek's wrists and pulls him painfully back to a standing position. Veronica knows he took that punch for her, spoke up as a distraction.

'*Je suis pas stupide,*' the one-eyed man warns him. '*Je te vois.*' Then he turns to the others. 'Fast. Fast, *vous comprenez?* You understand? We have no need of you all. You go fast now or you die.'

3

Jacob's scream is brief but blood-curdling, a high-pitched wail torn from his throat. He fights for freedom, his whole body thrashing, his face a twisted animal mask, but the men on either side are too strong for him, they hold him down. The one-eyed man draws the whip back with a casual and graceful movement. Veronica closes her eyes tightly, she doesn't want to look. She is close enough to feel the slipstream as the whip snaps through the air. Jacob howls four more times.

Then Derek says, sharply, 'No!'

Veronica opens her eyes. Jacob's head has been pulled back by one of the pygmies, and the one-eyed man has his panga to the lanky Canadian's throat, pressing hard enough that blood trickles from the line of contact. Veronica knows it won't take much more force to puncture Jacob's jugular vein. Derek's every muscle is taut as he stands beside her; he looks like he wants to throw himself at the one-eyed man.

'Please,' Jacob gasps, his body perfectly still. 'Please, no, don't kill me, please, I'll be fast, I won't fall down, I promise. Please, I swear to God, please, *please.*'

After a long moment the one-eyed man withdraws the panga, leaving a thin line of blood behind. Reluctance is evident on his face. Jacob fights his way to his feet. Derek relaxes a little.

'No more stops,' the one-eyed man hisses.

He angrily waves them onwards. The endless march resumes. Veronica trudges on painfully. She doesn't doubt that the one-eyed man is now ready, even eager, to kill anyone who slows them down.

Her shoulders are burning with agony, she is sure that by now they have actually been damaged. They aren't really walking that fast any more, they physically can't, but no matter how deeply she inhales she just can't get enough oxygen, this air seems almost too thick and damp to breathe. A crippling headache has grown behind her eyes. At least the blisters that line her feet have finally gone numb.

She doesn't want to die here. That is all she can focus on, the only thing that gives her strength. Maybe she will be killed when they reach their destination; maybe they will do things to her so terrible she will wish she had died on this march; but right now, it seems like the worst thing in the world, the most awful possible fate, to be murdered and left to rot here in this jungle.

What worries her most are her legs. She can't help thinking about the time she witnessed the home stretch of the Los Angeles Marathon, saw runners collapse less than half a mile from the end of the race because their legs simply stopped working. She thinks she may not be far from that point. She is limping badly, her left leg is cramping painfully, and her right leg worries her even more. It doesn't exactly hurt, but she doesn't think it can physically last much longer. Soon it will buckle beneath her and she will no longer be capable of walking.

At some point they stop for a water break. She can't remember how long it has been since the last one – time seems to have warped and melted as in that famous Dali painting. She looks up and her heart wilts. Through the curtain of canopy trees she sees the sun directly above them, obscured by a few fast-moving clouds. It's only noon. She won't make it to nightfall, not even close. Beside her, Jacob looks even worse than she does, confused and dazed. His eyes seem to have lost the ability to focus.

'I can't make it,' Veronica says dully.

Derek turns to her. Even he looks drained now, but his voice is still strong. 'Yes you can. It won't be much farther. We must be over the border by now. You'll be fine.'

She tries to laugh but it comes out as a whimper. 'I sure don't feel fine.'

'You will be. I promise.'

She manages a sick caricature of a smile. 'Thanks.'

'Breathe deep, into your belly. It helps.'

She nods and tries to follow his advice. After a few dozen inhalations it occurs to her that the water break should be over, the one-eyed man should be harrying them onwards. She looks around. Their abductors are staring warily into the sky, and there is a faint sound in the distance, odd yet familiar.

'Helicopter,' Derek breathes, and as he speaks she too recognizes the growing *whopwhopwhop*.

The one-eyed man issues a curt command. Someone grabs Veronica from behind and pushes her down. She doesn't need much encouragement to lie face down; taking her weight from her tortured feet is bliss. The mud is smooth and damp on her cheek, the earth smells rich and full of life.

The helicopter noise grows until it is directly overhead. Veronica wants to just stay where she is and rest, but she makes herself roll to her side and look up. The aircraft is flying low over the jungle, almost directly overhead, hanging in the sky like a huge white insect. The letters UN are written in blue on its side. She wonders whether it is a regular flight from the peacekeeping mission in the Congo, or if it is searching for them. That's possible. Eight abducted Western tourists will be big news, worldwide headlines.

She tries to hope, but she knows the helicopter won't see them. From above, this jungle looks like an opaque sea of green. But at least it's a sign that maybe someone is trying to rescue them. Maybe a group of park guards and Ugandan soldiers is trying to follow their trail right now. Maybe the rescue mission has pygmies too. Maybe they'll be here any moment now. If only they could somehow signal the helicopter, start a fire or something. There is a cigarette lighter in the half-empty pack of Marlboro Lights in the side pocket of Veronica's cargo pants.

She can feel the pack against her leg. She should have told Derek, he could have got it out, as he told her to get his Leatherman. But it's not like they could start a fire with these damp ferns and dripping vines anyway.

The helicopter drifts across the sky. Its noise diminishes. After a few minutes the prisoners are dragged back to their feet. Veronica whimpers as she is forced to start walking again. Her legs and lungs feel a little stronger, but her headache has grown so vicious it's making her dizzy, and the blisters on her feet have come back to life and are singing with renewed agony. If only she had broken in her new hiking boots before coming to Africa. If only they had not been kidnapped.

Veronica has given up any hope of this journey ever ending; she focuses now only on getting through the next few steps, and then the next few, and then the next. She seems to be losing sensation in her legs, but that must be a good thing, because the sensation is mostly pain. Her shoulders keep getting worse, and she is starting to feel pins and needles in her hands. Worst of all is her thirst. They are never given enough water. The searing pain behind her eyes is almost blinding now. She is vaguely aware this is probably from dehydration. Behind her Jacob is moaning with every breath.

They stumble forward in a collective stupor. Veronica slips and falls several times on the uneven ground, all of them do, but they are all quick to get up as soon as possible. Even in the abyss of their exhaustion they know that tardiness will be met with torture or murder.

Eventually she becomes vaguely aware of a noise like a sighing wind sweeping across the jungle. At first she thinks the drops of water on her face are wind-blown, but they keep coming, faster and harder, and when she looks up, she sees that the whole sky is dark and full of rain.

It takes less than a minute for this rain to turn into a hammering tropical downpour, falling in thick ropes from the canopy trees, reducing the earth to muck. Veronica is grateful for it. She cranes her neck back and lets the delicious water drip down her throat, easing her thirst. Better yet, it is slowing their progress considerably – they move no faster than a crawl as they slip and stumble onwards through the rain and the mud.

Slowly her head begins to clear a little. Her drenched clothes chafe uncomfortably, and the wet rope on her arms is painful; a ring of blisters has erupted around her wrists. She realizes that their abductors' sense of tense urgency has vanished; they are now laughing and joking with one another as they herd their captives onwards. Veronica moans with comprehension. No one will follow their trail across this melting earth; no helicopter can fly through this torrential storm. The rain has erased any chance of pursuit and rescue.

Jacob falls again. It takes him some time to struggle back to his feet, with shaking muscles and unseeing eyes. Diane is still half naked, her shirt still clumped around her wrists, she has been like that all day. She limps mindlessly onwards, her face blank, as if she is no longer really there in any way that matters. Michael behind her stares out at the world as if all he can see is ghosts.

The trail changes, becomes wide and flat and well worn. The trees too are different, they are all the same kind now, peeling brown trunks from which clusters of enormous tear-shaped leaves erupt like frozen green fireworks. Furled purple flowers dangle obscenely from the tops of the trunks, and tight clumps of bananas hang beneath the leaves. A banana plantation. They have left the wild Impenetrable Forest and entered the settled lands of the eastern Congo. If it makes any sense to call this land of blood and bullets 'settled'.

The rain begins to dissipate. Bolts of brilliant sunlight shine through rents in the dark clouds. The trail leads them up a steep ridge. They are allowed to climb it at their own slow pace, but they are not allowed to stop, and the gruelling ascent reduces Veronica to desperation; by the time she finally reaches the

summit, she is groaning with every painful step, wobbling on both legs. At the top the one-eyed man calls a halt.

Veronica blinks tears from her eyes and tries to catch her breath. The plantation ends at the ridge top, and she can see westward for several miles, across undulating hills partitioned into a madman's chequerboard of brown and green, cultivated plots and stands of banana trees. None of the plots is large; this is subsistence farming. She sees a few figures moving in the distance, working the fields. A faraway tin roof glitters in a shaft of sunlight. Much closer, on the downslope of the ridge, stands the most basic human structure she has ever seen, a misshapen one-person hut made of heaped mud and leaves.

The one-eyed man waits by the plantation's treeline, watching the sky carefully, listening. Then he hustles them farther onwards. The trail leads between fields of some knee-high, grassy crop. A little past the mud igloo they veer into the fields, down and then along the base of a steep and stony incline that eventually becomes a sheer rock face punctuated by a pale waterfall. They are led up to and then straight through this curtain of water. Veronica has no strength left with which to be surprised. She barely feels herself getting wet again.

There is a cave behind the water, a stone chamber the size of a ballroom. The light that filters through the water is dim and flickering. The cave is carpeted by unstable rocks the size of grapefruit, and Veronica falls almost immediately, bruising her hip. She struggles desperately back to her feet. The captives are led stumbling to the back wall. There is nowhere left to go, but Veronica stands uncomprehending for a long time, dazed and soaked, before she begins to understand that their awful journey is over, that this cave is their destination and their prison.

The gunmen sit in a tight circle near the waterfall. The eight captives sit in line near the back wall of the cave, as far from their abductors as possible. At first Veronica focuses on regaining her breath and strength. Her shoulders still hurt enormously, there is an odd crawling sensation all down her arms and hands, and her wrists have been chafed bloody by the wet ropes wrapped around them, but none of this matters compared to the sheer bliss of being able to sit in one place without standing or walking.

Eventually she recovers enough to wonder and fear what comes next. She looks warily at their captors. They too sit slumped on rocks, exhausted and triumphant. It doesn't look as if anything is going to happen any time soon.

On top of all her other agonies, she is direly hungry. She has two Snickers bars in her cargo pants, but no way to get them, unless—

'Derek,' she murmurs. They are all still roped together; he is perched on a rock only a few feet away.

He twitches as if roused from a trance. 'Yes?'

She hesitates. Maybe eating now isn't such a good idea. Maybe the candy bars will be needed more later. And bringing them out now will raise the issue of whether she should share them. On the other hand, she's sure at some point they'll be searched, and she doubts she'll be allowed to keep her Snickers then. 'I've got two chocolate bars in my pants. The side pocket, left side. Can you—'

He nods. She stands with a grunt, moves over to sit next to him, brings her leg against his hands. Her khakis are soaked, and torn in a dozen places. He reaches into her pocket, produces a Snickers bar, strips it quietly of its wrapper and lifts his bound arms up behind him as high as he can. She bends over, keeping her body between the treasure and their abductors, and grabs it with her mouth. Derek turns around to face her. She offers him the other end, leans her face towards his. He takes the other end of the chocolate bar in his mouth, bites it in half. It is almost a kiss.

They chew meditatively. It is the most delicious thing Veronica has ever tasted. At the other end of their group, Michael and Tom are with some difficulty re-dressing Diane in her crumpled shirt. Jacob has almost passed out where he sits. Susan and Judy are speaking, quietly, but there are tears streaming down Judy's broad cheeks.

'We should give the other one to the others,' Derek says quietly. She nods.

'Can you get my Leatherman?'

They twist their bodies again, arranging themselves so her hands can reach his belt. Her fingers are clumsy, it takes her a few attempts to open the button and pull out the multi-tool, but she manages to palm it.

'They'll search us eventually,' he murmurs. 'Hide it under a rock.'

She nods, selects an appropriately dark hollow and with some difficulty squats down and deposits the Leatherman there. Derek nods with approval as she sits back up on her rock. The tool is invisible to the casual eye.

There is a roar of delight from their African abductors. Veronica turns and sees that one of the pygmies has just entered the cave, carrying four large bottles of Primus beer in a woven basket. He speaks to the one-eyed leader in a dispassionate voice, conveying a message, as the beer is passed around. The leader frowns, dismisses the pygmy with a contemptuous wave, and looks over to his prisoners.

Veronica freezes as his eyes fix on her, and then move to Susan. A long moment passes. Then the one-eyed man gets to his feet, walks over to the prisoners and stops in front of the British girl. Susan stares down at the ground, as if pretending he doesn't exist. She is trembling. All conversation has ceased.

The one-eyed man grabs Susan by her hair and pulls her wincing to her feet. Then he draws out his panga, severs the ropes that connect Susan to Judy and Jacob, and begins to drag the blonde girl away, towards the waterfall. Veronica stares in horror. There is nothing they can do. She knows she will be next.

4

'No!' Derek shouts, leaping to his feet. 'No! Leave her alone!'

The one-eyed man stops, a little surprised.

'Come on, we have to stand together,' Derek says urgently to Veronica.

She hesitates for a moment; then she too stands and starts to shout, 'Let her go! No! You let her go now!'

Tom and Judy join in, bellowing and screaming, their voices surprisingly strong. Veronica grabs Jacob's shoulder and tries to pull him to his feet. His eyes open and stare blearily at her.

'He's taking Susan away, we have to stop him,' she hisses.

The message gets through, and Jacob lumbers to his feet. The one-eyed man begins to walk away, pulling Susan with him, but Derek leads Veronica and Jacob in pursuit, gets in front of him and blocks his path, and starts to shout again: 'No! Let her go! You let her go, you can't have her!'

'*Laisse-moi,*' Susan hisses to the one-eyed man, and Derek switches to French too: '*Laissez-la, maintenant! Maintenant!*' Then Veronica joins in the shouting, and so does Jacob, also in French. Tom and Judy add their voices, and look as if they would like to come and join them, but Michael and Diane refuse to get up.

The one-eyed man looks annoyed and perplexed by this cacophony of protest, as if confronted by buzzing mosquitoes. He glances over at the other Africans. They seem bemused, but also amused, and they do not seem eager to put down their beers and back him. He frowns for a moment. Then he releases Susan, grabs Derek by the throat and pushes him up against the wall of the cave, pulling Veronica along partway. He is amazingly strong.

Derek chokes for air, tries to kick and writhe out of the hold, but to no avail. The one-eyed man closes his other hand into a fist and slams it three times into Derek's midsection, and once into his face. Blood begins to seep from Derek's nose. Honour satisfied, the one-eyed man lets his victim drop to the rocky ground, and turns to Veronica. She quails – but all he does is shove her away, back towards the inner wall of the cave.

She and Jacob manage to half carry a stunned Derek back to the others. The one-eyed man retakes his position with his men, grabs a bottle of beer and drinks deeply. Derek drops heavily on to a rock, stunned, barely able to sit without falling. Veronica leans towards him and looks carefully into his eyes. To her relief his pupils seem undilated; he has not been concussed.

Susan sits beside them, keeping Derek between her and the Africans, looking as if she might shatter at any moment. She asks, hesitantly, 'Are you all right?'

Derek manages a smile that's mostly wince. 'I'll live. I think. We have to stick together. We can't let them divide us.'

'They're not going to kill us,' Veronica says, reassuring herself as much as anyone else. 'We're worth too much. They'll ransom us.'

'Not necessarily,' Jacob says quietly.

Everyone looks at him. Veronica is surprised he is making any contribution to the conversation at all. Jacob's face is still pale with exhaustion, both his voice and his whole skinny body are trembling, the back of his T-shirt is dark with blood that has leaked from his whip wounds – but his eyes are steady, and he no longer looks faint. He looks angry.

He says, in his faintly nasal voice, 'The reason we had guards today was six years ago a bunch of *interahamwe* came into the park and captured fourteen tourists. They eventually murdered eight. The English speakers. They let the French go.'

Susan's grip on Derek tightens. Veronica swallows. Everyone here is a native English speaker, although it seems Derek, Jacob and Susan can also get by in French.

Derek shakes his head. 'No. If these guys came intending murder we'd be dead already. They didn't march us all the way here for fun. I think Veronica's right. Ransom.' He takes a breath. 'But I also think if something goes wrong they won't hesitate to cut their losses.'

'Meaning . . .' Veronica's voice trails off.

'Meaning killing us all,' he says grimly. 'So our job is to try to make sure nothing goes wrong. I've been thinking this over all day. Escape, I don't think that's a realistic option. Sorry. We're too far from anything, we stand out too much. Even if we got away somehow they'd track us down too fast. There's no sense even trying, we'd just piss them off. But we do know people are looking for us. That chopper was flying too low for anything else. We need to keep our eyes out for opportunities to signal where we are, and to take any that come up, if we can do so safely.'

Veronica stares at him. The whole lower half of his face is covered with blood, but his voice is clinical, as if he is discussing business objectives, not their very survival.

'What?' he asks.

She shakes her head. 'You just . . . how can you be so calm?'

'I'm not. I'm a security professional, I was in the military, I've seen action before. You learn to suppress your panic reflex, that's all. I'm just as scared as you.'

Veronica doubts it.

Jacob says, 'They've got phones.'

Everyone looks at him, surprised.

Susan asks, 'Phones?'

'Guy over there has a cell phone, I saw it when we got up just now. He was reading a text message or something on it.'

'It can't actually work. Not out here,' Veronica says.

'It's not impossible. I work at Telecom Uganda. Their competitors provide service in the Congo too, with reasonable coverage from what I saw. And radio's a weird medium. If we're anywhere near a town, there might be pockets of service around.'

'But I thought . . . how do they have cell phones here? I thought there wasn't even any government.'

'There isn't,' Derek says. 'But there's still a lot of money out here, and there's not exactly a war any more. Just good old-fashioned anarchy. The UN keeps a pretty good lid on the cities, but we can't expect them to march out here looking for us. It's probably some local warlord's territory, they'd start a firefight if they came in.'

'Do you think that's who sent them?' Veronica asks. 'The local warlord?'

'I have no idea.'

'The point I was trying to make,' Jacob says waspishly, 'is that if we can get our hands on one of their phones, we can use it to call for help.'

Derek frowns. 'Remember that mud igloo we passed? This is the middle of buttfuck nowhere. I seriously doubt phones work anywhere near here.'

'Doesn't matter,' Jacob persists. 'They have them because they work *somewhere*. We get a phone somehow, we write a text message, it goes in the outbox, they recover the phone, they go to town or wherever, and the message gets sent as soon as they walk into signal range.'

There is a pause as the others absorb this.

'Not bad,' Derek concedes. 'But it'll be hard to grab one long enough to write a text. Probably the second most valuable thing these guys own, after their guns.'

'Anybody got a better idea?' Jacob asks.

Nobody does.

'OK. So keep your eyes open for their phones,' Derek says. 'But remember that priority number one is to make sure nothing goes wrong. We don't necessarily want army troops finding us and storming this cave. The best way out of this is to be traded for a big bag of US dollars. Until then we have to stick together and make sure they don't abuse us. We should go join the others.'

Veronica realizes she, Derek, Susan and Jacob have instinctively formed a tight group, a little apart from the other four. This makes sense – their foursome drove from Kampala together, Derek knew each of them before they came here, and they are all in their late twenties and early thirties, whereas the others are one or two decades older – but all eight of them need to be a single indivisible group. They get up and move across the cave, assemble into a rough circle.

'Love what you've done with the nose,' Tom says mordantly to Derek.

'Thanks. I always thought it was too straight. Is everyone OK?'

'We're fine,' Judy says, meaning Tom and herself. 'I may never want to walk another step again as long as I live, but otherwise fine. But Diane—'

Diane doesn't look good. She is sitting slumped on the floor, her back to the wall, breathing shallowly, her head lolling, her eyes unfocused.

'She needs a doctor,' Michael says to Derek. His voice is hoarse. 'Tell them that. Tell them we've got money at home, lots of money, we'll get them whatever they want. We have to get her to a doctor. If they just give me a phone I can get them half a million dollars.'

'I'll tell them,' Derek says. 'When I think they'll be receptive. That's not now.'

Michael looks like he wants to be furious but can't muster the energy. 'Listen, you son of a bitch—'

'Come on, man,' Jacob interrupts. He points out the line of blood on his neck. 'Don't kid yourself. You think they give a shit about us? They came this close to cutting my throat out there. They would have if I couldn't have made it. There's probably no doctor inside a hundred miles anyways. Best case, we're all going to be here for days, probably weeks. Don't start making trouble now. You'll just make things worse.'

'Trouble? *Trouble?* Look at my wife. Look at her. She might . . . she might be dying here. You have to go tell them to get help. You have to go tell them right now.' But Michael's voice sounds hollow, as if he knows in his heart that Jacob is right – pleading with their captors will be useless.

Veronica kneels next to Diane and examines her closely. The wounds on her back have clotted; blood loss couldn't have been that severe. She doesn't look dehydrated. Marathon runners sometimes die from hyponatraemia, the opposite of dehydration, but that's clearly not the problem either.

'She's in shock,' Veronica says. 'Does she have a heart condition?'

Michael shakes his head. 'No. Always been healthy as a horse.'

'Then it's probably not cardiogenic. Just psychological shock and exhaustion. I think she'll be better once she rests.'

Better but not healed, Veronica doesn't say; psychological shock often leads to post-traumatic stress disorder, and she has a nasty feeling there will be plenty more trauma to come before any of them get out of this.

'Are you a doctor?' Judy asks.

'A nurse. I used to work in an ER.'

Michael seems reassured. Veronica doesn't tell him she hasn't practised for seven years.

A figure breaks through the curtain of the waterfall, a strong man carrying a woven thatch basket strapped to his back. The cave fills with clanking noises as the basket is emptied. The one-eyed man takes a length of chain in his hands, stands and turns towards the captives. He is smiling. Veronica shivers.

They start with Derek. First they take his shoes, watch, belt and camera, his little day pack, and everything in his pockets. Then they wrap a length of chain tightly around his ankle, seal it with a small steel padlock and run the other end through a fist-sized natural hole in an oblong rock the size of a watermelon. Susan is next to be stripped of her possessions, which are piled with Derek's near the waterfall. Both the chains looped through the anchor rock are fastened to a large padlock, its hasp almost too big for the fingernail-sized links. The locks and chains are rusting but solid.

Veronica is next. She rises to her feet as the one-eyed man approaches, tries to be cooperative. She doesn't resist as he searches her roughly, not even when his hands squeeze and linger on her breasts and crotch. She tells herself at least he's only touching her through her clothes. She tries to pretend she isn't really there, that this is happening to someone else. Her pockets are emptied. Her second Snickers bar is taken. She wishes she and Derek had eaten it instead of saving it for the others. The cigarettes in her cargo pants are soaked, useless, and Veronica feels a sudden and powerful pang of regret that she hadn't smoked them. She would maim for a cigarette right now.

When he removes her belt he discovers the Celtic knot tattooed on to the small of her back, and traces its lines with his rough fingers. She stands motionless until he begins to probe beneath her waistband, then she pulls away and turns around, ready to shout and fight back at last – but he is already crouching before her, wrapping a chain around her left ankle, pulling it tight, locking it with one of the little steel locks. It won't impede circulation, but she knows it will chafe her skin raw, and there's no way she will get her foot loose. The other end of the chain, which is about twenty feet long, joins Derek's and Susan's chains on the big padlock. Veronica sits back down on her rock and stares dully at her new chain anklet. At least they have all been chained together, they will not be dragged away one by one. It is thin consolation.

Soon they have all been attached to the anchor rock, and the big chromed padlock is snapped shut. No key is in evidence. Veronica is thirsty again, and desperately hungry. She watches as all their possessions are collected in two jute sacks. At least she managed to hide Derek's Leatherman. That's something. Maybe Derek can pick or smash the lock and lead them all to escape. Maybe he's Superman and he can just fly them all out of here.

The one-eyed man produces his panga, and everyone tenses; but he uses it only to cut free their arms. The relief is acute. Her shoulders still feel wrenched in their sockets, and her hands are still full of weirdly damped sensations, but Veronica thinks, as she flexes her wrists, that maybe the damage isn't permanent after all. It feels strange, almost unnatural, to be able to hold her hands in front of her body again.

'À *demain*,' the one-eyed man says, after freeing Derek last; and he leads the rest of the Africans out through the waterfall, leaving the captives in the cave.

'What does that mean?' Michael whispers.

Jacob translates: 'See you tomorrow.'

The cave faces westward, and the red light of the setting sun shimmers gloriously in the waterfall, like flowing stained glass. It seems wrong that anything here should be so beautiful. The temperature is dropping with the sun. Veronica isn't cold exactly, not yet, but she is uncomfortably aware that all her clothes are still soaking wet.

No one speaks for a long time. Veronica doesn't know what to say or do. Nothing in her life has prepared her for this situation.

'Come on,' Derek says eventually. 'Let's move this rock to the middle so we've got more space.'

He and Jacob manage to carry it from the wall into the middle of the cave. By the time they have finished, the glistening red orb in the waterfall has been cut in half; they are almost on the equator here, and the sun sets with amazing speed.

'Any more bright ideas?' Michael demands of Derek, inexplicably hostile.

Derek shakes his head coolly. 'Not today. I think we should just follow your wife's example.' Diane has moved from shock straight into a nearly comatose sleep.

Michael glares back for a moment, then goes back to his wife, slumps to a sitting position beside her and covers his face with his hands. Veronica walks over to the waterfall and drinks deeply; the anchor rock is just close enough now for that. She hugs herself as she backs away from the water. She is now officially cold. Maybe she wouldn't be with dry clothes, but that's a moot point. The darkness is now almost absolute, except that their captors have set a fire on the slope just outside, and the flickering firelight radiates through the waterfall. Even if they were to somehow escape their chains, they are being watched; even if they somehow escaped their watchers, they are countless miles from anything they know. Derek is right. There will be no escape. There is only the hope of ransom or rescue.

'I'm cold,' Veronica says.

Susan nods. 'So am I.'

Derek says, 'We should huddle together. All of us, for warmth.

At least until we dry. And, shit, we have to clear rocks to make space, I should have thought of that earlier.'

Veronica doesn't like this intimation that Derek is mortal and makes mistakes. They labour in the dark at some length, groaning from their many agonies as they stumble and bump into one another, until they have finally cleared a flat patch of ground big enough for them all to lie down.

Veronica stays close to Derek, almost instinctively. When they all sink to the ground and tentatively pull each other close she is between him and Jacob. Derek's back is to Veronica; his arms are around Susan, who is sobbing quietly. Veronica feels angry, and jealous. She wants Derek's attention and his strength. She tries to tell herself it doesn't matter, this is about warmth, they have to all stay together. Susan needs him more than she does, and anyways being jealous here is totally ridiculous. She hugs Derek tightly and presses her face against his strong back. Jacob, behind her, is more tentative, and she reaches back to pull him closer against her. His long, lean body is bony and uncomfortable. The stone floor and the ankle chain are painfully hard.

'It's going to be OK,' Derek murmurs.

Susan sniffles a bit, then announces through tears, 'It better be.'

Everyone tries to laugh.

'I mean it,' Derek continues, louder. 'We'll be OK as long as we stick together. And I think we will. You guys have held up really well.'

'You were amazing too,' Susan says. 'You are amazing.'

'This isn't the worst thing that's ever happened to me. Top ten, maybe, but not even top three, not yet. Makes it easier.'

'It's easily the worst thing that's ever happened to me.' Susan is on the verge of tears again.

Veronica feels Derek tighten his arms around Susan, and hears him whisper to her, 'Things will look better in the morning. I promise.'

Veronica closes her eyes and hopes he's right.

5

For a long moment Veronica doesn't understand what she is doing lying on a stone floor pressed between two other bodies. Then memory jolts her like a thunderbolt and she moans with terror, instantly wide awake.

She hurts seemingly everywhere: badly blistered feet, cuts on her legs, a big bruise on her hip, a pulled calf muscle, aching shoulders, skinned wrists, chafed ankle, headache, hunger, thirst, stiffness everywhere, an overall feeling that she has been hit by a freight train. At least her clothes are now mostly dry. The cave is dark. She has no idea how long she has slept. Jacob, Derek and Susan seem asleep, albeit uneasily. She hears but can't make out soft, frightened whispers from Tom and Judy. Veronica wants to lie where she is and sleep for days, and she is so exhausted that despite the hard, cold, uneven stone floor she probably could, but she needs to pee. At least she isn't dehydrated.

Just getting to her feet feels like climbing K2, but somehow she manages. Her right calf won't flex at all, she can barely walk, but that hardly matters, the chain on her left ankle keeps her from going more than twenty feet from the anchor rock. She isn't sure where to go, but she has to go somewhere, so she limps near the waterfall. Her chain clanks bleakly behind her, as if she's the ghost in a ghost story. She doesn't want to pee so close to the others, but tells herself they can't afford niceties like personal embarrassment any more, and anyway the white noise of the waterfall swallows up the sound.

Veronica drinks from the waterfall, soothing her throat. The water feels cool and clear. She hopes it is also clean, that no upstream village dumps dead animals or faeces into the water. Dysentery is all she needs right now. Maybe she shouldn't drink from it, but she already did last night, what the hell. She feels her way back to her slot between Jacob and Derek, lies laboriously back down and starts to cry. It feels like an involuntary physical reaction, like sneezing. She can't stop, she starts weeping more violently. Derek wakes up and rolls over to face her.

'Sorry, I'm sorry,' she bleats.

'It's OK,' he mutters, and reaches out for her, wraps his arms around her, holds her close as she sobs against his shoulder. She tries to relax into his arms and let her exhaustion carry her back into sleep. It doesn't seem to work, she is not conscious of having fallen asleep, but somehow, when she next opens her eyes, the cave is filled with filtered dawn, the sun is on the rise, and others are up and moving.

The ceiling of the cave is barely high enough to stand, and except near the waterfall it is so dark she has to squint. Veronica moves as close to the light and the water as she can, as quickly as she can, heedless of the pain in her strained muscles. Being buried alive has long been her greatest fear. Yesterday she was too exhausted to react to her surroundings, and fear of imminent death trumped claustrophobic anxiety, but now just the thought of being in one of the dark corners of this cave makes her dizzily light headed and a little nauseous.

Once they have moved from lying on stone to sitting on a rock there is precious little to do. Jacob mutters, 'I'm hungry,' and there is general agreement. Otherwise everyone seems dazed and uninterested, too weak for conversation. Diane seems better, she's at least ambulatory, but she doesn't speak and her eyes are as wide as a child's.

'You have to tell them to get me a phone,' Michael says, breaking a brooding silence. 'I'll get them money. Tell them I can get them a million dollars if they let us go.'

Veronica wonders whether the *us* in question means all of them, or just Michael and Diane.

'I will,' Derek says. 'When they come.'

'I can do it fast. I can transfer fifty thousand dollars today, over the phone.'

'What makes you think they'll let you go once they have the money?' Jacob asks.

Michael flinches. 'What . . . why wouldn't they?'

'Wrong question. Why *would* they?'

Nobody has an answer.

The waterfall noise changes as two men push through its flowing curtain. One of them is the muscled one-eyed man. The other they have not seen before. He is even taller than Jacob, at least six foot six, he reminds Veronica of basketball players she has met. The cave is not quite big enough for him and he has to stoop. He wears sneakers, black shorts and a ragged blue T-shirt too small for him, and he walks with a pronounced limp. The one-eyed man carries a plastic bucket full of some pale paste-like substance, and a jute sack holding a half-dozen spherical things about the size of human heads. Veronica freezes in place as it dawns on her that they might actually be human heads. Both men carry pangas lashed to their belts.

'Good morning,' the tall man says, as the one-eyed man puts down his sack and bucket. His accented English is soft spoken and Veronica has to strain to hear him over the waterfall. 'My name is Gabriel.'

'I can get you money,' Michael bursts out. 'Give me a phone and I can get you a million dollars if you let us go.'

Gabriel examines him curiously. 'What is your name?'

'Michael Anderson.'

'You are a rich man, Mr Anderson?'

'Yes I am,' Michael says. 'And I'm ready to make you rich too.'

'*C'est vrai?* The Bible says it is harder for a camel to pass through the eye of a needle than a rich man to enter the kingdom of heaven.'

Michael stares at him. 'Don't you want money?'

'Of course I want money. But please, how is it you would give it to me?'

'I can do a bank transfer today, for fifty thousand dollars, I can do it in ten minutes if you give me a phone—'

Gabriel half smiles. 'Do I seem like a man who has an account at a Swiss bank? Please, Mr Anderson. Be sensible. Who will negotiate the arrangements? Who will transform the numbers in your bank account into dollars that I can hold? Such a magical transformation. Like water into wine. Who will bring me those dollars? Where will we meet? How will my safety be guaranteed? Are these arrangements that you can make today, in ten minutes, Mr Anderson?'

Veronica is relieved, listening to him. He doesn't talk like a brutal thug. He talks like an educated, reasonable man.

'I'll find a way,' Michael says. 'I'll work with you. We can make these arrangements together.'

'Thank you. But I prefer to work with professionals. Please, all of you, do not be afraid. Put your minds at ease. There is a long history in my country of trading tourists for money. Laurent Kabila, the lamented father of our president, he did this often when he was a fighter in the bush, like me. Today no tourists come to Congo, we must seek them out in Uganda, but the principles remain the same. Please. I will negotiate arrangements with your governments, not with you.'

Veronica takes a deep breath and lets herself look away from the sack full of head-like objects. She feels a little steadier. They will be ransomed. Everything will be fine. Or at least survivable.

'That all sounds terrific,' Derek says. 'But there's something you need to understand.'

Gabriel looks at him.

'Our governments will insist on verifying our well-being before they pay you one dime. And if we've been abused, they will come down on you so hard you won't know what hit you. Kabila kidnapped his tourists last century. The world is different now. You kidnap some Americans and Brits and Canadians, and then you ransom us unhurt, fair enough, you're not worth chasing down. But you hurt us again and you will die. That animal tried to rape her last night.' He indicates the one-eyed man and Susan. 'He pulls any of that shit again, he uses that whip again, anything happens to us, even if it's not your fault, even if one of us gets sick, then you and all your men will fucking die. Is that clear? Do you understand that?'

Veronica is awed by the intensity and casual certainty of his voice.

Gabriel seems less impressed. 'What is your name?'

'Derek Summers.'

The tall man nods. 'I see. Mr Summers. I have no intention of harming you. But not because of your ridiculous threats. For two other reasons. One is that I know you white people are like cut flowers, so weak that from only a little injury you wilt and die. The other is because I am not an evil man. None of us are. You called this man an animal. I know that is what you think of us. All Congolese, maybe all black men, we are all animals to you. I want you to think of this. I studied physics once, at a university. I travelled to Europe. Now my country is in ruins, my family is dead, I must fight and kill only to survive. That is why we have captured you. That is why we must have the money you will bring. Only to survive. This man Patrice, my friend, this man you call an animal, he was once the finest drummer in Nord-Kivu, maybe the finest in all the Congo, and though I doubt you know this, we Congolese are famous through all Africa for our music. He lost his music when he lost his eye, in battle, saving my life. He lives every day with terrible pain from those wounds. Crippling pain. Pain that would reduce you to an animal, I promise you that. But he is a man still. He is the most brave and most strong man I know. I want you to think of this the next time you call him an animal. You will not be harmed by my men, none of you, unless you bring it on yourselves. But if you do I will have no mercy. Because I think no better of you than you do of us. Is that clear, Mr Summers? Do *you* understand *that*?'

After a moment Derek says, quietly, 'Yes.'

Gabriel nods to Patrice, who draws his panga. Veronica freezes as Patrice reaches into the sack – and pulls out a pineapple, which he cuts into a dozen fragments, wielding the machete with a craftsman's mechanical grace. The smell makes Veronica's mouth water and her stomach cramp.

'You see,' Gabriel says, as Patrice arrays the wedges on a flattish rock and begins to chop up another pineapple. 'When you are here we treat you well. If there is trouble you will have yourselves alone to blame.'

Tom reaches his hand into the plastic bucket, withdraws another baseball-sized dollop of pocho, stares at it with a wrinkled face and announces, 'This is the worst bloody Club Med I've ever been to.'

Everyone laughs. It sounds almost like real laughter. Gabriel has kept his word, they have not been harmed further, and their bellies are at least half full. The pineapples were so deliriously delicious that Veronica now feels almost well disposed towards Patrice. But eating this pocho, a kind of banana pounded to the consistency of underdone mashed potatoes, is like chewing wet cardboard.

'You think the food is bad, wait till the activities begin,' Derek says, smiling.

'Everybody up for the sunrise flagellations!' Jacob adds.

'I'm definitely not going to tip the staff.' Diane's voice is quavery, but they are the first words she has spoken since entering the cave, and everyone laughs uproariously with relief.

'Pocho can be good,' Susan says from her seat next to Derek. She sounds oddly defensive. 'This just hasn't been cooked enough. And it usually comes with a sauce.'

'Tell Nigella, not me,' Tom says around a mouthful. 'This is one taste I promise you I will never acquire. Rather have a bucket full of Vegemite. Well, let's look at the silver lining. A few weeks here and we'll finally get our slender figures back.'

'Great,' Jacob said. 'I'll just start thinking of this as a whips-and-chains fat farm. We could probably market it when we get back home. People would pay for the experience.'

39

Judy takes a bite and her face wrinkles. She makes herself chew and swallow, then turns to Susan and asks, amazed, 'You actually eat this back in Kampala? By choice?'

Susan looks around uncertainly. 'Not Kampala. The camp where I work, near Semiliki. There's Western food if you like, but I try not to eat differently from the refugees when I'm there. I think it's patronizing, it reinforces the barriers.'

'Could do with a few more barriers at the moment,' Tom says drily.

'Do you speak the language?' Michael asks Susan.

She hesitates. 'Not really. There are so many of them around here, it's mad. In Zimbabwe there was only Shona and Ndebele. Here, I expect there's a dozen languages within a hundred miles. I can speak some Swahili. A little Luganda, not much, I've only been here eight months. I think the pygmies were talking Swahili to the men when we came here, but the men were speaking something else, not Luganda.'

'Kinyarwanda?' Derek asks.

'I don't know. I wouldn't recognize it. But I don't think they'd speak that around here.'

'They would if they were *interahamwe*.'

'If they were *interahamwe* I rather think we'd all already be . . .' Susan's voice trails off.

Michael asks, '*Interahamwe?*'

Derek looks at him as if he has just failed to recognize Kurt Cobain's name. 'You've heard of the Rwandan genocide?'

'Of course.' Michael sounds a little insulted.

Susan says, 'The *interahamwe* were the ones responsible.'

Derek frowns. 'Responsible's a big word. Ordinary Hutus did most of the killing. But it was the *interahamwe* militias who organized it. It's a Rwandan word, means "let us strike together". When the genocide was over, after Kagame took over the country, a million refugees ran away into the Congo. Specifically right here, North Kivu province, right next door. Remember those volcanoes we saw in the distance on the drive into Bwindi?

They're right on the Uganda–Rwanda–Congo triple border. Anyway, most of the refugees went home eventually, but the hardcore *interahamwe*, the real genocidists, the mass murderers, they stayed. There's still supposed to be about ten thousand of them in eastern Congo.'

'And you think these might be *interahamwe*?' Michael asks.

Derek hesitates, then shrugs. 'Probably not. Susan's right. We'd all be dead already. These guys are probably exactly what they seem. A local warlord doing a fund-raising drive with us as the poster children.'

'He seems like an OK guy,' Jacob says.

Derek's laugh has no warmth in it. 'Do me a favour. Don't get all Stockholm syndrome on me. Sure, he talks pretty. But let's hope real hard we never have to find out just how nice he actually is.'

After breakfast Veronica sits by the waterfall and does what she can for people's injuries. Her one tool is the plank of cheap purple soap Gabriel brought. She uses it to wash assorted cuts, bruises, blisters and whip wounds. Jacob and Diane shudder and groan as Veronica soaps their flayed skin. Diane once again doesn't seem as if she's all there, her eyes stare into the distance. There's no clean fabric for bandages; all she can tell them is to try to keep the wounds clean and dry until they scab over. Tom has somehow sprained a wrist, and Veronica ties his T-shirt around it tightly for support. Michael is still walking gingerly, but he doesn't approach her, and Veronica knows his swollen testes should be fine in a day or two without help.

When finally done she rinses blood from the soap. On impulse she sticks her head through the waterfall. Outside, the water plunges into a small pool that becomes a burbling creek, wending its way through little patches of beans and millet until it reaches a stand of banana trees. The ashen remains of a fire lie on a rock beside the pool. Two guards sit near by, carrying pangas but not rifles. Veronica thinks they were part of yesterday's kidnapping crew. They leap to their feet when they see her head emerge from the water, and one begins to shout in French. She recoils, frightened. The two guards storm in after her, yelling sternly but not angrily.

'In case their body language was somehow unclear,' Jacob says drily after they depart, 'they said we weren't supposed to go outside.'

Veronica swallows. Her knees are weak from the confrontation.

For a long time nobody says anything. Veronica wishes somebody else would talk. She can't do it herself. All the words in the world seem to have fled from her mind. Instead all she can think about is everything that might go wrong at any moment. If Patrice comes storming in drunk, murder and rape on his mind. If they are discovered, their location reported by some curious local child, and Gabriel decides to cut his losses before the UN arrives. If he is unable to make contact with their governments before *interahamwe* enemies come and take his prisoners for themselves. If the ransom exchange goes terribly wrong and ends in gunfire. If there is cholera in the water. These all feel like very real possibilities, far easier to imagine than returning to safety.

Jacob speaks deadpan into the silence: 'Well, now. I suppose you've all been wondering why I've asked you here.'

The laughter that follows is giddy to the point of hysteria.

'What you don't realize,' he continues, his voice rigid, 'is that this is the casting call for the world's newest and ultimate reality show. It's called *Survivor Congo*, and the big twist this season is we've replaced "getting voted off the island" with "getting your fucking head chopped off".' More laughter, not as loud. 'Of course, some of you will have to make ultimate sacrifices, but Jesus, people, just imagine the ratings.'

'Do I get a million dollars if I win?' Derek asks.

'No. You win *not getting your fucking head chopped off.*'

The laughter that follows is now thin and nervous.

'Sounds fair,' Derek agrees. 'See, this is why I invited Jacob to Africa in the first place. Black comic relief.'

'It's not really the right continent for racist jokes,' Jacob shoots back.

'You thought they were funny in high school.'

'That was a character. And a highly satiric one. Who I did only once.'

Derek smiles. 'Because DeShawn nearly beat the living shit out of you.'

'Discretion is often the better part of comedy.'

Veronica interrupts their repartee. 'You two went to high school together?'

Jacob nods. 'Twenty years I've known this guy. High school, university, now here. His fault I'm here in the first place. Talked me into an eighty per cent pay cut to work for some friend of a friend of his. I still can't believe I actually signed up.'

'Sure, it's all my fault,' Derek says darkly. 'Salesman of the century, that's me. Sand to the Bedouin, Africa to Canadians.'

'I want my money back. You'll hear from my lawyers.'

'What? Why? I promised you exotic adventure. If this doesn't qualify I don't know what does.'

Jacob snorts. 'Teach me a lesson. Jungle accommodation with a waterfall and a sunset view, you said. The company of beautiful women. A long walk through lovely rainforest with expert guides, culminating with quaint local rituals involving big fucking whips and machetes. Yep, definitely should have read the fine print.'

Their humour is forced, but everyone manages a smile.

'No, really, my own fault I'm here,' Jacob says bitterly. He takes a deep and shuddering breath. 'I keep thinking maybe this is a dream, and when I wake up tomorrow we'll be back in the park, or maybe in Kampala, and I'll say, hey, guess what, you'll never believe this dream I just had.'

'Yeah.' Veronica knows the feeling.

'These last few weeks already, most mornings I wake up and can't believe I'm in Africa in the first place. That was already surreal. This is even crazier. It's like I'm playing a video game inside a dream or something.'

'You've just been here a few weeks?' Susan asks.

Jacob nods.

'Me too,' Veronica says softly. 'Just a month.'

Judy asks her, 'You came as a tourist?'

Veronica shakes her head. 'I was working with this HIV research group.'

'We were supposed to fly home tomorrow,' Diane says. 'They took our tickets. It isn't fair. We're philanthropists. We would have been home tomorrow.'

Veronica sympathizes. She too probably would have been going home soon. Her month in Kampala has taught her that Africa isn't for her: too foreign, too chaotic, too poor, too intense. She was probably just weeks away from leaving. It doesn't seem fair that now she is trapped in this awful place instead.

Michael says angrily, 'I grew up poor, you know. I paid my own way through college. Now we give money to churches, orphanages, ministries all over the world. There are dozens of African children who rely on us to survive. Hundreds. We travel all over the world to inspect our good works and make sure our money isn't wasted. That's why we were here. We don't deserve this. We just don't deserve it.'

Susan looks like she wants to say something, but doesn't.

Jacob shrugs. 'It's like Clint Eastwood says. Deserve's got nothin' to do with it.'

'We would have been home tomorrow,' Diane repeats, as if she can make it come true by saying it often enough.

Judy says, 'You never think it will happen to you, do you? You always think this is the kind of thing that happens to other people. We're just tourists. Uganda was so lovely. We travel every year, never had a moment's trouble before.'

'We should have got married,' Tom says, very seriously.

Judy half laughs, half sobs. 'You've been saying that for fourteen years.'

He takes her hand gently. 'We get out of this, darling, first thing, I'm going to make an honest women of you at last.'

'Fourteen years?' Veronica asks.

Tom explains: 'It's been a very long engagement. Like that French film with what's-her-name from *Amélie*. I used to be a coal miner, up near Leeds, Jude here was a hairdresser. A month after we started going out, we were both sacked, on the same day. Fourteen years ago next month. The very next day we put our heads and bank balances together, started a delivery service. Nowadays we've got eleven vans, forty employees, it's a real going concern. But starting up shop was such a bloody bother we never found time to officially get married.'

As Veronica listens, she begins to feel a slippery looseness deep in her guts, a faint cramp. She swallows nervously. Just a little dyspepsia, she tells herself. You ate too much too fast. That water you drank was clean. You can't be sick. Not now.

'Every year we talk about it,' Judy says, 'and every year we decide we'd rather spend the time and money travelling.'

Tom rolls his eyes. 'She decides.'

'Come on, love. You've said yourself every trip's been better than a wedding. You hate weddings.'

'I'd rather get married than eat pocho again.'

'Fair point,' Judy concedes, and everyone chuckles.

'It's really not that bad if it's prepared correctly,' Susan protests, but she too is smiling.

Silence falls, and with it the almost-cheerful mood darkens again.

Eventually Tom says to Susan, 'What's your story, then, pocho-eater? What are you doing in Africa?'

'Me?' Susan looks around awkwardly, discomfited by their collective attention. 'Not half so romantic as yours. I used to be an actress. Not a very good one, I don't think. I went to all the right courses, did a few little roles in provincial tours, a few film walk-ons, but it never really happened for me. Fame. Success.' She shrugs. 'Then five years ago I came to Kenya for what was supposed to be two weeks, to help teach local theatre groups how to put on Aids awareness plays. The slums there, the way people live, I'd never seen anything like it. I'd never even imagined. And it's so *unnecessary*. The waste. The fucking *waste* of it all. Their government stealing their money, and the money that's supposed to go to them, just outright stealing it plain as day, thieves and murderers, killing their people in a dozen different ways, and all of them propped up by our governments, our aid organizations – we're helping to kill them too.' Susan glares at Michael and Diane as if they are personally responsible for Africa's poverty. Then she seems to come to herself, and her face softens again, her voice becomes shy and hesitant. 'I've been here ever since. Working at places I can believe in. Refugee camps, mostly. The aid industry mostly makes Africa worse. But in the camps I can make a difference.'

'Did the people at the camp know you were coming to see the gorillas?' Derek asks.

Susan considers. 'I told a few. The authorities must already know we're all missing, they took our passport details when we entered the park.'

Derek nods as if that wasn't quite what he was asking.

'How long have you been in Africa?' Tom asks Derek.

Derek too looks a little uncomfortable answering questions. 'Almost a year now.'

'You were in the service, you said? You've seen action?'

'Yeah. In Bosnia. I was a so-called peacekeeper. Ten years ago now. Private security, since. Iraq a couple years ago, working for Blackwater. Then Thailand before I came here. Beaches and girls. Probably should have stayed.'

'What you should have stayed in was university.' Jacob turns to the others. 'This guy was supposed to do a triple major in politics, philosophy and economics, while I did computer engineering. We were going to found a start-up once we graduated. The dot-com boom was just starting. We would have been millionaires. But loser-boy here had to go and change his major to drugs and girls.'

46

Derek smiles and quotes, 'Never let your schooling get in the way of your education. So I dropped out.'

Jacob clears his throat sceptically.

'No, I did. How many times have I told you this? You can check U of T's records. I officially withdrew a whole day before they would have expelled me.'

'And then you joined the army and went to Bosnia? Why?' Veronica asks, trying to ignore her increasing intestinal discomfort.

Derek says, as if it is all the answer the question requires, 'I was twenty-one.'

A hush falls over the cave. Nobody seems to have anything else to say. Veronica tries not to think about the slithering uneasiness in her belly, or about how many things could go wrong with their ransoming. She tries to think back to happier times. But those were too long ago to come into focus. She can't tear her mind away from being afraid; every time she tries to distract herself there is a sudden reminder: the tightness of her ankle chain, a groan from Diane, and Veronica gasps weakly as she remembers where she is, and her stomach writhes and twists anew. She feels like she is slowly sliding into a dark whirlpool that will swallow her whole.

'I'm sick,' she mutters. There is no longer any denying it. Her guts are lurching and roiling with illness, she can't hold out much longer. She rises weakly to her feet. 'Shit. Fuck. I'm sick.'

'What is it?' Derek asks, concerned.

'Just a stomach bug,' she insists. 'I've got to . . . I'm sorry.'

She grabs the empty pocho bucket and stumbles as far away as possible; only twenty feet, thanks to the chain. The others look studiously away as she squats over the bucket. Knowing that this could be cholera or dysentery, could actually kill her in a matter of days, somehow doesn't dull the humiliation. At least there doesn't seem to be any bleeding, at least not yet.

'I don't feel well either,' Jacob groans.

'Oh, Jesus,' Michael says, panicky. 'This is all we need. Tell them we need a doctor. Go tell them!'

Derek stands. He looks grim. 'I'll try. But Jacob's right, they're not going to care. Even if they did there's probably nothing they could do.'

6

Veronica spends the next three days in a haze of sickness, sometimes groaning weakly, sometimes staggering back to the toilet bucket. Between bouts of illness she lies on the ground and waits to die or get better. They seem like equally desirable options. At least she is not alone in her misery, Jacob is afflicted too. The others are unaffected: they are more travelled, or have been in Africa longer, and are thus less vulnerable to exotic stomach bugs.

Veronica soon begins to feel that she has been sick and chained to a rock in this cave for months. It doesn't take long for a routine to develop. They are woken by the shimmering dawn, rise and try to shake off their stiffness. Derek actually does calisthenics every morning. The two guards outside are changed. An expressionless teenager comes in laden with pineapples and pocho, and takes out the toilet bucket; and then nothing else of note happens until dusk, when the guards are changed again.

Veronica is vaguely aware that the tension and tedium would be excruciating if she were well. She watches blearily on both occasions that Derek ventures outside the waterfall to ask about Gabriel, and is chased back in with more shouts. She listens as the others speculate anxiously and endlessly about what's going to happen. But mostly she just lies there, weak and wretched.

After the first night they don't actually need each other's body heat, but they still sleep huddled up against one another. They need each other's closeness. Veronica understands now why solitary confinement can be such an awful punishment. Being alone isn't so bad by itself; but being alone in a prison, facing a dozen grim futures – she would lose her mind. Things are bad enough as it is. Veronica is almost grateful for the illness that keeps her mind mercifully fogged. Lucidity is the last thing she wants right now. What she wants is to close her eyes and go into a coma until one way or another this is all finally over.

She is aware, even in her fugue state, that Derek and Susan are now spending almost all their time within touching distance of one another. Veronica wishes he was spending his time with her instead. It isn't jealousy, not really. It's simply that being near Derek lightens her feeling of doom.

On the third day Veronica manages to rouse herself enough to inspect the others' wounds. They don't look good. The whip wounds on both Jacob and Diane are growing inflamed and filling with pus, clear signs of infection. Veronica doubts their systems will be able to fight off the infections unaided; Jacob is young but sick, Diane is old and weak, their environment is filthy, and neither is getting enough food. It won't be long before blood poisoning and gangrene become real concerns.

On the afternoon of the fourth day, Veronica lies half conscious, barely aware of a background conversation. It is a sudden transition to silence which rouses her. She looks up. One of their abductors has entered the cave. Veronica recognizes him as the first one she saw, emerging like a shadow from the jungle. Now instead of a rifle he carries a small steaming kettle and something wrapped in a piece of cloth.

The captives watch him tensely, as they might a wild animal, a leopard or a cobra. He makes his way straight to Veronica. Michael and Diane back slowly away. Derek takes a step forward. Veronica watches wide eyed as the man kneels beside her. She can see the vertical tribal scars on his face. He puts down the kettle and a small cracked cup, then uses his free hand to make wriggling motions in front of his belly, and mimes drinking from the cup. She stares at him, slowly comprehending. He repeats his motions.

'OK,' she says slowly. 'Yes. *Oui*. I understand.'

His smile reveals that he is missing several teeth. He puts down the rag and unwraps it, revealing a pineapple-sized clump of steaming plant matter, various grasses and barks mixed together and recently steeped in boiling water. He mimes cutting himself, then putting the plants on the cut. Veronica nods and repeats her understanding. Their abductor smiles goodbye, stands, turns and departs.

'Medicine,' she says. 'They brought us medicine.'

She and Jacob drink as much of the bitter tea as they can stand; then she applies the poultices to his and Diane's infected welts. She wonders whether the herbs actually work or whether they're just a totem for the placebo effect. Either way it's better than nothing.

She sits with her back against the wall of the cave. Jacob lies on his stomach beside her. They watch the shimmering curtain of the waterfall in companionable silence. After a while Veronica realizes that, placebo or no, she does feel more alert and less sickly. She feels almost as if she has woken from three days of sleep.

Jacob echoes her thoughts: 'I think I feel a little better.'

Veronica looks down at herself. Her skin is caked with dust and mud. She wonders how much weight she has lost in the last few days. Her belly seems to have retreated into her body, leaving taut skin behind. She hasn't been this thin since her modelling days. Jacob's long body, folded into a cross-legged position beside her, has gone from skinny to outright gaunt. His hair and goatee are half mud.

At length she says to him, 'You know, one thing you've never explained, why are you here?'

'I got kidnapped.'

She gives him a look. 'I mean Africa. Derek asked you to come, but why did you say yes?'

'I came for the waters.'

She smiles and quotes back: 'What waters? We're in the desert!'

50

'I was misinformed.' He considers for a moment. 'He happened to call me at a weak moment.'

'Weak how?'

'I turned thirty.'

'Oh. Yeah. That can be weird.' Veronica knows that all too well.

'And I had just broken up with my long-term girlfriend. We didn't even like each other any more, we were just staying together by default, you know? Momentum. That and neither of us wanted to have to look for someone new.' Jacob shrugs. 'We finally broke up and I suddenly realized I'd basically spent the last ten years watching movies and playing video games. Some other guys I graduated with, they moved to California, a couple of them are Internet millionaires now. And I'm a lot smarter than them. I used to think that mattered, being smart. But it doesn't. Not if you never do anything with it. I had a good job, but what for, right? I realized I had never actually done anything. Then Derek calls and says this is the land of opportunity. A whole continent leapfrogging landlines, new cell networks everywhere. And I figured, even if I miss the brass ring, at least I'll have gone and lived in Africa, right? At least I'll have done something more with my life than work and play *World of Warcraft*. So he found me a job at Telecom Uganda, at a mere eighty per cent pay cut. The grand plan was, I'd work there a year, figure the lay of the land, meet some funders, then we'd start a company here, try to build an empire.' He shakes his head. 'Now I just want to not die. How's that for perspective?'

'Yeah,' Veronica agrees.

'I must sound like a jerk, eh? You came here to help starving Aids orphans and here I am talking business opportunities.'

'You don't sound like a jerk,' Veronica said truthfully. 'And honestly, I didn't really come here for the orphans. I came because my whole life went to shit. Basically this was as far away as I could find.'

Jacob visibly decides not to ask for details. She likes him for it.

'I got divorced,' she says eventually. 'From a guy I should never have married in the first place.'

Veronica falls silent. She doesn't want to talk about it. Even now, even here, the hurt is still too fresh, that she devoted seven years of her life to Danton, abandoned her career and let her whole life fall into orbit around his, only to be discarded like used Kleenex when she turned thirty. Now that they're over it's almost like those seven years never really happened, like she somehow jumped from twenty-four to thirty-one overnight. That Rip van Winkle feeling was part of why she came to Africa. To start her life over, leave all her mistakes behind.

'I thought the hardest thing was going to be not being rich,' she says. 'Funny, isn't it. My ex was rich. Very. I never knew exactly how rich, he wouldn't tell me, but double-digit millions, at least. Inherited, he was an only child. I grew up poor, in Buffalo, my dad was on unemployment half the time and my mom was an artist, and even when I met him, I mean, I was doing OK, I was a nurse, I was even doing a little modelling too, that's how I met him, but it was still San Francisco, I was sleeping in a bunk bed. Then all of a sudden I moved to a mansion, got used to spending, I don't know, probably like a thousand dollars a day. I mean, that was nothing, I wouldn't even think about it. You get used to it. Believe it or not. Seven years of that and then, boom, divorce. I never missed him. Not for a fucking moment. I thought the hard part was going to be being poor again. Now here I am. Like you say. How's that for perspective.'

'You didn't get half, eh?'

She shakes her head. 'I signed a pre-nup. I should have known right then, huh? But I thought it was really his mother who was insisting. Then I think he was worried it wouldn't stand up, so he . . . he did some shitty things when we got divorced. Even before we separated. Private investigators, shit like that. Whatever. Doesn't matter now. So I came here, got a job at this NGO I used to do fund-raising for when I was a trophy wife, all full of big plans to reinvent myself, start a school for nurses, do some-

52

thing admirable. But I was about to give up that too. It was a crazy idea anyways, starting a college all by myself. And Africa, it's just too much, I can't live here.' She sighs. 'Never mind. None of that seems to matter much now, does it?'

Jacob nods quietly.

Veronica looks across the cave at Derek, sitting cross-legged next to Susan, and thinks of their first meeting, at a party at the French embassy. Incredible to think it was only ten days ago.

If she hadn't been at that party she wouldn't be here now, and she hadn't even wanted to go. Her three housemates were all attending, and Veronica had been looking forward to having the house to herself for once. It wasn't easy adjusting to having room-mates again, not after spending seven years as the reigning lady of a multimillion-dollar estate. But Bernard, the local managing director of HIV Research Africa, the NGO where Veronica worked, had made it clear he expected to see her at the embassy party, and so she found herself that night sitting with Belinda, Linda and Diane on the veranda of their shared house, a sprawling, musty colonial relic decorated with Persian rugs and mahogany furniture, waiting for their driver to arrive.

The unkempt grounds were surrounded by a high wall topped by broken glass, and an armed askari guard watched the gate around the clock. Kampala was not a particularly dangerous city, but Veronica was always grateful for his presence. He seemed to keep the real Africa outside. The real Africa was filth, beggars, anarchic shanty towns, cratered streets, teeming poverty, fat corrupt bureaucrats; a place where everything was ugly and shabby, and nothing worked. Their rickety house was filled with dust, cobwebs, creaky plumbing and uncomfortable furniture, but it still felt like an oasis, a sanctuary in a sea of chaos.

The car that came for them was a rusting, dented Suzuki with seats made mostly of duct tape. HIV Research Africa was small and poor, hired local drivers because it couldn't afford the customized SUVs and full-time chauffeurs that most African aid organizations boasted, but Veronica couldn't complain. No one else had offered her a job. What she did for them was largely make-work. Her reports could easily have been written in France or America rather than Uganda. She was in Africa only because Bernard had known Veronica when she was rich, and took pity on her when she fell from that state of grace.

The Suzuki bumped along Kampala's dark and uneven streets, with Veronica in the back seat pressed between Belinda and Diane, both sizeable women. She couldn't help but think wistfully of the private jets, limousines and Ferraris in which she had once ridden. Arrival at the embassy was a great relief. The stone-walled complex, adorned with sculptures, paintings and several tricolour flags, was crowded with well-dressed people sipping champagne. More than half the guests were white, and Asians outnumbered Africans. The servants and guards were of course all black. Beef, chicken and South African boerewors sausage were served up from a big propane barbeque, a colourful salad washed with boiled water was mostly ignored, and every guest in sight held a cold bottle of Nile or Bell beer.

She had been in Kampala for only three weeks but more than a dozen of the faces she saw were familiar. It was a city of millions, but expats lived in a tiny bubble: their own well-guarded homes and workplaces; a few dozen cafés, bars, hotels and supermarkets where they mingled; and drivers to carry them between the islands of their neocolonial archipelago. Africa was only a backdrop, they didn't really live in it at all.

Veronica couldn't shake the feeling that not much had changed from the colonial era. Half of the guests were NGO workers ostensibly here to save Africa from its misery, but they were still white people living like kings in an exotic land on the pretext of uplifting the locals. Only the justification had changed, from moral and religious conversion to aid and economic development. But from what Veronica had seen, most African aid benefited aid workers a lot more than the Africans.

She was making polite conversation with a half-drunk Brit named Simon when she heard a South African voice cut through the babble of conversation: 'What I wonder is if Africans are even capable of love. I've never seen it, not here. I've seen them spend their lives shagging like bonobos, I've seen them leave their babies to die by the side of the road without shedding a tear, but I've never seen love.'

Veronica excused herself soon afterwards, found her way to a corner of the yard, looked around and wondered what she was doing here, at this party, in this city, on this continent.

'*Excuse-moi, mademoiselle,*' a smooth male voice said, and a hand touched her shoulder from behind. '*Est-ce que je te connais?*'

He was tall, lean and muscular, with deep blue eyes, a sardonic smile and a Chinese dragon tattooed around his bicep.

'I'm sorry,' she said, 'I don't – *je ne parle pas français.*'

'No? I thought for sure you were French.'

'Not me. Born and raised in Buffalo.'

'Surprised to hear that. American women don't usually look like you do.' He seemed totally relaxed, a small smile playing on his lips.

She couldn't resist. 'What do I look like?'

He took a moment to inspect her. Veronica felt herself starting to blush and commanded herself to stop. This was ridiculous.

'Casually stylish,' he said. 'At home wherever you may find yourself.'

She couldn't help but laugh. 'I'm sorry, but that's *definitely* not me.'

He inclined his head. 'If you say so. I'm Derek.'

'Veronica.' After a moment she asked, 'What do you do?'

'I'm a security consultant.'

'What does that mean exactly?'

'I'm afraid in part it means avoiding specific answers to that question,' he said, smiling ruefully. 'I'm sorry. I don't mean to be rude.'

'No, not at all,' she said quickly.

A tall, thin, awkward-looking man with a goatee stepped up to Derek and muttered something in his ear.

'My friend Jacob,' Derek said to her, and she and Jacob shook hands. 'I'm sorry, we have to take care of something. To be continued?'

Veronica smiled, shrugged. 'Sure.' Not really expecting it to happen.

But half an hour later, there Derek was again, at her side with a full glass of champagne to replace her just-emptied one. They spent most of the rest of the night in conversation. She went home giddy. When he called her a few days later to invite her out to a weekend in Bwindi there were butterflies in her stomach for the first time since she was a teenager.

But Veronica knew at the same time it was crazy to be thinking about him. She would have to go home soon. The only thing she had really learned from her month in Africa was that she couldn't live here, not even in the expat bubble. She just wasn't tough enough, not any more.

'I always wanted to come here,' Veronica says softly, ending the lull.

Jacob blinks, looks back to her.

'Even when I was a kid. I saw *The African Queen* on TV once and I wanted to be a nun here like Katharine Hepburn. Then I read *Out of Africa*. When I graduated I applied to come here as a nurse with Doctors without Borders, but they turned me down. I mean, of course they did, I had no experience, but I was devastated. I was going to join the Peace Corps, but you can't control where you're assigned. I didn't want to end up in India or Peru. I wanted to come here.' She half laughs. 'So I finally made it here. And I hated it.'

Jacob doesn't ask why. She supposes the reasons to hate Africa are self-evident.

'I should have come when I was younger. I bet I would have loved it then. When I moved to San Francisco we hitchhiked all the way, me and my friend Rebecca, Buffalo down to Mexico, then back up the coast. We'd sleep outside, go days without showering, get in cars with strange men, we wouldn't care. Then in SF I was a real wild child – drugs, parties, go to bed at three, wake up at six and report to the ER. I was tough, back in the day, I could handle anything. Believe it or not.'

'I don't doubt it,' Jacob says.

'Yeah. Well. Not any more.'

Veronica thinks of the Ugandan guard who bled to death not five feet away from her, the day they were taken. If that had happened seven years ago Veronica would have rushed to his aid immediately, no matter what else was going on, she would have at least tried to save his life. She was a nurse, that was her job, her duty, to help the sick and wounded. Instead she just stood there, stunned and useless, while he bled to death.

'I've been thinking about how long they'll have to keep us here,' Jacob says. 'Assuming everything goes right. Let's just assume that for the moment.'

Veronica swallows. 'Yes. Let's.'

'I figure at least a few weeks. Probably more like a month.'

'A *month*?'

'Sorry. But Gabriel has to reach civilization, contact our embassies, show proof we're here and still alive, negotiate terms, make ransom arrangements. I've been here long enough to know nothing in Africa happens fast. Plus the whole time he has to be paranoid about them tracking him back to us. It'll probably be days before—'

Jacob falls silent for a moment as several figures step through the waterfall.

'Shit,' he mutters. 'I was just going to say, before we even see him again.'

Gabriel is instantly recognizable by his height. He is accompanied by a figure wearing a pale hooded robe that looks Arabic, not African. Veronica sits up with surprise, her weakness momentarily erased by adrenalin, and begins to pull her shirt back

57

on. The others stir too and turn towards their visitors. Gabriel looks cold and distant. Veronica can't see the other man's face at all through the shadow of his hood.

'Stay where you are,' Gabriel instructs them.

They obey. The hooded figure inspects each of them in turn. He seems to take a particular interest in Derek. When the hooded man comes near Veronica she tries to watch him carefully without looking directly at him. His robe is wet from the waterfall, and she can see through his half-fallen hood – actually a headscarf – that despite his dress he is dark skinned, ethnically African not Arab.

'How are things going?' Derek asks Gabriel, his voice controlled. 'Is there anything we can do to help?'

'Quiet,' Gabriel orders, distantly, as if instructing someone else's dog.

The man in the robe finishes his inspection, and their visitors depart.

It is Jacob who breaks the silence. 'Well. That was unexpected.'

'That was not good.' Derek's voice is grim. 'That was very not good. That was a dishdasha.'

'A what?'

'Dishdasha. What he was wearing. An Arab robe.'

'He was black, not Arabic,' Veronica says.

'Exactly. Ethnically African, culturally Arabic. Pretty small group of people fit that description, almost all of them in the Horn of Africa, which happens to be a thousand miles away over some of the nastiest terrain on earth. So what the fuck is this joker doing in Central Africa? And what the double fuck is he doing looking at us?'

Veronica realizes that the anger in his voice is masking fear. For the first time since their abduction, Derek sounds frightened.

'Maybe he's a trusted third party,' Michael offers. 'An arbitrator. To verify that we're OK and help both sides negotiate.'

'Maybe. And maybe he is the other side.'

Veronica blinks. 'What does that mean?'

'I mean maybe Gabriel isn't trying to ransom us back to governments. Maybe dishdasha man was here to inspect the goods he's about to buy. Us.'

'Us?' Tom asks, puzzled and alarmed. 'Why would he be buying us?'

Derek's smile is mirthless. 'Why indeed. What kind of Arabic-influenced organization would want to purchase a group of captured Westerners?'

Veronica doesn't understand. Neither does anyone else, except maybe Susan from the look on her face.

Then Jacob says, stunned, 'No fucking way.'

'I look like I'm joking?'

'How would he even have made contact?'

'Lot of Islamic influence in this region,' Derek says. 'Idi Amin converted and got a lot of money from Arab states while he was butchering Uganda. Muslims went untouched. There are mosques and Muslim schools everywhere over the border, nice places, well funded, well respected. Join Islam, join a strong community, get a quality education for your children, become middle class. Power-ful incentive. Especially if you're anti-Western to begin with.'

Veronica still doesn't get it. He's right about the Muslim influences, certainly. She remembers the mosque in Fort Portal, a city they passed through on the way to the Impenetrable Forest; its gleaming green minarets were so much cleaner and better built than the rest of that chaotic town, it looked as if it had fallen from a different world. She remembers the Muslim primary school in Butogota, the nearest town to the national park. But what kind of Muslims would want to ransom Western tourists, why—

'Oh my God.' The bolt of awful realization jolts Veronica up to a sitting position. She feels like she is going to throw up. 'No. You can't be serious.'

'They're definitely active in this region,' Derek says. 'I know that for a fact. And it wouldn't be the first time in Africa. Far from it. This is where they started. August 1998. Bombs go off at the American embassies in Kenya and Tanzania, killing hundreds, mostly Africans. For most people it was the first time they ever heard of Osama bin Laden.'

Diane gasps. Michael and Tom start with appalled understanding. The name hangs in the air.

'You cannot be serious,' Veronica repeats dully.

'What do we do?' Judy asks quietly.

Derek takes a deep breath. 'Not much we can do except hope I'm wrong.'

Veronica lies back down and tells herself this can't be happening. The African Arab is just an intermediary. Derek must be wrong. They are not about to be sold to Islamic terrorists.

7

Men appear outside, half a dozen, their silhouettes warped by the shimmering curtain of the waterfall. When they enter Veronica recognizes them as their jungle abductors. Two of them hold rifles; the others have pangas dangling from their belt. They are led by Patrice.

The one-eyed man produces a key, undoes their chains, withdraws them from the anchor rock, then reattaches them to the big padlock so the captives remain yoked together by their ankles. The others go among them, grabbing their arms and pulling them to their feet without niceties. It all happens very quickly. Veronica allows herself to be pulled along after Patrice, through the waterfall, out of the cave. The sudden sunlight is blinding.

They are led down along a muddy trail that winds through ragged plots of farmland worked by women, children and a few old men, all barefoot and dressed in rags. Some are half crippled by injury; others have misshapen goitres erupting from their necks. Some wield hoes with big metal blades that look like rusting shovel heads. The rest use sticks and bare hands. All watch amazed as the white captives are led through their fields like cattle being taken to slaughter. The occasional buildings are mud huts with misshapen walls and unevenly thatched roofs. Only a few scrawny goats and chickens are visible.

'*Vous voyez*,' Patrice says. He sounds angry. 'You see.'

Veronica is too caught up in her own misery to sympathize with that of these strangers. Her strength has ended; she is able to walk only because Derek is holding her up. They stagger to the bottom of the hill, to a broad, flat bean patch where Gabriel and the dishdasha man stand as if waiting for a bus. The dishdasha man holds a white telephone as big as a brick; it looks like a cell phone from the 1980s. The word *Thuraya* is embossed on its plastic shell.

'You see,' Gabriel says to them, indicating the fields around them, and their wretched inhabitants. His voice is serious, as if he is imparting great wisdom. 'This is my home. This is where I grew. Once there was a school and a church. Now they are ashes. The jungle has grown over the roads that once led here. We cannot grow enough to feed ourselves. We have no money for the market. We are too far from the roads to trade, we have no gold or gasoline to smuggle. We would leave our ancestors' land, but there is nowhere to go. Even the pygmies live better than us. We must have money. We must be strong. We have no choice. It is strength or death. You understand?' He sounds almost guilty.

The captives stare at him dully. He nods shortly, as if he has explained everything, and looks up to the western sky. Patrice produces lengths of mud-stained yellow rope and begins to go among the captives, binding their arms behind them as he did in the jungle. Veronica cries out as the rope tightens on her scabbed wrists, but she doesn't resist. There doesn't seem to be any point. Her fate seems preordained.

Once they are roped together again, into two groups of four, their ankle chains are removed and piled beside Gabriel. The man in the dishdasha walks among the captives, examining them carefully, as if looking for flaws. Veronica's shoulders and wrists are hurting again; she wishes their chains had not been replaced by ropes.

She hears a faint and familiar noise, the distant buzz of an approaching helicopter. Hope soars in her heart as she thinks of the UN helicopter they saw. But the buzzing aircraft that crests the hill, moving straight towards them like some gigantic June bug, is painted black, not UN white.

As the helicopter nears its noise becomes incredible, deafening. Its rotors are like smeared haloes. Crops ripple as it passes low above the fields, and the wind it generates is gale force; Veronica has to lean forward to stay upright as the helicopter stoops and lands in the bean field before them. The rotor wash crushes the nearby plants flat.

A watchful part of her mind notes the aircraft's streaked and peeling paint, the fading Cyrillic letters stencilled on its nose. The pilot is a white man, unrecognizable behind a helmet and bulky radio headset. The passenger compartment is occupied by three rusting metal benches. A man in a dishdasha, holding one of the rifles with wooden handles and curved ammunition clips – a Kalashnikov, according to Derek – sits alone in the back row.

The engine noise abates to a dull roar. The man with the Thuraya phone shakes hands formally with Gabriel. Then he produces a pistol from his billowing robe. The captives are pushed up on to the helicopter, forced to sit on the two front metal benches. The two dishdasha men sit behind them. Veronica is between Jacob and Derek in the foremost bench. She feels dizzy, and not just from sickness, or the powerful smells of rust and gasoline. This all feels so unreal.

The engine roar intensifies, swells into a pounding howl that seems to drown out all possible thought. Veronica tries to brace her legs against the steel wall in front of her. Her muscles have no strength in them. Then the aircraft lurches like an earthquake, they rise with sickening speed, and Veronica barely manages to lean over before vomiting on to the rusting floor.

She feels a little better when she sits up straight again. The aircraft pulses with the beat of its engine, rattling her bones inside her body, provoking all her wounds and blisters anew, and the wind blowing through the helicopter's open sides and broken windows is freezing, but at least her head has cleared somewhat. Beneath them the Congo is a rolling green carpet. They are flying north-west, low to the ground, following the contours of the hills and valleys. When they crest the hills, she can see the snowcapped Ruwenzori mountains to their right, their peaks mostly hidden by a dense curtain of crowds; and farther south, behind and to the right, the jagged Virunga volcanoes. Under other circumstances the panoramic view would be exhilarating.

They fly over tiny communities, clusters of mud huts hidden in the valleys of these rolling hills, connected by a network of red dirt trails like capillaries. Once they cross a larger road, big enough for two-way traffic, but only a few burnt-out wrecks are visible. Then for some time there is nothing, an endless, undifferentiable ocean of green hills carved by winding, silvery rivers. Only the occasional tin roof winking in the sunlight, or the sight of a canoe in a river, indicates that the land beneath them is at all inhabited. Veronica remembers reading that three million people have died in the lands below them over the last ten years, victims of civil war and anarchy. It is a terrifying thought.

The helicopter follows the path of a river that cuts its way through steep and rocky gorges, a gouged scar in the dense green jungle. They fly over a series of whitewater rapids and waterfalls until they reach a steep river gorge with a floor that looks like an anthill, a broad swath of red populated by hundreds of little black dots. There is nothing green left in this sheer-walled valley, it is little more than a swampy, fissured field of red mud and water-filled craters. Beyond this ravine the whitewater resumes.

As they grow closer the dots resolve into men. Few look up towards the helicopter. Most are busy working in the river bed. Others shoulder enormous burdens and climb laboriously up the side of the gorge, in a single-file line that reminds Veronica even more of ants, ascending dizzying switchbacks to the wide, narrow ribbon of green on the overlooking cliff. An airstrip, paralleling the edge of the ravine.

The timbre of the engine changes, and the helicopter begins to descend to the airstrip. A battered wooden building with a tin roof perches between the grass runway and the nearly sheer rock face. There is a satellite dish beside it. Some kind of settlement has grown on the other side of the airstrip, a collection of tent-like shelters, most of them little more than primitive tepees, canvas or plastic sheets draped over cut branches. Tendrils of smoke rise from open fires.

There are people moving amid the settlement. None pays much attention to the incoming helicopter. The landing is much smoother than the take-off until the final shuddering transition from airborne to earthborne. After the engine shuts off Veronica's ears keep ringing with its noise. Momentum keeps the rotors spinning.

The pilot detaches his headset, revealing a ragged beard and shoulder-length dark hair. He disembarks and walks to the sagging, weatherbeaten wooden building. The gunmen sitting in the back stay where they are, waiting for something. Boys begin to stream on to the runway, hooting and shouting with mocking triumph, boys armed with guns or pangas or both. Most are in their teens, but some look no older than twelve. Most are shirtless. Their eyes are wide and bloodshot. Dozens of them throng around the helicopter, waving their weapons in the air, pretending to shoot at their new captives, poking with gun barrels at those sitting on the sides of the benches.

Veronica looks beyond their homicidal welcoming committee, hoping for some reprieve. She sees a huge machine gun fed by long chains of bullets, and two rocket launchers, gleaming bulbous cones sprouting obscenely from tarnished tubes of dark metal, propped up against a big wooden crate. The ground is strewn with yellow plastic jerrycans, metal pots, empty bottles, coils of wire, charred bits of wood, unidentifiable debris. A few lean, feral-looking dogs prowl the open places. A scattering of older men sit and stand amid the shelters, dreadlocked men in their twenties and thirties, lean and strong, wearing rubber boots, red bandannas, necklaces of bones and bullets, pangas and rifles. They observe the airstrip with cold, flat expressions that make Veronica shiver. It is like staring into a nest of rattlesnakes. The exuberant frat-boys-gone-psychotic aggression of the teenagers is almost charming compared to the silent, predatory menace beyond.

Beside her, Derek says, his voice raw, 'I'm sorry. I don't think we're going to get out of this.'

8

Three men emerge from the wooden building: two in dishdashas, and a smaller man dressed neatly in hiking boots, jeans and a blue button-down shirt. The hollering teenagers fall silent and back away from the helicopter as these men approach. The smaller man wears glasses. His face is lined, his hair is beginning to go grey, but he is still trim and fit. Except for the little fur pouch hanging on a gold chain around his neck, he looks like a middle manager on casual day, would fit neatly into any Western street scene.

Veronica sees Derek start suddenly, as if remembering something. He says something that sounds like 'euthanasia'.

One of the two men in dishdashas is black, short but hugely muscled, like a professional wrestler. The other is lighter skinned, Middle Eastern. He shouts to the men in the back of the helicopter in a guttural language that must be Arabic. Veronica moans when she hears this. It feels like final confirmation that Derek's worst-case scenario is somehow, unbelievably, exactly what has happened. They have been seized by Islamic terrorists.

Derek turns to Veronica and demands in a shaking, angry voice, 'Was it you?'

She stares at him. He has gone pale, every muscle in his face is taut, he is trembling. She isn't even sure she heard him correctly in the wake of the deafening helicopter noise.

He says, louder, though she can still hardly hear him, 'You fucking answer me. Did you set me up? Was it you?'

'I don't know what you're talking about,' Veronica manages, totally baffled.

'Don't you lie to me.'

'I'm not lying. I don't—'

'Did your husband send you?' he demands.

'What are you talking about? I'm not even married.'

'You were. To Danton DeWitt. Did he send you?'

Veronica gapes at him. The world seems to spin around her. She has never spoken Danton's name to Derek or any of her other fellow captives. 'How . . . how do you even know who he is?'

'Did you know he was involved? Is that why you came to Africa?'

'Involved in *what*?' she bleats.

Derek looks at her, then back to the man in glasses outside the helicopter, who has withdrawn something metal and plastic, something familiar, from his shoulder bag. The device is so out of place it takes Veronica a second to identify it as a small handheld videocamera. He puts it to his eye and records as the black men in dishdashas grab the white captives and half lead, half drag them away from the aircraft. The Arabic man stays where he is, holding a curved and gleaming panga. Veronica thinks of the American hostages taken in Iraq, captured by insurgents and beheaded alive. She feels dizzy again.

The air smells of wet decay. The ground of the airstrip is not so much grass as dense weeds cut to ankle height, furrowed in places by muddy tyre marks. Dozens of gunmen surround them in a circle several rows thick, like an audience for a particularly good street performer. The Arabic man steps up to the roped-together line of captives. Veronica, who is at the front of the line, freezes as he lifts his panga. He cuts her free. Then he cuts loose Derek behind her, grabs him by the back of his neck, shoves him roughly to a point about ten feet away from the others, and gives his panga to another man in a dishdasha, the one who looks like a body-builder.

'This is a set-up,' Derek shouts to Jacob, the words spilling out of him, talking as fast as he can. 'This was never a random kidnapping, this is a fucking execution. Islamists and *interahamwe*, working together, that's exactly what I was here to investigate, someone set me up—'

The Arabic man punches him in the stomach. Derek falls to his knees on the airstrip, doubled over, the wind knocked out of him, gasping for air. Then the massive bodybuilder man lifts his panga high and brings it down in a glittering arc so fast Veronica doesn't even have time to scream. Blood spurts from the back of Derek's neck and he collapses on to his belly. His attacker drops to one knee and his panga rises and falls again, and then a third time. Veronica can't scream, none of them can, it is too awful, she can barely breathe. Derek's head rolls forward from his body, leaving a ragged, bloodsoaked discontinuity at his neck. Blood gouts on to the weeds. Veronica's mind reels, but she can't look away. It feels almost like there is something wrong with her vision, not with Derek, like if she looks hard enough, she will see his head above his shoulders, rather than the pale knob of his severed spine set in crimson flesh and torn flaps of skin.

Somebody grabs the back of Veronica's neck, pulls her around, leads her past the helicopter, across the airstrip, towards the edge of the gorge. She is vaguely aware that the faint animal keening she hears is coming from her own throat. The others are dragged behind her. The middle-aged man with the camera finishes his close-ups of Derek's beheaded corpse and comes up beside her, walking sideways, filming their staggering march like some kind of demented tourist. The Arabic man walks on their other side, in view of the camera. Veronica wonders whether they are going to be thrown off the edge of the gorge. It seems very likely, but she doesn't struggle. She feels as if she has been strapped into a runaway train, has lost even theoretical control over anything that happens to her. Derek is dead. They actually cut his head off.

Veronica knows intellectually she should try to fight, to run, but the idea seems ridiculous, she is helpless, escape is hopeless. It is easier to just detach herself from what is happening, to watch as if from a great distance, as if she is just a temporary passenger in this body.

There is a trail-head at the edge of the cliff, a narrow and treacherous path that zigzags and switchbacks down the steep and rocky slope to the muddy gorge below. Veronica is thrust on to the trail so hard that without her arms to right herself she very nearly overbalances and tumbles to her death. Instead she falls and scrapes her right leg bloody. She gets up and immediately begins to descend the trail, she needs no encouragement, all she wants is to get away from the horror she has just witnessed.

The valley floor below has been reduced to a swamp of red mud gouged into hills, mounds, fissures and craters. At least a hundred men are labouring here, digging from the river bed, dumping muck into what looks like giant wooden bathtubs, pouring water into those tubs with buckets, sifting through what remains. Others hold whips and pangas and move among the workers, watching hawk-like. Veronica sees a small group of armed men at each end of the gorge, where violent rapids begin. The base of the other side has been so hollowed out that the massive cliff above now forms a slight overhang. A ragged wooden shelter has been built in its shadow.

Veronica's feet squelch into wet mud. She has finally reached the bottom of the gorge. She looks up and back. The other captives are a minute behind her, still roped together, forced to move at the pace of their slowest member, probably Diane. The three men in dishdashas follow them, as does the small man in glasses. The videocamera swings on a strap from his shoulder as he navigates the steep trail.

The gorge is maybe a hundred feet across. Work near her has slowed or stopped as both labourers and overseers turn to watch their pale-skinned visitors. Veronica takes two deep breaths.

68

Then she starts to run. She doesn't think she has much of a chance, but she has to try, they're going to kill her.

The mud sucks at her feet, it's more a stumbling jog than a run. She angles towards the river, avoiding the nearby workers. Nobody seems to react for what feels like a long time; people stare but do nothing, as if she is a crazy person on the street, best avoided. Then she finally hears shouts from up above, and some of the overseers, the men carrying whips, move to intercept her. But they are too late, she has reached the main flow of the river. She dives into it with all the strength that remains in her legs. It is shallower than she hoped, only waist deep, with a bottom of mixed mud and gravel, but it flows fast enough to carry her past the first two overseers before they reach her.

She tries to kick and paddle, to accelerate downstream. It's hard to keep her head above water with her arms tied behind her back. Nobody seems to have jumped after her. She distantly remembers reading somewhere that most Africans can't swim. Then she remembers why, it's because their lakes and rivers are infested with crocodiles, but never mind that, she'll worry about four-legged predators once she gets away from these two-legged ones. She twists her body and lifts her head and catches a glimpse of the four gunmen at the end of the gorge, stationed just before the river plunges over a rocky cliff. The spray from the rapids beyond rises above their heads. She remembers seeing the valley from above, how it was bracketed on both sides by fierce white-water. If the rapids don't get her then the crocodiles and the Congo jungle probably will, but at least this way she has a chance, however small. She knows she won't be followed, it's like *Butch Cassidy and the Sundance Kid*, no one who didn't absolutely have to would go into these rapids.

The roar of the water quickly becomes thunderous, the river sweeps her downstream faster than she expected, the current is accelerating. She has to writhe for every breath, she can't hold a steady position. One of the gunmen steps into the river and reaches out to catch her. Veronica curls into a ball. He grabs at her – and her foot pistons out into his crotch. He lets her go immediately and sits down comically, clutching himself, and then her stomach lurches as the river sweeps her over a six-foot drop and into a deep, violent cataract of churning whitewater.

Veronica is flung in one direction, then pulled in another, scraped painfully along a jagged wall of rock, forced suddenly downwards and pinned on her back against the river bottom by a relentless jackhammering flow of water that feels like a wall. She can't break free, the water is far too strong, she isn't even sure which way is up. All she knows is that she is trapped and she is running out of breath.

Don't panic, she tells herself. *If you panic you're dead.* Her arms are behind her. That's something. She grabs at the darkness and her fingers close on sharp rock. She tries to pull herself sideways, crabwise, instead of fighting the full brunt of the current. She isn't strong enough, not even close, she exerts all her remaining strength and succeeds in shifting herself only an inch – but this is enough to break the equilibrium. Suddenly she is torn from the watery prison and catapulted back up to the surface, just long enough to grab a breath before she is dragged back into the river. Its power is overwhelming, she is like a feather in heavy surf, the notion of fighting for any kind of control is laughable. She will go where the water takes her. Veronica curls into a ball and hopes for the best. Seconds later her head slams into solid rock and everything goes dark.

9

The world is bouncing up and down. No: she is bouncing up and down. Her head hurts beyond description, it feels as if it has been split open, like a coconut. Veronica opens her eyes and is amazed to find they still work. She is hanging upside down, draped over the shoulder of some strong but dangerously thin man. They are climbing an uneven scree of rocks and tangled bushes. Her head is level with his thighs. Veronica opens her mouth and throws up weakly all over the back of his legs. He doesn't even break stride. His ankle is marked by a ring of scar tissue. She wonders dizzily if he was the one who found her, whether he drew her from the water and saved her life, or whether she clawed her way on to dry land herself, semi-conscious. She can't remember. She feels physically broken, a rag doll barely strong enough to breathe, but she doesn't feel dazed, her mind isn't rattled, her thoughts are sharp and her memories intact up to the moment her head hit rock.

Watching the world upside down is a queasy and headache-worsening experience. She keeps her eyes closed during the journey. She can tell the man carrying her is near the edge of his endurance too, his muscles are quivering. Finally he stops, drops to his knees and dumps Veronica ungently on to mud.

She opens her eyes and her heart sinks. She is back in the gorge, in the shadow of the overhanging cliff. There is another man in front of her, standing above her, holding something. The little man in glasses, filming her with the videocamera. A hand grabs Veronica's hair and pulls her up to her knees. She moans, her voice weak and hoarse. She does not resist as someone behind her wraps a rusting chain tight around her neck and locks it with a battered brass padlock. Maybe thirty feet away, in the ragged wooden structure at the base of the cliff, the other captives huddle, watching aghast.

The man with the camera approaches her, zooming in.

'Fuck you,' Veronica says dully, and tries to spit at the camera.

The man behind her, the muscular man who killed Derek, pulls hard on the chain around her neck. She falls on to her back, gagging. Three men in dishdashas stand around her. One kneels behind her head, holding her chain. Another sits on her legs, pinning them. The third, the Arab, draws the panga from his belt. Veronica hears herself moan. The cameraman films the Arab as he poses dramatically, then lowers the blade to Veronica's throat. She feels the cold metal against her skin. The mud is soft and damp beneath her. She can't breathe.

'Please, no,' she whispers.

The camera turns to her. The panga rises into the sky. The Arab tenses, waiting like a home-run hitter ready for a fastball. Veronica starts to cry. This can't be happening. This can't be the moment of her death.

'No, please,' she weeps. 'Please, I don't want to die. I'll do anything you want. You can do anything you want to me. Just please don't kill me, please, anything you want, anything, just please don't kill me, please, please.'

Her voice dissolves into racking, incoherent sobs. The cameraman grunts, a satisfied sound. The Arab lowers the panga. The man on her knees gets off, and the man behind her gets up and yanks on the chain he holds, pulling Veronica brutally to her feet. She is led like a dog over to the structure where the others huddle. It covers a space about twenty feet by ten, made of thick branches lashed together by vines, roofed by a ragged patchwork of canvas and plastic tarpaulins. Two plastic buckets sit by the cliff wall.

Veronica collapses to the ground. She can't stop crying. Her head hurts and when she puts her hand to her face she discovers her head is half covered in dried blood. Jacob comes to her, takes her in his arms, holds her wordlessly. The others too have been leashed, and then padlocked to a huge cinder block half sunk in mud. Veronica's chain is added to the tangle. Then the men in dishdashas and the cameraman walk away, back towards the trail that climbs to the airstrip.

Veronica holds Jacob tightly, like a frightened child. Judy sits next to them. She too has been crying. She puts her arms around Jacob and Veronica, and then Tom joins their communal embrace. Michael and Diane stay back. It takes a long time before Veronica's sobs peter out into silence.

At length Veronica whispers, 'What happened to Susan?'

Jacob shakes his head. 'They took her away.'

Slowly they disentangle.

'I wish I knew where we were,' Tom says sadly. 'I'd just like to know where I am.'

Veronica thinks it a very strange sentiment, but Judy nods her understanding.

'I can tell you exactly where we are,' Jacob says bitterly. 'The heart of fucking darkness. The perfect storm of bad guys. The guys with guns are *interahamwe*. The ones in dishdashas are terrorists, probably fucking al-Qaeda, for real.'

'*Interahamwe?*' Judy asks. 'Are you sure? Some of them are teenagers. The Rwandan genocide was eleven years ago.'

'I saw Derek's face. He wasn't guessing. He *recognized* the guy with glasses, he knew him. But you're right, not the kids. The *interahamwe* are the older ones with dreads. Ran away from Rwanda ten years ago and been killing their way across the Congo ever since. The kids must be local recruits. Probably taken away after their parents were murdered, raised by monsters. But the ones in dishdashas, speaking Arabic? They're not *interahamwe*. The Muslims were the only group in Rwanda that *didn't* participate in genocide. It's perfect, when you think about it. The terrorists have money, weapons, international connections. The *interahamwe* have muscle and places like this.' Jacob waves at the scores of men working in the red mud around them, digging and sluicing and sifting. 'They run these slave-labour open-pit mines, fucking fifteenth-century technology, then smuggle what they get to the Islamists, who sell it in the Middle East. I figured this was a gold mine at first, but I've been looking at what they keep, and it's not gold. I think it's coltan.'

He sounds as if he thinks it matters that he has figured out who has captured them and what is being mined here.

'Coltan?' Tom asks.

'World's most efficient heat conductor. Used in cell phones, PlayStations, advanced electronics. Eighty per cent of the world's supply comes from the Congo. Shit, I've *designed* chips that had to use coltan in the heat sinks, I've written it down as a requirement in the specs. Never even thought about where it came from.' Jacob looks around. 'Hell of a way to find out. Karmic payback or something.'

'Look,' Judy says suddenly, straightening up and pointing.

Everyone looks to the trail that leads up to the airstrip. Susan is at its base, being led across the gorge by the Arab man. She walks like a sleepwalker, hunched over in a kind of dazed shuffle, dragged along like a recalcitrant pet. The men in dishdashas follow. There is blood around Susan's mouth, and she no longer has a bra on beneath her torn T-shirt.

The Arab man attaches Susan's chain to the cinder block. She crumples to the ground, her face slack and her eyes unfocused. Veronica wonders distantly why she hasn't yet been raped herself. Maybe she looks too wretched to bother with. Maybe they just wanted the blonde girl first and are saving Veronica for later.

Judy goes over to Susan, tries to hold her, somehow comfort her. Susan recoils from the contact as if Judy is some kind of loathsome insect. Judy hesitates, then returns to the others.

The Arab man produces a key and begins to unlock chains from the cinder block. Veronica tenses as Michael and Diane are detached from the anchor.

'No,' Diane says, frightened. 'No!'

The strongman who killed Derek takes the end of their chains and begins to pull them away.

'You're not taking us anywhere,' Michael says like a petulant child. He grabs his chain and Diane's and tries to pull them free. 'No. We're staying. We're staying here. Don't be stupid. I can get you money. I can get you a million dollars.'

The man with the camera barks an order. Another dishdasha man takes the panga from the Arab, walks up to Michael and unceremoniously thrusts the weapon into the American's stomach. Veronica gasps. Michael lets go of the chains and grunts as if with mild surprise. The blade doesn't penetrate very far, only a few inches, pangas are designed for slashing not thrusting, but Veronica knows that's enough to perforate the intestine.

Michael stares disbelievingly down at himself as the blade is withdrawn and blood gouts forth. Diane begins to scream. The strongman yanks hard on their chains, choking her silent and

74

pulling Michael to his knees. Then he has to scramble to his feet again as he and Diane are forcibly dragged away from the wooden shelter, across the ravine. The cameraman and the other men in dishdashas follow. The trail of blood Michael leaves behind glistens in the sun.

On the other side of the gorge he collapses like a toy whose battery has run out. The other prisoners stare, silent and aghast, as the Americans are carried up the trail that ascends to the airstrip.

'I just want to go home,' Veronica whispers, but no one seems to hear her.

10

'They won't come for the rest of us yet,' Jacob says thoughtfully, in his slightly nasal voice, as if proposing a solution to an interesting puzzle. 'Not today. They'll want to maximize the media coverage. They have enough now to make a big splash, they'll want to draw it out as long as possible.'

'Media?' Judy asks.

'That's why we're here. That camera. It's like those hostages in Iraq. al-Qaeda doesn't just kill the people they grab, they kill them *on video*. And not for *Taliban's Funniest Home Videos*. For CNN. Bet you a million dollars the footage from that camera will be edited and released to al-Jazeera some time this week. They know what they're doing. Dead bodies are a story that runs once. Live hostages have legs.'

'Then we've got a chance,' Tom says desperately. 'People are looking for us. They could have tracked the helicopter. They might know we're here.'

Jacob shrugs. 'I doubt it. Everyone gets around by air in eastern Congo, they have to, there aren't any roads. I'm thinking, if they couldn't find us at Gabriel's, they won't track us down now. Maybe that's why they kept us there for a few days, let the trail cool down. Or maybe Gabriel decided to renegotiate his price after he grabbed us. Either way, I strongly doubt anyone knows we're here.'

Veronica sags to the ground, defeated. There is no out, no escape from the terrorists. Some time in the next few days, maybe later today, they will all be killed. She will be beaten and gang-raped and murdered with a panga.

Then Jacob says, 'But maybe we can tell them.'

After a communal moment of silent surprise, Tom asks, 'How?'

'That satellite dish up there. All I need is five minutes alone with it. Or with that Thuraya satphone of theirs.'

'Up next to the airstrip?' Tom shakes his head, and his chain rattles. 'Might as well be in Timbuktu, mate. Unless you have a way to get free of these bloody chains.'

Jacob has no answer. The hope that briefly flowered in Veronica's heart quickly wilts. She turns and stares dully at the river. The workers are keeping their distance from the white prisoners; the nearest team of men is a good hundred feet downstream, digging near the riverbank, filling hand-woven baskets with red mud. They are desperately gaunt, they remind Veronica of Holocaust pictures, but they work ceaselessly under the sharp eye of their whip-wielding overseer. Veronica can't believe she is in this horrific place. She can't believe a place like this even exists.

'They didn't even leave us guards,' Jacob says. 'Nobody's watching us. They're overconfident. There has to be some way out of here.'

But nobody has any suggestions.

'Look on the bright side,' Tom says to Jacob. 'You're Canadian. They might let you go. Not us, not her, but maybe you.'

'Derek was Canadian.'

'Yes, but he . . .' Tom hesitates. 'I thought he said he was set up.'

Jacob nods slowly. 'Yeah. He did.'

Veronica blinks. A memory creeps through her despair and into her pounding head. Derek's last words, shouted to the others: *This was never a random kidnapping, this is a fucking execution. Islamists and* interahamwe, *working together, that's exactly what I was here to investigate, someone set me up—*

And before that, in the helicopter, even more mystifying: *Was it you? Did your husband send you? Danton DeWitt. Did he send you? Did you know he was involved? Is that why you came to Africa?*

'This isn't coincidence,' Jacob says. 'Derek gets kidnapped by the same people he was investigating? No way that happened at random. He was set up. We all were. Someone knew he was going to Bwindi and wanted to stop him before he found something.'

'Investigating for who? Who did he work for?' Tom asks.

Jacob hesitates. 'Private security consulting company called Azania. It was just him and his partner, guy called Prester. Doesn't really matter now. We're here. He's dead. The why stopped being relevant a while back.'

Veronica opens and then closes her mouth. She wants to tell them he mentioned Danton's name, but Jacob is right, it doesn't matter any more. Still, the question nags at her. She never mentioned Danton to Derek at all. She certainly never mentioned her ex-husband's full ridiculous name. So how did Derek know it?

Could Danton have been involved with terrorists? No, the notion is ridiculous, laughable, obviously false. Danton is not a nice man, their divorce proceedings made that abundantly clear, but there is no way he supports Islamic terrorists. It's true that he has African connections – it's even true, in a roundabout way, that Veronica is in Africa thanks to those connections – but Danton is a commodities trader, not some kind of international terrorist financier. She shared his life for seven years. She ought to know.

She can't come up with any answer that makes sense. Her head hurts too much to think clearly. Anyways, it doesn't really matter.

The Night Of Knives

Derek is already dead. She will join him soon. Veronica almost wishes they would come right now and get it over with. She is so weak and miserable, her head hurts as if her skull has been fractured, her ears are actually ringing with the pain, and her skin is riddled with innumerable other gashes and bruises and blisters, an inescapable, discordant symphony of pain. In many ways the end will be a mercy. Maybe she should try to find some way to finish it herself, suicide as a final act of defiance, a way to avoid whatever they will do to her before they kill her.

Veronica wonders who will really grieve when she is dead. Her parents, of course. They are old and frail, they married late and had her late in life, she is their only child, the shock of it might kill them. Nobody else. After marrying Danton she drifted slowly away from all her friends.

The daylight begins to fade. They hear and briefly see the helicopter fly away. A boy with a gun brings them a bucket of rice. They eat in silence, except for Susan, who doesn't eat at all. The rice is dirty and undercooked, and Veronica doesn't feel the least bit hungry, but she forces herself to eat nonetheless. She wonders why their captors are bothering to feed them at all. Maybe so they won't be too weak to scream and plead when they are executed.

At least her sickness has abated. A small mercy, if a mercy at all. It was easier to cope when her mental acuity was sapped by sickness. This endless gruelling fear is crippling, both mentally and physically, her stomach muscles cramp violently every time the image that has conquered her mind recurs: herself forced to kneel on the red river mud, naked and bloody and violated, as a man in a dishdasha stands above her, a machete in his hand. That is what will happen to her soon. Not a nightmare but a near-certainty.

Then Susan says, quietly, 'It's not over.'

Everyone turns to stare at the blonde British girl.

She says, 'Derek gave me something.'

*   *   *

'He gave it to me in the cave,' Susan says, looking down at the Leatherman multi-tool in her hands. 'They never . . . they never bothered to search my clothes.'

Tom shrugs indifferently. 'Lovely. What do you intend to do with it? Have a go at stabbing them all to death?'

'No,' Jacob says sharply. 'She's right. We can use it.'

'How?'

'These locks.' He fingers the little brass padlock on his neck.

'You can pick locks?' Judy asks.

'What I had in mind was more brute force and ignorance.' Jacob reaches for the Leatherman. Susan gives it to him. He opens the multi-tool's handles and snicks out one of its blades. 'Look at this hacksaw blade. Derek was showing it off to me last week. Hardened steel impregnated with diamond dust. Should be able to cut right through brass.'

'Then what?'

'Go up to the dish, call for help, run like hell, and hope the good guys find us before the bad guys do.'

'Not much of a plan,' Tom says doubtfully.

'Anybody got a better idea?'

Nobody does.

'He could have broken out any time,' Veronica says, amazed. 'Even back in the cave.'

'Sure,' Jacob says. 'Once. But then what? Run for it? They would have caught him. He was waiting for opportunity, but it never knocked.' He looks up to the top of the canyon. 'We have to make our move as soon as it gets dark.'

The first stars have already appeared in the sky. Down the length of the gorge, the slaves are beginning to cluster and huddle in little groups; apparently they sleep out on the mud. Most of the overseers are climbing back up to the airstrip, leaving only a skeleton crew of overnight guards at either end of the gorge. No one is paying any attention to the white prisoners, they aren't part of this ecosystem. A dim hope begins to flicker within her.

The sky reddens and darkens. It doesn't take long. At these equatorial latitudes night falls as suddenly as a stage curtain. Soon the strip of velvet darkness above is stuffed full of stars. Veronica can clearly see the gossamer ribbon of the Milky Way stretched across the night sky.

'All right,' Jacob says. He threads the hacksaw blade into the hasp of the padlock at his neck, and smiles thinly. 'You know, if this actually works, it'll be the greatest customer testimonial of all time, eh? My Leatherman got me out of the clutches of homicidal terrorists! Don't you *dare* leave home without it!'

No one else smiles. Jacob begins to work, holding the padlock with one hand, sawing rhythmically with the other. It doesn't take long before he begins to tire and slow. Veronica can't help but resent him for it a little. She feels like Derek, if he were still alive, would have cut through all their locks in a matter of minutes.

The rasping noise of metal biting metal seems very loud, she is frightened that someone will hear it, but nobody intrudes. Veronica waits tensely as the minutes drag by. She is very tired, she cannot remember a more draining day, but she is too nervous to sleep. Instead she lies on her back and stares up at the stars. She never realized how beautiful they could be. She promises herself, God, the Tao, whoever is listening, that if she gets out of this somehow, she will pay more attention to the beauty of the world, she will appreciate every golden moment of the rest of her life.

She falls into a dazed and trance-like state until a brief clatter of metal brings her back. 'Got it,' Jacob mutters triumphantly, breathing hard as he detaches his chain, then hands the Leatherman over to Tom. The portly British man seems stronger and works faster than Jacob, but Judy takes so long that Veronica actually falls asleep.

'Come on,' Jacob says, prodding her awake. 'Your turn.'

Veronica looks around wildly before coming to her senses. It is almost pitch dark. The others are all free. She takes the Leatherman in her fumbling fingers, remembering how she freed it from Derek's belt. The memory is somehow comforting, steadying. She inserts the blade into the lock at her neck and begins sawing back and forth. At first it doesn't seem to bite at all, and she begins to fear the hacksaw has worn smooth, but then it catches on the brass, rasps loudly as it begins to abrade and then to cut. Her forearms and biceps are already cramping. She switches arms, then switches back. Soon she has to rest between arms. A small eternity seems to pass, but when she pauses to inspect her work, only a shallow notch has been carved into the brass.

'What time is it?' she asks the darkness.

'No idea, love,' Judy says. 'They took our watches.'

Veronica swallows. 'If it starts getting light, go without me.'

'Don't say that. Get back to it.'

She obeys. Her muscles fall into a rut of sawing. She is getting clumsy now, keeps stabbing herself with the end of the hacksaw blade, and though it is dull she draws blood from her neck at least once, can feel it dripping slowly down her skin. Her mind seems to retreat from her, take a few paces back to observe, and she almost bursts out in giddy laughter. Here she is in a slave-labour mine, sawing at her chain, about to attempt a desperate escape: a situation so wrong, so ridiculous, so not the kind of thing that happens to people like her, that she has to bite her tongue not to laugh.

The moment passes. Veronica has to close her eyes and grit her teeth against the pain in her arms. She tries to belly-breathe, as if this is some kind of demented Lamaze class. But there seems to be no more strength left in her. She is about to ask someone for help when suddenly the hacksaw blade breaks free and the lock swings open.

Veronica's arms feel as if they are about to fall off, she can barely pull the chain from her neck, she is panting as if she just ran a marathon. But it feels so good to be free.

The starlight is not enough to navigate across the gorge. They have to crawl like animals, feeling their way through the mud. The river water feels very cold, and when they climb out on the other side Veronica starts to shiver. As if she didn't have enough problems already, now she has to worry about hypothermia.

It takes ages to locate the trail that leads up to the airstrip. It seems unguarded. Veronica supposes the last thing escaped slaves would do is climb to the *interahamwe* settlement above. Somehow they manage to ascend the treacherous switchbacks out of the gorge without tumbling to their deaths. It helps that they crawl. Veronica has to; her legs are too weak to climb. At least the exertion keeps her warm.

The trail seems endless, she feels like Sisyphus, doomed to climb until the end of time – and then suddenly she crests the cliff edge and sees the airstrip spread out before her, and above it a half-moon hanging in a canopy of stars, shedding enough light to make out even distant shapes. Veronica remembers the equatorial full moon from a couple of weeks ago, fat and radiant; remembers standing on a hilltop in Kampala with her housemate Brenda, reading a newspaper by moonlight just to prove that it was possible. It feels like remembering a past life.

She forces herself back to the present. Red embers are visible on the other side of the airstrip, in the *interahamwe* settlement, where something is flapping in the warm night wind. Veronica is glad of the wind, it swallows other sounds. Along the cliff edge to their left they see the wooden building, and beside it, looming in silhouette, the pale arc of the satellite dish.

'We have plenty of time,' Jacob mutters. 'It's just past midnight.'

'How can you tell?'

'Astronomy. The stars rotate around Polaris during the night, they're like a clock. Come on.'

The satellite dish is mounted on a metal pole set in the earth. Three metal arms project from the lip of its pale bowl, holding a small box at their apex a few feet above the dish. Three cables run from this box into the wooden building. The dish is mounted near the edge of the gorge, on the edge of an overhanging cliff. Jacob looks around as if something is missing.

'What's wrong?' Veronica whispers.

Jacob says, low voiced, 'We need power. There must be a generator, or batteries.' He touches one of the cables that leads to the wooden building, so old and weather beaten that its planks sag towards the ground. 'Inside.'

They look at one another.

'It's not like we have a choice,' Susan says.

She pulls open the single misshapen door as gently as possible. The one-room space beyond is obviously used mostly for storage; the walls are lined by piled bags, boxes, jerrycans, tools and random debris, looming shadowed and mysterious in the moonlight. There is a desk in the middle of the room, and on it a laptop computer. Jacob walks in and begins to feel around. After a moment Susan joins him.

'Wish we had a light,' Jacob mutters under his breath. 'Maybe turn on that laptop—'

'Here,' Susan says. 'Look. There's a phone.'

Green monochrome light blooms inside the hut, emanating from the clamshell cell phone Susan holds. Jacob kneels beside a tangle of wires, plastic and metal at the edge of the room.

'Here we go,' he says triumphantly. 'Car batteries. Must be seriously jury-rigged. But it will do if there's any juice left.'

He takes up two wires. A spark flickers between his hands, then another, and another; then three more, with longer pauses between; then three more, in quick succession.

'What are you doing?' Tom asks.

'Turning it off and on again.'

'That's all? That's our signal?' Veronica feels betrayed.

'Morse code,' Jacob clarifies. 'I'm doing some SOSes. Then I'll tell them what's happening, our names, everything.'

'Them who?'

He hesitates. 'Hard to say. The NSA is supposed to pick up every satellite signal on earth, and they should be looking for us. Also the satellite company might pick up on it, lots of guys who work there are ham-radio types, they'll know Morse code when they see it, and they probably have the lat–long coordinates of this dish. I never said this was guaranteed. But it's a chance.'

Veronica doesn't complain. Some hope is infinitely better than none. She goes back around the building, just to be sure, and when she sees a little green LED winking on and off above the dish, her heart soars. It seems incredible that they can communicate across the world with nothing but that box full of electronics, the ceramic dish below and the few stacked car batteries inside the building.

Susan joins her, still holding the terrorists' phone, now folded and dark. They wait in silence. A long time seems to pass before Jacob emerges from the building.

'OK,' he says shakily. 'Might as well stop, I'm getting too sloppy.'

'What do we do now?' Tom asks.

'Run. And pray.'

Jacob staggers with every step, and in the growing pre-dawn light Veronica can see that his face and arms are covered with blood and muck. She supposes she looks much the same. The world has begun to swim dizzily around her. Her throat is as dry as desert rock, she aches for water. She keeps having to reach for branches and tree trunks to steady herself. Luckily there is no shortage of those, and she has been pierced by so many jungle thorns in the last few hours that she has almost stopped feeling their white-hot bites. Behind them, Tom, Judy and Susan trudge mechanically onwards through the thick and trackless African bush.

'I don't understand why they keep biting me,' Jacob groans. 'I can't possibly have any blood left.'

Veronica says, 'We all have malaria by now. Guaranteed.'

'Ten-day onset time. If we're still alive in ten days I will treat cerebral malaria as a cause for rampant celebration.'

They reach another thicket so dense it is practically a wall. Veronica wants to go around, but murderous gunmen are surely on their trail already, and they have decided to continue due east no matter what, for fear of going around in circles. She groans, covers her head with her arms and forces herself into the bush.

The vegetation around here isn't like Bwindi. This soil is too stony to support huge canopy trees. Instead, low palms and vine-covered leafy trees stand above an amazingly dense underbrush of ferns and grasses, which in turn conceal creeper vines or thorn bushes that seem to reach out with stealthy fingers to grasp at passing ankles. The trees block out most but not all of the sun's dawning light. They have heard a few rustles of animals fleeing their noisy approach, and once something small and slimy, probably a frog, bounced off Veronica's arm, but otherwise there have been no signs of animate life. Unless she counts mosquitoes. Their ceaseless buzzing and biting threaten to drive her mad.

'Hey,' Jacob says wonderingly. He has stopped walking and is staring up into the air. 'You guys hear something?'

'Yes,' Tom grunts. 'Mozzies.'

'No. Listen. I think I hear a plane.'

Everyone stops and looks into the sky. Veronica realizes he's right, not all the buzzing is insectile, there's an airplane approaching – and suddenly it flashes past, as white as a cloud, half obscured by palm leaves, maybe a thousand feet above the ground. They glimpse it just long enough to register its odd shape. Its wings seem very long and narrow for its body, and two wide struts extend downwards from its tail, like a bipod support.

'Holy shit,' Jacob breathes, his voice full of hope and wonder.

'What is it?' Judy asks.

'Predator. Unmanned airplane. US military. They found us. They must have got the signal. They fucking found us.'

Hope erupts like flame in Veronica's heart. Rescue is on the way.

'We should signal,' Tom says, 'build a fire or something—'

Jacob shakes his head. 'No. They're not the only ones looking, remember? No point bringing them all the way here just to take pictures of us all getting shot. Just keep running and hope they find us first.'

The Night Of Knives

They push onwards. Just as Veronica begins to think they can't make it through this thicket, they will have to turn back and go around, her foot lands unexpectedly on smooth, bare dirt. It is only a foot wide, but it is unmistakably a trail, marked with prints of bare human feet.

'Do we follow it?' Judy asks. 'Or do we keep going east?'

Everyone looks to Jacob. He hesitates, then decides, 'There's a camera on that Predator. They won't see us in the bush, but they might on this path. We'll stay on it until it flies over again.'

They proceed north along the path. It is so much easier than fighting their way through the thorns and vines of the jungle, but even so Veronica doesn't think she can stay on her feet much longer. Her legs are starting to feel as they did on the death march from Bwindi, increasingly less responsive to her mind's commands. She wonders whether maybe it would be best to split up. Together they must be easy to track. Alone maybe at least one would get away or be rescued. It makes sense, like a kind of pre-emptive triage, but she doesn't want to be the one to suggest it. She doesn't want to be alone out here.

The black men with rifles who rise up from either side of the trail appear so suddenly and unexpectedly it is like they just winked into existence, were beamed down from some *Star Trek* spacecraft. There are six of them, in rubber boots and ragged khaki uniforms. When she sees them Veronica's legs give way with shock, and she half falls backwards, sits down hard on the ground. She feels frozen inside, as if her lungs and spine have turned to ice. It's over. They have lost.

But the black soldiers do not seem eager to kill or capture. Instead they stare at the five filth-smeared white people for a moment, then begin to speak excitedly to one another in soft words that sound unlike any African language Veronica has yet encountered. It slowly occurs to her that their uniforms are nothing like the crimson headbands and bullet necklaces of the *interahamwe*.

She looks around, confused. The others sway on their feet, looking as dazed as she feels.

Then one of the gunmen says, in strangely accented but understandable English, 'Everything is OK. Everything is a hundred per cent. We come to help you.'

'Who are you?' Jacob asks, his voice rasping.

The man says, as if it explains everything, 'From Zimbabwe.'

The Zimbabwean soldiers mutter to each other in low voices, tense but not frightened, as they move along the trail. Veronica doesn't understand what they are doing here, but she supposes right now that doesn't matter. It takes all her concentration just to keep pace with the soldier half carrying her. The trail has led them into another banana plantation, and the waxy leaves around them rattle in the wind. They stop every so often for one of the soldiers to shout into a massive old radio that looks like something from a Vietnam movie. It distantly occurs to Veronica that it might actually have seen service in Vietnam, and then been donated or sold to Zimbabwe as surplus. Whatever its provenance, it doesn't seem to be working.

When her legs finally collapse it is like it is happening to somebody else; she watches the ground rise to meet her as if she is riding in an airplane. Rough, strong hands grab and lift her. She wonders if this is what shock feels like, or if maybe she is dying, if all her life's strength has finally been spent.

She emerges from something between a daze and a blackout just as the trail opens into a hilltop clearing dotted by a few dozen thatched mud huts with sagging walls. Goats and chickens pick their way along the narrow dirt paths that connect the huts, run through the small agricultural patches that surround the hill and disappear into the bush all around.

The village itself seems empty of humans; but in the bean field beneath the hill there is a huge helicopter, painted khaki, covered with bulbous, streamlined projections. This ultramodern vehicle seems wildly out of place here, as if it has travelled in time, is taking part in an invasion of the eleventh century by the twenty-first. There are men milling around the bean field, a few white men in military fatigues and body armour, and many black soldiers in ragged khaki. The helicopter is embossed with an American flag and the words AIR AMBULANCE.

The sight of the American flag is like a jolt of electricity, makes Veronica's heart soar with the most intense joy she has ever experienced. She has never been so happy to be American. America has reached across the world to save its daughter. She can barely move, but she feels alive again, alive and triumphant.

Two men in civilian clothes, a wiry black man with dreadlocks and a tall grey-haired man with an acne-scarred face, supervise as she and the other survivors are strapped on to stretchers and lifted into the helicopter. A man with a red cross on his camouflage uniform stoops beside her and begins speaking to her in a Southern accent. She can't make out what he says, partly because the engine roars to life beneath them, partly because her mind has lost its ability to comprehend. It doesn't matter. She is safe now. She has been rescued. She can let herself go. The rotors of the helicopter begin to spin, and Veronica feels as if her mind is spinning with them, corkscrewing up into the blue sky and the dark void beyond, losing all awareness of the world and time.

11

She wakes to bliss. There are sheets over her body, pillows beneath her head, and her body is free of pain for the first time in recent memory. It feels like floating in a warm bath. She rolls on to her side, keeping her eyes closed, trying to draw out this deliriously wonderful daze as long as possible – but there is something against her arm, some kind of thin plastic tube. She tries to push it away but it seems stuck to her wrist. In fact it feels stuck *in* her wrist.

Veronica opens her eyes, alarmed. She is in a room decorated with wicker furniture, a big TV, a ceiling fan and a leopard-print blanket. It looks like a hotel room except for the wheeled cart next to her bed and the IV drip in her arm. She doesn't understand where she is or why. Her memory is a jumbled collage of nightmare images, blood and slaves and feral teenagers with dead eyes, chains and guns and pangas, Derek's severed head, their desperate escape through thickets of thorny bush.

Recollection trickles slowly into her muzzy brain. She lifts up her blanket and peers beneath. Somebody has dressed her in a hospital robe. Her numberless wounds have been treated and dressed with white gauze bandages, although several are already dark with seeping blood. She feels oddly dissociated from her body, like it used to belong to someone else. Veronica puts her hand to the side of her head and feels fresh stitches. It doesn't hurt. She's drugged, she realizes distantly; that IV is overflowing with analgesics, maybe even morphine. Which is fine by her.

She lies in bed for a long time before deciding to mount an expedition for the TV remote control. It lies tantalizingly close, on a table not ten feet away. Sitting up is hard. Swinging her legs over the side of the bed is harder. Standing up is nearly but not quite impossible. She grabs the IV rack and uses it as support as she shuffles dizzily across the room. Through the window she sees daylight and palm trees. She wonders where she is. Maybe she's been flown back to America and that's Miami outside. She could look, but the window seems so far away. The TV will tell her. She harvests the remote control and is on her way back to bed when the door opens.

'Well, aren't you a lively one,' the plump, middle-aged black woman says cheerfully. She wears an army uniform and speaks with an American accent.

'Where am I?' Veronica asks.

'You're safe. I'm your nurse, my name's Irene. Let's just get you back to bed.' She helps Veronica back to a horizontal position. 'How are you feeling?'

'I feel great,' Veronica says enthusiastically. 'What are these drugs?'

Irene laughs. 'The works. Analgesics, antimalarials, vitamins, minerals, we've put together a real party cocktail for you. You just sit tight. I'll be back right away. They'll be glad to know you're awake.'

She leaves without explaining who *they* are. Veronica turns on the TV. The entertainment selection consists of CNN, some French equivalent of the Discovery Channel, a soft-core porn channel and a very strange, cheaply made black-and-white movie which seems to be about genies who appear out of thin air and shower African crowds with money. Clearly she's still in Africa, some French-speaking nation. The third time she flips to CNN she sees Michael and Diane's faces on-screen above the words BREAKING STORY. Veronica nearly screams before she realizes they aren't ghosts, they are actually the subject of the piece.

The anchorwoman says, 'Mr Anderson and his wife were millionaire philanthropists who had come to Uganda to tour the missions and orphanages they funded. CNN has learned that earlier today America's special forces, aided by a local militia, mounted a dramatic assault on the terrorist headquarters in which dozens of terrorists were killed. The US government reports that all the other hostages have been safely rescued and are being treated in an undisclosed location. In a related story, well-known video-sharing website YouTube has agreed to remove the videos of these hostages that were uploaded to their site, several of which are already among their most viewed videos ever, but copies are still reportedly widely available on similar sites worldwide. Some of these videos portray the beheadings of Mr and Mrs Anderson, and of Derek Summers, a Canadian citizen.' Derek's picture appears on-screen. 'CNN has elected not to show any footage filmed by terrorists and we call on other news organizations to join us in this decision. Up next, sports and entertainment.'

Derek's face is replaced by that of David Beckham. Veronica switches off the TV and stares at its dark screen. Her head is starting to hurt, both inside and out, and her blistered feet too; but at the same time, her mind is beginning to clear. She almost wishes it wouldn't. She can hardly believe what she just heard.

The door opens and two men enter. One is white, tall, lean and middle aged, with greying hair, a badly acne-scarred face and jewel-blue eyes. He looks as if he has spent most of his life working outside. He wears nondescript jeans and a T-shirt, and holds a small metal briefcase. The other man is black, small, slim and strong, with dreadlocks cascading down his back, late thirties or early forties, dressed in black jeans, a Diesel T-shirt, North Face hiking boots, a diamond earring, a gold necklace and a chunky gunmetal watch. Veronica remembers vaguely that both these men were on the rescue helicopter.

'Miss Kelly,' the white man says. 'Are you well enough to talk?'

'I guess.'

'Good. My name is Strick. I work for the State Department.' His clipped voice has a military cadence. 'This is Prester. He was Derek Summers' colleague.'

'Pleased to meetcha,' Prester says, in a laid-back American accent.

Strick sits on a chair beside Veronica's bed, then opens his briefcase, withdraws a small electronic device and places it on the bedside table. His scarred face and icy blue eyes are mesmerizing. 'We'd like you to tell us everything that happened in your own words. Mr Rockel has told us his version already. Then we have some pictures we'd like you to look at.'

'Mr Rockel?'

'Jacob,' Prester clarifies.

Veronica nods, hesitates, stares at the voice recorder. She isn't sure what to say. Prester sits across the room on a wicker chair, watching carefully.

Strick cues her, 'Just begin at the beginning. You were in the Bwindi Impenetrable Forest, and—'

'No,' Veronica interrupts. 'I don't think that's where it started. Did you find Derek's body?'

Strick nods slowly.

'We found all of him,' Prester says softly. 'The Andersons too. They put their heads up on stakes by the airstrip.'

Veronica groans and closes her eyes. She opens them again in time to see Strick staring at Prester.

The black man shrugs. 'You want me to candy-coat it? After what they've been through I think we owe them the whole truth.'

Veronica says, 'He was set up. Derek. It started before we ever got to Bwindi. He was in Uganda to investigate links between terrorists and *interahamwe*, wasn't he? That's what he said, just before he died. It couldn't have been coincidence they kidnapped him.' She hesitates for a moment. 'And it wasn't coincidence he invited me. He thought my ex-husband was involved.'

Strick blinks with surprise, and Prester says incredulously, 'Your *ex-husband?*'

'Danton DeWitt.'

The name appears to mean nothing to either of them.

'When did he tell you all this?' Strick asks.

'Right before . . . before he died.'

'What did he say? What were his exact words?'

She recounts what she remembers. When Strick asks what happened next, she tells them of her desperate flight into the river valley, her escape into whitewater, how she was knocked out.

'We saw,' Strick interrupts, when she gets to the part about them holding her down and threatening her life.

It is her turn to stare with surprise. 'You *saw?*'

'The whole world saw,' Prester says. 'YouTube and the like. The greatest video hits of your abduction got uploaded from a Malaysian Internet café. Current theory is the terrorists who grabbed you emailed the footage to their buddies in Malaysia via that satellite dish you signalled with. Ain't the twenty-first century a kick? And guess what, you were a hit. Not a blockbuster, not exactly front-page news, but solid middle-page coverage around the world, and four of the top forty YouTube videos of all time.'

'Prester,' Strick says. 'This is a debriefing, not a gossip session.'
Prester rolls his eyes but shuts up.

Strick says to Veronica, 'That was the only time Derek mentioned your ex-husband's name.'

'Yes.'

'And minutes later you suffered a severe head injury.'

'No,' she says, knowing where he's going with this. 'I mean, yes, but it wasn't like that—'

'I understand you're an ER nurse. So I don't need to tell you how concussions can jumble the memory.'

'Derek said Danton's name,' Veronica insists. 'I'm sure of it.'

'What exactly does your husband do?'

'Ex-husband. He's a commodities trader.'

'I see. Where?'

'Legally, Texas, but really he divides his time between New York and Marin County.'

'And do you have any other reason to believe your *ex-husband* was involved in your abduction by Islamic terrorists and an *interahamwe* militia?' Strick's voice is rich with disbelief.

She swallows. 'No.'

She wants to argue, but at the same time she knows he's right, it doesn't make any sense at all. There's just no way Danton would ever have conspired with Islamic terrorists. So why did Derek suggest he was involved? How did Derek even know his name?

Strick nods, jots down a few words and says dismissively, 'We'll look into it. As for Derek being targeted, yes, obviously. Hard to say who by. Advance bookings are required to see the Bwindi gorillas. Any number of people could have known. Now please, Miss Kelly, go back to the beginning and tell us just what you experienced personally.'

Veronica decides she doesn't like Mr Strick at all. But he works for the State Department, his is the voice of authority, it is his job to avenge Derek. She accedes to his request and tells him everything that happened. It seems to take a long time.

'I don't understand,' she says when she finally reaches their rescue. 'Zimbabwe's a thousand miles south of the Congo. They don't even share a border. So what were Zimbabwe soldiers doing there?'

It is Prester who explains: 'Mugabe, Zimbabwe's president, he sent his army here to back Kabila against the Rwandans back in '99. After Kabila won he let the Zimbos stay – smart move, seeing as how he was in no position to kick them out – and granted them some seriously large land concessions. General Gorokwe, the guy who helped us get you out, is the personal overlord of a chunk of real estate the size of Delaware. And he sends most of the money he's squeezing out of the Congo back to *his* big boss, Mugabe, who these days needs every hard-currency penny he can get. It's all very feudal around these parts, case you hadn't noticed. Anyways, Gorokwe volunteered his troops to help out the special forces. Good thing too. They're jungle vets, they know the territory, we probably couldn't have extracted you without them.'

'Yes, thank you,' Strick says sharply to Prester. He turns back to Veronica, reaches into his briefcase and withdraws a black binder. 'We'd like you to look at these pictures and tell us if you recognize anyone.'

Veronica takes the binder. Prester walks over to look over her shoulder as she flips through it. The pictures are head shots of candid moments, blown to 8 × 10 size, often taken from across the street or across the room, some of them almost too blurry to be useful. There are no labels or captions, only a number in the top corner of each page. All the subjects in the first half of the book are black men. She stops about a third of the way through.

'That's him,' she says. 'That's the leader, in the glasses, the one who had the camera.'

'You're sure?' Prester asks sharply. 'You're absolutely sure?'

She says, 'Yes.'

Prester and Strick look at one another. Then Strick announces to the voice recorder, 'Miss Kelly has identified figure number thirty-one as the leader of their abductors.'

'Who is he?' Veronica asks.

'Please continue,' Strick says.

She doesn't. '*Who is he?*'

Prester and Strick exchange a look. Then Prester says, in a low voice, 'His name is Athanase Ntingizawa. He was one of the chief architects of the Rwandan genocide.'

Veronica remembers Derek starting with recognition, and saying something like 'euthanasia'. *Athanase.*

'Please continue,' Strick repeats.

Veronica turns the pages of the photo book. The second half of the binder is populated by Arabic men, but the terrorist who held a panga to her throat is nowhere to be found. She goes through the binder again, slowly, double-checking, before returning it.

'You got them, right?' Veronica asks. 'They're all dead?'

Prester shakes his head.

'But . . . they got away? CNN said—'

'Yeah. I saw. CNN said dozens dead. Which is true. But not Athanase, not the Arabs, none of the senior *interahamwe.* Just kids with guns. The real bad guys got away to play another day.'

Strick is staring angrily at Prester.

Prester shrugs. 'Never mind. What do you care? You're going home. I think we're done here, right?'

'Very,' Strick says curtly. He snaps his briefcase shut and stands up. 'Get some rest, Miss Kelly. We'll explain your options when you're more fully recovered.'

By the time it occurs to Veronica to ask what he means by *options*, or where exactly she is right now, they are already out the door.

12

Veronica disconnects her own IV. She knows when the drugs wear off she will start to hurt all over, but she wants to be able to think clearly again. She fights her way back to her feet and shuffles to her window. Her room is on the second floor of a walled and gated hotel complex screened by palm trees. A half-dozen military-drab Land Cruisers and Hummers are parked in its gravel parking lot. Two white soldiers in American uniforms guard the gate. She hears aircraft above, both airplanes and helicopters, a near-constant buzz of aerial traffic.

Irene comes in while she is on her feet.

'Just can't keep you down, can we, hon?' she says. 'Those poor feet of yours need a few more days off, you ask me.'

'Later,' Veronica says. 'Do you have any clothes?'

Irene purses her lips. 'Suppose we can track some down.'

'Could you? I can't stand hospital robes.'

'All right, will do.' But she doesn't move. She just looks at Veronica.

'What is it?' Veronica asks.

Irene says, 'Don't know if this is the right time. I'm not really trained for this kind of thing. But, listen, hon, we have specialists coming here to take care of you. We have a highly trained trauma counsellor, and another who specializes in counselling victims of sexual abuse. I'm sorry, hon, but I have to know, what did they do to you?'

'To me?' Veronica half laughs. 'Nothing.'

Irene looks at her sceptically.

'No, really. They . . . I think they raped Susan. The British girl. But me, I mean, they weren't exactly friendly, they put a fucking leash on me, and a machete to my throat, but physically, honest, I got out OK. Just what you see, cuts and bruises and blisters, and I was sick, I've probably lost a lot of weight, but I wasn't . . . nothing awful happened.'

'Sounds pretty awful to me.'

'It's over now. I don't want to see any counsellor. I'm fine.'

'I'll ask you again when you're sober.'

'I'm fine,' Veronica repeats. 'Could I just get some clothes?'

'I'm on it, hon.' Irene leaves quickly.

Veronica ventures into the bathroom. She wants to shower, but the idea of climbing in and turning on the water seems horrendously difficult and complex right now. There are a pair of flower-patterned slippers inside. She decides to try to go for a walk before the drugs wear off.

The door opens to an exterior walkway that connects the rooms, as in a motel. She's glad she's in a decent buttoned-up hospital gown, rather than a cheap backless one. There is a soldier at the end of the walkway, and she freezes in place, afraid she is violating some rule, but he just nods to her stiffly. He looks Latino and about nineteen. A small strip of tall ferns and palm trees grows just outside, and through them she can see some large body of water. It isn't the ocean, there are no waves.

She proceeds down the walkway until she reaches a covered patio full of tables and chairs. All are deserted except one table heaped with scrambled eggs, fresh fruit, French bread and coffee. Jacob is sitting there, his tall, gaunt body folded into a small chair, dressed in a hospital robe and bandages like hers, eating like he is trying to win a contest. Veronica's stomach lurches with desire.

He waves her over without stopping eating. She joins him and the next several minutes are devoted to food. At one point a formally dressed waiter comes up the stairs that lead to the patio and refills their coffee and orange juice.

'Where are we?' Veronica asks, when the ravenous void in her gut has been sated, for the moment.

Jacob points northwards. 'Pretty sure it's Goma, from the lake and those volcanoes.'

Veronica looks and sees jagged mountains rising into the sky above a ramshackle city, the same mountains they saw from the helicopter, a few days ago. She remembers looking at the Michelin map of East Africa as they drove from Kampala to Bwindi, less than a week ago; remembers Derek pointing out the Congolese city of Goma, right on the Rwandan border, a hundred miles south of the Impenetrable Forest, nestled between vast Lake Kivu and the towering Virunga volcanoes. It feels like a memory from long ago, from her childhood.

'Makes sense,' Jacob says. 'Goma's the headquarters of the UN peacekeeping mission. Probably the safest city in the whole Congo. Not that that's saying much.'

'No.' Veronica looks at the armed guards at the hotel gate. 'I think we're pretty safe here, though.'

'Yeah. They can't let us get abducted twice. Just imagine the headlines.'

'Have you seen any of the others?'

'No. I think they'll be in bed another day or two. They're older. Except Susan, and she . . .' His voice trails off.

Veronica nods. 'Did they offer you a trauma counsellor too?'

He nods. 'I told them no.'

'Me too. I don't know.'

'I read a study once they did of World Trade Center survivors. Those who went to analysis and counselling and joined survivors' groups and made cathartic art and so on were still totally screwed up three years later. The ones who just sealed it off and didn't talk about it and moved on were fine.'

Veronica nods. 'Yeah. It'd be like picking at a cut before it's even scabbed over.'

'Right.'

They sit in silence for a while.

Then Jacob says, 'I'm going to find them. Whoever did it, whoever set him up. I'm going to find them.'

Veronica looks at him. She doesn't know what to say. She would dismiss it as bluster, but Jacob doesn't seem like a blusterer. She settles on asking, 'How?'

'There are ways.'

She doubts it. But he has reminded her of one nagging question. 'Did Derek ever tell you why he invited me along?'

'No. Why?'

'I don't know exactly. But—' She hesitates. Maybe she shouldn't tell Jacob, shouldn't add fuel to his already burning desire for vengeance.

'But what?'

Veronica decides she owes him the truth. He's a rational, logical man. Once he recovers from this period of shock he'll surely come to his senses, do the reasonable thing and go back to Canada. 'On the helicopter, right after he saw Athanase – did Strick and Prester come to you too?'

'Yeah. They debriefed me. I knew Prester already, he was Derek's partner, I met him in Kampala. What happened on the helicopter?'

'Derek got all . . . weird . . . and asked me if it was me who set him up.'

'If it was *you*?' Jacob asks incredulously.

'Yeah. And when I said it wasn't, he asked about my ex-husband. He said his name. Danton DeWitt. I'd never told him or any of you about Danton, not by name.'

Jacob stares at her.

Veronica continues, 'He must have known before he ever invited me to Bwindi. Probably before he ever met me. I think . . . I think maybe that's *why* he met me. We were at a party, he seemed to, like, single me out.' She grimaces. 'I thought he liked me. Now I think it was because he knew I was Danton's ex-wife.'

'Danton DeWitt,' Jacob repeats. 'Tell me about him.'

'There isn't much to tell. He's not interesting. He's rich, he was born rich. He's a commodities trader. He is involved in a lot of African charities, his mother was born here. That's kind of why I'm here, I got involved in them, and then after the divorce I sort of talked one of them into bringing me over. I'm sure they ran it by him first. He probably okayed it because he didn't want me around. Too embarrassing.'

'Did you tell Strick and Prester?'

'Of course. But they don't believe me. They think it was my head injury, my memory got messed up. But it wasn't. He said

Danton's name, I'm sure of it. But listen, I promise you there's no way Danton is involved with terrorists. There's just no way. Derek must have made some kind of mistake.'

Jacob says, 'We'll see.'

Footsteps click up the stairs that lead to the patio, and Irene appears, holding a big bundle of clothing.

'What's this? Flying the coop?' she scolds them gently. 'I brought you clothes, but I'm not giving them to you until you're back in bed where you belong.'

Feeling a bit like a high-school student caught cutting class, Veronica shuffles guiltily back to her room. Jacob is two doors over. Pain is beginning to gnaw at her from a dozen places. She lowers herself wearily back to bed, turns on CNN and lets sleep wash over her again.

When she wakes up Veronica doesn't know how long she has slept, whether it has been hours or days. The light and TV clock tell her it is late afternoon. She hurts almost everywhere, inside and out, but she feels a little stronger too, the food helped. She decides to get dressed. When she strips off her hospital gown she sees that her body has shrunk amazingly, she has lost at least ten pounds in only a week.

The clothes Irene brought are ill fitting but better than nothing. She dons the slippers and shuffles back outside. No one is in sight on the walkway or the deck. Stairs lead downwards, and she descends them with the banister's help. At their base, a leopard-skin rug awaits, complete with head and jaws. Beyond is the small, clean hotel lobby. The sign on the desk indicates that this is the Hotel VIP. The young well-dressed woman behind the desk watches her with undisguised curiosity. Jacob sits on the couch near the main entrance, reading a thin, cheaply printed French-language newspaper.

'Hey,' Veronica says. 'What's news?'

'Hard to say. This is two months old, and my French isn't great. From what I can tell it's mostly complaints about how the elections aren't worth the paper the ballots are printed on.' He puts down the newspaper. 'Prester's going to take me to an Internet café to check mail and make some phone calls. The lines here aren't working, some technical glitch. Want to come?'

She nods and sits next to him. They don't speak, but their silence is companionable. After what they have been through together she feels closer to Jacob than to any of the friends back in America she has known for many years.

She wonders who she should call. Her parents, she supposes. She hasn't spoken to them much for years now, since her marriage. Her ageing ex-hippy parents hated Danton, took her wedding as a slap in their face. When the divorce hit she couldn't bring herself to go to them for support. It would have been too much like admitting they were right all along, and she had just crumpled up and flushed away the prime of her life. She tried to leave everything behind when she went to Africa, including her family, but they're still her parents, they must be deathly worried about her, and right now it feels like they're the only people in all the world who might care what happens to her.

Prester appears at the entrance, jangling keys in his hands. He doesn't look enthusiastic about Veronica's presence, but accedes to her company and leads them out into the parking lot. Two jeeps full of American soldiers are waiting for something, along with the two guards at the gate. Prester leads Jacob and Veronica to a green Mitsubishi Pajero. The American soldiers nod at Prester and swing open the hotel gate, and they advance into the streets of Goma. To Veronica's amazement, the two jeeps of soldiers roll out behind them. A military escort.

The Hotel VIP is an island of luxury in a sea of poverty. They turn on to a boulevard divided by a wide grassy meridian strewn with trash and plastic bags, occupied by vendors selling airtime cards, cigarettes and avocados as big as grapefruit. They share the potholed road with trickling streams of ragged pedestrians, hordes of cheap motorcycles, battered cars, less battered SUVs and a few angelically white UN jeeps. The high walls of the estates on either side are topped by barbed wire and broken glass. Curiously, Veronica doesn't feel overwhelmed by the in-your-face poverty, the way she always did in Kampala. It doesn't seem so bad compared to what she's seen in the last week.

She sees a helicopter pass above, heading south, towards the lake. The sun has disappeared behind the high bluffs to the west. The boulevard ends at a large roundabout surrounded by big colonial-era buildings that claim to be banks, a post office and the Hotel du Grands Lacs, but whose shambolic, half-collapsed appearance makes Veronica doubt they function at all. The roundabout also boasts a brightly coloured Vodacom store with glossy new ads and posters advertising new SIM cards for two US dollars.

'Dollars?' Jacob asks, pointing out Vodacom as they pass. 'Not francs?'

Prester says, 'It's a dollar economy. You only use francs for small change.'

As Veronica stares out of the window she begins to realize Goma is not quite the wretched wasteland it first seemed. Its buildings are low battered concrete, mostly unfinished, but some of these drab shells contain flashy boutiques selling stuffed toys or designer clothes. The streets throng with pedestrians: gangs of skinny teenagers selling gasoline from yellow jerrycans, men in sharp suits, young women with basins full of goods on their heads and babies strapped to their backs, elegantly dressed women hiding from the sun beneath rainbow-coloured parasols. A man chatting on a brand-new Razr cell phone is surrounded by street urchins playing soccer with a ball made of rags. It is a surreal melange of hypermodern and post-apocalyptic, but it's not nearly as overwhelming as it would have been just a week ago.

There is an Internet café next to the shuttered marble building that was once a post office, when the Congo was a nation-state in more than name. Shrivelled beggar women nursing malnourished infants hiss at Veronica, Jacob and Prester as they enter. One jeepful of soldiers remains outside; the others enter and take up stations at the door. The other customers look up briefly, then go back to their work. Detachments of armed men are apparently not unusual here. The café's fifty computers are named after the US states, and CNN plays on TVs in the corners. Veronica is glad to see that neither she nor Jacob is on-screen.

The bored young woman at the counter wears Parasuco jeans, a Versace shirt and diamond earrings. Her entire right eye is obscured by a milky cataract. Veronica writes down her parents' phone number and goes into a tiny phone booth. A minute later the phone rings, and when she picks it up, her mother is on the other end.

'Hello,' Veronica says. 'It's me. I'm fine, I'm safe.'

'Veronica?' her mother gasps. 'Oh, Veronica, oh, thank God, oh, thank *God*.'

Their conversation is brief. Her mother's voice is difficult to decipher, partly because it is tinny and faraway, partly because she starts weeping almost immediately. When her father takes the phone he too is crying. Their voices are frail, and Veronica knows it isn't just the connection. Her parents have grown not just old but feeble, fragile. She hasn't talked to them much in the last seven years. Maybe it happened then and she didn't notice. Maybe it happened this week, and the catalyst was the very public kidnapping and presumed murder of their daughter. Veronica has to cut the conversation short, she can't bear it. She puts down the phone feeling like a miserable failure as a daughter and a human being.

When she emerges from the phone booth, Prester gives the one-eyed girl a five-dollar bill, and she returns four filthy hundred-franc notes. He offers them to Veronica. 'Keep 'em. Souvenir.'

'Thanks.'

They return to Jacob, who is sitting at the computer labelled IOWA.

'Have a seat, check your mail, but make it fast,' Prester says quietly. 'I want to be out of here in five minutes.'

'What for? We just got here.' Jacob looks upset.

'We need to talk. In private. Without them listening.'

Veronica stares at Prester. 'Them who?'
'Strick and his boys.'
'Talk about what?'
'Five minutes,' he repeats.

13

The Pajero, followed by the two jeeps, drives along a crowded road, past vegetable and cigarette stalls, until the street commerce suddenly ends and is replaced by – nothing. The road opens into a vast blasted field of jet-black rubble. A few shattered, burnt, half-buried skeletons of houses emerge from the dark landscape, as do, unexpectedly, a few bright new half-constructed buildings. Men with picks chip languidly away at ridges and shoulders of the black rock. The field is littered with neat piles of shadow-coloured stones the size of watermelons; the walls going up around the new houses are made of those stones, mortared thickly together. In the pinkish sunset light the whole scene seems eerily unreal.

'What is this?' Jacob asks, astonished.

Prester halts his vehicle in the middle of this strip of wasteland that runs through the heart of Goma like an inky river, all the way to Lake Kivu, severing the city into two halves. It is wider than a football field. To the left, the waterfront is dominated by a massive, black-walled complex surrounded by a rickety collection of crude huts where women sit mending fishing nets. Farther inland, the rusted remains of several dozen vehicles lie jumbled like children's toys. The wide strip of jagged black continues inland towards the nearest mountain: a huge, looming, flat-topped presence maybe fifteen miles north. A plume of cloud rises from the edge of its summit.

'Mount Nyiragongo,' Prester says, pointing at the mountain. 'You've read your Tolkien? Four years ago Mount Doom went boom.'

Veronica understands. That isn't cloud above the mountain. It is smoke rising from a live volcano. Four years ago it erupted, disgorged a red river of lava that cut this city in two and cooled into the field of black rock around them.

'Let's go for a walk,' Prester says. 'But first, do me a favour, go through the pockets and seams of your new clothes, check your slippers, everything, see if you find anything hard and metal.'

Jacob stares at him. 'What is this?'

'Humour me.'

Jacob begins to feel along the seams of his clothes. Veronica does the same. Neither of them finds anything.

'Maybe I'm just being paranoid,' Prester says. 'Maybe not. Bet there's something in the car.' He chuckles. 'Which totally makes my day – it'll piss Strick off no end to know we talked but not know about what. Come on. Walk with me.'

First he goes over to the jeeps, which have stopped behind them, and explains that they're going for a short walk; then he leads Veronica and Jacob over the uneven, night-dark terrain. Veronica has to walk slowly and carefully in her thin slippers. Jacob at least has sandals. The vast field of black lava with the blue lake beyond, all limned in crimson sunset light, is beautiful in a stark and inhuman way. The workers are packing up their picks and departing. They walk about two hundred feet inland, to the piled mound of rusting vehicle carcasses that emerge like dinosaur bones from the solid lava.

'Goma's one tourist attraction,' Prester says. 'The car graveyard. Lava came spilling down, ran right through and blew up all the gas stations, picked up all these cars and for some reason dumped them all here. There's probably dozens more underneath.'

'What's that big compound by the water?' Jacob asks.

'MONUC headquarters. The UN peacekeeping mission.'

As if to underscore his words, the gates to the complex open, and three huge white UN vehicles, an armoured personnel carrier followed by two oil tankers, begin to climb towards them along the road carved into the lava field.

Prester offers them cigarettes. Veronica accepts. Prester lights up and looks around as if he is staring into a parallel dimension. Veronica shudders minutely as the smoke abrades the back of her throat, and again as the nicotine hits.

'So why did you drag us out here?' Jacob sounds a little exasperated.

Prester takes a long drag on his cigarette and says, distantly, 'Sometimes I think this whole country is cursed. First the Belgians, then Mobutu, now sheer fucking anarchy. Even nature. You see the lake? Pretty, ain't it? That's Rwanda across the bay there. See that hotel? That's where they planned the genocide. Well, that pretty lake builds up volcanic gases inside, and every thousand or so years they blow, suffocate everything within a hundred miles, then wipe it all clean with a tidal wave. Could happen any moment if there's an eruption beneath the lake. Would kill two million people in ten minutes.' He shakes his head. 'Some ultra-badass witch doctor must have cast the spell to end all spells on the whole Congo watershed. We had one hope, Lumumba, fifty years ago. But the CIA took care of him in a hurry.'

'We?' Veronica asks curiously. 'I thought you were American.'

'Kinda. I was born here. Kinshasa anyways, the capital, not that it's really the same country, that's a thousand miles west, there aren't even any roads there from here. But we moved to New York when I was eleven.'

'What brought you back?'

Prester sighs. 'I used to deal on the Lower East Side. Had to do it to pay my way through Columbia. Just little stuff at first. Then more and bigger. Then one day I had to get out, and all America was too fucking small. Came back here, never even got my degree. That's me in a nutshell. I'll spend my whole life two credits short of the Ivy League. Ain't life a joke?'

'Hilarious,' Jacob says curtly. 'Why are we here?'

Prester favours him with a dark look. 'You got somewhere else to be?'

'I'm just wondering if you have a point.'

'I'll get there when I get there. I'm doing you a fucking favour, man. I shouldn't be talking to you at all.'

Jacob looks unconvinced.

'Prester,' Veronica says the name slowly, remembering something. 'Prester John was a king, wasn't he?'

Prester blows a smoke ring. 'That he was. The legendary king of a fabulous Christian nation hidden deep in the dark continent. A kingdom of peace and love where the roads were paved with ivory and gold. Never existed, of course. But a whole shitload of crazy motherfuckers came here to look for him. And just look what they found instead.' He waves his arm to take in all of the country around them. 'Found and founded. Genocide and civil war. About four million untimely dead in the last twelve years, between Congo and Rwanda.'

For a little while he and Veronica smoke in silence.

Jacob asks, 'And now you work for the US government?'

'No, no, no. Bite your tongue, wash out your mouth. Not for. With. Independent contractor. Professional go-between. Protocol man. Human bridge between the Congo and America, providing that invaluable extra edge of local knowledge, cultural understanding and, most important of all, connections to everyone who's anyone. Least that's what it says on my business cards. Azania was a two-man shop. Me the protocol guy, Derek the security expert.' Prester hesitates, and his voice drops. 'We had real clients. Mining companies. But mostly, in practice, for real? Me and Derek were a deniable front for the CIA.'

The three letters seem to echo.

'You wouldn't believe all the shit going down out here nowadays,' Prester says. 'The new race for Africa is on. America, Britain, France, China, Russia, the Saudis, the South Africans, there's a whole new twenty-first-century Great Game going on, and everybody wants to win. That's the thirty-thousand-foot view. Sounds romantic, don't it? But zoom in close enough and what you see on the ground is a whole lot of people getting very fucking dirty.' He smiles sardonically. 'The funny thing is, Strick thinks I'm one of them. He will be so pissed that I'm talking to you *in camera*. But Derek said you were his best friend.' He turns from Jacob to Veronica. 'And if you were faking it when they put that panga to your neck, then you deserve all the Academy Awards ever made. So what the hell. Let's spread a little home truth around for once.'

'What truth?' Veronica asks.

'Ay, well, there's the fucking rub.' Prester drops his cigarette and grinds it out beneath his heel. 'Derek was set up. You know that. He knew too much. But what did he know? Not that terrorists were working with *interahamwe*. They went out of their way to make that very public themselves, didn't they? Told the whole fucking Internet. No, what Derek knew was that one of our bosses, one of our real bosses, in Charlie India Alpha, was covering up a small mountain of smuggling money. Just imagine. An American intelligence officer raking in profits from illegal cross-border trading by *génocidaires*. Working hand in hand with Athanase Ntingizawa, Captain *interahamwe* himself. Definite first-ballot member of the all-time bad-guy hall of fame, even before he jumped into bed with al-Qaeda. Bit of a résumé stain if that comes out, you know? The kind of thing that might drive the officer in question to some seriously extreme extremes, in order to sweep all the blood back under the carpet. Like cutting a deal with Athanase to murder the guy investigating the smuggling.'

Veronica opens her mouth and shuts it again. She can't believe she's hearing this, especially not here in this surreal place. She feels like she's in a movie, as if some director is about to shout *Cut!*

Jacob says, 'You mean Strick?'

'No. Strick is many shitty things, but on the take is not one of them. He's an asshole but a clean one. All God and country and ramrod up his ass. No, it's gotta be some shark in a suit farther up the food chain. Someone in Kampala, in the embassy. That's all I can tell you, I don't have any names.' He looks at Veronica. 'But you had one for me, didn't you? Danton DeWitt.'

'Danton's not in the CIA,' she says shrilly. 'This is ridiculous.'

'No. He'd be the outside partner. I looked him up today. Commodities trader, right? Legal smuggler, in other words. With lots of holier-than-thou charitable interests in this here dark continent, right? And an Old Rhodey mother? Makes sense to me.'

'No,' she insists. 'Danton's not . . . he's a selfish prick, but he's not *evil*. He wouldn't have worked with monsters like that. No. It's not possible.'

'I bet he didn't know,' Prester says softly. 'That's how it works around here. You don't ask where the diamonds and the gold and the coltan and the timber came from. You don't ask where your good buddy got all those dollars, or why he needs all those guns and pangas and whips. You don't ask how many slaves died and how many women got raped and how many children got press-ganged. You don't want to know.'

Veronica shakes her head. 'No. I still don't believe it. Danton wouldn't get involved with this.'

'Yeah? You think he's too goody-two-shoes? That surprises me. His daddy made all the money, didn't he? I've met lots of spoiled rich kids, and none of them ever struck me as particularly lawful good.'

'No. You don't understand. Danton wouldn't do it because he'd think it was beneath him. He already has money. What he wants is to be a big shot. Smuggling gold or whatever in Africa would be too small-time for him. Too pathetic.'

A moment of silence hangs over the apocalyptic wasteland.

Then Jacob says to Prester, intently, 'What else do you know?'

Prester shrugs. 'That's all I got. The good is oft interred with their bones. So let it be with Derek. He kept his whole life close to his vest.'

'So what do you expect us to do now?' Veronica demands.

'Do? Nothing. Quite the opposite. The whole reason I'm telling you this is to keep you out of trouble. I heard you talking earlier, on the patio. I'm warning you. Don't do it. Don't go poking around wondering what happened to him, or what your ex-husband was up to. Not even when you get back home, and definitely not here. This cover-up added up to at least six corpses already. Once you've gone that far it's real easy to add two more. And you ask me, our terrorist friends are far from finished. You know what was in the phone that British girl picked up in their camp? Cell-phone numbers for two hundred Western NGO workers in Congo and west Uganda.'

Jacob sucks in breath sharply.

'Yeah. We figure they were going to try to lure them into ambushes, capture more hostages. We should be able to stop that, but I expect they've still got plenty up those long sleeves. So you go home. Leave the intelligence to the professionals, be glad you've still got your heads on your shoulders, and don't go asking anyone any awkward questions. You are way out of your league here. Clear?'

Neither Jacob nor Veronica answers.

'I'm sorry. He was a good man. He loved Africa. And not in that let's-fix-it way most white folks get when they come here. He loved it for what it is. More than I can say.' He takes one last look around the lava field. 'Come on, let's head back. Be dark soon. Strick's made arrangements for you both to fly out tomorrow, collect your shit in Kampala, then fly back to New York. First class, on the government dime. Enjoy the ride. I figure you've earned it.'

Veronica can't sleep. Partly because she can't find any position that doesn't aggravate one or more of her blisters and bruises and wounds. Mostly because she can't stop thinking.

She knows she should go home. It is the right thing to do, the safe thing. The idea of staying is crazy. She can be on an airplane out of Africa tomorrow. But an airplane to where? She has no idea where home is any more. The black hole that was her marriage consumed her career and most of her friends. The whole point of coming to Africa in the first place was to forge a whole new life for herself.

Eventually she gets up and goes for a walk, makes her way down the walkway to the patio, careless of the pains that stab through her feet. A warm breeze wafts through the night air. Occasional airplanes groan along the flight path directly above the hotel. To the north, a livid crimson glow hangs in the night sky, emanating from the summit of volcanic Mount Nyiragongo; red light burning from a sea of molten rock seething within an open crater. Prester was right when he called it Mount Doom.

She supposes she should feel miserable. She's gone through unspeakable horror, been wounded and traumatized, and now she's supposed to abandon her new life. But standing here, in this surreal, cinematic place, breathing the night air of Africa, Veronica feels strangely jubilant. She came so close to death that every breath now seems a precious gift. She feels as if some kind of shell has been burnt away from her, leaving her lighter and freer, even younger. The downward spiral of her life during the last year, the divorce, her return to relative poverty, her inability to cope with life in Africa – these things all seem so trivial now. She's young and healthy and alive. That's all that matters. Not a divorce from a man she never really loved.

Danton. Derek thought, and Prester thinks, that her ex-husband was somehow involved in her abduction; that he was the partner of a corrupt American intelligence agent in the Uganda embassy who knew that the *interahamwe* smugglers were harbouring Islamic terrorists, and who ordered the capture and murder of Derek, and anyone unlucky enough to be with him in Bwindi, before Derek discovered too much. But the more Veronica thinks about that theory, the more it sounds both crazy and wrong. There's just no way Danton would have been involved in anything like that. Either Derek was just plain wrong about Danton, or there's something else entirely going on here. But what could that possibly be?

She shakes her head angrily. It shouldn't matter what Danton is doing. He's not supposed to be part of her life any more. Seven years of her life wasted, and now these seven days of horror, and the awful death of a man she could have fallen in love with. Except it seems even Derek was interested in her only because she was Danton's ex-wife. It feels like that's all she will ever be for the rest of her life. Especially if she goes back to America.

Veronica can't think of any reason to go back. There's nothing waiting for her there. It would feel like surrender. She came to Africa to reinvent herself. Just because she went through one awful week of torment doesn't mean she has to abandon that dream and go home to whatever squalid life awaits her in America. She can stay here now, she's sure of it. Life in Kampala will be a breeze after this week. She's taken the worst Africa can throw at her, and she's still standing. She doesn't have to give up now just because everybody assumes she will. That's just another reason not to go.

The sun has not yet risen over Rwanda when Jacob and Veronica arrive at the helipad just outside peacekeeping headquarters. Strick shakes their hands goodbye while the bored-looking Indian UN soldier inspects their orders.

'Don't take this the wrong way,' Strick says, 'but I don't ever want to see either of you again. Go home and don't come back.'

He turns and walks away before they can respond. The Indian officer hands them back their paperwork. Veronica was surprised to receive actual military orders, on an A4 sheet with her name and new passport numbers printed beneath official UN and MONUC logos, along with an official UN boarding pass, a brand-new passport good for one year, a first-class British Airways ticket from Kampala to JFK via Heathrow, and five new twenty-dollar bills in an envelope labelled 'per diem'.

'Wait,' the Indian soldier says, and directs them to a gaggle of troops, all of them Indian too, sitting cross-legged in the shade of the nearest big white helicopter. Jacob and Veronica join them. Strick drives away in his jeep. Two soldiers in blue berets appear with a plastic bag full of still-warm chapatis and a samovar full of sweet Indian chai. They eat and drink gratefully. The soldiers look at them sidelong but do not otherwise interact with them. Veronica supposes she and Jacob must look somewhat grotesque; her head is still bandaged, and they are both moving stiffly and covered by scabbed-over cuts and scrapes.

Eventually an officer stands and begins to bark loud orders in Hindi. The Indian peacekeepers climb into the helicopter and begin to strap themselves into the fold-down seats around its cargo area. After a few confused moments Veronica and Jacob join them. The seats are surprisingly comfortable. The cargo space is full of all manner of boxes, crates and bags, enough for a small truck, all tied down with netting. There are about forty passengers. Only a few seats are left folded up and unoccupied.

'I wish we could have said goodbye,' Veronica says. They tried, but Tom, Judy and Susan were still under sedation.

Jacob nods.

'Are you going back to Canada?'

'No.'

'I'm not going back either.'

He looks at her, surprised. 'Why not?'

'Because I don't want to.'

Jacob doesn't say anything.

'Are you still going to try to find out who did it? After what Prester said?'

He says, simply, 'Yes.'

The pilots are the last to board. Doors are closed, interior lights come on, the engine shudders into life, and the big chopper's two rotors begin to spin. A peacekeeper gives Veronica and Jacob earplugs. Even with them it is soon too loud to think. The rotor above them becomes a translucent blur.

The world wobbles for a moment, and then the ground falls away. Veronica's stomach lurches, but after the first few dizzying moments the flight is surprisingly stable. The sides of the helicopter are open and she can see Goma to the north, divided by the jet-black lava field that snakes in an unbroken line up to smouldering Mount Nyiragongo. On the other side lies placid Lake Kivu. Veronica thinks of what Prester said about the tons of lethal gases trapped in that lake, how it too is a killer. She is glad to be leaving. She reaches out and takes Jacob's hand, and he squeezes hers comfortingly.

They fly north, between two of the spectacularly jagged Virunga peaks, and over a sea of rolling hills. At one point they pass right over a particularly deep and dense patch of green, and Veronica sucks in breath sharply. Beyond the Bwindi Impenetrable Forest a red lacework of roads begins. The helicopter continues east above the roads and emerald hills of southern Uganda, and then across the huge blue expanse of Lake Victoria, so vast that water is all they can see in every direction for some time. It takes them about an hour to reach Entebbe.

Kampala's airport is an enormous field of tarmac dotted by buildings, airplanes and vehicles. They land on the military side of the airfield, and the helicopter powers down. The soldiers allow Veronica and Jacob to disembark first. Strick told them that a jeep would take them to customs and then Kampala, but nobody seems to be waiting for them.

'Military efficiency,' Jacob mutters. 'Hurry up and wait.'

They sit in the shadow of the huge helicopter and watch their fellow-passengers file across the tarmac to one of the long, low buildings on the periphery. Peacekeepers walk and drive up to and around the helicopter, load and unload cargo. They hear the white-noise scream of a jet taking off on the other side of a huge hangar. Veronica feels like an ant that has found its way into the innards of some vast and incomprehensible machine.

At length she says to Jacob, 'Listen. I don't think you should get any more involved in this.' She knows he doesn't want to hear it, but feels that she has to try. 'Prester was right. It's too dangerous. You're not . . . you're not trained for this. Think about it. I mean, rationally. You're an engineer. All this crazy stuff, spies, al-Qaeda, smugglers, war criminals, genocidal killers – I mean, no offence, but honestly, Jacob, what do you think you can really do except get yourself in more trouble?'

He smiles darkly. 'More than you might expect.'

It sounds like empty bravado. Veronica shakes her head and looks away.

'More than anyone expects, now that Derek's gone.'

She blinks and turns back. 'What do you mean?'

Jacob says, 'I mean there's a reason Derek asked me to come to Uganda. Just like there was a reason he invited you to Bwindi. I'm not here just because he wanted my smiling face around. I'm here because he knew what I can do.'

'What can you do?' Veronica asks, curious despite herself.

A Humvee pulls up beside them, driven by an Asian man, maybe Filipino, in a military uniform.

'Tell you what,' Jacob says. 'Come by my place some time and I'll show you.'

II Uganda

1

Veronica wakes to clammy heat. The power has gone out, the creaky generator in the basement has once again failed to automatically kick in, and the ancient air conditioner set in the window beside her mahogany bed is silent. Kampala is a kilometre above sea level, but it's right on the equator, and the mid-morning heat and humidity are oppressive. Her sheets are damp with sweat.

She feels enervated, all she wants to do is lie where she is, but she makes herself stand up and walk to her bathroom. The floorboards creak beneath her feet. It has been five days since her return to Kampala, but her legs are still wobbly, and when she looks in the mirror her body is still covered by purple and yellow bruises. At least the cuts and scrapes on her face have diminished from scabs to blemishes.

She brushes her teeth with bottled water and cools down with a quick shower. When she emerges she feels much better, almost good enough to go into work, but she decides against it. Maybe tomorrow, for half a day. Maybe not until her face is fully healed. Bernard told her she could have as much time off as she wanted.

Bernard also told her that journalists have been calling for her, and a British tabloid has actually offered money for her story. The notion repels Veronica. It would feel like blood money, and people who pay for a story will tell lies to make it better. The offer wasn't even for very much. She supposes the gory details are already available on YouTube for free, and besides, most Westerners don't much care about anything that happened in Africa.

The Night Of Knives

Downstairs the maid is mopping the kitchen's tiled floor. Veronica can never remember her name. The maid smiles but keeps a respectful distance as Veronica starts the generator, makes coffee, takes some bread from the fridge and goes out to the veranda. Their askari gate-guard waves at her, and she waves back. At least the servants are treating her normally again. Her housemates have reacted to her return with awkward and increasing discomfort, as if Veronica might have contracted some hideous and hyper-contagious disease in the Congo, become a carrier of Ebola virus. Twice she has walked into the living room and caught Belinda, Diane and Linda speaking in whispers.

Veronica sees a huge marabou stork standing by the hedge in the corner of the property, feeding on something. Kampala is infested by hundreds of these storks, carrion-eaters with eight-foot wingspans and sharp beaks the size of meat cleavers, standing on spindly legs to nearly half Veronica's height. Their scab-encrusted heads and the huge gullets of pink flesh that dangle from their throats make them look obscenely diseased, like pigeons grown to gargantuan proportions by a mad scientist who didn't care about cancerous side effects. But they keep Kampala relatively free of refuse. Like those birds that clean crocodiles' teeth. Veronica has a sudden image of a dozen marabou storks feeding on Derek's headless corpse, and turns away.

After breakfast she lights a cigarette and considers the day ahead. The heat makes her weak and listless. Maybe she will just sit in the house and watch satellite TV all day, again. She feels like she should go somewhere, do something; but the idea of arranging for a driver seems hideously complex and oppressive, and their house is too far from any destination to walk, at least in her current condition. Maybe she could walk to Makerere University, but there's really nothing there to do, and everyone will stare at her.

Veronica returns to the living room, switches the television on and turns up the volume to drown out the generator. She channelsurfs between CNN and BBC World for some time, paying little attention until she flips to CNN and sees the graphic behind the news anchor has changed to a picture of Osama bin Laden inside the outline of the African continent. The caption says: AL-QAEDA IN AFRICA.

'Last week's Congo hostage-taking may have been only the opening skirmish in a new front in the War on Terror,' the pretty Asian woman says. 'Several jihadist websites have reported that Osama bin Laden's al-Qaeda network has claimed responsibility for the attacks. Meanwhile, American special forces, aided by Zimbabwean soldiers, are in hot pursuit of the terrorist leaders who escaped last week's dramatic rescue of five Western hostages. Three other hostages were murdered before the rescue. CNN today has an exclusive interview with General Gideon Gorokwe, the Zimbabwean general who commands the allied force. Nigel Dickinson has the story.'

The picture cuts to two men in comfortable chairs. One is a grizzled, ponytailed white man in khaki, the other, presumably General Gorokwe, is built like a heavyweight boxer and dressed in an expensive suit. He looks relaxed and comfortable. The decor behind them is blandly expensive, like a room in a luxury hotel.

'This is General Gideon Gorokwe,' the white man says to the camera. His accent is British. 'A general in the Zimbabwe army whose soldiers have been based in the Congo for years. Last week, after al-Qaeda kidnapped eight Western hostages and took them into the Congo, General Gorokwe volunteered to help American forces track them down, and his soldiers were instrumental in their rescue. He did this even though General Gorokwe, like all senior Zimbabwe government and military figures, is under American sanctions that specifically prevent him from travelling to or trading with America or Europe. General, let me just begin with some background. Our viewers may be wondering, why exactly are your soldiers in the Congo in the first place, a thousand miles away from home?'

'Of course, Nigel, and thank you for this opportunity,'

Gorokwe says with a smile. His voice is warm and powerful, his
mild accent almost aristocratic. 'As you know, the Congo has
been racked by civil strife for many years. We came here as
peacekeepers.'

'You volunteered your soldiers to help America fight al-Qaeda
even though you personally are specifically targeted by American
and European sanctions. That's a surprising decision. Could you
explain your reasons?'

'I would hope the reasons are obvious.' Gorokwe seems slightly
surprised. 'It's true my country has been the victim of American
and European sanctions, but the fight against terror is everyone's
fight around the world, far more important than whatever
differences we may have. I see it as my moral duty to help
America in this war. And I personally hope also to show Americans that Zimbabwe is not your enemy and these sanctions are
the result of a misunderstanding. I studied in America, at the
University of Michigan. I admire America. I am a friend to
America. And I truly believe Zimbabwe and America can be
great friends as well.'

'What does your President Mugabe think about all this? He has
repeatedly condemned America in his speeches.'

Gorokwe's face clouds slightly. 'I have not yet consulted with
him. He's presently away at a summit in China, and my command
here is quite independent. But I'm sure he would agree that we
cannot allow the scourge of Islamic terror to spread into Africa.'

'Thank you, General. For CNN, this is Nigel Dickinson.'

Veronica wants the interview to continue, she'd like to hear
more from the man who was so instrumental in her rescue, but
CNN switches back to the anchor desk and a new story about
military deaths in Iraq. Restless, Veronica turns off the television
and wanders back out to the veranda.

She wonders whether staying in Kampala was such a good idea
after all. She feels as if her Congo ordeal should have been
followed by ceremonies, press conferences, ticker-tape parades.
Maybe it would have been, if she had flown back to America. She

could have been a guest on morning shows and Larry King, big-name newspapers would have hounded her for interviews, she might have had to hire a press agent. America loves its victim-survivors. And she's still wounded. Her cuts have scabbed over but there's plenty still wrong with her. Surely what she needs most right now is rest and recuperation, a long vacation in a secure, comfortable place.

No: what she really needs is a time machine. A giant rewind button for her own life. She would go back a long way, if she had one. Eight years. It would be so good to be twenty-four again, to live as if life was an adventure and the world her playground, to live fearlessly, as if she had for ever in which to undo whatever mistakes she might make. When she was twenty-four Veronica believed it was better to regret something you had done than something you hadn't. Now she knows better.

She was a better person when she was twenty-four. Hard to admit but true. Not just tougher, but also kinder, more forgiving. Then for seven years she spent money without knowing or caring where it came from, had her bed made and most of her meals prepared by servants, lived in a world where inconveniences were outsourced. It made her lazier, weaker, more selfish, less under-standing, shade by incremental shade. She didn't even notice it happening until she was suddenly expelled from that world. Now when she looks at herself she hardly sees the girl she used to be at all. Though maybe she's come back a little in the last two weeks. Maybe that's the only good thing to have come out of the Congo.

When she was twenty-four the world seemed so full of op-portunity, a cornucopia of possibilities. Now Veronica feels as if she has only one or two chances left to get her life right. If Africa doesn't work out, she doesn't know what she'll do. She supposes that's why Derek made such an impression on her, even though she hardly knew him. It wasn't just that he was dashing and handsome, there was something about him that hinted at an opportunity to get things right at last, some fairy-tale notion of falling in love, for real this time, and living happily ever after.

Her cell phone rings. She looks at it, doesn't recognize the number, answers.

'Veronica? How are you?'

'Oh, hi,' she says, surprised, recognizing Jacob's faintly nasal voice. 'Fine. You?'

'Pretty good. You busy?'

'Not really.'

'Want to come over? I've got something you might be interested in.'

She hesitates, not sure that she wants to see Jacob and be reminded of Derek. 'I'm kind of stranded today. No driver.'

'No problem. I'll send mine.'

After a pause she says, 'OK. Sure.' She can't hide in her house for ever.

Jacob's driver is a quiet, bespectacled middle-aged man with a pot belly named Henry. His vehicle is a slightly dented but clean Toyota. Veronica wishes she had a driver of her own. During her marriage she travelled everywhere in luxury automobiles. Danton had a Jaguar and a chauffeur, a Ferrari, a Lamborghini. He loved driving hyper-powered sports cars, and so did she, it was one of the few things they had in common.

Their route takes them through downtown Kampala's densely packed warren of shops, hotels, banks and government buildings, all perched on the most central of the city's seven hills. The Sheraton Hotel looms atop this hill. On the other side of downtown they pass the concrete-walled complex of the US embassy: the workplace, if Prester was right, of the person ultimately responsible for what happened to them in the Congo, a traitor conspiring with terrorists for his or her own gain.

Then along the Jinja highway and through the vast shanty town that surrounds Kampala, thousands of tiny, misshapen wooden huts leaning drunkenly on one another, their tin roofs patched with garbage bags and weighed down by rocks. Children play soccer on narrow, uneven dirt roads, women sell food from cloths laid out on the muddy ground, men sit or lean in the shade, doing nothing, as if waiting for a messiah to come. When Veronica first came here it seemed an abyss of misery, but witnessing the Congo's real wretchedness has opened her eyes to its merits. Most shanty-town inhabitants do not live in interminable suffering. Some do – refugees, Aids orphans – but most are just poor. Very poor, desperately poor, and with little hope of ever being wealthier, but it's still much better than life in the Congo.

The New City complex stands on a hill above the shanty town like a mirage in a desert. Henry continues past this gleaming, modern shopping mall into a leafy and exclusive suburb. Jacob lives in an apartment complex that wouldn't look out of place in the West, except for its guardpost and barbed-wire fences tastefully hidden by bushes and trees. His askaris look at her curiously. They've probably never seen such a dire-looking *mzungu* woman before. It isn't until she's at the door to Jacob's apartment that she begins to wonder why he invited her.

2

Jacob says, 'These are all of Derek's phone calls.'

He looks from the computer screen to Veronica. Her expression is hard to read, the half-healed cuts on her once-perfect face make her look like an extra in a zombie movie. Jacob supposes he still resembles an acne-scarred teenager himself. At least his goatee conceals the worst of the damage.

He wishes he'd cleaned up his apartment a little before she came over. It's a nice enough place, two bedrooms all to himself, but it isn't really ready for guests. His bedroom is strewn with scattered clothes and books, and the rest of the place is devoid of furniture except for his computer desk and a couple of chairs. The white walls are bare, the kitchen cabinets are empty, and most of his possessions are still piled in suitcases and toiletry bags. He doesn't even ha* bookcases yet: dozens of science-fiction novels and technical texts sit in stacks on the carpeted floor of his computer room.

Jacob looks back to his computer, and to the Google Map of Uganda on its screen, a map half covered by little orange and red balloons that serve as place markers. Red outnumbers orange by a wide margin. Most are clustered in Kampala, but there are a fair number out west, near the Congo border, and a few orange balloons scattered in other places as well.

'Red is Derek,' he explains, 'orange is the other participant, if they're on Mango.'

'Where did this come from?' She sounds more perplexed than impressed.

'Oh.' Jacob realizes he has been remiss in providing context. 'Derek had a Mango cell phone. Mango is a division of Telecom Uganda. I work for Telecom Uganda and have admin access to their databases. And the reason they hired me is there isn't much I don't know about mobile communications systems. This is what I've got so far. Would have been more, but I spent my first three days back basically fully zoned out.'

Veronica nods with understanding.

Jacob switches briefly to a black window full of orderly rows and columns of text. 'The records of every call Derek ever made or received, including,' he points at columns on the screen, 'the other number involved in that call, Derek's location and, if the other participant also had a Mango phone, their location as well. I converted this data to XML and plugged it into a Google Map. *Et voilà.*'

'Location? You can actually track cell phones? I thought that was just in movies.'

'No, you can, for real. What happens is, we record which base stations handled the call, and the signal strength they got from your phone. Base stations are the cells, the fixed antennas your phone talks to. We know their exact location. So if three or more were in range, we can triangulate a phone to a single patch of real estate.'

'How close can you get?'

'Well, it varies.' Jacob decides not to get into too much detail. 'Depends on how many base stations and how far apart. Error margin is probably somewhere from forty metres in downtown Kampala to half a kilometre in rural areas. It's not quite like the movies, you can't actually track individuals, because the closer you can get, the more densely populated the real estate, they get lost in the crowd. But you can get a pretty good idea of their general vicinity.'

'And you have names too? You know who he called?'

'No. Unfortunately. Mostly. If they're actual Mango subscribers, yes, but almost every phone in Uganda is prepaid, not subscription. But I bet if we look hard enough at this list we'll find some interesting stuff.'

'This is why Derek brought you to Africa,' she says slowly.

'Exactly. To track the call records of whoever he was interested in.'

'You really think you can find out who set him up from this?'

'There's a lot more I can do than just this. But it's a good place to start. Retrace his steps, work out who he's been talking to.' Jacob switches back to the Google Map. 'Red is where Derek was during the call, orange indicates the other person's location, if it was a Mango-to-Mango call. I can't track people on other networks.'

'So that red marker up at the Congo border means Derek was out there?'

He nods. 'Yeah. Good example. Let's take a closer look at that.'

He scrolls over and zooms in. One red and one orange balloon, both labelled with question marks, float over the Semiliki district, right up against the Congo border a good three hundred kilometres north of Bwindi. Jacob clicks on each marker and examines the call data that pops up on the side of the screen.

'He was there three weeks ago,' he reports. 'Or at least his phone was. And this orange one there, this other number, it's Mango too, he called it repeatedly over the last month.'

'Prester said there was a smuggling ring,' Veronica remembers. 'From the Congo to Uganda. And Semiliki's right near the border.'

'Exactly.'

'What do the question marks mean?'

'Geographical uncertainty. If there's only two base stations in range of a phone, then you can only track it to one of two locations, where their circles of coverage meet. But Semiliki is way out there. Only one base station.'

'So we can't tell where exactly he or the other phone was.'

'Probably not. Unless . . . let me check.' Jacob switches back to the black window full of text, and opens up an SSH connection to Telecom Uganda's master database server. His fingers rattle with machine-gun speed over his keyboard as he composes a moderately complex database query, calling up the exact details of all calls involving Derek made near Semiliki.

He runs the query. Telecom Uganda's servers ponder the question for a few seconds; then rows of numbers begin to scroll rapidly down the screen. Jacob peruses them. After a moment he grunts with surprise. Both the handsets in question, Derek's and the other one, were used far enough away from Semiliki station that their signals regularly arrived twenty microseconds out of sync from their allotted time slot. That's something. Radio waves move at the speed of light: three hundred thousand kilometres per second, aka six kilometres per twenty microseconds. There's no way to work out the handsets' direction from the station when they were used, but Jacob knows they were exactly six kilometres away.

He relays this information to Veronica, and adds, 'Semiliki's a small town, more like a village, there's nothing else out there. And the base station's right in town. So what was Derek doing that far out?'

'Maybe that's the smugglers' hideout?' Veronica suggests tentatively. 'Maybe Derek went out there, and that's how he found out too much?'

Jacob frowns. It sounds a little too neat. 'Maybe. I don't know. It's not like a secret terrorist cell would have called up a white boy and invited him out to come look at their operation. Tell you what. Let's take a look at what's out there.'

Jacob launches Google Earth. A new window opens up on his computer screen, and within it an image of the world as seen from orbit. He copies and pastes data from the other window, instructing the software to traverse the six-kilometre loop around the coordinates of the Semiliki base station. Veronica murmurs with surprise as the image zooms in towards the earth, as if the window were a camera on a falling satellite.

The virtual eye in the sky swoops downwards from orbit, towards Africa, into Uganda. They see roads, forests, clouds over the bristling Ruwenzori mountains south of Semiliki, the blue expanse of Lake Albert to the north, the grey grid of Fort Portal. The virtual camera levels off a few thousand feet above ground and begins to fly in a tight loop. Jacob smiles at Veronica's surprise.

'This is the six-kilometre radius around Semiliki base station,' he explains. 'What you're seeing are real recent satellite photos, stitched together auto-magically into a single landscape. Pretty cool, eh? It's like having your very own Pentagon war room, for free.'

Hilly terrain scrolls past, and is interrupted by what looks like a wide red scar in the green earth, a blotchy discontinuity several square kilometres in size. The resolution is too vague to see details, but within the red smear, oblong green and grey shapes are arranged in vaguely geometric patterns that suggest human habitation.

'What's that?' Veronica asks.

Jacob freezes and peers at the display. 'Must be some kind of town. Weird. Deeply weird. It looks way bigger than Semiliki, but it's not on any of the maps. Let's do a quick Web search on latitude and longitude and see what we get.'

He launches a Web browser.

'Fast connection,' Veronica observes. 'Mine's really slow.'

'Yeah. There's no fibre link to East Africa yet, everything's through satellite, it's a pain in the ass, high latency. But this computer has a DSL connection to the hub, and I've given my personal data the highest priority on their satellite link. Making this literally the fastest Internet connection in Uganda.'

He goes to Dogpile.com and types in the geographical coordinates of that mysterious settlement near Semiliki. Dogpile delegates the request to all of the world's major search engines, and assembles the collective results into a single list. The first entry is entitled *UNHCR Semiliki*.

'UNHCR?' Jacob asks, perplexed.

'I know that one.' Veronica leans forward, interested. 'United Nations High Commission for Refugees. It must be a refugee camp. Didn't Susan say the camp she worked at was in Semiliki?'

'Did she? But that's not Susan's number.' Jacob double-checks. 'No. She's not on Mango. This is another phone. Someone else at that camp.'

'Someone else.' Veronica considers. 'Maybe Susan knows who. Maybe Derek didn't invite her to Bwindi just because she's blonde and pretty. Maybe she was a lead.'

'Huh.' Jacob leans back instinctively to think, winces as the pressure causes the five whip wounds on his back to flare up, and hunches forward again. He closes his eyes and tries to arrange all the facts swimming in his mind, order them into some logical sequence. 'OK. So Derek was investigating a smuggling ring and rumours they were connected to terrorists. He invites you and Susan to Bwindi because he wanted to make friends and sound you out, Susan because she worked at the camp, you because of Danton.'

'Where else?' Veronica asks. 'Where were his other calls? Where in Kampala?'

Jacob switches back to the map full of balloons, and zooms in on the Google street map of greater Kampala. There are markers almost everywhere in the city, both red and orange, but a few dense clusters stand out.

'This is here,' Jacob says, indicating a little cluster on the east side of the city. 'Calls to my phone. This is Derek's apartment, by the Sheraton.' A dense clump of red near the centre of town. 'And here's his office.' A thick cloud of red and orange to the north. 'Those orange markers in his office, that other number, that must be Prester.'

'What about this?' Veronica asks, pointing at a pile of orange markers a little south of downtown, between the Sheraton and the taxi park.

'No idea. They're all the same number. Not Prester, not the Semiliki number, someone else.' He checks back against the raw data. 'He started calling that number three months ago, and he's been calling them ever since, a couple times a week. What do you think that means?'

'I don't know. None of this makes any sense to me.' She looks at him. 'Why are you showing me all this?'

He hesitates. 'I thought you'd be interested.'

'I am, I guess. But why not take it to Prester or the US embassy or something? Or did you already?'

'No. We can't do that.'

She blinks. 'Why not?'

'Think about it. Derek was set up by someone he was working for. Or with. I take this to the wrong person, they find out what I can do, they'll cover their trail and I'll just be getting myself into more trouble. I go to the Canadian or British embassy, they'll just pass the word on to the USA. The real reason I'm showing you is because you're the only person I know I can trust.'

Veronica shakes her head. 'You're being paranoid. I'm sure Prester or Strick—'

'You know what Derek was doing in the last couple months before we got grabbed? Investigating Prester.'

Veronica stares at him.

'Yeah. Some big boss in the CIA, I don't know who, Derek never told me details, found out there was something rotten in the state of Uganda and sent Derek to investigate. When I got here Derek had me track Prester's phone calls. And in the last week before we went to Bwindi, you know what? He had me tracking Strick's calls too.'

'But – no. Not Prester. He told us what was happening. He was trying to help us.'

'Or he was telling us what he wanted us to believe. Plus a few things we would have figured out or found out by ourselves anyways, but we heard them from him first, so it looks like he's a good guy. And while he's at it he just so happens to warn us to stop poking around and get the hell out of Africa for our own good. Just like Strick. They both wanted us gone.'

'Maybe because they want us safe,' Veronica says.

'Maybe not.'

'They don't even like each other.'

'They're intelligence professionals,' Jacob says. 'They know how to seem like something they're not.'

'You sound totally paranoid.'

'Only the paranoid survive.'

'Come on,' she objects. 'This is crazy. I mean, even if you're right, like you say, all you're doing is just getting yourself into more trouble. You want to know what I think? I think you should stop playing Sherlock Homes and go home.'

'He was my best friend,' Jacob says sharply. 'Someone set him up. And us too. Someone *murdered* him, someone he was working with. I'm not just walking away.'

A long moment of silence passes.

'You seriously think Prester and Strick might be working with al-Qaeda?' Veronica says, incredulous.

'I doubt whoever it is knew their smuggler friends were in bed with al-Qaeda until after we were taken. And now they'll be extra desperate to cover their tracks. Maybe it's just one of them. Maybe neither, and Prester was telling the truth, it's somebody at the embassy.' Jacob pauses. 'Derek thought your ex-husband was involved. There might be something there.'

'Like what?'

'I don't know,' he admits.

'Did Derek tell you about Danton?'

'No. All he told me was what phone numbers he wanted information for. He wouldn't give me details, he said it wasn't safe.' Jacob spits out the last few words angrily. 'If he'd told me, maybe I would have seen it coming. Or at least now I'd know what he knew.'

'Or whoever set him up would have found out you knew too much too,' Veronica points out. 'And you would have been number two on the chopping block.'

Jacob pauses. She's right. Derek's secrecy may have kept him alive.

'So what are you planning to do?' Veronica asks.

'What we need is evidence,' he says. Veronica raises her eyebrows sceptically at the *we*. 'Once we've got hard actual evidence of who it was, then we can go to the embassy, take it straight to the ambassador, make it public.'

'You really think you'll get hard evidence out of this?' She points to the computer screen. 'Tracking a bunch of phone calls?'

'I think we're finding lots of stuff out already.'

'Stuff that doesn't make any sense.'

'It will eventually,' he says confidently. 'We just have to be methodical. Gather data, make a hypothesis, test it against the evidence, repeat until understanding is attained. The scientific method. It's cracked problems a lot harder than this one.'

Veronica shakes her head. 'Jacob, you want to know what I think, you should just go home. Maybe both of us should.'

Jacob can't help but wonder whether she's right. Living in danger, investigating mysterious conspiracies – that was Derek's line of work, not his, he's just a techie, of unusual ability, to be sure, but he's no swashbuckling superspy. It's true he came to Uganda to help Derek, and it was exciting knowing he was really working for the CIA, it felt like a big, wonderful adventure, like being in a movie, a supporting character to Derek's starring role. But Jacob never dreamed he might find himself in real danger. Until Bwindi. Until it turned into a horror movie.

The safe thing to do is to stop investigating and hope the authorities can find Derek's killer. But he can't turn his back on the murder of his best friend. It wouldn't be right. It wouldn't be *honourable*. Jacob has always thought of himself as someone who would do the right thing, *in extremis*. He supposes most people do. But most people never actually have to find out. He does, and right now. His whole life, quiet and ordinary until now, has in a way just been a prelude to this. What he chooses to do now is the measure of who he is. And if he fails, if he gives up and goes home, he will feel that shadow hanging over him for the rest of his life. He has to at least try.

Jacob tries to think of some way to convince Veronica to stay and help. He can trust her. He doesn't want to have to deal with this alone. And if Derek was right, Veronica's ex-husband is somehow involved in all this. But no brilliant insight or debating tactic that might convince her comes to mind.

Veronica's gaze drifts back to Jacob's computer, to the Google Map full of markers that indicate where Derek placed and received his phone calls.

'Wait a minute,' she says, sitting up straight, suddenly alarmed.

He blinks. 'What?'

'That terrorist phone Susan picked up. By the satellite dish. Remember what Prester said? It had two hundred phone numbers for Westerners in Congo and west Uganda.'

Jacob nods. 'And?'

'So they could track those phones like you tracked Derek's calls, right?'

He hesitates. 'If they had access to the databases, yes. But like I said, the higher the geographical precision, the denser the population. You can't locate specific individuals, they inevitably get lost in the crowd.'

'Not in Africa. Not if they're white and the rest of the crowd is black.'

Jacob opens his mouth but says nothing at first. She's right. The industry truism that cell phones can't be used to track down their owners is in this case false. White people stand out in Africa, especially rural Africa, like pink paint on black canvas.

'You think they're planning to—' He shakes his head. The idea is too huge to accept all at once. 'You think al-Qaeda are going to try and hunt down all those people. Using their cell phones. That's . . . no, that's crazy. How would they get access to the databases?' Jacob answers the question himself. 'Oh, no. Holy shit. Through their partner in the CIA.'

They stare at one another.

'Derek thought whoever he was investigating had an in at a phone company,' Jacob says. 'The first thing he did was have me make sure Mango was safe for him to use, check that nobody else was tracking his calls.'

'We have to tell someone,' Veronica says. She looks shaken.

'Don't panic. Not yet anyways. It's just a theory. And I'm sure the powers that be have thought of it too by now.' Though Jacob is not at all sure of this. 'We don't have any evidence. And I still can't believe a CIA agent would work with al-Qaeda.'

'They would if they were being blackmailed,' Veronica suggests. 'Help track these phones or we reveal how you were the smuggler who set up the kidnapping and murder of your own agent plus two other Americans.'

Jacob nods slowly.

'Two hundred people. A lot of them, like Peace Corps types, out in rural areas, totally on their own. My God, they'll kill them. Or take them hostage first, like they took us. We have to do something. We have to go to someone.'

He shakes his head. 'With what? We have zero evidence. Just theory and supposition. And go to who? If we pick the wrong person, if they find out we're chasing their trail and I was working with Derek all along . . .' He hesitates. 'They might come after us.

They probably would. Whoever it is, they're not fucking around, we know that already.'

Veronica swallows. 'So what do we do?'

Jacob looks back at the computer screen and considers. 'There's still too many unknowns. We might just be jumping at shadows here. I say we try to find out more before we do anything.'

This time Veronica lets the *we* pass unchallenged. 'How?'

'Go back to Plan A. Retrace Derek's steps, find out what he knew.' Jacob points to the cluster of orange markers on the map near Kampala's taxi park. 'I'd like to know who this is, for starters. Must be a friend of Derek's, they talked a couple times a week, every week. Frequently immediately before or after calling the number in Semiliki. What do you say we go pay them a visit?'

Veronica looks at him uneasily.

'Come on,' Jacob says. 'Downtown Kampala, broad daylight, a friend of Derek's. It's not dangerous in the slightest. I promise.'

3

Downtown Kampala is an area of wide, scarred boulevards intersected by narrow side streets, clogged by choking squalls of traffic and dense clouds of pedestrians, lined by a dizzying array of African commerce: *nyama choma* street meat braziers, *boda-boda* motorcycle taxis, newspaper hawkers, bakeries, bookshops, Internet cafés, pharmacies, stationery shops, cell-phone stores, fast-food stalls. The grassy meridians of the boulevards are fenced by ankle-high barbed wire. Huge concrete monoliths rise above the retail level, banks and government buildings. Posters advertise Sleeping Beauty cosmetics and Celtel phones.

'I guess this is it,' Jacob says, looking up at the rotting concrete stairs that lead upwards beneath the hand-painted sign HOTEL SUN CITY, then down to the hip-top computer in his hand, and the tiny Google Map of Kampala on its screen. He can't imagine why

Derek would have had anything to do with this place, but according to the hip-top's GPS receiver, the Hotel Sun City is the real-world establishment that best overlaps the cloud of orange dots that correspond to Derek's twice-weekly calls to a handset located in this region.

Jacob closes the hip-top's clamshell case and looks around. His shirt is already damp with sweat. The street they are on is one of the busiest in Kampala. Buzzing pedestrian traffic, aggressive sidewalk vendors, protruding metal signs, dangling vines of casually strung electrical cables and occasional stands of bamboo scaffolding combine to make walking a hazardous business. The opposite side of the boulevard, across a churning river of smog-belching traffic, is occupied by Kampala's central taxi park, a gargantuan and mind-numbingly busy triangle of dirt occupied by hundreds if not thousands of *matatus*, East Africa's ubiquitous minivan shared taxis, and their associated passengers, drivers, vendors and askaris. On reflection Jacob can think of two advantages to this location: anonymity and quick getaways.

'All right,' Veronica says doubtfully. 'Let's take a look and get this over with.'

Jacob follows her up the cracked and uneven stairs, and despite the uncertainty of their situation, as he climbs he can't help but be distracted by Veronica's trim, swaying hips. He's half amused at himself, half pleased that life is coming back to him; he hasn't thought about sex since the Congo, but clearly he is recovering fast, and Veronica is easily the most beautiful woman he's ever spent an extended amount of time with. Not that he has any illusions that anything is going to happen between them. He's a geek; Veronica is a former model who married a multimillionaire. Jacob is ruefully aware that she is way out of his league.

They ascend to a glassed-in security box manned by a woman who awards them a hostile glare.

'We want to see a room,' Jacob improvises, 'we might stay here tonight.'

The receptionist frowns suspiciously and passes him a key. 'Number three-oh-seven. Ten minutes.'

They advance into the hotel's labyrinthine interior. It's much bigger than it looks on the outside, six storeys tall and occupying almost the whole block. The interior arrangements are gloomy and bizarre: a half-dozen interior stairways connect only two or three storeys apiece, hallways terminate at doorless walls, benches and chairs sit in dark alcoves. Water drips from leaky pipes. Except for themselves the halls are eerily empty. Jacob is reminded of *Gormenghast*.

They glance into Room 307 out of curiosity. It's barely big enough for its rickety bed. There are roaches on the filthy floor and the even filthier mattress. The mosquito net is full of holes. The shower is a nozzle set in bare concrete, the toilet has no lid, and there isn't even a light, just a bundle of torn wires protruding from a hole in the roof beside a fan that doesn't work.

'I sure hope it's cheap,' Jacob says, appalled. He can't imagine any less desirable place to stay in Kampala. Even a shanty-town hut would be better than this.

Veronica closes her eyes. She is breathing hard.

He looks at her. 'You OK?'

'Fine,' she says without opening her eyes. 'I just don't like tight spaces.'

'Oh.' A few seconds pass. Jacob doesn't know what to say. 'Maybe you should wait outside, or—'

'I'm fine. It's no big deal.' She takes a deep breath, opens her eyes, looks around again and shakes her head. 'Look at this place. Why would Derek—'

'I have no idea. And not just once. A couple times a week for six months.' He hesitates, then draws out his hip-top again. It doubles as a phone. 'One way to find out.'

'You're going to call them?' Veronica looks around nervously. 'I don't know if that's such a good idea.'

Jacob understands her reluctance. He doesn't particularly want to make contact with anyone here either. This rotting wreck of a hotel feels like the kind of place where people die. But if they turn back at just the implication of danger they'll never uncover the truth. He tells himself to think of this as a test, like an obstacle in a video game.

'It's just a phone call,' he says, trying to convince himself as much as Veronica, and he dials.

After three rings a woman answers in a breathy voice. 'Hello?'

'Hello,' Jacob says. 'Hi, um, who am I speaking to?'

'My name is Lydia.'

'Hello, Lydia. Where can I find you?'

'The Hotel Sun City, darling. Room two-one-one. Come by any time.'

Jacob blinks with surprise. 'Room two-one-one. OK. I . . . I guess I'll be there soon.' He hangs up and looks at Veronica. 'Well. That was easy.'

'Too easy.'

'Come on. It's broad daylight. She sounded harmless.'

Veronica reluctantly acquiesces. They find their way to Room 211 after a few missteps. Jacob stops in front of it and looks back at Veronica. He is nervous now. She's right, this is too easy. She shrugs but says nothing. He takes a deep breath and knocks on the door.

The woman who answers the door is tall and remarkably beautiful, except for her oddly bloodshot eyes. She makes Jacob think of Iman, the model. She is heavily made up, with braided hair, in high heels, a leather miniskirt and a form-fitting long-sleeved tiger-striped shirt. The room behind her is relatively clean, and empty but for a shabby bed. It smells of perfume.

'Lydia?' Jacob asks.

The woman nods. She seems surprised to see them.

'I just called.'

'Yes. How did you get my number?' Her voice is low and doesn't sound Ugandan, the accent is more French.

'From Derek.'

Lydia's face flickers. Then she smiles broadly. 'Oh yes. A

naughty man who likes *very* naughty girls. Girls like me. But I'm sorry, I don't entertain couples.' She frowns at Veronica.

'Oh,' Jacob says. Embarrassed understanding floods into his mind. 'Oh. Right. I'm sorry. I think there was a misunderstanding. We should be going.'

'Perhaps you should. Today is very busy for me. I don't like having my time wasted.'

'Sorry.'

Lydia closes the door. Jacob retreats hastily, and Veronica follows. He can feel his face burning.

'I guess that explains it,' he says, speaking quickly. 'Maybe we shouldn't have, uh, shouldn't have pried. I mean, into his private life. I'm surprised. But I guess, you know, it was hard for him to maintain healthy relationships, with his lifestyle, and I'm sure he's hardly the first guy to move to the Third World and let himself go a little, and he was in Thailand before he came here, I'm sure after a little while it's just normal.'

'Normal?' Veronica asks. She sounds amused despite herself.

'Well, not actually normal, but I can see, not see, but I can imagine how after a while it would seem that way, I mean, if you live an abnormal life,' he flounders. 'Let's just go home, OK?'

They are at the top of the hallway that leads to the bulletproof reception desk when Veronica suddenly stops walking and says, 'Wait a minute.'

Jacob stops too. 'What?'

'Her eyes.'

'What about her eyes?'

'She wasn't hung over. Those weren't burst capillaries. Those were *lesions*. Kaposi's sarcoma.'

'Lesions?'

'Aids,' Veronica says softly. 'Late-stage. She's very sick. Probably dying.'

'Aids? And . . . and Derek was sleeping with her?'

'That's what I'm wondering.' She pauses. 'Any chance he was HIV positive?'

Jacob shakes his head, astonished. 'No. He had a bag of his own blood in his fridge, for transfusions, so he wouldn't get HIV if he had to go to a hospital here.'

'Then he wouldn't have been having sex with a prostitute with Kaposi's sarcoma, would he? He would have known. She must have other lesions on her too, it wouldn't just be her eyes, that'd be very unusual.'

'I wouldn't have thought Derek would ever have slept with a prostitute at all.' Jacob isn't sure exactly how true this is. Derek never exactly treated women respectfully, and he spent a year in Thailand, world capital of prostitution, just before coming to Africa. But at least he never talked about it.

Veronica turns around. 'We let her get rid of us too easy.'

'My rule for couples has not changed in five minutes,' Lydia says. Her voice is cool and distant, but Veronica sees wariness in her eyes.

'We'd like to ask you some questions about Derek.' Veronica indicates Jacob. 'He was Derek's best friend.'

Lydia frowns. 'He has never spoken to me of any friends.'

'What did he speak to you about?'

'I think it is time for you to go.'

'We're not going anywhere until you start talking.'

Lydia takes a step back and begins to close the door. Jacob jumps forward and interposes himself before it closes.

'If I raise my voice my protectors will come running here in two minutes!' Lydia says sharply. 'With knives and guns! They will—'

Jacob says, 'Derek's dead.'

Lydia stops in mid-expostulation and stares at him as if slapped.

'Haven't you heard?' Veronica asks, amazed. 'It's been all over the news. Especially here. TV, newspapers, everything. He was one of the tourists kidnapped in Bwindi and taken into the Congo. So were we. We were with him.'

Lydia shakes her head faintly. 'I do not read the newspapers.'

'But he should have called you by now, shouldn't he?' Veronica guesses. 'Doesn't he call you every week?'

Lydia says nothing, but her expression is confirmation enough.

'I'm sorry,' Jacob says gently. 'It's true. He's gone.'

After a moment she asks, desperately, 'If you say you were his friend – then what was the name of the girl who gave him his tattoo?'

'Selima. In Sarajevo. She died the next day. There was a picture in his apartment.'

Lydia stares at Jacob and Veronica as if they are not just messengers but avatars of death. Then she sags backwards and sits down hard on the bed. Veronica sees for the first time how frail and sickly she is, how gaunt.

Veronica enters the room. Jacob follows her and starts to close the door, but she grabs it before it shuts, it's bad enough being in this tiny room with an open door – bad, but she doesn't feel in danger of a panic attack. She's too intent on what she's doing, they're so close to finding out something important, she can feel it.

'You did something for him, didn't you?' Veronica asks Lydia, in the soft voice she used with anxious patients when she was a nurse. 'Not sex. You were a friend. You did him favours.'

Lydia doesn't answer.

'We're his friends too. We're trying to find out who was responsible for his death.'

'What will I do?' Lydia asks plaintively. 'What can I do?'

'Was he supporting you?'

She laughs bitterly. 'What do you think? Who else would have? I am illegal, from the Congo. I have no family here. I am too weak to work, I am dying. I have no clients any more, everyone can see I am sick. Derek brought me the new medicines, but it is too late for me, they don't work for me. He paid for this room, for my food, my life, everything. Without him I have nothing. I will die alone on the rubbish heap.'

'We'll take care of you,' Jacob says. 'Trust us.'

142

'Trust you.' She sounds as if she wants to spit.

Veronica says nothing.

When Lydia eventually speaks there is an awful resignation in her voice, as if she knows these are her last words. 'He kept another room here. He came twice a week. He pretended that he came for me. Sometimes he brought his computer, but it is not there now. Yesterday I looked to see if he had come. It is almost empty now. A mobile phone, some papers.'

'A secret office,' Jacob breathes. 'No kidding. Let's go see this cell phone.'

'And papers,' Veronica says.

Jacob nods perfunctorily, as if paper is only an antiquated afterthought.

4

'It's a Mango phone,' Jacob reports happily, as he types on his computer and interprets the results that scroll across his screen. They have taken the fruits of their investigation – a wrinkled notebook and a cheap Nokia phone – back to his apartment. 'Activated three months ago. Involved in a very small set of calls. None to me, none to Prester, none to that refugee camp, no overlap whatsoever with calls from his other phone. He made sure this one was totally separate. Calls to a Celtel number in Jinja, and get this, to a bunch of international numbers. Tanzania, Kenya, Zimbabwe and the USA. Virginia area code. He received calls from the Zimbabwe number too. Those were the only incoming calls.'

Veronica stops leafing through the spiral-bound notebook. 'Prester.'

'Prester?'

'Look.'

She shows him the notebook. The front and back pages are empty; but a single page of enigmatic point-form notes is hidden in the middle, written in a close, spidery hand.

'That's Derek's writing,' Jacob confirms.
The single sheet of scribbled notes says:

- *Prester? Langley thinks yes*
- *plausible: method, motive, opportunity*
- *plus he's long-term consultant to Kisembe*
- *$50 mil exports, 'negligible' production, one conclusion*
- *Coltan too*
- *Ultimately minority owned by Selous Holdings – D.*
- *Who is Zanzibar Sam? R. says arriving Kampala in a few weeks*
- *Need second-source confirmation – wait on L.*
- *Zanzibar – connection to Muslim world – Arab gold buyers in Congo*
- *interahamwe smuggling unquestionable, Islamists only hear-say*
- *Western connection likewise, likely through deniable cut-outs*
- *Freeze bought-off locals' bank accounts, see who they call?*
- *Need. Hard. <u>Evidence</u>.*

'It'd be nice to find something that actually answers more questions than it asks.' Veronica gloomily rereads the notes for the third time. 'Zanzibar Sam? D and R and L? Kisembe? Langley?'

'We'll make sense of it,' Jacob reassures her. 'We just have to be methodical about it. The scientific method.'

Veronica frowns. This doesn't feel anything like science to her. It feels more like trying to assemble a jigsaw puzzle with most of the pieces missing, without even knowing what it's meant to represent.

'Langley,' Jacob says, rereading the notes. 'Of course. That one I know. Langley, Virginia. CIA headquarters.'

'How do you know?'

'I watch a lot of movies. Kisembe sounds like something we can Google.' He opens a Web browser, types, reads, nods. 'A Ugandan gold mine. Which Derek thought was being used to hide gold smuggling. Minority-owned by Selous Holdings.' He types again, and frowns. 'Which is not Googleable. Maybe on Edgar, or some other financial database—'

'No,' Veronica says suddenly. 'No, you won't find anything. Selous is based in the Cayman Islands.'

Jacob turns and stares at her. 'How do you know?'

'Because I remember Danton talking about it. With business associates. At dinners and conferences. It was one of . . . I don't know if it was his, exactly, but it was a company he was involved with.' She stares at the *D.* scrawled next to *Selous Holdings*. D for Danton. That D is her connection to Derek, the reason he invited her to Bwindi, the reason she was abducted, the reason she is here.

'L for Lydia?' Jacob suggests. 'Maybe she knows more than she's saying?'

'I think she would have told us,' Veronica says faintly. She feels dizzy.

'I guess there're a lot of Ls out there. Don't suppose you got Mr Strick's first name, back in Goma?'

She shakes her head. She feels warm fury beginning to burn inside her. Danton. This is all his fault. Their kidnapping, her week of horror, Derek's death, whatever the terrorists are plotting now – none of this would have happened if it wasn't for her ex-husband's squalid, criminal greed.

'Wish we knew when this was written,' Jacob muses.

Veronica takes a deep breath and looks back at Derek's notes with new resolve. After a moment she says, 'Does it really matter? Never mind all the complicated stuff. He was set up by whoever was making money off the smugglers. Look. First name on the sheet. First word. Prester.'

Jacob inclines his head slowly. 'Yeah. Yeah, it all makes sense. Derek gets sent here to look for evidence that al-Qaeda are working with *interahamwe*, smuggling stuff in from the Congo. Then he starts suspecting his new partner is working with the smugglers too. That explains why he sets up a secret office in the Sun City. He went out to that refugee camp because that's where the smuggling happens. He makes some international calls from the Sun City and finds out that your ex's company is taking the gold and coltan, pretending they mined it here legally, and exporting it. With the help of some high-up Ugandans, see that last line? "Bought-off locals?" And remember how Prester said his other clients were mining companies?' He shakes his head angrily. 'Fifty million dollars. That's a lot of money. Plenty of profits for everyone. Except the Congolese slaves, and who gives a fuck about them, right? Derek gets too close, Prester finds out, and gets his *interahamwe* friends to grab us all in Bwindi. Maybe he knew they were best friends for ever with al-Qaeda, maybe not. Anyway, they outsource it to *their* friends, Gabriel and Patrice and company. It all makes perfect sense. Prester. It was all Prester all along.'

Veronica thinks of Prester in Goma, of the genuine grief in his voice when he talked about Derek. Suddenly she isn't so sure. It feels like they're forcing together two pieces that don't quite fit. 'Except there's no evidence.'

'It's all circumstantial,' Jacob admits. 'But it all points his way.'

'Yes, but . . . I don't know. I don't think Prester is the type.'

'The *type*? What do you know about the type?'

She smiles bitterly. 'I was married to one, remember?'

Jacob doesn't say anything.

'Maybe we should go to Strick,' she suggests.

'No. For all we know Strick is in on it too. Even if he isn't, like you said, we don't actually have any evidence yet. All we have is a hypothesis, now we have to test it. We need hard data before we can go to the authorities. Something inarguable. Like he says here. Hard evidence. Proof.'

'Proof? How?'

He says, 'Prester has a Mango phone.'

'I can't believe you can do this,' Veronica says.

Jacob shrugs. 'A cell phone is just a two-way digital radio. The service provider controls the software. I have admin access to the service provider's systems. We can do pretty much anything we want.'

'But even when it's not turned on?'

'Oh, it's on. It just looks off. From now on, when Prester pushes the off button, his screen goes dead but his phone stays active. It'll burn through juice faster than a phone that's really off, he'll have to recharge it more often, and the battery might stay warm. But the new Razr has good battery life and heat sinks, he probably won't even notice. His own fault for having a flashy new phone, really. I don't think I could do this to an old phone, their OS can't handle it.'

Veronica shakes her head wonderingly.

'It's voice-activated, too,' Jacob explains. He seems very proud of the surveillance software he has uploaded to Prester's cell phone. 'Basically it comes to life when it hears something loud enough to understand. Otherwise it would chew through the battery in just a few hours, and we'd have to sift through endless junk. There's enough junk as is.'

That much is true. They have already spent most of an hour listening to Prester flirt with a girl at the post office, order a coffee somewhere, discuss Arsenal's Champions League prospects with an opinionated Chelsea fan, and complain to Uganda Online about DSL failures: not exactly the stuff of thrilling espionage stories.

'I looked up Derek's calls from his secret phone,' Jacob says. 'The ones to Tanzania were actually to Zanzibar. It's like a province of Tanzania, but it's all Muslim. His notes talk about Zanzibar Sam, and Zanzibar as a gateway to the Islamic world. I figure this Zanzibar Sam is the link between the *interahamwe* and al-Qaeda.'

'Makes sense.'

'Yeah. Almost everything makes sense. Almost.'

'What doesn't?'

Jacob says, 'Zimbabwe.'

Veronica looks at him, confused. 'Zimbabwe? What do you mean?'

'It just keeps popping up. Derek's calls to and from Zimbabwe. Those were the only calls he received on that phone. Those soldiers that rescued us, and their general. Susan used to work in Zimbabwe. And Danton's mother was born there, right?'

'Sort of. It was called Rhodesia back then.'

Veronica tries to remember what she knows about Zimbabwe. Until a decade ago it was a wealthy and prosperous nation, by African standards. Then its president, Robert Mugabe, went crazy and evicted almost all its white landowners, their farms were ruined and feel into disuse, the violence stopped tourists from coming, and Zimbabwe's economy nosedived. Now it has the lowest life expectancy in all of Africa.

'Maybe it's just coincidence. But it's kind of weird. I was thinking of calling that number there, seeing who answered.'

'You think that's a good idea? What are you going to say to them?'

'I don't know. Now that Prester's back I figure we should wait on him. He's our best bet for a breakthrough.'

A long silence ensues.

'I went to the Speke Hotel for a beer last night,' Jacob says. 'Started wondering about what this place was like when Amin was in charge. I read about him before I came here. He ran the whole country into the ground. You couldn't even get candles or light bulbs, so almost everything was dark at night. And in the day they didn't have air conditioning, so they kept all the windows open in the government buildings. They'd torture people to death every day there, and the windows were open, they had to be, otherwise it was too hot to torture. People sitting in the fancy hotels across the street, diplomats and mining executives and journalists and so on, they'd hear the screaming, and they'd just keep on eating their lunch. Crazy, eh?'

Veronica grimaces.

'The more I know about this continent, the crazier it gets. Have you actually gotten to know any Africans? I mean, personally?'

She thinks for a moment. 'No. Not really. Lots of expats and NGO workers. I live in a bubble. We all do. There are lots of Africans at work, they're big on local hires, but I don't really talk to them.'

'Did you notice Henry has a furball dangling from his rear-view mirror? Like fuzzy dice. He says it's *muti*, magic, a fetish, keeps the car safe. And he's a Jehovah's Witness. I figure, OK, basically no formal education, ignorant cultural superstition, right? But these African guys at work, they're Western educated, university degrees, super-smart. I started talking to them about it, and they got all weird. Like scared. Changed the subject, walked away.'

'Athanase had a little fur pouch around his neck,' Veronica remembers.

'Derek said it was a big deal around here. Black magic and witch doctors. No one talks about it to Westerners, but it's a huge, huge influence. And tribes too, tribal politics, their tribe matters to them a lot more than their country. Why shouldn't it, it was Europeans who mapped out their borders, right? Derek said a lot of the things that apparently don't make sense in Africa, at least to our eyes, are actually down to black magic and tribal politics.'

'Yeah, well, he's dead now, isn't he?'

Jacob stares at her.

'Sorry. I don't want to talk about Derek. I know you were his best friend. I'm sorry.'

'It's OK.'

'I hardly knew him, right? I shouldn't care.' Veronica sighs, decides to confess. 'I had this monster crush on him. I didn't even want to admit it, not even to myself, but, like, the morning after I met him, I woke up with part of my mind imagining our future together. That kind of crush. You know what I mean?' Jacob nods. 'Like he was the man I should have married. It was crazy. I'm sure it was just, I don't know, rebound, psychological reaction to divorce, whatever. But it felt like he was all I ever should have wanted in the first place.'

Jacob shrugs. 'Well, if it's any consolation, he was a great guy, but I never thought he treated his girlfriends particularly well. Actually he was kind of an asshole to women. Sorry.'

She doesn't say anything.

'I knew him since I was eleven. We were the two biggest geeks in junior high. We used to spend every lunch hour playing Dungeons and Dragons. Just the two of us, because no one else would talk to us. We were best friends the whole way through high school. Even in university, even when he got into drugs and flipped out, we still hung out all the time. He even got me laid. Quite a feat back in those days.'

'I can imagine,' Veronica says without thinking.

Jacob laughs good-naturedly. 'You have no idea.'

'Then he went to Bosnia?' she asks, interested despite herself.

'Yeah. He must have barely passed the physicals. But when he came back he'd turned into, like, a Superman action figure. All muscle. Like you saw.' Jacob pauses. 'He was different when he came back. I don't know. Haunted. But we were still friends. I don't know if we would have been if we had met then for the first time, but we had momentum, you know? So we stayed pretty tight.'

Veronica nods.

'And it was cool being friends with him. I'd brag on him all the time, my adventurer best friend working in all these crazy places. Haiti, Thailand, Iraq, then here. The last five years, we didn't see each other much, he didn't get along well with his folks, he'd come back to Canada maybe once a year. I was so looking forward to coming out here and hanging out with him. I was kind of sick of living vicariously, you know? This was supposed to be my big adventure. It was going to be so great. And now, *bam*, he's gone. If he'd gotten cancer or something there would at least have been some warning, you know? It feels like he's not supposed to be gone. I keep half thinking like somehow he actually faked his death and he's going to pop up any moment with a big grin on his face and tell me the whole story.'

Veronica can't think of anything to say.

The computer speakers come to life. Both of them twitch with surprise, lean towards Jacob's laptop and listen intently. The sound is muffled, like that of an accidental pocket-call from a cell phone, and further blurred by engine noise from some kind of vehicle, so Prester's voice wavers between clear and indistinct:

'Just got back into . . . halfway from Entebbe . . . tomorrow night . . . Yeah . . . No shit. Well, I'm ready to bring in Zanzibar Sam. Tonight? Usual time and place, then. Cheers.'

The computer goes silent.

'Zanzibar Sam,' Jacob mutters. 'Tonight.'

'It sounded like he's on the phone.'

'I think he was. But not his Mango phone. We would have heard it loud and clear. All his calls are now conferenced to and recorded on this computer. He's got another phone. Like Derek did.'

'Half the people where I work have more than one Ugandan phone,' Veronica points out.

'It's not uncommon,' Jacob concedes. 'Three different networks here, three different coverage maps. Phones are cheap, if you travel a lot it makes sense to have one of each. That's true. But how does he know about Zanzibar Sam?'

'Maybe Derek told him.'

'If Derek told Prester everything, why did Derek have a secret office?'

Veronica doesn't have an answer for that. Maybe Jacob is right and Prester is guilty of Derek's death. But it's still hard for her to reconcile that possibility with the way Prester talked in Goma.

'We should take all this to the embassy,' she says. 'Let them handle it.'

'Take what?' Jacob sounds exasperated. 'What do you want to do, go knock on their door and say, listen, we happen to think that two of your CIA agents are actually smugglers who had Derek killed, and are now being blackmailed by al-Qaeda into helping them kill two hundred Western NGO workers. And by the way, Veronica here thinks her ex-husband is in on it too. Oh, but you know what, all we have for proof is a bunch of Derek's scribbled notes, a few cryptic phone records and a whole lot of speculation. Can you just drop everything and arrest Prester and Strick right now, pretty please with a cherry on top?' He shakes his head. 'I seriously doubt they'll listen. Even if they did, there's no way Prester and Strick wouldn't find out. We'd have shown our hand for nothing, they'd hide their tracks. I mean, if they actually are corrupt. We don't actually know that, you know. We don't know anything. We just suspect.'

'But it makes sense.'

'To us. I seriously doubt we can convince anyone else with what we've got.'

Veronica considers. 'Where's Prester now?'

Jacob flips to a Google Maps window that displays a single red marker on a map of Kampala; Prester's current location. 'His office.'

'Is anybody else there?'

'Nobody with an active Mango phone. That's all I can tell you.'

'But he didn't sound like he was with someone.'

'No,' Jacob admits.

'When he goes out, we should follow him.'

'*Follow* him?'

'What do you want to do, wait around until he happens to speak clearly into his phone that he's the guy who set up Derek? If this Zanzibar Sam guy really is some kind of al-Qaeda terrorist contact, the embassy will probably have his picture. Remember that binder full of Arab faces? I bet they'll start taking us seriously once we can pick him out of a line-up. Unless you can make Prester's phone take his picture for us.'

'I probably could trigger his camera phone remotely,' Jacob says thoughtfully. 'Interesting.'

'But you wouldn't know when to do it, unless you were watching.'

'No. But . . . were you just listening to what you were saying? *Al-Qaeda terrorist contact*. You want to go following a guy like that? You and me, in Kampala, where we happen to stand out like Michael Jordan at Albinos Anonymous? Stop me if I'm wrong, but weren't you the one not long ago at all who wanted to give up and go home because this was too dangerous?'

'We have to do *something*. We're talking about two hundred lives in danger here. At least. And as far as we know nobody else even suspects.' She thinks of the NGO workers in the Congo and western Uganda, digging wells, installing solar panels, providing medical care. 'I'm not talking about endangering ourselves. This is Kampala, not the Congo. We'll stay in busy places, we won't take any chances, no dark alleys. But if we can't take what we've got to the embassy, then we have to get more evidence ourselves.'

Jacob reflects. 'I suppose that is actually logical. Insane, maybe, but logical.'

'If we can actually see Zanzibar Sam, even from a distance, then we've got something.'

He nods slowly. 'Fair enough. And now that you mention it, this does sound like the perfect time to break out my digital SLR and telephoto lens.'

5

The rest of the day passes slowly. Prester, or at least Prester's phone, does not leave his office. He has a few conversations on his Razr, most of which deal with a complicated contract for a pilot project to mine dissolved methane from Lake Kivu, a venture that doesn't appear to have anything to do with Derek or al-Qaeda or the *interahamwe*. From what Veronica can gather, officials in Kinshasa and Goma have raised many objections to the proposal, most of which are actually coded demands for bribes that must be paid before the project can proceed.

She and Jacob quickly grow bored. Veronica passes the time reading an oddly fascinating science-fiction book called *Lord of Light*. In the early evening she has Henry take her to New City, where she buys sandwiches and a bagful of snacks from the huge Game supermarket. She spends a good hour just wandering around Game, revelling in its towering, well-lit racks full of First World products. She never imagined when she came to Africa that an air-conditioned supermarket could seem so poignant.

Jacob spends the afternoon working on a way to make Prester's Razr take a picture with its on-board phone, and then upload it to Jacob's computer, without Prester ever noticing. He is utterly lost in his technical world, seems unaware of Veronica's presence. She has never seen anyone so engrossed. She has certainly never experienced anything like it herself; even when she worked as a nurse, it was more a question of doing the rounds, filling out forms and responding to crises and demands, rather than embarking on projects of her own. She wonders what it would be like to be so absorbed by her work.

It is amazing what Jacob can do. Veronica wonders how many other people would be capable of these feats, tracking calls, reprogramming phones, using someone else's cell phone as a remote camera. Probably very few. No wonder Derek wanted Jacob on his side. She is in the presence of a kind of modern-day wizard.

The sun is setting, and Veronica is about to propose that they call it a day, when Jacob's computer bleeps a warning sound. He blinks, looks up from the online technical documentation he is studying and switches windows to the Google Map of Prester's phone.

'He's on the move,' Jacob reports.

Veronica looks outside. It will be dark soon. She hadn't really considered the possibility of following Prester at night. But they have a car; as long as they stay distant, they should be fine. 'All right. Let's go find him.'

Jacob nods and grabs his hip-top.

'You take that everywhere,' she observes.

'Not to Bwindi. Figured a disposable phone would be fine there. But almost everywhere, yes. Don't leave home without it.'

'I thought that was the Leatherman.'

'I've got that on me too. Souvenir. And you never know, it might come in handy again.'

Veronica frowns. 'Let's hope not.'

'No, wait, go back,' Jacob orders, looking up for just a moment, then back to his hip-top's shining screen. He soon realizes it's almost useless; none of the real-world roads around him appears on the online map. Kampala wasn't planned or surveyed, it just grew. 'The other way. South-west.'

'I have no compass, sir,' Henry says. 'You must give me roads for directions.'

'I can't. According to this map, we're in the middle of empty wilderness.'

'Go straight and then left,' Veronica tells Henry.

'Thank you.'

They turn off a paved boulevard on to a wide dirt road without electrical power; neither town nor shanty town, but a region between. The buildings here are low and lit by flickering candles. The Toyota's headlights briefly illuminate shadowy figures walking or standing along the road. The dirt thoroughfare is pitted and rutted, scattered with entropic debris and pools of stagnant water. A few piles of organic trash have been set by the road to burn. The last line of street lights dwindles behind them, and Jacob begins to feel uncomfortable. He is on the verge of suggesting they turn around when Veronica says, in a relieved voice, 'That must be it.'

The *it* in question is an island of light in the sea of darkness; a large property illuminated brightly from within, surrounded by a wooden fence. Cars ranging from rusting *matatus* to gleaming black BMWs are parked on the streets and in vacant lots all around. Thatched roofs arranged in a U shape sixty feet square are visible within the wall, and the open gate reveals a thronging crowd of Africans beneath those largely open-walled roofs. It's some kind of outdoor nightclub; half the people inside are dancing ecstatically, giving themselves totally to the music. Nearly every-body is holding a bottle or a cigarette or both. The babble of conversation is audible a hundred yards away, mixed with the thumping beats and lilting melodies of African music. Four burly men at the gate watch carelessly as people pass in and out. Others congregate at the nearby *nyama choma* grilled-meat stand.

Henry pulls to a stop about a hundred feet away and looks around to be sure all the doors are locked before he switches off the lights. 'This is a place for bad people,' he says, worried. 'The men who come here are drinkers and fornicators. Ganja smokers. They have closed their eyes and ears to the Lord's message. They have no discipline, no restraint.'

'Sounds like my kind of place,' Jacob jokes.

Henry looks at him with sad disapproval. It is like being glared at by a priest. Jacob wants to apologize but decides to just shut up. Henry always makes Jacob a little uneasy. He's still not accustomed to having a servant, and being called 'Mr Rockel' by an older man.

'Can you hear anything from his phone?' Veronica asks.

Jacob frowns. 'Doubt it. It should turn on by itself if it picks up any usable audio. The software's not perfect, but I'm guessing there's too much background noise in there . . .' He taps at his hip-top, and the car suddenly fills with loud, muddy music. Jacob quickly turns it off. 'Nope. He could recite *Kublai Khan* at maximum volume and we wouldn't pick it up. We won't get anything from in there unless he actually uses his Razr. Maybe not even then.'

'Shit.'

'Yeah. We can't follow him in there. Not surreptitiously. We're probably the only white people within half a mile. Well, maybe we'll get lucky and he'll develop a hankering for *nyama choma*.' Jacob produces his Canon Rebel camera and a long lens from his backpack, assembles them, lowers his window just enough for the lens to pass through, and peers through the viewfinder at the nightclub. It's hard to make out individuals amid the constant motion. He sees a few men with dreadlocks, but none is Prester. He's short for an African, next to invisible in a crowd like this.

'Is there enough light to take a picture?' Veronica asks.

'I don't know. The window works as a poor man's tripod, that helps. Let's see.' He sets the camera to its maximum ISO level, takes a test shot and examines the resulting image. 'Hey, that's actually not bad. Good enough to recognize faces.'

Jacob goes back to surveying the crowd through the telescopic lens. It feels like he is in a movie, but at the same time he feels coolly confident, ready for anything, as if he has been training his whole life for this pursuit of al-Qaeda down dark African alleys. Maybe he has: maybe every movie, book and video game he's ever seen, read and played has honed his instincts and his strategies, maybe this is the triumphant advantage of having lived a Western pop-culture youth, that all the ten thousand made-up adventures he has seen and lived on screen and page have prepared him for this real one better than any formal training ever could.

'Can I see?' Veronica asks after a few minutes.

'Sure.'

She has to lean over him and press her body against his to get a decent view, and when she does, Jacob goes still. She is amazingly warm. It feels as if a long time passes before she withdraws from the camera and sits back in her seat.

'I guess we wait,' Veronica says.

Time passes. Jacob wishes he had thought to bring a jacket. By day, Kampala's equatorial heat is oppressive, but the night air is cool.

'Lot of mosquitoes out here,' Jacob says, slapping at his shoulder.

Veronica produces her pack of Marlboro Lights. 'Don't worry. I'll smoke them out.'

'Can I have one?'

She looks at him. 'I didn't know you smoked.'

'I may as well start. We've got bigger problems than lung cancer.'

It feels like sucking air from a car's exhaust pipe, he hacks and coughs on the first couple of puffs, but Jacob keeps going, although he stops inhaling. Soon his fingers are tingling and he feels a little sick.

'Veronica,' Jacob whispers. He puts his hand on her shoulder and shakes her, gently at first, then firmly. 'Veronica, wake up.'

She gasps and sits up, eyes wide, alarmed. 'What is it?'

'It's OK. You fell asleep. He's outside.'

Prester has emerged alone from the fray of the nightclub, and is buying a skewer of grilled meat from the *nyama choma* stand. Veronica, Jacob and Henry watch intently. When Prester goes back inside Jacob groans and slumps back into his seat.

'Jesus,' Veronica mutters. 'I never knew following someone could be so boring. How long have we been here now?'

Jacob checks his hip-top. 'Almost five hours.'

'Christ.'

Henry says, unexpectedly, 'The patient in spirit is better than the proud in spirit.'

Jacob blinks. 'Says who?'

'Ecclesiastes, chapter seven, verse eight.'

'Wait,' Veronica says. 'He's coming out again,'

This time Prester keeps walking, and disappears into the night. Jacob and Veronica are still considering their options when Prester's familiar green Mitsubishi Pajero emerges from the darkness and drives right past the Toyota. Jacob yanks the camera away, and he and Veronica crouch down in the back seat as Prester's headlights sweep over them.

'Do you think he saw us?' Veronica asks.

'No,' Henry says.

She and Jacob exchange glances.

'All right,' Jacob decides. 'I've always wanted to say this. Follow that car!'

*   *   *

Prester drives back to the paved road and turns left, away from downtown. Jacob is relieved to be back among street lights. They enter a quasi-industrial zone of warehouses and car repair shops, properties fenced with barbed wire or concrete topped with broken glass, some guarded by askaris or dogs. Then, when the road forks, Prester bends left where all the other traffic goes right. The left-hand fork is paved but has no street lights.

'Turn our lights off,' Jacob orders. 'Keep following.'

Henry hesitates before obeying. Jacob is glad he had Henry drive. Henry was born in Kampala, he must know the city like the back of his hand, surely he won't allow them to drive into disaster.

'Where does this road go?' he asks.

Henry shakes his head. 'I do not know.'

Jacob winces and looks down at his hip-top. The map is utterly blank.

'He is slowing down,' Henry says softly. He is leaning forward and squinting in order to see the road ahead of them.

'Keep back,' Jacob says. 'Don't let him see us.'

Prester's lights begin to bounce and jostle. Seconds later they feel the smooth pavement beneath them end, the Toyota begins to rattle violently along rutted dirt. In the moonlight Jacob sees shacks strewn haphazardly alongside the road, closed and dark as coffins. He hears the snarl of a feral dog as it leaps out of their way. They are in the shanty town. Jacob knows the smart thing to do is to retreat. This isn't just shady, this is outright dangerous. But they are so close.

'I don't think this is a good idea,' Veronica says nervously. 'We should go back.'

'I think the lady is right,' Henry quickly agrees.

Jacob hesitates, then capitulates. 'Yeah. Fuck. OK, let's turn—'

'Behind us!' Henry says sharply.

Jacob turns around. Another set of headlights is roaring up behind them.

Ahead of them, Prester's Pajero stops and begins to reverse towards them.

'Oh, no,' Jacob breathes. The moment of awful realization is like an abyss opening up beneath his feet, like the moment he looked into the Bwindi jungle and saw men with Kalashnikovs emerge. 'It's a trap.'

6

'Turn around, turn around!' Jacob cries out.

Veronica can hardly breathe. Her lungs feel trapped in an icy cage.

'There is no room,' Henry says.

He's right. This dirt path is only a single lane wide, the shacks here are too close together. The vehicle behind them is big, another SUV. Prester's Pajero stops twenty feet away. They have been boxed in.

'Call the police,' Veronica says hoarsely.

Jacob picks at his hip-top, then stares at it, disbelieving. 'No service. How the fuck? We're in range, we've got to be.'

They hear doors open on the vehicle behind them.

'The Lord Jesus will shelter and guide us.' Henry's voice is low and strained. 'Holy Jesus, pray for us sinners, now and at the hour of our death.'

'Run,' Veronica says, 'we have to run.'

Jacob looks at her helplessly. 'Where? How?'

Prester gets out of the Pajero and walks slowly back towards the Toyota. The gun in his left hand shines darkly in the head-lights of the vehicle behind them. Veronica feels paralysed. She can't even turn her head to look at Jacob.

Prester bangs on the car window beside her with his gun, so hard that he almost breaks the glass. 'Out of the car. *Now.* There are two hard men with Kalashnikovs right behind you. If you don't do this my way, you *will* do it their way. Your call.'

After a second Veronica forces herself to move, reaches out with a trembling hand, unlocks the door.

Prester yanks it open and orders, 'Out.'

Veronica obeys. She is trembling, wobbling on her legs, she feels like she hardly has the strength to stand. She half expects to be pistol whipped or killed on the spot – but Prester just gapes at her. Jacob follows her out and takes a step forward past her, half interposing himself between Veronica and Prester.

A long moment passes. Prester stares at them as if he's never seen white people before. Then he demands, 'What the fuck?'

Veronica and Jacob don't know how to respond. Prester looks into the vehicle, sees Henry. 'Who's this?'

'My driver,' Jacob says weakly. 'Henry. He doesn't know anything, he doesn't have anything to do with this.'

'Anything to do with what? Why are you following me?'

Veronica realizes they should have come up with some kind of cover story, some explanation, however thin. Now she can't think of anything but the truth.

'Give me a fucking answer. Who put you up to this?'

'Nobody,' Jacob says, startled into the truth. 'It's just us.'

Veronica gives him an alarmed look. Jacob just admitted that no one knows where they are or what they are doing, and that no help is on the way. His face falls as he realizes the same thing.

'Holy shit.' Prester's expression brightens with understanding. 'Holy shit, you thought it was me, didn't you?'

They don't dare answer.

'You think I set Derek up.' He shakes his head wonderingly. 'You fucking idiots. This is why I told you to go home. You stupid fucking amateur-hour morons.' Prester starts to laugh. It's a relieved laugh, not a mocking one, and after a moment Veronica allows herself to smile with the hope that Prester is actually not a bad guy, she and Jacob are not actually about to die.

'I should have known,' Prester says, and now he sounds amused and confident. 'You drive right up to the club and think no one will notice a white couple just down the street with a camera big enough to choke a crocodile. Then you think I won't notice you following me. Turning your lights off in the middle of the road. Jesus. And I was actually worried. What a fucking joke.'

He calls out to the SUV behind them, speaking mostly in an African language, but Veronica hears the word 'jammer'. A moment later Jacob's hip-top, still sitting in the back seat, bleeps with approval. Prester digs out his phone and dials. Jacob freezes; and as Prester speaks, again in an African tongue, his own voice emerges from the hip-top, it's like listening to him on a surround-sound system. Prester stops talking, lowers the phone and stares at Jacob.

'We, um, we bugged your phone,' Jacob says apologetically.

'No shit.'

'Let me just get that.' Jacob dives back into the Toyota just long enough to switch off the hip-top. Prester finishes speaking into his phone, hangs up and examines Jacob and Veronica again, this time more carefully.

'Sorry,' Veronica says. 'I guess we were wrong.'

After a moment Prester says, 'Come on. Follow me. Let's go get a beer. We need to talk.'

The bar he takes them to was once a house, and might still be used for accommodation, Veronica isn't sure. Men and women sit on rickety chairs and couches, stand in the kitchen or loiter on the barren dirt outside the building, drinking and smoking. Dreadlocks and Rasta caps are over-represented among the crowd, and reggae music pumps through air thick with the sweet smell of marijuana. The chief distinction between this and a house party, from what Veronica can tell, is that the pretty, bare-bellied young woman who walks around distributing beers and joints collects money from their recipients. When they enter, Prester hugs the hostess familiarly, exchanges complicated handshakes with a half-dozen other men, purchases three beers and two joints, and then leads Veronica and Jacob to a small room upstairs.

The walls are of barren, splintered wood; the only furniture is a low table and a half-dozen torn cushions. The windows are empty of glass and a low babble of conversation filters up from the yard. Prester motions them to sit, cracks open the Nile beers with his teeth and stations them around the table. Veronica doesn't like how close the walls are, but the open windows make the room tolerable.

'Your driver's going to sit it out?' he asks.

'He's not part of it. He's a Jehovah's Witness,' Jacob says.

'Yeah. And he's just your driver, not an actual human being, right?'

Jacob blinks.

'You want to get yourselves in deep shit, go right ahead, but if he's not part of it, you should have left him out. He would have died just like you if you'd actually been right about me.'

Jacob wordlessly acknowledges Prester's point. Prester lights up a joint, takes a drag and offers it to them. Jacob declines. Veronica does not.

'Derek was investigating you,' Veronica says, after she finally exhales. She ignores Jacob's glare. Prester has proven himself trustworthy. 'We found his notes.'

'Really? Where? How?'

Jacob explains his cell-phone wizardry and their expedition to the Hotel Sun City.

Prester nods slowly. 'I'm impressed. Yeah. Somebody at the embassy is making millions off smuggling, and either Langley really thinks it's me, or whoever it is decided I was the perfect fall guy. Which is true. Criminal record, complicated history, nobody's going to believe I'm pure as the snows of Kilimanjaro, you know? Which I actually am, not that I expect even you to believe. It's like Saddam and the WMDs, the more they don't find anything, the more they assume I'm hiding something big.' He shakes his head, half appalled, half amused. 'I need to be corrupt in order to be less suspicious. It's so tragic it's almost hilarious. So they sent Derek to investigate me. I knew that. But instead he found out something else.'

'What?'

'Don't know exactly. He never trusted me. Or anyone. I gathered, from what he let slip, probably to see how I'd react, he was looking for some guy named Zanzibar Sam, who he thought was the connection between the Arabs and the *inter-ahamwe*. Sound familiar?'

Jacob hesitates, but Veronica has decided to tell Prester the whole truth. He had them at his mercy and let them go; that's good enough for her. 'Yes. It's in his notes.'

Prester takes a swig of his Nile and a puff from the joint. Then he says, 'The Arabs who come to the Congo, all the ones I've met, they come for gold. Locals pan gold from rivers up by Bunia, just like the Old West, complete with shitloads of bad guys with guns. Ever see *Treasure of the Sierra Madre*? Bogart. Great movie. Arabs come here, buy gold for a hundred bucks an ounce, then get it overland to Zanzibar or Sudan, cross to Yemen or Dubai on a dhow, sell it at market rates. Which last I checked were well north of five hundred an ounce. Damn fine profit margin, especially if you happen to cut out customs. But the locals, they've got cell phones, they've got the Internet, they know the price of gold. So as you might imagine you get some tension between them and the Arabs. So a lot of the Arabs start working with local warlords to keep the labour in line. People don't complain so much about being underpaid when the buyer has a gun to their head. Marx and Mao can tell you all about it. All control of the means of production comes out of the barrel of a gun.'

'What about the UN peacekeepers?' Jacob asks.

Prester almost laughs. 'Something like one peacekeeper for every hundred square miles around eastern Congo, and most of them stay in town and don't get out much. Can't say I blame them. They have about as much influence on day-to-day life in eastern Congo as the Kinshasa government does. Which is to say, very fucking little. Shit, I shouldn't need to tell you guys this, you were *in* one of those mines.'

'Don't remind us,' Veronica mutters.

'Trouble is, seems the CIA is now half convinced that *I'm* the connection between al-Qaeda and Athanase. Same mistake you made. They've got dozens of spooks and special forces in the Congo right now, looking for the bad guys. I should be with them. I'm the fucking local expert. But instead I find myself *persona* not particularly *grata*. Who needs me when you've got General Gorokwe, right?' He grimaces. 'That lucky bastard should do very well for himself out of this. Current Washington policy, when fighting in unstable nations, is to find sympathetic local strongmen like him and use them as an instrument. If the instrument in question isn't a complete idiot he comes out smelling of roses and Old Glory and thousand-dollar bills. Karzai in Afghanistan. Chalabi in Iraq, until he got too greedy. And now Gorokwe in the Congo. A week ago he was an evil general from a pariah nation. Today he's a peacekeeper and a valuable ally in the War on Terror, he's been shaking hands with high-level diplomats and getting shipments of all manner of shiny new guns to hunt and kill al-Qaeda. And the *interahamwe*, if they happen to get in the way, not that anyone really cares about them, they're yesterday's bad guys. My suspicion is the general sees no real reason to hurry the job.' Prester finishes the joint. 'But never mind him. It's my own future I'm worried about. So I spent the last few days looking for Zanzibar Sam myself, to try to clear my name. This whole deal has made me start to seriously wonder about my future. I mean, it's fun playing James Bond, but it's a lot less fun when you suddenly find out M and Q and Moneypenny are suddenly lining up to stab you in the back. I don't want to spend the rest of my life dealing with this kind of bullshit. If all you do is use people and be used, you forget how to have friends. I know a million people here, some of them real big men, it's not ego when I tell you I'm a serious player. I can make a phone call and have someone killed or have a briefcase full of cash delivered. But you know how many real friends I have? Zero. No room for 'em. Beginning to think that calls for a certain re-examination, you know? Whole new lifestyle, maybe. Whole new life. Again.'

Prester falls silent. For the first time since Veronica met him he looks old, there are lines graven on his face. She realizes his eyes are red not just with smoke but with sleep deprivation; he's been awake for a long time, maybe days.

'Very moving,' Jacob says, 'but what does it have to do with us?'

'With you.' Prester considers. 'That remains to be seen. But for one thing,' he looks at Veronica, 'I found out a little something about your ex-husband.'

'Danton?'

'The same. He, or at least somebody by his name, flew into Kampala yesterday, first class of course, checked into the Sheraton's presidential suite. Kind of a funny time to take a vacation in Uganda, don't you think? Unless, of course, you just found out that you and your CIA smuggling partner are being blackmailed by al-Qaeda to cooperate with them or be revealed as having conspired with genocidal war criminals to smuggle slave-labour minerals out of the Congo. Nasty moral dilemma, that. Assuming you have any morals.'

Veronica stares at him. She doesn't know what to say or think.

'Do you think it might be Strick?' Jacob asks.

Prester rolls his eyes. 'No. That's the one thing I am certain of. I've told you. Strick is a prick, but he is not dirty. I've worked with him for years, I would know. And he's not senior enough to have gotten away with this. No, it's somebody higher. Some suit in the embassy.'

'OK. And Zanzibar Sam?'

'Zanzibar Sam, I learned at the club, tonight, from an extremely fucking scary man, and for a painfully large fee, Derek was all wrong about. It's not a person. It's a package. Zanzibar *Sams*, plural. And they're supposed to arrive in Kampala tomorrow, for one night only, before being shipped off again the next day.'

'Where to?'

'I have no idea. But would I ever like to know. The what it is, and the where it's going, and especially the who it's going to. And you know what else? I'm actually glad you two lost your minds and decided to stay and play Hercule Poirot and Miss Marple. I'm beginning to think you might be able to help me out.'

7

'These are expensive,' Jacob says, looking at the two iPod-sized lozenges of black metal on the desk in his study, sitting beside a metal box as big as a toaster that bristles with electronic apparatus and LCD screens. 'The GPS trackers are five hundred US each. If I don't get them back inside a week I'll have to pay for them myself. And the spectrum analyser's more like ten thousand. That's like half my annual salary here.'

'If we get the evidence, those most high will cover your expenses, I promise,' Prester says. 'They've got plenty of black-book discretionary slush funds.'

'Why don't we just go to the embassy now?' Veronica asks. 'We must have enough to convince them something's going on. They'll listen to all three of us.'

Prester shrugs. 'I doubt it. Take it from me, put not your faith in the American intelligence services. They're not much sharper than any other batch of bureaucrats, and they're already half convinced I'm the bad guy. But even if they do listen, then what? We don't even have a name. All we know is Derek got set up by somebody in the chain of command. If they find out we're poking around, they'll pull the plug and, poof, we got nothing but conspiracy theories and a cheese omelette on our face. We need names, dates, pictures, verifiable evidence. With any luck these little toys will help get us that tonight. Without . . . well, there's always Plan B. Your ex.'

Veronica frowns. She doesn't want to crash Danton's hotel and start demanding answers. She came to Africa to get away from her ex-husband and everything he represents. She doesn't want to see him ever again, not unless and until she has the advantage. She can't even really imagine what that would be like. Danton always has the advantage. That's what it means to be rich.

'Shouldn't be necessary,' Prester says reassuringly, reading her face. He seems more cheerful today, and more rested. 'Tonight should be plenty. Even if we can't plant these trackers, your amazing little number harvester should be highly helpful.'

'It's not just a number harvester,' Jacob objects. 'It's a full-feature GSM spectrum analyser. Practically a mobile base station. And it doesn't actually register cell-phone numbers. Just handset and SIM card IDs, and signal strength. We can only get the numbers of Mango phones.'

'Mango or Celtel or MTC.'

'Celtel and MTC are whole other companies. I don't have any access to their database.'

'Celtel is minority owned by a CIA front,' Prester says casually. 'And we got an MTC engineer on our payroll too. There's a reason Derek recruited you to work at Telecom Uganda. Same reason we both got Mango phones once he started getting suspicious. It's the only cell company here we hadn't wormed our way into yet.'

Jacob stares at him.

'More things under heaven and earth, son.' Prester is considerably shorter than Jacob, and Veronica doubts he is more than five or ten years older, but right now the diminutive seems appropriate. 'You're playing in the big leagues now. So don't get sloppy. Now what's the range on your precious spectrum analyser?'

'Maybe a hundred metres.'

'OK. Should be ample. You've only got two GPS trackers?'

'That's all I could manage.'

Prester frowns. 'Well, we'll make do. With luck whoever's smuggling these Zanzibar Sams won't have more than two vehicles. Strong magnets on these, right? All I have to do is put them somewhere on the chassis and they'll stay there, even on bumpy African roads?'

'Not a problem.'

'They text their coordinates how often?'

'It's configurable. Right now every ten minutes.'

'And if they don't have a cell signal?'

'They store their locations in local memory, times stamped, and send them all in one burst the next time they get into coverage.'

'Good.' Prester nods and turns to Veronica. 'I need him with me, but you can sit at home.'

She hesitates, then shakes her head. 'No. I want to come with you.'

'Sure?'

'Danton might be there.'

'Not likely.' Prester considers. 'But not impossible. Seeing as how we have no idea what exactly these Zanzibar Sams are or why somebody seems to think they're so important.'

'Are you sure you know where they're going to be?' Jacob asks.

'For the price I paid I better fucking not be led astray. But no, I'm not sure. People like this, you're never sure until the time comes.' He looks at his watch. 'Which is all too soon. Let's saddle up.'

Prester navigates his Pajero through a huge market of rickety wooden stalls, colourful pyramids of vegetables, dangling carcasses of meat, bowls of spices, sacks of grains and all the world's cheap clothing and plastic crap. They crawl slowly through the market's clogged streets, and then through ten minutes of grimy shanty town, as the sun hides itself behind the western hills.

'Shouldn't we wait until dark?' Jacob asks from the back seat.

Prester shakes his head. 'We'll stand out more if we wait too late. Not much traffic in this area after sunset. Besides, I want to get the lay of the land.'

Veronica is riding shotgun, which in this vehicle is the left-hand seat; Ugandans theoretically drive on the left, and this Pajero came from Japan. She looks around at the shanty town and winces when she sees a child with a large goitre bulging from her throat. All it would take to cure her is a little iodine.

The Night Of Knives

Every day this ramshackle sea of desolation expands farther into the green landscape around Kampala, swollen by unemployed *bayaye*, the Ugandan name for disaffected youths and families who stream in from poor rural villages to this city that offers them neither work nor shelter – but it doesn't seem as bad to her as it once did. Veronica understands now that most Africans, even in shanty towns, are not trapped in relentless disaster and tragedy. They build houses, raise families, hang out with their friends, visit the big city, work when they can, play music, drink, gossip and basically live normal, recognizable lives. But what they lack, desperately, is healthcare and education. If Veronica could actually fund and build a school for nurses here, it would help, it would make a real difference.

They finally reach Kampala's small industrial belt of warehouses and repair yards. Here the foot traffic streams back towards the shanty town, tired men walking home after a hard day, and Prester has to nose the Pajero upstream through this human river like a salmon seeking spawning grounds, until he finally says, 'Here.'

There is a scrapyard the size of several football fields ahead and to their right. It looks like a muddy parking lot hit by a massive artillery shell and left to rust, littered with the rotting hulks of cars, motorcycles and other unidentifiable machinery, surrounded by a chain-link fence topped by a single strand of barbed wire. In its centre there stands a single wide, low building, basically a hollow concrete block. Clusters of rebar sprout like some kind of steel vegetation from its roof. The yard's only visible inhabitant is a bored-looking watchman sitting behind the main gate, which is locked with chains and padlocks.

Prester drives past the yard without slowing down, until they have gone over another small rise; then he stops the car in front of a motorcycle repair shop. Ditches full of plastic bags and rotting trash cut through the vacant lot of gouged mud across the street. The few Africans still on the road look at the Pajero curiously, then move on, hurrying back to the market and the shanty-town houses beyond. It is apparent that this quasi-industrial zone is largely deserted come nightfall.

'Any phones around?' Prester asks.

Jacob examines the screen on the spectrum analyser. 'Just ours.' Then he digs out his hip-top and taps at it briefly. 'But there's a Mango phone alive inside that scrapyard.'

'That so? How convenient.'

'We should get closer. The analyser isn't in range.'

Prester says, 'Wait until dark.'

The sun falls over the horizon. It takes only a few minutes for the darkness to deepen into night. The few street lights that work shed barely enough light to see the outlines of the buildings around them. As they wait, Prester reaches inside his shirt collar, withdraws a little pouch of pale leather that hangs on the golden chain around his neck and twirls it absently between his fingers. It has been sewn shut with silver thread.

'What's that?' Veronica asks.

Prester looks down at the pouch as if he hadn't noticed it. Then he says, calmly, 'The little finger of a stillborn child.'

She stares at him.

'*Muti?*' Jacob asks, incredulous and revolted. 'You actually believe in that black-magic shit?'

'I live here. I can't afford not to.'

'But, come on. You're an educated man.'

'And you're a tourist. More things under heaven and earth, like I said. You'd never believe some of the things I've seen.' Prester takes a deep breath and tucks the pouch back under his shirt. 'Never mind. We're wasting time. Let me just go over the plan again. The objective here is to collect information, not get in trouble. I'm going to find a place to park which is both secure and has a view of the yard. You will call me if you see something I need to know about. My phone is on silent.' He double-checks this. 'You two will stay in the vehicle, no matter what. You're not trained for this and I've got enough problems without babysitting. I'm going to station the analyser by the gate, close enough to harvest their numbers when they come out, then go into the yard and put trackers on their vehicles. If something goes wrong, just get the fuck away and call for help, either the police or Strick, depending on what's happened. Is that all clear?'

Veronica nods, wide eyed.

'Clear,' Jacob rasps.

'Good. Let's do it.'

He turns the Pajero around and drives back past the scrapyard. Their headlights cast long, distorted shadows from the ruined machines sprawled on the vast field of fissured mud. There is a light on inside the building in the heart of the yard, and two vehicles are parked outside, a white Land Cruiser and a black Mitsubishi pick-up. Neither was there when they passed by before. The scene is eerily post-apocalyptic, like a night shot from *Mad Max*. Veronica is beginning to wish she'd told Prester she didn't want to come. It's far too easy to imagine being killed here by terrorists.

The watchman at the scrapyard gate looks at them with indifference as he is lit by their headlights. Prester drives back over the hill, then switches off all the Pajero's lights, U-turns, goes off-road across cratered mud and parks in a vacant lot atop the ridge that overlooks the scrapyard, almost level with the roof of the yard's single building. The street lights are distant and they can barely see more than silhouettes.

'That analyser ready?' Prester asks.

Jacob checks. 'Yes. Scan-and-record mode.'

Prester takes it and orders, 'Stay.'

Then he steps out of the vehicle, closes the door by leaning on it slowly so as not to make any sound. Veronica sees him get about twenty feet down the ridge, heading towards the scrapyard gate, before he disappears into darkness.

'No problem,' Jacob says, trying to be reassuring. 'He's not doing anything really risky. Just one lousy askari. No big deal.'

A long, slow silence passes. Veronica and Jacob watch the scrapyard like hawks. She blinks and squints at the black pick-up.

She can't tell for sure, the light is too dim, but did something just move?

'Did you see that?' she asked. 'By the pick-up?'

'No.'

'There it is again.'

'I don't see anything.'

'It's there,' Veronica insists. 'Something moving. In the pick-up, in the back.'

'Maybe it's him. Putting the trackers on.'

'It's too soon, I don't think he could have gotten there that fast – oh shit. Call him, call him!'

'What is it?' Jacob asks, reaching for his hip-top.

'Dogs!'

But it is too late. Before Jacob can dial, the two lethal-looking guard dogs leap out of the pick-up truck and charge towards a ruined truck, howling for blood. Then Veronica sees motion near the truck carcass. Someone running from the dogs, pelting towards the scrapyard fence. It must be Prester. He's not going to make it.

8

Jacob takes a deep breath. He doesn't want to intervene. He wants to run. But Prester has a problem, and Jacob has a solution. 'I'm going out there,' he says, and opens the door. 'He won't make it. I can help.'

He takes a second to close the car door quietly behind him, no sense advertising their presence, then he draws out his hip-top and rushes down towards the fence. The dogs howl for blood. Behind Prester's fleeing form, light spills out of the scrapyard building as a door opens. The ground is ridged and uneven and twice Jacob stumbles and nearly falls. Several men advance from the open door into the scrapyard. At least one is holding a rifle. Jacob slows halfway long enough to push the right buttons on his hip-top, it takes maybe three seconds but that seems like an eternity, the dogs are right on Prester's heels. Jacob sprints towards the fence, holding his hip-top above his head as if to announce its presence to the world. Prester's almost at the chain-link barrier, but he can't climb over barbed wire, and the slavering dogs have almost reached him—

But then Jacob reaches the fence, and the dogs come within range of the repellent sounds his hip-top is projecting at maximum volume in frequencies only canines can hear, like an anti-dog whistle. Their howls wilt into whines, and they slacken their pace and slink away, back into the shadows. Prester and Jacob come to a halt across the fence from each other. Jacob sees the GPS trackers in Prester's hand, and his heart sinks. Prester didn't even have a chance to plant them, this was a total failure.

'They're coming,' Jacob hisses, meaning the men behind Prester. They have guns and at least one flashlight, he can see a beam of light stabbing at the scrapyard wreckage as the men approach the fence. Their eyes won't have adjusted to the dark yet, but Prester is on the wrong side of a chain-link fence topped with barbed wire, Jacob has to stay close to him in order to keep the dogs away, and they have maybe twenty seconds before the gunmen discover them. He can't think of any way to get Prester out.

Headlights blink into life behind Jacob.

He turns and watches, amazed, as the Pajero accelerates downhill towards the scrapyard fence, its engine roaring, its undercarriage rattling and clanking against unseen obstacles on the uneven ground, until it slams into the fence with enough momentum that three fence posts come straight out of the ground and the chain-link folds backwards. The Pajero's horn bleats briefly at the moment of impact; then the vehicle drives right over the flattened chain-link and barbed wire into the scrapyard, and keeps going straight.

The broken shell of what was once a boat looms up in its headlights. As far as Jacob can tell Veronica never even touches the brakes. The Pajero ploughs into the ruin of the boat with a loud *crunch* and carries it some distance across the yard before both vehicles come to rest. Light from one still-functional headlight blazes off the boat's torn and twisted fibreglass hull, illuminating the accordioned metal of the Pajero's hood intertwined with the wreckage of the boat.

Jacob and Prester both sprint to the new gap in the fence. When they meet, Prester grabs the hip-top from Jacob's hands, hisses 'Be right back,' and disappears into the scrapyard before Jacob can protest.

He thinks Prester has gone crazy, there are men with guns in there, albeit distracted by Veronica's dramatic entrance. Jacob looks over at the Pajero for a moment and hesitates. She needs help, but if he goes to her aid he'll expose himself to the gunmen. Before he can decide what to do, the Pajero's door opens, and he sees Veronica's lithe form stagger away from the vehicle and into the darkness.

Veronica trips on a rut and falls hard to the hard-packed dirt; her hands and knees scrape painfully against the ground but then she is up again, still moving. A rattling fusillade of gunfire echoes in the distance, some kind of automatic weapon echoing across the scrapyard. She keeps sprinting across the moonlit yard, half expecting to be shot dead within seconds. She can't believe everything has gone so wrong so fast. She can't believe she actually drove the Pajero through the fence into the scrapyard instead of following Prester's instructions and fleeing to the embassy for help. She feels dazed, her forehead smacked into the middle of the steering wheel when the Pajero slammed into the fence, rattling her consciousness, but she thinks she's more or less OK, no concussion. She's just lucky the fence didn't stop the car; she should have taken two seconds to put on her seat belt. On the other hand those two seconds might have been crucial.

No more shots come. She hears shouts, in the middle distance, baffled and alarmed voices calling out in some language that is not

English. Her eyes adjust enough to see something looming ahead of her, the mangled remains of some kind of vehicle. Once past it she comes to a halt and looks back. No one seems to be chasing her. She crouches, hiding behind the wreckage, and examines her palms. They are raw and bleeding slightly but not too bad. Her jeans are torn but saved the skin on her knees. She is grateful she didn't fall on any shards of glass or metal.

Veronica hears barks and moans under her breath. She had forgotten about the dogs. She hears motion and voices, but none seem to be coming near. Her eyes slowly readjust to the night. She has taken cover behind a *matatu* that appears to have gotten into a stomping match with Godzilla. Veronica squats there for a good thirty seconds, staring out around the corner of the wreckage, trying to see what's going on, before she becomes aware of the two sets of pale eyes staring up at her from beneath the ruined vehicle.

She jumps back and very nearly screams. It takes her a heart-thumping moment to realize there is no immediate danger. There are two children huddled under the wrecked *matatu*. They are very small, certainly less than ten. They stare wide eyed at Veronica. She wonders for a moment what kind of game they are playing. Then she understands: they live here. This heap of torn metal is their home. She puts her fingers to her lips, hoping the symbol is universal. The children wriggle their way deeper under the wreckage, out of sight. She can hear their fast, frightened breaths. Veronica looks around and wonders with something like horror how many more of the scrapyard's hulks of twisted steel serve as homes for Aids orphans.

She hears a loud clank of metal on metal in the distance, and a few moments later, another. Beginning to hope that the men and dogs will not pursue her, she scuttles to the other side of the *matatu* wreckage and peers out. There are a half-dozen men around the Land Cruiser and the pick-up, watching warily, weapons ready, on guard. One of them holds the two growling guards on leashes. The pick-up has been loaded with two big metal boxes that look like coffins. As Veronica watches, the men climb into the two vehicles, the engines roar to life and the Land Cruiser and pick-up truck roll slowly away, to and through the now open scrapyard gate; turn to the right, away from central Kampala; and vanish into the night.

After a few more breaths Veronica dares to stand up and look around.

Then Jacob cries out, from maybe a few hundred feet away: 'Veronica!'

She hesitates to answer, but no one and nothing reacts, the scrapyard appears empty. Even the askari by the gate is gone. 'What? Where's Prester?'

'He's right here,' Jacob says hoarsely. 'They shot him.'

Prester lies on his side, in a shining, swelling pool of his own blood. It is so dark Veronica can hardly see him. Jacob stands helplessly over him. Veronica pushes Jacob aside, drops to her knees beside Prester and checks his airway. He's unconscious but still breathing.

'Get the first-aid kit,' she snaps at Jacob.

'First aid? Where is it?'

'The back of the Pajero. Go!'

While Jacob is gone Veronica strips Prester's shirt off and uses the light of her phone to inspect him. The ends of his dreadlocks are soaked in blood, as is his little leather fetish pouch. His breathing is shallow and laboured. The entrance wound below his left shoulder blade is relatively innocuous – but as Prester breathes, little bubbles rise from the centre of the dark stain spreading across his chest from the exit wound, and Veronica goes cold with dismay. Those bubbles are the classic symptom of an open pneumothorax, better known as a sucking chest wound.

'Call for help!' she shouts into the night at Jacob. 'And bring a blanket!'

Prester at least had the good sense to crawl into a little ditch before he passed out. Veronica lifts his arms and legs up on to the lip of this ditch, above his heart, so that more blood will flow to his head and upper body. She ransacks her mind for how to treat a pneumothorax, and remembers: tape something non-porous and airtight over the wound, leaving one corner unsealed to allow trapped air to escape. Some kind of plastic square would be perfect. She digs into her money belt and produces a credit card.

'Hurry!' she almost screams.

Jacob stumbles into sight, holding the first-aid box. 'I couldn't find a blanket.'

'Fine,' she says, popping the box open, opening gauze and tape. 'Did you call for help?'

'There's an ambulance on the way.'

'Good.' She tapes the exit wound, using her credit card to seal it off, bandages the entrance wound, and then stacks gauze on top on his chest and tries to apply pressure. It isn't easy with him on his side, but they can't risk changing his position, his neck or spine might be damaged. She works quickly, old reflexes re-emerging – it's been seven years since she worked in an ER but her hands have not forgotten. Veronica's finger is pricked by a damp splinter of bone from a shattered rib. She winces and hopes Prester isn't HIV positive. His blood loss is serious but not critical, not as bad as the guard who died at her feet in the Bwindi jungle, the man Veronica didn't even try to help. Unlike him Prester at least has a chance.

'What shot him? A handgun or a rifle?' she asks, after sucking at her pricked finger and spitting out the blood.

'I think a rifle.'

'Shit.'

'Is that bad?'

'Rifles are high velocity. They tumble in the wound, they have much higher energy transfer, you get indirect trauma, you can get small entry and exit wounds either side of a massive wound cavity, he could fucking die on us any second. It isn't a good sign he's unconscious.'

'I don't know it was a rifle for sure. After you crashed through the fence, he ran back out, grabbed my hip-top and went back in. I guess he figured they were distracted and wanted to take the chance to plant the trackers.'

'Fucking idiot,' Veronica mutters.

'Yeah. We're lucky they were even more scared of us than we were of them. Prester was conscious when I got to him, he said something to me. I'm not sure exactly what. I think he said . . . it doesn't make any sense, but I think he said, "The Sams are Igloos."'

Veronica almost releases the pressure bandage. 'Igloos? What does that mean?'

'You got me.'

'Take your shirt off.'

'What?' Jacob asks, amazed.

'*Take your shirt off.*'

He obeys.

'Now hold down this pressure bandage. Firm but not crushing. I'm going to tape it down to make it easier.'

Jacob obeys. Once the gauze is half taped in place – it's a sloppy job, with all the blood, but it should at least help prevent the bandage from slipping away – Veronica drapes Jacob's shirt over Prester's torso, then takes her own shirt off and uses it to cover his midriff. The night is cool, and blood loss saps body heat with dangerous speed. She considers trying to cut down on the blood loss with indirect pressure, pinching shut the major blood vessel that's feeding the wounded area, but it's been so long since she's practised she can't remember the details of the procedure, and she has a vague memory it might make things worse not better.

'OK,' she says. 'I think that's all we can do for him. Now we just wait. And hope the ambulance gets to us before whoever shot Prester decides to get curious and come back here.'

But neither the ambulance nor the gunmen reach the scene before the police arrive. Veronica has never been so glad to hear howling sirens.

*   *   *

'Please, I don't understand,' Jacob says wearily. 'What are we under arrest *for?*'

The big policeman looks at him as if his question is senseless. 'You are under arrest,' he repeats.

'I don't think they need a charge,' Veronica mutters through clenched teeth. Her eyes are closed and she is breathing hard. Her claustrophobia, Jacob supposes.

'Oh, the charge!' the policeman says, understanding at last. 'Your charge will be determined later. Before you go to a judge.'

'We have the right to call our embassies.'

'Yes, yes. After you are charged. I will see you tomorrow.'

The policeman leaves and closes the door behind him. Jacob and Veronica look at each other. She reaches out and takes his hand, clutches it so tightly it's almost painful. He squeezes back in what he hopes is a reassuring manner.

'It could be worse,' she says, as if trying to convince herself. 'We could be in the real jail. I think I would have gone batshit in there.'

Jacob nods. That would be worse. Much worse. They passed through the jail on the way in; lightless, overcrowded cages so crammed with men that some had no room in which to lie down or even sit, cells that stank of vomit and diarrhoea, fear and despair. Some of the prisoners were naked. All looked slumped and listless, uninterested in their visitors. Jacob supposes they don't get enough food, that's one way to keep your prisoners weak.

The cage in which they now sit is inset into a small room with cinder-block walls, a brick floor and a barred window. The ceiling is so low that Jacob has to stoop. The air is painfully stuffy and smells almost as bad as the jail. A number of disturbing stains smeared across the cage's rusting walls make Jacob suspect that Ugandan interrogation techniques have not advanced much, ethically speaking, since the days of Idi Amin; but at least they have the room to themselves, and are being treated with distant courtesy. He doesn't want to imagine what their fate would be if they were black and Ugandan.

'At least they gave us something to wear.' Jacob looks down at his T-shirt, which says FOR AN AIDS-FREE GENERATION, obviously a bulk donation from some Western aid organization. It actually fits him fairly well, but Veronica's is several sizes too large. He searches for any other silver lining, something cheerful to say. 'Nice driving back there, by the way.'

'Thanks.'

'You think Prester will make it?'

She takes a deep breath and visibly forces herself to think. 'I think he's got a good chance. The ambulance people actually seemed pretty on the ball.' By the time the police drove them away from the scrapyard Prester had been carried into an ambulance.

'They're a private service, they contract out to the police for emergency calls.' Jacob's first job for Telecom Uganda was the prioritization of the ambulance cell-phone service on the Mango network.

'They'll have to fly him out. He needs a real hospital.'

'Will they? I don't know if he's even an American citizen.'

Veronica blinks. 'But . . . but he works for the CIA.'

Jacob shrugs. 'So did Derek, and he was Canadian. Deniable front, that's what Prester said, remember? They hire non-Americans as a cover. They might just cut him loose.'

'Shit. What about us?'

'I don't know.' He considers saying something comforting, but decides to go with the truth. 'But I think we might be staying here for a while.'

Veronica's face tightens. Jacob wishes he could help her somehow but doesn't know how. He supposes holding her close is exactly the wrong thing to do.

A minute later the door opens, and the big policeman comes back in, leading a lean, grey-haired white man with a scarred face.

'All right,' Strick says. He sounds disgusted. 'Let's get you two out of here.'

9

Entering the American embassy is like teleporting back into the First World, into an office complex occupied by some moderately successful business. Everything is clean, new, imported from the USA.

It takes five minutes to get past the security gauntlet of razor wire, concrete barriers and guardposts. Strick parks, leads Jacob and Veronica through a side door, up a staircase and into a meeting room dominated by an elliptical wooden table surrounded by big office chairs. One wall is a large whiteboard. The other three are lined with folding plastic chairs, maybe thirty in all. A sleekly designed conference phone sits in the middle of the table. Strick reaches over, pushes a button on that phone, sits down and motions for them to do the same.

Once they are all seated Strick says, his voice controlled, 'This is the part where you tell me everything. And don't you dare leave anything out.'

Jacob thinks back to what Prester said: *Strick is a prick, but he is not dirty. That's one thing I am certain of.* He begins to tell the whole story. Veronica chimes in from time to time. Strick listens without asking questions. Jacob thinks his expression softens slightly as they tell their tale.

'I hope you still have those airline tickets,' is all he says when they are finished.

They nod.

'Being full-fare first-class tickets, they're good for a year after purchase. I can't actually make you use them tomorrow. But I very strongly suggest it.'

'And then what happens?' Jacob asks.

'And then we take care of things. It's a matter of priorities. There are a lot of innocent lives at risk. The first thing we do is take care of al-Qaeda in the Congo. We can put our own house in order later.'

'What if they're planning something?' Veronica asks. 'What if they're blackmailing whoever set up Derek to help them?'

'We're well aware of that possibility and we're taking measures to ensure that doesn't happen.'

'What measures?' Jacob demands.

Strick fixes him with a cold stare. 'Classified measures.'

'Classified my ass,' Jacob says, his anger finally bubbling over. 'You aren't well aware of shit, and you aren't the least bit interested in who set up Derek, or you wouldn't be hearing about all this from us. This is insane. You're telling us to go away? You should be asking us for help. I've found out more sitting at my computer than you have with the whole American intelligence budget behind you. Derek was murdered by one of you. By someone he was working for. But you don't actually want to find out who it was, do you? All you want is to use your pet Zimbabwe general to clean up in the Congo, collect the hosannas, then make your own problem go away before it makes you all look bad for not having noticed, this whole fucking time, that one of your own guys was in league with terrorists and genocidists. Never mind that they might be planning something in the meantime. The important thing is to keep your dirty laundry private, isn't it? You're nothing but a useless bureaucrat.'

Strick recoils slightly, as if he has just been slapped. He looks at Jacob for a long moment. Then he says, in an oddly gentle voice, 'I know he was your friend. But you have to let go.'

'No, actually, I don't.'

'Let me tell you a story.'

Jacob opens his mouth to say he doesn't want to hear it. Veronica kicks him in the shin. He looks at her and subsides.

'I knew a woman once,' Strick said. 'A Kurdish woman. I was there on duty, this was between the Gulf Wars. We were going to be engaged. That is, we were engaged, but it was secret. We couldn't tell anyone. Then one day she disappeared. I didn't take it seriously for the first couple of days. I thought she'd come back. It wasn't the first time. She had a history. Fits of madness. I guess you're not supposed to call it that any more. Madness. She was younger than me. Sometimes it hits women in their twenties.

Especially trauma survivors. Her family was all murdered in the eighties.' He takes a deep breath. 'But this time it wasn't madness. She told her cousin, who told her uncle, they took her away and killed her. Honour killing. So-called.'

Jacob and Veronica stare at Strick.

'I could have gone after them,' the grey-haired man says. 'I could have had my revenge. I wanted to. But it would have ruined everything both of us had worked for. And what good would have come from it? What good would have come?'

They have no answer.

'So I let her go. You want to help. You want to know what happened to you and your friend. I respect that. But I'm sorry. You can't. Let it go. Leave it to the professionals. Don't interfere. No good will come of it. People like you, well-meaning amateurs, you can't do good here, not in Africa, the place isn't built for it. The harder you try, the more you fail. You almost died tonight, both of you. Please. Go home before it's too late.'

Strick gives them a car and driver to take them home.

'Maybe he's right,' Veronica says to Jacob, as they sail through Kampala's empty streets. 'It sounds like they've got the whole al-Qaeda angle under control. Maybe we should just go.'

'Maybe we should. But I'm not going to.'

'Why not?' she asks, frustrated, and still a little angry at him for losing his temper at the embassy. 'I mean, honestly, what do you hope to get out of it? You really think you're going to get enough evidence to put somebody in jail? Here? With all this complicated mess? Come on.'

'I'm going to find out who it was.'

'And then what?'

'That is the what. *I just want to know.* Maybe I won't do anything, maybe that won't be possible. I understand that. But I want to know who and why. And I want them to know that I know.'

'That's crazy.'

'You think so? Then you better get on the plane tomorrow.'
'Maybe I will.'

He looks at her with an opaque expression. 'I hope you don't. I really . . . Veronica, I really hope you don't. But I have to see this through, you understand? He would have done it for me. And we're close. Can't you feel it? We're so close.'

'Close? What do you mean, close? We don't have anything.'

Jacob digs his hip-top out of his pocket.

'I thought Prester took—' Veronica says, and falls silent when she sees the blood, Prester's blood, smeared on the device's plastic carapace and LCD screen.

'He did. I found it next to him, he must have dropped it. I thought they'd take it from us in the jail. I guess the cops here are more honest than I figured. Brutal but honest. Or maybe only with white people. Or maybe just incompetent. They didn't even take the Leatherman.'

Jacob cleans the hip-top with the lip of his shirt and begins tapping away at its tiny keyboard. Veronica wonders what it says about Jacob that he picked up the hip-top before she even got to Prester. Is it a credit to his presence of mind, that he remembered to do it between calling for help and tending to the victim? Or was it the first thing he did?

Jacob spends the rest of the drive back to his apartment typing into and staring at the glowing hip-top. He grunts with surprise a couple of times. Veronica doesn't try to initiate conversation, she just stares out the window. It is past midnight and the main streets of Kampala are entirely deserted, as if some plague has wiped out every inhabitant but for them.

'I'll call you tomorrow,' Veronica says, when they reach Jacob's apartment complex.

'No,' Jacob says sharply. 'Come in for a moment. I'll get Henry to drive you home.'

'No, Jacob, he's sleeping, he's a human being, you can't just treat him as—'

'*Come in.*'

She looks at him. His face is pale and deadly serious. 'OK.'

The driver is content to let them go together. Jacob's sleepy askaris wave them through.

'What is it?' she asks, as they walk up to his apartment door.

'Let's go in.' Jacob hesitates. There is a strange and wild look in his eyes. 'No. Actually, on second thought, let's go sit on the lawn.'

'What? Jacob, it's midnight, this isn't—'

He grabs her hand. 'Follow me.'

She allows him to lead her into a dark corner of the groomed lawn that surrounds his apartment. He tugs her down to sit beside him on the grass, shifts over until their legs are actually touching, leans over to her and puts his head so close to hers his chin is on her shoulder. At first she doesn't know how to react. Then she realizes he isn't making a clumsy pass. This is something else.

'They called Strick,' Jacob whispers. She can feel his lips brush against her ears, but he is so quiet she can hardly hear him.

'What?' she asks, not understanding but instinctively whispering back.

'You remember I said there was a Mango phone in that building? One of theirs. A phone belonging to one of the men who shot at us. That phone called Strick's number before I called the ambulance.'

When Veronica understands the implication of that she starts as if shocked by a thousand volts.

'It's Strick. He's on their side. He's the smuggler. He's the guy who set up Derek. He's the one working with al-Qaeda.'

'Oh my God.'

'And there's something else. Good news. We're getting messages from one of those GPS trackers. Prester managed to tag one of their vehicles. That must have been when they shot him.'

'After,' Veronica says softly, thinking of the exit wound in Prester's chest. 'When he was getting away. He was shot from behind.'

'For all we know Strick was actually in the building.'

She shakes her head. 'I saw all the men there. They were all black.'

'Well, he's involved somehow, he has to be.'

For a second Veronica wonders whether Jacob is inventing all this just to keep her from leaving, or whether it's some sort of paranoid fantasy – but no, this isn't the sort of thing that men like Jacob lie about, it is falsifiable, at least in theory, he's talking about facts not interpretations, it would never cross his mind that she doesn't know enough about the technology to prove or disprove his claim no matter how many screens full of numbers he showed her and patiently explained. He isn't crazy, and he wouldn't lie. Not to her. She knows that. She trusts him.

'Where is it going? The tracker?'

'Shh. Quiet as you can. West. Towards Semiliki. The refugee camp.'

'You think they've bugged us?'

'I think we can't be too careful. Especially when Strick finds out we didn't get on the airplane tomorrow.'

Veronica swallows. He is taking it as a given. And maybe he is right. She is starting to feel angry, a warm and soothing rage deep inside.

'We should go to Semiliki first thing in the morning,' he whispers.

'No,' she says.

'But—'

'Second thing. There's something else I have to do first.'

'What?'

'Danton.'

10

Of course Danton is staying in the Sheraton. Kampala arguably has one or two finer hotels, but none more central, and Danton must always be at the centre of things. The staff at the Sheraton recognize Veronica, she comes here for lunch at least weekly. She doesn't need to ask what room he's in. The presidential suite, the penthouse. Nothing less would be acceptable to her ex-husband.

The elevator opens on to a narrow hallway covered by leopard-patterned carpet, overseen by framed explorers' maps and sketches of nineteenth-century Africa, and by a pair of mounted elephant tusks. Two security guards stand on duty. Four mahogany doors lead out from the hallway. Veronica steps out, not allowing herself any hesitation, and demands, 'Which door for Mr DeWitt?'

The guards look at her for a moment. Her face is almost healed from her Congo ordeal, the scabs have flaked off, the bruises are fading back into healthy flesh, and she is a well-dressed white woman. They aren't about to challenge her.

'This way, madam,' one says, and opens the door for her. She enters the suite's antechamber, basically another hallway with a closet. Veronica closes the door behind her and opens the one ahead without knocking. Her hand is trembling slightly. Danton is sitting and reading the *International Herald Tribune* by a huge window with a magnificent southern view that extends all the way to the blue expanse of Lake Victoria. He is of average height but thick and wide, built like a pit bull; he lifts weights religiously. His pot belly has grown since she last saw him, his hair has thinned, and his face is grizzled and stubbly. He wears khaki slacks and a vest of many pockets, as if he is about to go on safari, it makes him look ridiculously colonial, all he needs is a pith helmet. She recognizes his Ecco shoes.

'Jesus,' he says, amazed; he nearly drops the newspaper.

'No. Just me.'

Veronica doesn't know what else to say. She tries to resurrect the rage she felt last night, but all she feels is horribly out of place, awkward, embarrassed. She shouldn't have come. This was a terrible mistake. He still has all the power.

It takes Danton only a moment to readjust. 'I heard what happened, of course. I'm glad you're OK. But Veronica, if there's something you want to see me about, you should call ahead. You should call Julia. I'm on a very busy schedule, I really don't have time to chat.'

His mention of Julia reawakens Veronica's rage. Julia is one of Danton's personal assistants. It was Julia who informed Veronica that Danton had decided to divorce her. He couldn't even be bothered to tell her himself.

'I'm sure you're very busy,' Veronica says. Her voice sounds shrill even to herself. 'Is there trouble with Selous Holdings? Out at the Kisembe mine? Is Athanase giving you some kind of problem?'

Danton's expression doesn't waver, and it is that which convinces her she's right. If he actually didn't know what she was talking about he would have reacted somehow. 'I'm sorry, I don't understand.'

'Did you know I was in that group, in Bwindi? Did you know and go ahead and say it was OK anyways?'

He blinks with surprise at the accusation, and she realizes no, he hadn't known. But that doesn't mean he wasn't responsible. It's like Prester said. He didn't know because he didn't want to.

'Veronica, I don't know what you're talking about, and I don't think you do either. It's time for you to go. You should go home. You've been through a traumatic experience and I think your mental health has suffered—'

'You're fucking right I have. Being married to you.'

'Veronica, please. Don't make me call security. Don't make me humiliate you like that.'

'Oh, come off it. You can't wait to humiliate me. You never could. Seven years and you throw me out like a . . . like a used condom.'

'I'm not going to waste my time justifying myself to you. You know what I think?' Danton sounds angry now. 'I think you knew all along you were infertile. You knew and married me anyways.'

The accusation is so outrageous Veronica can't find the right words to respond.

189

'So don't you come to me talking about things you don't understand. You're not getting any more money from me. You've gotten more than enough already. Seven years of the high life is more than most women like you get. Plus alimony for life. You should count yourself lucky.'

'Lucky? *Lucky?* You piece of shit. You *piece of shit.*' She can't believe she used to tell this man she loved him, that she slept beside his hairy, walrus-like body most nights for seven years and told herself she didn't mind his snoring, didn't mind the carelessly indulgent way he treated her, as if she was more pet than wife, didn't mind the selfish, mechanical way he fucked her on the rare occasions he was roused to sex. She can't believe she once hoped to bear his child. She wants to walk over and smash his face, crush his testicles, gouge his eyes out.

Danton's face hardens. He reaches for the phone on his coffee table.

'They're blackmailing you, aren't they?' she asks. 'The terrorists. Blackmailing you and Strick. What are they making you do? What do they want?'

Danton freezes. Then he turns and stares at her as if he has actually noticed her presence in a way he never has before, as if he is really looking at her for the first time ever. Veronica realizes she has just made a mistake, maybe a terrible one, in her effort to score a point and make him feel something. She shouldn't have given away what they know.

'You don't know what you're doing,' Danton says quietly. 'If you keep playing with fire, you will get burned alive.' He pushes a button on his phone, waits only a moment; of course his call is answered immediately, all his calls are answered immediately.

'Get over here,' he says to the phone. 'I have a security situation.'

'You can't do it,' Veronica says. 'Whatever they want you to do. People will die. Innocent people. God knows how many. You have to turn yourself in.'

Danton looks at her, considering. For a second she wonders whether he's going to allow her to depart.

Then he says, 'You know why I'm here, Veronica? To *save lives*. I suppose I might as well try to save yours too. You should be grateful. I'm giving you one last chance. Stop interfering and go home. Today. No one's going to warn you again.'

'To save lives?' Jacob asks, puzzled. His hands falter in mid-gear-shift and the Toyota nearly stalls. He isn't accustomed to piloting a right-hand-drive stick-shift. 'That's what he said? I mean, even if he's lying—'

'There's no if about it.'

He decides not to argue the point. 'Fine, but it's kind of a weird lie to tell, don't you think?'

Veronica shrugs.

'You didn't find out anything else?'

She hesitates. 'Not really. I think he might suspect we know about Strick.'

Jacob starts. 'What? How?' If true, it's disastrous. The element of surprise is almost the only thing in their favour.

'Just his attitude, his face when he said he had friends in the US government.'

'What were his exact words?'

She shrugs. 'I don't remember. I was too wound up.'

Jacob frowns. There's something about her body language. 'You didn't give anything away, did you?'

'I don't know. I don't think so. But, I mean, we were married. He's supposed to know me pretty well. Maybe not, though. He never paid that much attention to me.'

'He never paid attention to you?' Jacob asks incredulously.

'Not after we got married. The way he saw it, his wife's job was to impress his friends, keep him warm at night, run the occasional errand, bear his children and acknowledge his supremacy. Not someone to have a meaningful relationship with.'

'Jesus. Why did you stay?'

She sighs. 'I don't know. I mean, for a long time I really believed he loved me, in his way, he was just distant and hard working and reserved. The lies we tell ourselves. And . . . you know, being his wife was the good life. Villas, penthouses, yachts, private jets, expense accounts, beautiful people, amazing parties. He went away on business a lot and it was all mine. I guess on some level I must have known what I really was. And I guess I was OK with it. It was his idea to get a divorce.'

'He dumped you? Why?'

'I can't have children. Endometriosis. I didn't know, whatever fucking conspiracy theory he wants to believe. You know what I think? I think when we found that out, he decided right then, that day, that moment, he would divorce me when I turned thirty. I'm pretty sure he hired a personal trainer to try to seduce me. He was worried the pre-nup wouldn't hold up in court. He definitely hired a private investigator to take pictures of me taking drugs. They were in the divorce papers I got served with two weeks after my thirtieth birthday.'

After a moment Jacob says, angrily, 'Well, you're almost lucky.'

'Lucky?' She half laughs. 'How you figure?'

'You deserve a lot better than him.'

They drive on in silence for a while through the breathtaking Ugandan countryside. Rolling hills drift past, thick green vegetation laced with red-dirt roads, maybe half of it occupied and farmed. All colours are brilliant under the searing equatorial sun. Everything seems airbrushed, too vivid to be real. Even the cultivated areas are beautiful, geometrically patterned fields cut by shining irrigation ditches, dun-coloured zebu cattle with scimitar-shaped horns as thick as elephant tusks, little clusters of round bamboo-and-mud *bandas* in the shadows of tall trees. The ugly towns they pass through are like scars on a supermodel's face; brutal concrete shells and wooden huts in fields of filth-strewn dirt, as furrowed and uneven as a frozen ocean, littered with piles of bricks and clumps of filth.

The road is good, but there isn't much traffic. A few private cars; a few of what Derek called NGO assault vehicles, white 4WDs with logos painted on their doors and six-foot radio antennae attached to their front bumpers; one bright red EMS Postbus; and dozens of sixteen-seat minibus *matatus* hurtling past in both directions, with toppling mounds of baggage roped precariously to their roofs, stopping without warning anywhere and everywhere to absorb and disgorge passengers. Spike belts and yellow metal barrels indicate the police roadblocks that are ubiquitous on all African highways. To Jacob's relief, all the police wave them on without inventing some traffic transgression and demanding a 'fine'.

Jacob remembers what he wanted to tell Veronica. 'Derek's phone rang this morning. His other phone. The one from the Sun City.'

She blinks, looks at him. 'Who was it?'

'That number in Zimbabwe.'

'Did you answer?'

'No. They didn't leave a message.'

Veronica shakes her head. 'This doesn't make any sense. Zimbabwe, Danton, Strick, al-Qaeda, *interahamwe*, Zanzibar Sams that are actually Igloos, it's like something out of Lewis Carroll, none of it makes any sense.'

'It does to someone.'

'Why are we even going to this camp? What are we possibly hoping to achieve?'

'Understanding,' Jacob says sourly.

'You really think we'll find something?'

'Susan works at this refugee camp. That's why Derek brought her to Bwindi. He visited this camp, and made phone calls to someone else there. Whoever shot Prester is going to this camp. Whatever's going on, it's all going on there.'

'And we're driving straight into it. And we know from that phone Susan picked up that they were already planning some kind of attack in western Uganda.'

Jacob shrugs, annoyed. He's not going to back out now. He's already made that perfectly clear. 'You want to get out and take a *matatu* back to Kampala, go ahead.'

He waits tensely while Veronica thinks.

At length she says, 'No. I want to know. But first thing we do is go to Susan, make sure someone knows we're there. And we don't do anything crazy. We definitely don't go back over the border. I'm not going back into the Congo.'

Jacob half smiles, relieved. 'Yeah. Been there, done that, got the bloodstained T-shirt. No more Congo. It's a deal.'

They stop for lunch in Fort Portal, a small collection of low, dusty buildings in the foothills of the cloud-wreathed Ruwenzori mountains. The town's two significant buildings are the local tribal chief's hilltop castle, which looks like a modern Western university building, and the town mosque. Veronica sees that mosque and thinks of the Arab man who held a panga to her throat. She, Derek, Susan and Jacob stopped in Fort Portal for lunch on the way to Bwindi, at the same hotel where he parks now, the Ruwenzori Travellers' Inn. She opens her mouth but leaves her protest unspoken. No sense running away from memories. And they know the food here is good.

They eat beef stew with rice and chapatis. Outside, peasant farmers walk rusting bicycles used for cargo; each supports four or five beer-keg-sized bundles of bananas fresh off the tree. A group of women obviously from Kampala, wearing bright clothes and mobile phones on lanyards, their hair cut fashionably short or braided with purple highlights, pass through the more soberly dressed local foot traffic like swans through ducks. Their amused-by-hicksville expressions are the same as those of New Yorkers in Iowa.

'I'm thinking of calling Zimbabwe,' Jacob says, after tapping at his hip-top for a bit.

'Zimbabwe?'

'That number Derek used to call. The one that called him this morning.'

'Why?' To Veronica it sounds like asking for trouble.

'It seems like it's all going down at this camp, doesn't it? Any information we can get before going there might help.'

'What if whoever it is is on the other side? What if he figures something out and calls them to warn them?'

'He can't,' Jacob says. 'Unless they've got a satellite phone.'

'I thought there was cell service up by the camp.'

'There is. But only a single Mango base station, the other networks don't reach it at all. Probably half the reason Derek got me my job. I just disabled incoming calls and texts via that base station for every phone but yours and mine.'

'What? When?' Veronica asks, amazed.

'Just now, when you were ordering.'

'But, Jacob, that's a refugee camp. People's lives could be in danger.'

'Right now I'm more worried about our lives,' he says sharply, and then in a softer voice, 'It's no big deal. Outgoing calls still work.'

'Huh.' Veronica shakes her head. Jacob's abilities, and their ramifications, continue to astonish her. 'OK. I mean, yeah, I'm sure curious, so why not. What the hell. Let's call Zimbabwe.'

Jacob starts to dial, then looks around. 'Once we're back in the car. Privacy.'

'Be funny if the call didn't work,' Veronica says sourly, once they have paid the bill and returned to the Toyota. 'Half my international calls from here never get through.'

Jacob smiles. 'Not me. All my calls are flagged as highest priority . . . Here we go.' He taps at his hip-top, switching it to speakerphone, and she hears the doubled rings of a phone call to England or a former English colony; then the click of an answer.

'Hello?' asks a plummy English voice that sounds both eager and wary.

Veronica looks at Jacob and realizes he has no idea what to say.

'Hello?' the voice repeats, more wary this time.

She takes the initiative: 'We're returning your call from this morning.'

A brief pause. 'And with whom exactly do I have the pleasure of speaking?'

'My name's Veronica Kelly. I'm with Jacob Rockel. We were friends with Derek.'

She ignores Jacob's appalled stare. There's no point in complicated lies and evasions. The truth may set them free; even if it doesn't, lies won't do them any good.

'Veronica and Jacob,' the voice says doubtfully. 'I seem to recall from YouTube that you were with him in the Congo.'

'Yes.'

'I called this morning to speak to his partner. Prester.'

'I'm sorry,' Veronica says, 'Prester isn't available. He's . . . he's been shot.'

'Shot? I see. An accident? Or an act of malicious intent?'

She pauses. 'Intent.'

'By whom?'

'We're not sure exactly. That's what we're trying to find out. We think,' Veronica says, flinging caution to the wind, 'it has something to do with the Zanzibar Sams, which are actually Igloos.'

After a long pause the voice says, 'I think we may have a bad connection. Could you repeat that?'

'Zanzibar Sams, which are actually Igloos.'

'Ah. No, the connection is fine. What in God's name are you talking about?'

'We're not really sure,' Veronica admits. 'We thought you might know.'

'There are two of you there?'

'Yes,' Jacob contributes.

'And why did you think I might know?'

Jacob answers, 'We have access to cell-phone records. We know Derek called you, and you called him, repeatedly, over the last few months.'

'Mobile phone records. I see. Who do you work for?'

'Telecom Uganda.'

'That's not what I mean,' the voice says, a little testy. 'Why do you have this phone? Why are you involved in this? Why are you even still in Africa?'

'I was his best friend,' Jacob says. 'Who exactly are you?'

A long silence. Veronica is afraid the man will hang up.

Eventually he says, grudgingly, 'Let's just say Derek and I were in some ways compatriots.'

'What did he call you about?' Veronica asks. 'We know he was investigating a smuggling ring. We think he found out someone American was involved, not Prester, and that's who arranged for him and the rest of us to be abducted.'

After another pause, the man acknowledges, 'That was what I understood as well. From inferences. He told me very little directly.'

'Very little like what?' Jacob asks, exasperated.

'Pardon me, Mr Rockel, if that is actually your name, but why should I tell you anything? How am I to know under what auspices you acquired this phone?'

Jacob hesitates. 'You can't.'

'Precisely,' the voice says. 'Pleasure talking to you.'

'Wait,' Veronica says. 'Why did you call? What did you want to talk to Prester about?'

Another long pause. 'I suppose the question itself is harmless. I called to ask for Derek's professional next of kin.'

'Excuse me?' Jacob asks, befuddled.

'Either you really are an amateur or you play the part well. I mean the name of whoever has inherited Derek's work. I have something for him or her. My more official request seems to have become lost in a bureaucratic labyrinth, and I thought I might speed up the process a little.'

'I'm sorry,' Veronica says, 'we don't have any idea who that might be.'

'Pity.'

'Wait,' Jacob says desperately. 'You're saying you have something meant for Derek? What is it?'

'Information.'

'What kind of information?'

'Now that would be telling,' the man says, amused. 'Goodbye.'

The road from Fort Portal to Semiliki weaves through the lush green hills of western Uganda, past misty crater lakes, placid villages, tiny roadside markets, vast tea plantations, a cement factory and eleven million banana trees. Sometimes the road is wide and paved, well signed, with painted lane markers and roadside gutters to carry away rainy-season overflow; sometimes it is well-worn red dirt; sometimes it is heavily potholed asphalt, far worse to drive on than dirt. They stop in Semiliki for gas, Snickers bars and Cokes, and for Veronica to take the wheel. By the time they finally see the sign that says UNHCR SEMILIKI beside an otherwise unremarkable road of pitted laterite, the sun is low above the western hills.

'Are we even sure this is the right road?' Veronica asks, as Jacob produces and consults his trusty hip-top.

'I'm sure the tracker is that way. Right now I'm not sure of much else.'

Veronica takes a deep breath. It occurs to her that UNHCR Semiliki is miles away from civilization, home to numerous white NGOers, and very near the Congo border. They already know that al-Qaeda are planning attacks on western Uganda. This camp, so close to Athanase's smuggling route, will certainly be at the top of their list. And maybe they've just been waiting for the Zanzibar Sams to arrive before they strike.

But it's too late to back out now. She grips the wheel and the gear-shift, puts her feet to the clutch and gas pedal, and steers the Toyota towards the refugee camp.

11

The red dirt road is terrible, carved with more craters and ravines than the surface of Mars. It takes thirty bumpy minutes to drive the eight kilometres to the refugee camp. Entrance is barred by a pair of concrete guard huts and a steel bar across the road, manned by uniformed Ugandan soldiers, and for a moment Jacob is worried they will simply be denied access and sent back; but when he invokes Susan's name, the soldiers' faces clear with recognition, and they raise the bar to allow the Toyota access.

UNHCR Semiliki is an encyclopedia of suffering, a tent city of misery in a small valley surrounded by steep and largely denuded hills. A half-dozen brick buildings cluster in the middle of the settlement. The camp proper boasts a smattering of thatched mud huts. But most of its thousands of shelters are blue plastic or green canvas tarpaulins stretched over frames made of tree branches. Whole families live in each. A few roads radiate out from the brick buildings at the centre of the camp, but in the anarchic wedges between those roads the tents are packed so densely that there is rarely enough room for more than two to walk abreast. There are people everywhere, the camp seems flooded with them, mostly dressed in rags. A few goats and chickens pick their way through the dirt. Jacob wonders what they eat; the ground throughout the camp is entirely mud, even weeds have been trampled to death. He doesn't want to even imagine what the camp is like in rainy season.

There are more women than men, and amazing numbers of children. A few have the distended bellies of malnutrition. Many children, and a few adults, turn and wave, smiling hopefully as the Toyota passes. Others stare with lifeless eyes. A few look angry, hostile. Jacob hears snatches of French through the open window. The air holds a stale, faintly rancid smell of smoke and filth. He sees a huge tent beneath which a teacher teaches mathematics to several hundred children, in the failing red light, with no aids but chalk and a single blackboard. He sees and smells a long, low, filthy building labelled LATRINE, its wrecked door hanging open like a broken jaw. Old women lug yellow jerrycans full of water, and others queue to fill theirs from rusted taps that protrude from the ground. Pots boil over open-pit fires next to wood-and-canvas shelters.

The brick buildings with tin roofs in the middle of the camp seem like an island of peace and civilization. Here the soft background chatter of the refugees is drowned out by the hum of multiple generators. Veronica parks the Toyota at the end of the row of cars in front of another guard hut, populated by a half-dozen Ugandan soldiers. Jacob wonders whether these soldiers, and those by the gate, are intended more to protect the refugees, or to keep them in the camp and under control. He wonders how effective they would be against Athanase's veteran *interahamwe* force.

'Susan Strachan, please, can you direct us to her?' Jacob says to the soldier who comes to investigate.

The soldier nods and leads Veronica and Jacob between two of the permanent buildings to a large shade structure made of metal struts and a green plastic ceiling. Several dozen desks are arranged underneath it, adorned with lights and laptop computers connected to a central generator via an interwoven tangle of power cords clumped on the dirt floor like old spaghetti. It is like some kind of surreal parody of an open-concept office plan. Susan sits at a desk crowded with papers near the edge of the tent. When she sees Veronica and Jacob her mouth literally drops open with astonishment.

'Surprise!' Veronica says, trying for enthusiasm.

'Bloody hell,' Susan manages. 'What are you two doing here?'

'It's a long story,' Jacob says. He wishes they had gone to Susan earlier, before she left Kampala. He'd intended to, but then events overtook them; he'd forgotten all about her and the Semiliki refugee camp until he saw where the tracker was going. 'You have a moment?'

Susan shakes her head, still amazed. 'I suppose I must, for you two.'

Veronica says, seriously, 'In private.'

Susan opens her mouth and then closes it again. 'I see. Yes.' She stands up. 'In that case, let's take a walk.'

Susan leads them out into the camp, on to a road leading away from the gate. The long fingers of clouds above are reddening with sunset. Refugees cluster and watch as if Veronica, Jacob and Susan are A-list celebrities. It occurs to Veronica that just a month ago she would have been far too intimidated by this camp and its densely packed tragedies to go out and walk among the refugees like this.

A cloud of children surround and follow them, crying out for largesse: 'One pen!' '*Donnes-moi d'argent!*' '*Un bic, monsieur, madame, un bic!*' 'Give me money!' 'What is your name?' '*Quel est ton pays?*' Despite the children's entreaties, Susan and Jacob act like they are on a stroll through an empty field. Veronica tries to do the same, but it isn't easy.

'How are you?' Jacob asks.

'I'm well enough, I suppose,' Susan says. 'It's good to be back here. It's the right place for me. I don't think I'll leave any time soon. Why are you here?'

'We were abducted because somebody wanted Derek dead. We're trying to find out who.'

Susan comes to a halt and turns to stare at Jacob. 'That's mad.'

'No, it's not,' Veronica says. 'We've found out a lot of things.'

'But what are you doing *here*?'

'Somebody brought something to this camp last night,' Jacob says.

'What?'

'We don't know. But there's a tracker on it, we can find it, we don't need you for that. We need to know, have you seen anything? Anything that might imply there's some kind of smuggling going on between this camp and the Congo?'

Susan considers. 'I couldn't tell you. It's not like this place is tightly policed. Look around, it can't be. There are tribal gangs in the camp. Some mornings we find bodies. Not from natural causes. But nobody ever saw anything. Nobody ever dares bear witness. People disappear all the time. Some run away to find a job. Some never existed in the first place. False identities to get extra rations. Some go back to the Congo, yes. That's where most of these people are from, you know. They ran away from the civil war, and now there's nothing left to go back to. But a smuggling ring? It's possible. I don't know.'

'Derek invited you to Bwindi for a reason,' Jacob says.

She twitches with surprise. 'What reason?'

'There's someone else in this camp that he's been in touch with. Derek even came here, a month ago. Did you see him then?'

Susan looks astonished. 'No.'

'Did he talk to you about that at all?'

'No. He met me in Kampala, he invited me, I knew he knew I worked here, but he never asked me anything.'

'Me neither,' Veronica says. 'I guess he never got the chance.'

'Have you seen any American visitors here lately?' Jacob asks. 'Have you heard anything about General Gorokwe? Do Zanzibar Sams or Igloos mean anything to you?'

Susan shakes her head three times, increasingly perplexed.

'All right. Shit. Well, never mind.' Jacob looks at his hip-top. 'We're not far from that tracker. Let's take a look before it gets dark.'

Susan looks nervous. 'Maybe we should wait. I should ask some other people.'

Jacob shakes his head. 'It's less than a thousand feet away. In fact,' he says, turning back towards the centre of the camp, following the directions on the hip-top's screen, 'it's right back in the middle there.'

He leads them at a brisk pace back towards the brick buildings, almost bowling over two children surprised by his sudden direction shift. Veronica follows closely. Susan trails behind. Jacob rounds the corner of one of the brick buildings and comes to a sudden halt so fast Veronica nearly bumps into him.

The black pick-up from last night is there, parked in another row of vehicles, most of them white four-wheel-drives. Its cargo bed is empty. Jacob rushes over to it, drops to his knees, reaches beneath it and detaches the GPS tracking device that has clung magnetically to the underside of the pick-up.

'Where did this come from?' Jacob demands, indicating the black vehicle, as Susan arrives.

'Oh, the pick-up,' Susan says, as if everything suddenly makes sense. 'Let's go back to my desk. I'll find someone who knows.'

'The bureaucrats in New York don't believe what I'm doing is particularly valuable, so I don't qualify for a wall,' Susan says, leading them back to her desk inside the shade structure. 'They think perpetuating what you see here is more important than building a way out. Mail, bus services, mobile phones, the Internet, connections to the rest of the world, we can't have those, can we? Because then they might use them, and stop needing UNHCR, and we *certainly* can't have that. You soon find that the first priority of almost every aid organization in Africa is to perpetuate their own necessity, actually helping people is decidedly secondary. And the Ugandan government doesn't want these dirty Congolese refugees anywhere near the rest of the country either. So I got pushed out here. Not that I mind having a view, but in the rainy season, when the wind blows, we all have to huddle in the middle or we get soaked. I'm sorry. You don't care. Do you want some food? A cup of tea? We've even got a few solar showers.'

'I just want to know where that pick-up came from,' Jacob says.

'Yes, of course. Lewis!' she calls out.

The same guard who escorted them to Susan walks over. He looks about nineteen. 'Yes, Miss Strachan?'

'That black pick-up. Did it arrive last night?'

'No, Miss Strachan. This morning. I was at the gate myself.'

'What was in it?' Jacob asks eagerly.

Lewis looks at him, surprised. 'Nothing. It's a new vehicle for the camp motor pool. We did not requisition any supplies.'

'You're sure? There weren't any big metal boxes in the back?'

'I am quite certain.'

'Shit,' Veronica says. 'Too late. They're gone.'

She and Jacob exchange dejected looks.

'I suppose you're spending the night,' Susan says. 'I'll rustle you up a tent and a couple bedrolls. Oh, and a flashlight. Remind me to show you where the latrines are. And you must be hungry. The canteen will be serving for another hour or so. Pocho, I'm afraid.'

'Pocho,' Jacob says dourly. 'Can't wait.'

The tent is perched on the thin strip of no man's land between the administrative buildings and the refugee camp proper. It is small and bedraggled, and the sleeping bags are moth-eaten, but Veronica supposes she can't complain, not when she is literally surrounded by tens of thousands of refugees sleeping in even more uncomfortable shelters. She doesn't feel hungry or tired yet, she's too keyed up from the day, but she knows she will after half an hour of inaction.

'Are you going to be OK in there?' Jacob asks, worried.

She looks at him without comprehension for a moment, then realizes he's referring to her dislike of tight spaces. 'Oh. Yeah, no problem. Tents are fine. Don't ask me why.'

'Oh.' He looks baffled. 'Well, I guess it's irrational by definition, right?'

A little annoyed by that, Veronica stoops and tosses her day pack into the tent, then stands, looks up at him and says, 'We should go eat.'

'Not yet.'

He disappears into the tent without another word, taking the flashlight with him. It takes his gangly body a moment to negotiate the door flaps. Veronica looks around. She is dimly lit by the electric lights of the central buildings and the open flames that dot the refugee camp. Mosquitoes are buzzing everywhere, she's glad she brought insect repellent, and the background hum of conversation in the distance is ever present, like static. Veronica doubts she has ever been in a more densely populated patch of real estate that didn't involve skyscrapers.

She follows Jacob inside. Being in a tent, lit by flashlight, feels like being back in summer camp, when she was a teenager, when the world seemed bright and full of promise. Jacob has unpacked and turned on his bread-box-sized spectrum analyser, has both it and his hip-top out, and is examining the readouts on their respective screens.

'Did that thing get anything useful from the scrapyard?' Veronica asks.

Jacob, studying his hip-top, shakes his head. 'A few phones. None Mango except the one I already knew about.'

'What are you doing?'

'Checking the GPS record. They didn't go over the border. The pick-up went off-road just before the turn-off to the camp, at about six this morning, stopped there for twenty minutes, then came back.'

'So they're gone,' Veronica says.

'Maybe not. I don't think they would have crossed the border by day. They would have waited until tonight. Probably the middle of the night, a few hours yet.'

'You want to go back out there now? I . . . no. No. Absolutely not. Jacob, we agreed, we wouldn't do anything crazy, and going out to where these things are hidden in the middle of the night all by ourselves is crazy.'

'That's not what I want to do right now. I want to find Derek's contact.'

'Who?' she asks.

'The other phone signal from this refugee camp, remember? Whoever it was that Derek came to visit. Wasn't Susan. Somebody else. Somebody here. Maybe they know something.'

'I thought you said you couldn't track locations out here. Only one base station.'

'Right. That's why I brought this.' Jacob taps the spectrum analyser as if he's petting a good dog. 'It acts like a portable base station all by itself. It also boosts the signal from the existing station, which allows my hip-top to connect over GPRS to Kampala and the Internet, which is pretty amazing all by itself, if you think about just how deep in the middle of nowhere we are right now. I just checked the central database to see if Derek's contact's phone is here and active. Guess what? Yes it is. Somewhere in this camp, right now.'

'Great. How do we find it?'

He pets the analyser again. 'We get this within a hundred metres of that phone, close enough to triangulate its location.'

'Oh.'

'So let's go take this puppy for a little walk.'

Veronica leads the way with their flashlight. Jacob carries the heavy and cumbersome signal analyser, and has strapped on his day pack as well, full of other equipment. They walk in a slow circle around the camp's administrative centre. Nobody asks them what they are doing; nobody else is out and about. He isn't surprised. Outside of major cities, Africa lives on a dawn-to-dusk schedule.

The spectrum analyser picks up plenty of cell phones within its range, almost all of them Mango, but none is the phone that Derek called. Soon they are back at their tent and the analyser is running low on power. Jacob wishes he had thought to charge it fully before leaving Kampala. He brought a hand-crank recharger with him, but they don't really have time for it.

'No good?' Veronica asks.

Jacob shakes his head.

'Maybe it's not in the camp. We didn't know exactly where that phone was, right? We just know it was six kilometres from the base station.'

'Right. But everything else six klicks out is just bush. It has to be here. Nothing else makes any sense. Let me make sure it's still alive.' Jacob puts down the spectrum analyser and logs on to the Kampala master database server with his hip-top, via that same base station. The GPRS connection is painfully slow, but he's only sending and receiving text; once connected it doesn't take long to establish that the phone in question was active and six kilometres from Semiliki base station as of fifteen seconds ago.

Veronica turns to look at the overcrowded sea of refugees. Most of the fires are dying down now, the camp is mostly darkness.

Jacob nods. He's thinking the same thing. 'It's out there. Let's go find it.'

Veronica hesitates.

'Nothing's going to happen to us. We're *mzungu*. We can shout for help. There are soldiers, they'll hear us. We'll be fine. Anybody asks, we're just going for a walk. Come on.'

She reluctantly accedes. They venture out into one of the roads that radiate out from the centre of the camp. Veronica keeps her flashlight aimed at the road, which is remarkably clean. Jacob supposes there's no such thing as debris out here. These people have so little that every rag and scrap is valuable.

Occasionally he sees people sleeping out in the open beside the road. Their eyes gleam in the light and they stare at him and Veronica but do not react. Some of them are children sleeping alone. They seem to Jacob like ghosts, somehow, insubstantial, so unrooted to the world that he can almost believe that after he walks past them they will actually cease to exist.

The camp doesn't actually end, it just bleeds into scarred plots of scraggly-looking farmland, and the number of visible goats and chickens slowly increases. Veronica and Jacob decide not to cut through the inhabited wedges; instead they return to the centre and try another of the eight radial roads, moving quietly, whispering to one another, as if something terrible might awaken. He knows it's ridiculous but he can't shake the feeling.

Midway down the third road Jacob's spectrum analyser suddenly bleeps. Veronica starts as if at a gunshot. Jacob crouches over its screen excitedly. They've made contact. The cell phone in question is within range.

Jacob goes forward twenty paces along the road, slowly rotates, goes back another twenty paces and repeats, studying the analyser the whole time. Radio is a weird and unpredictable medium and it isn't easy to work out where the signals are coming from, but they seem to get stronger to the south. He walks off the road and into the densely populated shelters, holding the analyser ahead of him as if it's a gigantic compass. Veronica follows.

The shelters are so tightly packed together that Jacob has to be careful where he steps so as not to tread on a person or a structural support. The refugees around them begin to come to life; a soft hum of surprise radiates out from Jacob and Veronica as they make their way through the settlement. People sit and kneel up and stare at the two white people as they pick their way through the shelters; they have a murmuring audience of hundreds, maybe more. Jacob pretends not to notice, but he is breathing fast now, and the hairs on his neck are prickling. All this attention is eerie and maybe dangerous, they won't have time to yell for help if these refugees decide to jump them and take all their things, but they can't go back now. His arms are aching, and the analyser's battery monitor is flashing red.

Suddenly the signal strength begins to dwindle. Jacob stops and rotates until it regains its strength, then walks in the new direction until the signal diminishes again. They slowly spiral inwards until Veronica puts her hand on Jacob's shoulder to stop him and he looks up from the analyser's screen.

'That tent,' she says.

It is the only actual tent within fifty feet, made of ancient, much-repaired canvas, leaning drunkenly on sagging poles. Its door hangs open; the zips are broken. Veronica stoops and aims the flashlight inside. Jacob crouches beside her. There is a man sleeping within, lying diagonally on the uncushioned floor, and a small pile of belongings beyond.

'Excuse us,' Veronica says tentatively, aiming the light at the man's head.

His eyes open and he immediately sits straight up, shading his face with one hand, reaching instinctively into his small pile of possessions with the other. He is short, compact and muscular, with a broad nose, low forehead, deep-set eyes and very dark skin, almost like some bigoted caricature of an African. Jacob guesses his age at thirtyish. After a second he utters something curt, half question, half demand. His voice is gravelly, his eyes and face are flat, expressionless. Jacob doesn't understand his language.

'Excuse me,' Veronica says soothingly, and aims the flashlight at herself for a second, then at Jacob stooping next to her. 'Can we talk to you for a moment?'

The man says nothing.

'Do you have a mobile phone in there?' Jacob asks, wondering whether the man understands English at all.

'No. No phone. Why do you come here?' His voice is hostile. His accent is French, which makes sense – most of these refugees are from the Congo.

Veronica looks helplessly at Jacob. He hesitates, then realizes what he should have done some time ago: he puts the analyser down on the dirt, pulls out his hip-top, opens it and simply dials the number of the phone they seek. A second later the bundled clothes that serve as the man's pillow begin to vibrate, subtly but unmistakably.

The man's expression hardens. He rises from his seated position into a crouch, ready for action. Jacob flinches and puts his hand on Veronica's shoulder, about to pull her away.

'We're friends of Derek,' Veronica says quickly. The man's expression flickers, he knows the name. 'I'm Veronica, this is Jacob. What's your name?'

He answers, eventually, 'Rukungu.'

'Rukungu. Hi. It's nice to meet you. Can we come in and talk?'

After another long, wary moment Rukungu says, 'No. I will come out.'

*　　*　　*

'Where is Derek?' Rukungu asks, when they get back on the road.

He turns towards the perimeter of the camp. Veronica and Jacob follow. She tries to think of a way to break the news gently.

Jacob says, 'Derek is dead.'

Rukungu's pace doesn't even falter. 'How?'

'He was abducted. We were too. Taken into the Congo. He was killed by al-Qaeda and *interahamwe*.'

'It was all over the news,' Veronica says lamely. In this refugee camp the rest of the world might as well not exist.

'How did you find me?'

'I was Derek's best friend,' Jacob says. Veronica winces at this avoidance of the truth.

'Derek said he told no one about me. No one.'

Jacob hesitates. 'He didn't. We followed your phone.'

Rukungu looks at him and says nothing.

Veronica says, 'We need your help. We need to know what's going on.'

'I will speak only to Derek.'

'You can't. I'm sorry. Derek is dead.'

'Then I will speak to no one,' Rukungu says flatly.

'We're trying to find out who killed him. Who was responsible,' Jacob says. 'I was his best friend.'

'So you say.' Rukungu stops and turns on Jacob, steps into his personal space, moving so suddenly that Veronica takes an alarmed step back. He looks ready for violence. 'But how can I know this is the truth?'

Veronica can't think of any way to break the tense silence that follows.

Then Jacob smiles, as a light bulb visibly goes off in his mind. 'I'll show you.' He reaches for his hip-top. 'Look.'

Rukungu looks suspicious but grudgingly circles around to look as the much taller man punches buttons.

'This is us at university,' Jacob says. 'At a Nirvana concert, six months before Kurt Cobain killed himself. Twelve years ago now.'

Veronica leans in, curious despite herself, and sees a picture of two kids barely out of their teens; one is tall and skinny, the other shorter and pudgy, with unkempt hair and sallow skin. She recognizes both, but only barely.

'This is Derek?' Rukungu asks, and his voice echoes her own amazement.

'Yep. And this is him when he got back from Bosnia.' Jacob pushes keys, and then Derek appears again, still young but trim and muscular now, she can see the man he will become within his not quite fully formed features. His dragon-tattooed arm is around a slender redhead. 'And here's us in Thailand, a few years ago. Not my most flattering picture, but hey.'

It's true: Jacob is lying on a beach, pale and pasty and rail thin, staring up at the camera with bloodshot eyes. Derek is beside him reading a Martin Cruz Smith novel.

'I was badly hung over. His then girlfriend took it. Then they broke up while I was there, it was awkward.'

Rukungu looks at the pictures, then at Jacob, not quite convinced.

'Come on,' Jacob says, exasperated. 'What do you want, a notarized statement? We were best friends for twenty years. Ask me anything.'

The African man asks, 'Do you know Lydia?'

Jacob looks at Veronica, surprised, then back to Rukungu. 'You mean the . . . the lady in the Hotel Sun City?'

'Yes. Yes, the Sun City. Is she still there? Is she well?'

'Sure. We saw her last week. We gave her money, I'm sure she's fine. But, I mean, you know she has . . .'

'Yes,' Rukungu says shortly. 'I know. Is she still strong?'

'Strong enough,' Veronica says gently. 'Do you know her?'

He doesn't answer.

'Is that why Derek was taking care of her? Because you asked him to?'

'She could not come here.'

'Why not?'

'There are *banyamulenge* here who know her.' He uses the word like an epithet. Veronica doesn't know what it means, and from his expression neither does Jacob.

'What did you do for Derek?' Veronica asks. 'Why are you here?'

Rukungu looks at her, then at Jacob, and comes to some decision. 'I was waiting for Derek. He said there would be a transfer this week, and he would come. I was to take him to bear witness. He was right. Tonight is the new moon. There will be a transfer.'

'How do you know?' Jacob asks.

'Because I was one of them.'

'One of who?'

Rukungu looks at Jacob as if the question is stupid. 'One of Athanase's men.'

Veronica sucks in breath sharply.

'I can take you to the transfer,' Rukungu says. 'It is not too late. It will happen at midnight.'

'No,' Veronica says quickly. 'No, it's too dangerous.'

'There will be no danger. I can take you to a place where they do not see us. But you can see them. You will see everything.'

Veronica looks at Jacob. She wants him to say no.

'You trusted us,' Jacob says. His voice is quiet but Veronica can sense his excitement. 'We ought to return the favour.'

12

Jacob, Veronica and Rukungu march through the night. When Jacob shines his flashlight around them he sees that these hills above the refugee camp have been stripped bare of trees, ravaged by the demand for firewood and arable land. The resulting erosion has obviously eaten away the soil; jagged rocks protrude with increasing frequency as they climb the steep slope. Jacob wonders whether rainy-season landslides will soon threaten the camp itself. The trail they follow leads them through tiny, ragged and ever less fertile plots of farmland.

Rukungu moves slowly but unstoppably, and carries the spectrum analyser as if it is a balloon. Veronica is beginning to wheeze. Jacob too is soon exhausted; his muscles have not yet recovered from the Congo, and this climb is gruelling. He forces himself to continue on weak and rubbery legs, aiming the flashlight straight down, to illuminate the ground on which they walk. He wonders whether its light is visible from below. At least it is a good flashlight, a small but durable Maglite that shows no signs of darkening.

'I have to stop,' Veronica pants. 'I can't make it all the way up without a break.'

'Me neither,' Jacob gratefully seconds.

Rukungu turns to them. 'Go slow. Softly, softly. But do not stop.'

They follow his advice, take smaller steps. For a while it works. Then both lungs and legs begin to burn again. Jacob is on the verge of demanding another halt when Rukungu stops on a flattish patch. While Jacob and Veronica catch their breath, Rukungu kneels beside a large boulder, carefully thrusts his hands beneath and withdraws a dusty panga.

'What's that for?' Veronica demands nervously.

'For making a path. Come.'

'Five minutes,' Jacob grunts.

Rukungu nods. Jacob turns off the light and focuses on his breath. Eventually the stars stop swimming in the sky and fix in one place. He is ravenously hungry, he wishes they had stopped long enough to eat, right now he would devour pocho as if it were made of chocolate truffles.

'What time is it?' Veronica asks Jacob.

He consults his hip-top. 'Ten.'

She turns to Rukungu. 'How much farther?'

'Myself, thirty minutes. With you, I think one hour.'

They continue, leaving the farming plots behind; the slope has become too steep and stony to eke out any crop. There is no longer any trail, they have to improvise their route through bushes and rocks. Jacob is glad the refugees have cut down all the trees for firewood or construction. Thick forest would take hours to climb through.

When they finally reach the crest of the ridge the night is so dark they see nothing of the hills around them at all, nothing but the distant glow of the few electric lights in the camp's administration centre. At least the mosquitoes are now few.

'There is a road,' Rukungu says, pointing downwards, away from the camp. 'Past the road there is a river. Past the river is the Congo.'

Rukungu takes the flashlight and begins to lead them downhill. Jacob follows uneasily. They are placing an enormous amount of trust in this man they have just met. He could take the light and leave them and they would probably never find their way back. He could turn on them with his panga and kill them both. Jacob supposes that if Rukungu were going to do these things he already would have. Somehow this is unconvincing comfort.

He is beginning to wish he had declined Rukungu's offer. He hadn't quite realized it would mean marching for hours through barren African wilderness in the moonless dark. And now that it's actually happening, the idea of spying on a rendezvous between smugglers and al-Qaeda on the very border of the Congo, with no recourse if something goes wrong, seems completely insane.

Well, you always wanted your big adventure, he thinks to himself. *Adventure, noun. Long periods of tedium interspersed with brief moments of terror.* Except Jacob has learned this *Devil's Dictionary* definition is incomplete: in real adventures, the tedium is usually coupled with total physical exhaustion, and the terror never really goes away, it's always there in the background, gnawing at him like sandpaper.

'Look,' Rukungu says softly.

Jacob looks. Lights in the distance, headlights, bouncing up and down; the road is clearly as bad as that leading into the camp.

Rukungu immediately switches off the Maglite. The vehicle rounds a gradual curve until it parallels the ridge they have just crossed.

'We must hurry,' Rukungu says. 'This torch is too bright.'

He gives Jacob back the flashlight, produces his Nokia phone and uses its screen to light their way down the ridge. Veronica follows, with Jacob behind her, using his hip-top as light. They follow a narrow path that seems to have barely worn its way into the thick trees and bushes. Jacob twice sees footprints too small to be Rukungu's. Prints left by a child's feet. Or a pygmy's. The vegetation here is thin, Rukungu doesn't need to use his panga. Jacob wonders why he brought it, then. Maybe for self-defence. Maybe this isn't as safe as he promised.

As they descend, the vehicle pulls off-road and stops, almost directly beneath them. They are only a few hundred feet away now. Jacob's muscles are taut, almost cramping with fear and adrenalin. He has to force himself to breathe slowly, quietly.

The vehicle's engine is switched off, its doors open, and Rukungu stops so suddenly that Veronica almost collides with him.

'What is it?' Veronica whispers.

'You are very loud. We must wait for more noise.'

'From where?' Jacob asks, low voiced.

'The other vehicle.'

'We're almost in range of the analyser,' Jacob says. 'Just twenty metres closer.'

'No.'

Jacob doesn't argue. Ahead of him Veronica is breathing fast. Jacob reaches out and takes her hand. She squeezes back tightly. Then Jacob lets go, shrugs his backpack off as silently as he can, and kneels. He gently opens his pack, withdraws camera and lens, and begins to assemble them by touch, working slowly and gently. His heart is thumping but his hands are steady. He remembers soldering circuit boards together, back in university, he was always good at that. Twice he slips slightly, metal clicks against plastic and Veronica inhales sharply, but Jacob isn't worried, they're surely far enough away that the men in the vehicle can't hear anything. Those men are speaking, conversing in low voices, but he can't make out any words or even the language.

'They come,' Rukungu mutters.

Jacob looks west and sees two more headlights in the distance.

Rukungu says, his voice so low Jacob can barely hear him, 'You must be silent. Absolutely silent. No light.'

He begins to move farther downslope. Veronica takes a deep breath and begins feeling her away along the path too. Jacob follows, but he can't move quickly with the camera, and soon she and Rukungu have disappeared into the darkness ahead.

Veronica's outstretched hand touches something warm and she almost gasps before identifying it as Rukungu. He is crouched behind something, a rock outcrop. Beyond a dirt slope drops maybe twenty feet to the road, lit by the approaching headlights. Veronica huddles next to Rukungu. At least the outcrop, plus the low trees and bushes on this stony ridge, should screen them from view. She can smell cigarette smoke. They are almost directly above where the first vehicle is parked. The men there are smoking, she can see the incandescent red dots of their cigarettes. Veronica badly wants one herself.

The second set of headlights wash over the first vehicle, a *matatu* like any other. Four men loiter around it, standing or leaning against the vehicle, smoking and waiting. They could be the same men Veronica saw last night in the scrapyard, she can't be sure. Light reflects from the white *matatu* on to the second vehicle as it pulls in alongside. It is big, blocky and angular – a Humvee. Its doors open and three men emerge. Veronica squints. The headlights are aimed away, and the diffuse light isn't enough to recognize faces, but one of the men is small but built hugely, like a bodybuilder. Veronica shudders. It's him, she can't recognize his face but she's sure of it; there, only fifty feet away, stands the al-Qaeda terrorist who beheaded Derek.

The two groups of men engage in a brief and businesslike discussion. Veronica does not understand their language. She wonders whether Rukungu does. If so he makes no obvious sign of it, just watches patiently.

Veronica is suddenly aware of someone on her other side. She twitches, turns her head and is relieved to see Jacob kneeling next to her, holding his camera with zoom lens attached. He rests it cautiously on the edge of the outcrop, aims it down at the two vehicles and seven men, and pushes the button. Veronica stiffens, but no sound or light emerges from the camera. Jacob must have switched it to some kind of stalker mode.

The smokers below carefully crush their cigarettes beneath their feet. Then the short, wide man who killed Derek opens the back of the Humvee, revealing a forest of yellow jerrycans. All seven men begin to move the jerrycans out on to the road. Veronica can smell gasoline.

Jacob leans over to whisper gently into her ear. 'I read about this. Gasoline smuggling. That gas actually got trucked in through Uganda in the first place, but there's no government in Congo, so no taxes, so the price there is so much lower it's cheaper to bring it back in from the Congo than to buy it in Ugandan gas stations.'

Veronica doesn't care and wishes Jacob didn't either. She wants to snap at him to focus. This isn't a time to be interested in the economics of smuggling. This is exactly the kind of knife-edge dangerous situation he promised they wouldn't get into.

Below them, the rear doors of the *matatu* are opened. Veronica breathes in deeply as she sees the two coffin-sized metal boxes within, the same boxes she saw on the pick-up last night. She sees something written on them, stencilled letters she can't quite make out. Jacob returns to his camera. The metal boxes are heavy, it takes four men to carry each from the *matatu* into the Humvee. Once they are loaded, the bodybuilder and two other men get back into their vehicle and drive away, heading west again, towards the Congo. Veronica watches their tail-lights disappear.

She feels relieved but also disappointed. They are safe, but they haven't learned anything new. She was expecting something more important, more decisive.

The four men from the *matatu* load the vehicle with jerrycans. Jacob reaches out to adjust the zoom. The camera lens extends outwards – and knocks loose a pebble that rattles loudly down the rock outcropping.

Veronica freezes as one of the men below turns around to stare at the unexpected noise. Her skin tingles with acid electricity, her heart fills her throat. The man stares into the darkness for a second, then says something and points, directly at them. The others stop working and follow his lead. She feels like they're staring straight at her. She couldn't breathe even if she dared.

Then Rukungu opens his mouth and an inhuman sound emerges, a warbling, high-pitched animal noise, some kind of mammalian chitter. The men below visibly relax, and one chuckles. Veronica starts to breathe again, shallowly and silently. The man who pointed at them is the last to turn away. He goes to the *matatu*'s passenger-side door and gets into the vehicle. The last few jerrycans are loaded, the rear doors are slammed shut.

The passenger door opens again and the man emerges with a flashlight in his hand. Veronica's heart convulses again as he shines it into the darkness. She crouches lower, as do Jacob and Rukungu; all three are fully obscured by the rock outcrop.

But Jacob's camera is still perched on the rock, its lens aimed straight at the man with the flashlight.

Veronica closes her eyes. They won't see it, she tells herself. It's too dark.

Then she hears a surprised and outraged shout, and an icy fist clenches at her gut.

'Run!' Rukungu orders.

Jacob grabs the camera and sprints noisily back up the trail. More shouting erupts below. Veronica stays where she is, hunched over, she feels paralysed, like a rabbit caught in headlights, until Rukungu shoves her so hard she almost topples over.

It breaks the spell. She too turns and rushes uphill, stumbling on the uneven ground; in the darkness she can't make out the path. She hears Jacob running above her and deliberately turns diagonally away. They're better off splitting up.

Then she hears the firecracker noises of gunfire behind her, an automatic weapon. She throws herself to the ground, heedless of the thorns and branches that claw at her face and arms. The gunfire continues briefly. Then she hears running noises from below. They are following. Veronica considers trying to flee, but she'll make too much noise, they're too close, and they're faster and stronger. Best to hide and hope.

She curls up in a ball and looks behind her, down the ridge. Two lights are coming up the path. She is less than twenty feet away from the trail, not nearly as far away as she hoped. She can see the face of the man holding the first flashlight, the form of the second man behind him, and the rifles they carry. They rush right past her, pursuing Jacob; but the other two-man team, with the second flashlight, is climbing much more slowly, and examining the ground as they come. Both hold drawn pistols.

Veronica stays rigidly still and silent. She wants to run, to leap to her feet and scramble away, but it is too late now. She can't bear to watch, she wants to close her eyes, but doesn't let herself, she needs to know what's happening. She tries to tell herself that she will be fine, that somehow this will all be over soon.

The two men with pistols veer off the path, straight towards her. Veronica twitches with dread. She has to hold her breath to keep herself from moaning with terror. Their light is aimed at the ground, they are studying that circle of illumination carefully. They are thirty feet away, maybe less, they will see her in seconds.

Light flickers from up the ridge, light as from a gunshot, but there is no sound. The two men following her turn to look. There is another flash, and another, they seem to be coming every two seconds. The men speak briefly. Then they return to her trail. They heard her, she realizes too late; they noticed that somebody stopped running after the gunfire. They know she is close to the path.

Light from their flashlight washes over her. She cringes away as one of them exclaims triumphantly, and suddenly they are both standing over her, aiming their light directly at her face, speaking to one another in surprised tones. Veronica curls into a foetal position. All she can see of them is that they wear jeans and leather boots, good quality, these men aren't poor. One stoops, grabs her arm, pulls her roughly to her feet.

'No,' she says weakly, knowing there's no use in fighting back, trying to resist by going limp, like a child. 'No. Let me go. Let me go.'

She makes a pathetic attempt to pull away. In response the pressure on her increases, her arm is pulled behind her back and forced upwards until she cries out from the pain. Her shoulder feels as if it is on the verge of dislocation. She is hyperventilating, panting like an animal. It is all she can do not to stumble and fall as her abductors march her back to their vehicle.

13

Her captors are laughing now, exchanging eager banter. They propel her across the road and shove her hard against the side of the *matatu*; she gets her free hand up just in time so that it instead of her face absorbs most of the impact. Then that arm too is grabbed and forced painfully behind her back. She is dragged alongside the *matatu* and bent head first over its hood. She kicks out feebly, tries to wriggle free, but it is no use, and then her arms are forced higher, agony arcs through both her shoulders, and she screams.

Her arms are allowed to drop a tiny amount. Veronica stops trying to resist, she just lies there numbly, moaning, her arms held behind her back, the *matatu*'s hood against her face. Its engine is still warm from the drive. A single powerful hand pressing down on her arms keeps her pinned face down. Her captors discuss something. She doesn't understand their words, but she gets the idea that one of them is arguing in favour of something, and the other is reluctant, but eventually gives in.

Moments later something metal touches her temple. She swivels her head instinctively so she can see what it is. A gun, a pistol, held to her head. The second man fumbles with the zip of her jeans. Veronica tries to think of something to say to make them stop but the only sounds emerging from her mouth are helpless animal grunts. She tries to fight but there is too much weight on her; the more she tries to wriggle free, the more her shoulders howl with pain.

The button pops free. She whimpers as her jeans and under-wear are yanked down to her knees. She hears a loud grunt then, and unexpectedly some kind of warm, thick liquid splashes over her lower back, and the flashlight that has illuminated her goes careening into the night. The hand on her wrists and the gun against her head pull suddenly away. As Veronica reflexively stretches out her arms, releasing her tortured shoulders, she hears a horrible gurgling sound, and then a man falls right on top of her, his whole weight pushes her into the hood for a moment before he rolls limply away, leaving her free.

Veronica stands, turns and screams again. In the dim light of the fallen flashlight she can see there is blood everywhere, blood all over her legs and lower body, and two men lie dead at her feet. A third stands in the darkness, she can't see his face but the panga in his hand is wet with blood. She instinctively turns to run, but her jeans trip her up and she falls hard on one of the bodies. Veronica scrabbles away, clumsily pulling her jeans and under-wear back up, gasping with shock and horror. The third man picks up the fallen flashlight and illuminates himself. It is Rukungu.

'Be silent,' he hisses.

Veronica somehow manages to get to her feet. She is shaking so violently that she has to lean on the *matatu* to steady herself.

Rukungu inspects her. 'Are you wounded?'

She shakes her head.

'The other men will return. They have Kalashnikovs. We must run, not fight.'

Veronica takes three deep breaths, recovers enough of her self-possession to stand unsupported. 'Yes. OK. I'll follow you.' Her voice sounds foreign to herself, an old woman's voice.

By the time Veronica and Rukungu begin their descent back to the refugee camp, his water bottle is empty, her throat aches with thirst, her head hurts and she is dizzy with exhaustion. Her adrenalin has drained away, she is covered with the blood of two dead men, all she wants is a Gatorade and a shower and a warm bed. She forces herself to keep marching onwards after Rukungu. Going downhill requires less effort but more attention, and she staggers frequently. Every step causes both her shoulders to pulse with dull pain, but she doesn't think there's any serious damage or dislocation; both her arms seem to work fine, they just hurt.

'Veronica,' a cautious voice calls out. 'Rukungu.'

Veronica stops, amazed. Rukungu aims the flashlight and picks out Jacob, seated slumped on a big boulder, covered in dirt. Veronica sways with relief. He's OK. He got away. She finds the strength to rush up to him and hug him.

He hugs her back clumsily. 'Are you OK?'

'Fine.' She manages a smile. 'Lot better than I look. How'd you find us?'

She is not terribly surprised when he holds up his trusty hip-top. 'GPS. I backtracked to our route up, recognized this rock.'

She looks down and realizes that this boulder he is sitting on is the same one beneath which Rukungu's panga was hidden. She also sees Jacob's water bottle, still half full. She grabs it, takes a few deep swigs and passes it to Rukungu, who finishes it.

Jacob says, 'I had to dump my camera. I turned on the flash and put it on automatic, threw it downhill. They went after it instead of me.' Veronica nods; those were the flashes she saw. She's impressed by his presence of mind during a crisis, but then she's seen it before, in the Congo. There is an iron core beneath Jacob's geeky exterior. 'Had to leave the spectrum analyser too. That's fifteen thousand dollars down the drain.'

'You're alive.'

He smiles. 'Good point. Cheap at the price.'

'Never mind the pictures. We got away.'

'Oh, I've still got the pictures, I took out the memory card before I tossed the camera. What happened to you?'

'Two of them got me.' Veronica turns to look at Rukungu, who waits silently a little distance away. 'He killed them.'

'Jesus.'

'Yeah.'

'What do we do now?' Jacob asks.

'I think we should go. Just go, right now. They'll know we went back to the camp. Rukungu messed up their *matatu*, they'll be stuck there for a while, but I think we should get out of town before they call for help.'

'They probably already have . . . oh, right. I blocked incoming calls at this base station. Maybe they called Kampala for help, but they can't have called anyone local. See, I'm a genius.'

Veronica smiles wryly. 'I never doubted it.'

'All right. Let's get the hell out of Dodge.'

Veronica and Rukungu wait on the road that leads to the gate while Jacob returns to the administrative centre for the Toyota. She can't be seen there covered in blood, and while Rukungu has restored his panga to its hiding place, he too might provoke unwelcome questions. She wonders what Susan will think of the sudden disappearance following their sudden appearance. They'll have to send her a text message or something, try to explain.

Headlights bob and jostle down the road from the camp. Veronica breathes with deep relief. She was worried the soldiers wouldn't allow Jacob to depart by night. The Toyota pulls up beside them. Veronica opens the passenger door – and Rukungu opens the back door behind her.

She stops and looks at him, surprised. 'Are you coming with us?'

Rukungu looks betrayed. 'Derek said he would take me back to Kampala.'

Jacob looks like he wants to protest, but the man just risked his own life to save Veronica's, she isn't about to argue. 'Fine.'

They both get in. Jacob gives her a Snickers bar with a *ta-da!* flourish. She groans with desire, rips it open, then hesitates, breaks it in two and gives half to Rukungu, who accepts it without a word. She suddenly remembers sharing a Snickers bar with Derek in the Congo, in that cave behind the waterfall. Their one almost-kiss. It is like remembering a high-school boyfriend.

There's a blanket in the back seat, and Veronica drapes it all over herself and checks the mirror. Fortunately there's hardly any blood on her face, and a little spit clears it off. She and Rukungu pretend to sleep, which is not at all difficult, as Jacob drives up to the gate. The gate guards are initially reluctant to allow them to depart, and demand to see all their ID cards. Jacob first claims they have lost their ID, and must rush to a sudden emergency in Kampala; when that fails, he offers them a *kutu kidogo* – meaning 'little gift', or more loosely 'bribe' – of two fifty-dollar bills. The restrictions on who may exit UNHCR Semiliki are suddenly relaxed and the Toyota waved through. Veronica suspects Jacob overpaid; this is a refugee camp, not a prison.

'You can wake me up in an hour or so if you need me to drive,' she says as they bump down the roller-coaster road that leads away from the camp. She doesn't really mean it. She just wants to close her eyes and wake up in civilization. It is too easy to imagine obstacles that might leap into their path: road disasters, mechanical problems, more gunmen. They are in wild lands on the very edge of civilization and anything could go wrong. All she wants is to get safely away from the Congo border to Fort Portal.

When Veronica finally opens her eyes again, woken by the dawn, she sees, to her piercing relief, that that is exactly what has happened. She would never have believed that the sight of this dirty, dusty town would be so welcome. She feels like a passenger on the last helicopter out of Saigon.

'You should sleep,' Veronica says.

Jacob shakes his head. 'There's an Internet café down the road. I want to go see what we've got.'

They are back in the restaurant at the Ruwenzori Travellers' Inn. Veronica feels almost alive again: freshly showered, dressed in clean clothes, at least halfway rested, and there is a plate of toast and a cup of Nescafé on the chequered tablecloth before her. Jacob sits opposite her.

'When was the last time you slept?' she asks.

'Don't worry about me. I'm used to all-nighters. As you can see.' He indicates the trilogy of caffeine before him: his own Nescafé, a cup of 'African tea' – English Breakfast steeped in boiled milk – and a cold bottle of Coke. 'Maintaining productivity while sleep deprived is key to hacker credibility. I feel like I'm back in university.'

Veronica looks at him suspiciously.

'Really, I'm fine. While you were showering I texted Susan, told her we had to head back to Kampala because you were malarial, and I turned on that base station again. Let me just finish these and we'll go see if they've opened. Their hours say they opened half an hour ago, but, you know, Africa.'

'Where's Rukungu?'

Jacob shrugs. 'Up in his room, I guess.'

The Travellers' Inn is under construction, half the building is blocked off by sheets of canvas hanging on two-by-fours, they were able to annex only two rooms when they checked in. It was somehow wordlessly understood by all of them that Veronica and Jacob would take one and Rukungu the other. The reasonably comfortable rooms cost ten dollars a night and boast balconies that look on to the cloud-capped Ruwenzori. The bathrooms are a little primitive, but to Veronica's joy, soap has been provided and the hot water seems everlasting.

'He said he was one of Athanase's men,' Veronica says. Jacob nods. 'Do you think that means he was . . .'

'I don't know. But he's old enough. And it would explain why he's so good at killing people. Does it matter?'

Veronica doesn't answer. She owes the man upstairs her life. But she can't shake the awful suspicion that Rukungu is *inter-ahamwe*, that he participated in the Rwandan genocide, massacred helpless innocents, women and children, just for belonging to the wrong tribe. Surely that has to matter.

'Rukungu's the least of our problems,' Jacob says. 'He's the only person other than Prester we know for sure is on our side.'

'How do we know that?'

'Because if he wasn't we'd be dead right now, wouldn't we?' Jacob finishes his coffee, drops five thousand shillings on the table and picks up his Coke bottle. 'Let's go.'

The Internet café is small but clean. Its six monitors are hidden beneath a big glass table, tilted up towards the user. Jacob ignores the monitors and drops to his knees next to the nearest computer. The nursing mother who runs the café watches him curiously as he peers at its carapace. To his relief there is a USB port. These machines are old but not antiques.

Veronica sits down at the next computer over.

'Don't log into your email,' Jacob cautions her. 'Strick might be looking for us, they could conceivably track your Internet use to Fort Portal. And keep your phone off, don't make any calls. I'm pretty sure Mango is safe, I monitor who accesses that system, but no sense pushing our luck. And calls to anyone else would definitely be trouble.'

He reaches into his pocket, pulls out the memory card rescued from his camera and folds it in half, revealing a USB connector. He plugs the card into the computer and sits at the monitor.

'How much trouble do you think we're in?' Veronica asks uneasily.

226

'I don't know. Maybe I'm being paranoid. Maybe we're actually on the run. Whoever those guys were last night, they have high-level connections, and it won't take too much asking around the camp to find out who came to visit and then suddenly disappeared. Strick probably already knows what happened.'

'Shit.'

'Well, maybe it was worth it. Let's see what we've got.'

The first few pictures are fuzzy and useless, blobs of orange light outlining vaguely human shapes and the white blur of the *matatu*, and Jacob fears the worst. Then they began to resolve into much better, in-focus shots. He grunts with relief as he scrolls through the pictures. About thirty are usable.

'Go back through them,' Veronica says when he is done. 'There's one in the middle. Back a couple. There!'

Jacob nods. 'Good eye.' This is the only in-focus shot where the short but immensely muscular man is turned towards the camera with his face lit. He taps at Photo Viewer's magnifying-glass icon, zooming in, pans up to the face.

'That's him,' Jacob says dully. 'That's the guy who killed Derek.'

'Yes.'

'Fucker took his dishdasha off for this job. Wonder why. There was one shot after this . . .'

He scrolls a few pictures forward, to a moment when the metal boxes are in the Humvee but the doors have not yet been closed, and a flashlight is being shone on their coffin-sized shapes. Jacob taps the magnifying glass again, three times, to maximum zoom, and pans right over to the boxes. The writing on them is too blurry to read, and Veronica groans – but when Jacob zooms out one step, the four largest figures suddenly condense into something readable, if mysterious:

И Г Л А

'Looks like Greek,' Veronica says, perplexed.

'Or Russian. Cyrillic. Let's get Google to translate.' It takes Jacob a little while to find the characters in a configuration that can be pasted into Google's online form. 'Here we go. Means *needle* in Russian.' Jacob shakes his head, mystified. 'Needles in a haystack, eh? Seriously big ones if they need boxes that size to carry them.'

Veronica says, 'Wait a minute. What's the phonetic translation?'

'The phonetic? Why?'

'Is it Igloo?'

Jacob brightens, nods. 'Wikipedia should have a cross-reference page.' They have to wait a few seconds, the Internet connection is slow, worse than a phone line. 'Here we go. Bingo. You're almost a genius. Not Igloo, *Igla*. Whatever that means. I guess we can Google and see . . .' He switches back to Google, types 'igla', and hits Return.

'International Gay and Lesbian Aquatics.' Veronica reads the first result aloud. 'Somehow I don't think that's it.'

'No. But look, here's Wikipedia. '9K38M Igla-1, which has the NATO reporting name SA-16 Gimlet.'

He clicks on the second link. The page loads. As Jacob reads, his eyes get very wide.

' "The 9K38 Igla is a Russian/Soviet man-portable infrared homing surface-to-air missile," ' Veronica reads aloud, softly. 'Oh my God.'

Jacob feels dizzy. Zanzibar Sam. SAM. Surface-to-Air Missile. The enormity of this discovery is far beyond what he expected. 'Holy fucking shit. *Boxes* of them. Look at this picture, they're not that big, there must have been probably four in each of those boxes.'

'Oh my God,' Veronica repeats.

'This is a big deal. This is a really big deal. If those are going to the terrorists—'

'Going? They're *gone*. They've got them. They're in the Congo already.'

'They can shoot down helicopters with those. Or airplanes. Smuggle them into Kenya or back to Entebbe and blow up whole airliners full of tourists. Al-Qaeda on the loose with two boxes of man-portable anti-aircraft missiles. I'd say that's pretty fucking close to a worst-case scenario.'

She says, 'We have to tell someone.'

'Yes. Of course. We have real evidence now, pictures of missiles being smuggled. And Prester saw them too.'

'Let's show these to Rukungu, see if he knows anything. He might recognize some of these guys.'

'Good idea. Then we better get some rest. Long drive ahead of us. Back to Kampala and straight to the embassy. Sooner we tell the whole fucking world about this the better.'

'Strick's at the embassy.'

'Not for long,' Jacob says grimly. 'Not by the time we're done.'

'Yes,' Rukungu says tersely, looking at the hyper-muscled man on the computer screen. 'I know this man.'

Veronica looks at Rukungu and wonders what he's thinking. When she knocked on his door and entered his room he was standing on the balcony, staring at the Ruwenzori mountains. The bed was mussed, and there was water on the shower floor, but otherwise there was no sign that his room was occupied. She wonders why he didn't even collect his possessions before leaving the refugee camp. As far as Veronica can tell he has his clothes, his phone, his rubber boots and nothing else in this world.

'Who is he?' Jacob asks.

'His name is Casimir. He is from Rwanda.'

Veronica blinks. That wasn't the answer she expected. 'He's Muslim?'

Surprise flickers across Rukungu's face. 'No. No, Muslims are with the *interahamwe*.'

'He came with the Arab man, right? He and his three friends? Maybe earlier this year?' Jacob asks.

Rukungu looks at Jacob, perplexed. 'No. Casimir has been with Athanase for many years. Since we left Rwanda. There are no Muslims. The only Arab who comes to Athanase is a man who comes to buy gold. That man has no religion but money.'

Veronica looks away. *Since we left Rwanda.* That's all the confirmation she needs. Rukungu is *interahamwe*, a mass murderer.

'That doesn't make sense,' Jacob says, puzzled. 'Your buddy Casimir here is the guy who killed Derek. Chopped his fucking head off with a machete. If he's not Muslim, why was he wearing a dishdasha? Are you totally sure this is him?'

'This is Casimir. I have no doubt. I have known him for twelve years.'

Veronica frowns. 'Then why was he in a dishdasha?'

Jacob reflects. 'Maybe for TV. Maybe they didn't have any real terrorists handy who were willing and able to swing the panga, so they dressed up the big *interahamwe* guy for the camera.'

Something about his phrasing nags at Veronica. She tries to figure out what it is exactly, but it won't come to her.

'Figure it out later,' Jacob says. 'Let's sleep on it. I'm beat. And we should keep a low profile anyways. I saw a couple other white folks earlier, but we still stand out too much. I vote we stay here until nightfall.'

Rukungu glances from one of them to the other, looking perplexed. She supposes they're speaking too quickly for him; his English is good but slow, every sentence is carefully thought out before he speaks.

'And just hope Strick doesn't find us before then?' Veronica asks.

'I think he'll figure we've gone straight back to Kampala.'

She stares at him. 'You think? That's the best you can do?'

Jacob shrugs. 'Sorry. I'm all out of guarantees.'

14

Veronica is bored and frightened. There isn't anything to do in their hotel room, no TV, not even a Gideon Bible to read. Jacob sleeps peacefully on the queen-sized bed beneath the wobbling blur of the ceiling fan, but Veronica feels too wired for sleep. She wants to go out and explore the streets of Fort Portal, but she doesn't dare. She allows herself to go to the balcony, listen to the chatter and watch the bustle on Fort Portal's main drag, and look south-west, past rolling hills covered with banana trees, to where the otherwise blue sky is occupied by thick clouds clinging to the Ruwenzori, entirely covering the so-called Mountains of the Moon. But even this radiant view eventually grows boring. She wishes she had thought to bring a book from Kampala.

She sighs, lies down on her side of the bed, closes her eyes, tries to make herself sleep. It doesn't seem possible. She should be tired, yesterday was truly draining and she slept for only a few hours in the car, but she feels much too keyed up to fall asleep. If not for Rukungu she would have died last night. And they're still a long way from safe.

She opens her eyes, rolls on to her side and watches Jacob. He looks peaceful in his sleep, like a little boy. She wonders whether he's as frightened as her. Probably not. To some extent Jacob seems to be treating all this as some elaborate game, an intellectual challenge to overcome. He's working on the assumption that he's much smarter than their antagonists, and therefore safe. The assumption is probably true, but Veronica isn't at all sure about the conclusion. It is amazing, however, what Jacob can do with just a few pieces of electronic equipment. His hip-top is like Batman's utility belt.

Jacob shifts a little, opens his eyes and looks at her blearily; his subconscious must have noticed he was being watched. She smiles. He reaches out a long arm and pulls her close to him, and she lets him, fits her body against his, puts her head on his shoulder and holds him tightly. He grunts with sleep satisfaction and closes his eyes, and she does too, and they lie there for some time. He is warm and comfortable, and comforting. Veronica's breath and heartbeat begin to slow down in time with his. She dozes.

When she opens her eyes she isn't sure how much time has passed; the room is still full of sunlight, but not as bright. Jacob has gone to the bathroom. He returns to bed and this time it is she who reaches out for him. They nestle together again, this time with their eyes open, their faces close to one another. Neither of them speaks. Veronica feels Jacob's heart pounding as he lifts his hand, reaches out a trembling finger, touches and traces the line of her cheek. When she does not pull away he leans forward and kisses her. She closes her eyes.

They kiss for a long time before he dares to slip his hand beneath her shirt. At first she isn't sure she wants this. He senses her hesitation and pulls back. A minute later she decides, and pulls her shirt off herself. He fumbles awkwardly with her bra strap before it finally opens. Veronica moves on top of him, feeling his long, lean body beneath hers as his hands and lips come to her breasts. She pulls away long enough to pull his shirt off too, and presses herself against him, luxuriating in the bliss of skin on skin. She stays on top. The sex is slow at first, tender, unhurried, but gradually becomes urgent and passionate, and she loses herself in it, forgets everything but pleasure.

Afterwards they lie naked together, both limned in sweat. Jacob looks a little stunned and Veronica has to keep herself from giggling. She feels irrationally giddy, like a teenager.

'I don't know about you, but I feel *much* better,' she says, stretching catlike.

He laughs. 'Me too.'

'It's kind of been a while.'

'Me too.'

They lapse into silence. Jacob rolls on to his elbow and looks at her closely, as if inspecting her. Then he reaches out and touches her very gently, running a still-tentative hand up and down the curves of her body. She murmurs appreciatively.

He says, wonderingly, 'I honestly never thought I'd ever sleep with anyone as beautiful as you.'

'Aw. You're going to make me blush.'

'I suppose I should have brought condoms, eh?'

She almost laughs again at his concerned expression. 'Funny how you didn't think of that in the heat of the moment,' she mock-scolds. 'They'll throw you out of the Boy Scouts if you don't watch it.'

'Actually, they kicked me out for hacking into their computers.'

'Oh. Well, anyways, I think we've got much bigger things to worry about.'

'True. Until tomorrow anyways.'

'When did you want to leave?'

Jacob thinks. 'After it gets dark.'

'Good.' She snuggles up against him, puts her open palm on his damp chest, feeling his breath and heartbeat. 'That gives us time for more.'

Jacob reminds himself that his life is in real danger and he should not feel giddily triumphant. But it's hard not to grin as Veronica walks naked from the bathroom back to the bed and curls up in his arms again. She's addictive, he can't stop looking at her, can't stop running his hands all over her perfect body, hardly believing she's allowing him to do so.

'Mmmm,' she says, arching her back at his touch. 'I almost wish we could stay here longer.'

'Me too. But we can't. It's hard for us white folks to hide in Africa. If they're looking for us, I think they'll find us pretty soon. Maybe tomorrow. I was thinking we should call Prester.'

'What for?'

'We know he's on our side,' Jacob says. 'And he seems to know everyone in Kampala, he can give us some names to go to for help, if there's any trouble.'

'If he can even answer. If his phone's in his hospital room. Or if he isn't . . . I mean, we don't know his condition.'

Jacob digs his hip-top out of his jeans pocket. 'Worth a try, though.'

'You sure they can't track that?' Veronica asks worriedly. 'Or my phone?'

He smiles. 'Good thinking. But no. I've erased all traces of our phones from Telecom Uganda. We're invisible.'

Jacob dials Prester. His phone rings five times but there's no response. He tries again; same result. 'His phone's on, but he's not answering.'

'Can you track him? Where is he?'

'I can track his phone.' Jacob connects to the Telecom Uganda master switching database and runs the shell script he's written that plots a Mango phone's current location on a Google Map. He peers at the hip-top's small screen. 'Huh. That's weird.'

'What?'

'According to this, Prester's phone is in the middle of nowhere. An empty space on the map about fifty K north of Kampala.'

'What does that mean?' she asks.

'I have no idea.' Jacob sits up cross-legged on the bed, peering down at his hip-top. 'Google Earth won't work on this. I could maybe get some satellite photo. Or, no, wait a minute. That idea you had.'

'What idea?'

'About triggering his camera phone remotely. Let's see if that code I wrote actually works.'

Jacob has tested the software in question, but not in a real-life situation, so he is very pleased when the hip-top's screen begins to fill with a picture silently taken by Prester's phone, at Jacob's behest, and then sent over Uganda's cellular network. It's a blurry picture, the victim of a lossy compression algorithm, but Jacob can make out a table lamp, viewed from below, and wooden slats above, arrayed circularly like spokes in a wheel. Prester's phone must be lying flat on some table with the camera lens aimed up.

'A *banda*,' Jacob realizes aloud. One of the circular huts that dot Uganda's landscape, wooden or bamboo frames filled with mud.

'A *banda*? He should be in a hospital,' Veronica says, shocked. 'He was shot in the chest two days ago, he has a perforated lung. What's he doing in a *banda*?'

'I don't know. He's not answering.' Jacob hesitates. 'Wait a second.'

He sets Prester's camera phone to take a picture every half-second for the next twenty seconds, then dials its number again. If there's anyone there, maybe they'll at least look at the phone to see who's calling.

It takes a full minute for each picture to be uploaded from Prester's phone and downloaded to Jacob's hip-top. The first three contain nothing unusual. But the fourth displays a familiar face.

'Oh, no,' Jacob says, as the new picture fills his hip-top's screen. 'Oh, shit.'

Veronica sits up quickly, grabs his arm, looks and gasps. The picture that has been taken is a somewhat warped view of Strick, viewed face-on from below.

'They got him,' she whispers.

'Maybe they just got his phone. Let's see.'

They wait anxiously. Seconds crawl by. The next picture is also of Strick, but this time a white-haired white man with a thin face is looking over Strick's shoulder. Jacob has never seen him before. Neither has Veronica.

Three similar pictures later, they finally get a partial shot of the phone's surroundings. It's at an angle, and blurry, the phone must have been in motion when the camera fired, maybe it was being put back on the table. Light streaming from an open window drowns out almost all the rest of the picture. But this light clearly illuminates, in one corner of the frame, a dark-skinned wrist handcuffed to a metal bed frame, and a few loose cables of dreadlocked hair.

'No,' Veronica says. 'Oh, no. That's him. That's Prester.'

Jacob nods grimly. 'And they think he knows where we are.'

'Oh my God. What do you think they're—'

'I think I don't want to know what they're doing to him,' Jacob says harshly. He shakes his head. 'Sorry. Shit. We have to get to the embassy as soon as it opens. That's all we can do.'

*   *   *

235

The Night Of Knives

The darkness outside their car is almost perfect. There are no street lights on Ugandan highways, and almost no night-time traffic. Earlier they drove through a swarm of tiny flies as dense as fog, and then a hammering tropical downpour, lightning flickering around them two or three times a second, illuminating the ghostly silhouettes of roadside *bandas* and tin-roofed huts. Now the clouds have cleared and the pale skein of the Milky Way is visible in the moonless canopy of countless stars above. They pass through dusty villages so quiet by night that they look deserted, across tumbling rivers that glitter in the headlights. There are only a few roadblocks, and the police who man them seem tense and nervous, as if whoever drives by night carries the devil as a passenger. Jacob and Veronica are waved past without inspection.

They stop for Veronica to relinquish the wheel. Both she and Jacob are exhausted, but neither can sleep. As they resume their motion Veronica looks over her shoulder at Rukungu, lying sprawled across the Toyota's back seat, sleeping like a baby. She thinks of what she has read about the Rwandan genocide in which he participated.

There were eight million people in Rwanda, seven million Hutu and one million Tutsi, when the Hutu leaders decided to murder all the Tutsi. The weapons of choice were clubs and machetes. In the cities, *interahamwe* death squads hunted door to door, killed whole families in their homes, dragged them out to be executed in public, stopped carloads of Tutsis at roadblocks and slaughtered them on the spot. Children proudly told passing death squads where their neighbours were hidden. Doctors invited them into hospitals to murder their patients. As the weeks of genocide progressed, Hutus increasingly eliminated the middleman, killed their Tutsi acquaintances themselves and moved into their houses. In rural areas Tutsi were hunted down like vermin – hunting parties went out every day to find the 'cockroaches' hidden in fields and forests, slaughtered man and woman and child alike. Tutsi women, famous for their beauty, were usually gang-raped before they were slaughtered.

The survivors of the first few weeks congregated in caves, churches, schools, stadiums, with no food, no water, no hope. Some tried to flee to cities not yet affected, but genocidal bloodlust spread inexorably through the nation like a virus. The slaughter at some of the sanctuaries lasted for weeks. Massacring people by hand is hard work. Sometimes, too exhausted to actually murder those trying to escape, the killing mobs just severed their victims' Achilles tendons, then came back to finish the job in the morning. Dogs and crows multiplied, fed on the countless bodies that littered the nation's streets and fields.

Meanwhile, every government official, every radio host, called for the completion of the genocide. 'Exterminate the cockroaches,' they said. 'Wipe them out. Every one of them. To your work, all of you. The graves are not yet full.'

Athanase was one of those leaders, one of the chief architects of the genocide. Rukungu was a member of one of the *interahamwe* death squads who spearheaded the genocide. Veronica wonders how old he would have been at the time. Late teens, maybe. She wonders how many women he raped, how many children he murdered, both in Rwanda and afterwards, when the *interahamwe* were finally driven out into the Congo, where their campaign of murder and rape continued. Probably dozens. Maybe hundreds. Any reasonable person would call him a monster. But she owes him her life.

Jacob and Veronica wait in the same embassy meeting room where they talked to Strick. Veronica's eyelids feels like anvils, and she is not so much sitting as drooping on her chair. They drove all night across half of Uganda to get here, taking turns at the wheel, and then fought their way through Kampala's rush hour to drop Rukungu off at the Hotel Sun City. But they made it. If they're safe anywhere in Africa, it's here in the US embassy.

Jacob reaches out and takes her hand, lifts it to his face and kisses it. She smiles back absently. Part of her is already wondering whether this sudden relationship is going to make any sense when the extraordinary circumstances that threw them together are gone. She squelches that notion. She will worry about the future next week. This week she will pretend the future never existed, she will just enjoy being alive.

The door opens.

'My name is Julian,' says the man who enters. He's in his thirties, with a square jaw and a crew cut. 'I'm the assistant deputy head of mission.'

Jacob says, 'We need to speak to the ambassador.'

Julian shakes his head. 'The ambassador isn't in today, he's at a ceremony in Jinja, his schedule is fully booked for the whole week. I'm sorry, I know you said it's urgent, but I'm as good as you're going to get on such short notice.'

'Does Strick work for you?' Veronica asks.

Julian looks sour. 'Gordon Strick works at this embassy for the State Department. He does not report to me.'

'What about Prester?'

Julian blinks. 'Who?'

'He worked with our friend Derek,' Jacob says. 'For Strick, indirectly. He was shot the night before last.'

'Is he an American citizen?'

'I don't think so.'

'Then I wouldn't know anything about him. Please. We're wasting each other's time. Why are you here?'

Jacob and Veronica look at one another. She nods.

'All right.' Jacob speaks in a clipped, factual voice, an engineer reporting on the data. 'We have proof, we have pictures of Russian surface-to-air missiles being smuggled into the Congo last night.' He puts down a CD-ROM he burned at an Internet café before coming to the embassy. 'We have physical evidence that Derek Summers believed a company run by Veronica's ex-husband Danton DeWitt was involved with this smuggling ring, there's a scan of his notes on that CD, you can check it against his handwriting. Derek said just before he was executed that he was set up, and he accused Danton of being involved. We have

238

telephone records, also on that CD, strongly implying that Mr Strick and Athanase Ntingizawa were conspiring to smuggle goods from the Congo and Uganda, and photos showing that Strick has since kidnapped and tortured Prester.'

Julian stares at Jacob.

'We also have beliefs and conclusions we've drawn, but I want to stress that what I've told you so far isn't just suspicion, there's evidence on that CD, hard evidence.'

'Christ,' Julian says, in a very different tone of voice than that in which he began the conversation.

'In particular, we believe that al-Qaeda has been blackmailing Strick into giving them material assistance for an attack they are planning in the very near future.'

'Wait,' Julian says, holding his hands up as if a wall is about to fall on him. 'Wait, slow down, please.'

Jacob falls silent.

'I need to go get my boss,' Julian says. 'Stay right there. I'll be right back.'

He all but scampers out of the room. Veronica and Jacob look at one another.

'Well,' she says, 'at least they're taking us seriously.'

Less than a minute later the door reopens and a thin man in his fifties enters the room. The white-haired man's skin seems unnaturally pale, and even his facial features are thin, seem slashed into taut skin. He is the same man they saw yesterday, in the picture taken from Prester's camera phone. His appearance is surreal, it's as if he has stepped out of that picture into real life.

'I'm Dr Murray,' he says, 'the chief of mission here. I under-stand—'

Then he recognizes them and suddenly falls silent. Veronica gapes at the white-haired man. For a heartbeat he is no less surprised to see them, his eyes widen and his step falters, but he quickly recovers his possession and continues smoothly, 'Mr Rockel. Miss Kelly. I wasn't told it was you. We're all so glad you're safe after what happened.'

Jacob and Veronica are too stunned to speak.

'Is something wrong?' Dr Murray asks. His voice is like warm silk.

'No,' Jacob manages. 'No, we're just very tired, we drove all night to get here.'

'Drove from where?'

Jacob flashes a panicked look at Veronica. She doesn't know how to respond. Her mind is whirling. It doesn't seem possible that this Dr Murray is in league with Strick and al-Qaeda. But there's no other explanation. Yesterday he was in the same room as Prester's phone, a room where Prester was handcuffed to a bed, those are established facts.

'From the border,' Jacob says haltingly. Veronica supposes there's no point in hiding that now. They have just admitted everything. 'Near Semiliki.'

'Indeed. And what were you doing there?'

After a long moment Jacob begins to tell the story, speaking slowly, starting back in the Congo, expounding on irrelevant details while leaving out as much as possible. Veronica realizes he's stalling, playing for time. They have to do something. Murray already knows they know too much. They have to get out of here.

'Where's the bathroom?' Veronica interrupts.

'Just down the hall,' Dr Murray says absently, his thin face rigid with contemplation.

Veronica slips out of the room and closes the door behind her, dizzy with exhaustion and panic. She walks down the hall, barely aware of the world around her, walks right past the bathroom and has to double back. She's thankful it's empty. She sits in a stall, locks the door, covers her face with her hands, and tries to think.

Her gut tells her to run, to escape and leave Jacob behind. Murray won't allow them both to leave. He'll think of some reason to have them arrested, their evidence will be destroyed. She has to get out before he calls security, once he does that it's all

240

over, the US embassy is probably the single most secure building in all of Kampala. Jacob knows all this. He wants her to escape right now, without him, she is sure of it.

'Jacob, I'm sorry,' Veronica whispers aloud.

Then she gets up and walks fast out of the bathroom, heading for the exit. She passes an Asian woman holding a folder of papers. She reaches a T-junction, turns left – then stops and turns back towards the junction.

For a moment she stares at the little red fire alarm hanging on the wall there. Then she walks back, looks around to ensure no one is watching her, reaches out and pulls the alarm. It is harder than she expected, she has to use much of her strength before the little lever pulls free. A single moment of silence passes. Then a siren begins to whoop.

Veronica quickly scuttles away. About ten seconds pass. Then doors begin to open up and down the corridor, and people begin to stream out, most of them white and well dressed, wearing resigned or irritated expressions, most holding papers and cell phones and Palm Pilots. She joins the throng as they file sedately out of the building into the parking lot, then makes her way inobtrusively over to Jacob's Toyota. Now if only Jacob can find a way to get away, and surely he will think of something, he probably has some embassy-escape function on his hip-top—

'Come on, let's go,' Jacob says urgently, behind her, and Veronica sags with relief. Saved by American fire-safety standards.

They dive into the Toyota. He reverses out; they have to move slowly, their path is blocked by the fringes of the crowd. Veronica looks around, afraid that Murray will suddenly loom out of the assembled masses, but he is nowhere to be seen. The office workers around them make way for the vehicle. Then they are at the security gate – and they are waved past. This security system is built to keep terrorists out, not white people in, and Dr Murray doesn't yet know that they know he's conspiring with Strick.

'How'd you get away?' she asks.

'Halfway out I said I'd left my hip-top, ran back before he could say anything, found another set of stairs. But he got the CD.'

'Shit.'

'I've got other copies. Online and off.'

'I can't believe it. Not just Strick, but the deputy chief of the embassy.'

'They were both smuggling,' Jacob says grimly. 'And now they're both being blackmailed.'

Veronica nods, but somehow that doesn't sound quite right. Would a man like Dr Murray actually have met with Athanase, and put himself in a position where he could be blackmailed, if he had Strick to do the dirty work for him? And Danton too? Any two of them, maybe, but all three – it doesn't sound right, it feels like a jigsaw piece that doesn't quite fit. But it must be true. What other reason could there be for Murray, Strick and Danton to conspire?

'They'll be looking for us,' Jacob says. 'We have to get out of here.'

'How?'

'Entebbe. The airport. We have to get out of the country before they can find us.'

He has just turned on to the Entebbe highway when his hip-top rings. Jacob puts it to his ear for a moment, listens. 'Are you sure?' he asks. Then, in a taut, brittle voice, 'All right. Thank you. It's a misunderstanding, Henry. Don't worry. It will all be cleared up soon.'

He hangs up. Then he pulls the Toyota over to the side of the highway and brakes so hard the tyres screech and Veronica is thrown up against her seat belt.

'What is it?' she demands.

'That was Henry,' Jacob says, his voice weak. 'He says the police just came to his house. You and I are wanted for the murder of John Katumbi, aka Prester John, whose body was apparently discovered in my apartment.'

Veronica feels like she is falling. 'Oh my God.'

'They'll have notified the airport. We can't fly out.'

She thinks for a moment. 'We have to drive to the border. To Kenya.'

'There's a half-dozen police checkpoints on the Jinja highway alone. And that's on a normal day. Probably twice that when they're actually after someone. We're lucky he called before we reached one on this road. The police have cell phones, they'll broadcast our descriptions via text message. A runaway white couple isn't exactly hard to find in Uganda.'

'Can't you do something about the broadcast?'

Jacob hesitates. 'Not if it's already gone out – but maybe.'

He grabs his hip-top, tries to log in to Telecom Uganda's master database server – and stares at the words LOGIN FAILURE. He retries, typing his password very slowly and carefully. Same result.

'They locked me out,' he says dully. 'Maybe last night, maybe just now. Prester must have told them what I could do. I never put in a back door. I should have, of course I should have, but I never thought I'd need it, I just never imagined we'd find something this big. What a fucking *idiot* I am.'

'It's OK,' Veronica says.

'No, it's not. We have to turn our phones off, all of them. I made them invisible but if they look hard they'll be able to reverse that and track us. Take the battery out too. Just to be sure.'

She nods quietly. Cars whizz past in both directions as they remove the batteries from their cell phones. Veronica feels like they are rearranging the deckchairs on the Hindenburg. She wonders how long before a police car passes and notices the two white people pulled over on the hard shoulder.

'How can they do this?' Veronica asks. 'How can they make the Uganda police come after us?'

'Because they have friends in high Ugandan places. Remember what Derek wrote about bought-off locals?' Jacob takes a deep breath. 'This is bad. This is extremely bad. If the police find us, no way we live long enough to tell our story to anyone who cares. We'll be shot trying to escape or something. Like Prester.'

'Then what can we do? Where can we go?'

Jacob shakes his head. 'I have no idea.'

15

Jacob stares out at the Kampala–Entebbe highway, stretched before them like a black ribbon laid across Uganda's green hills, and tries to think of a way out. No solution is apparent. Despite the equatorial heat he feels cold, his heart is thumping, panic is threatening to swamp his mind like a tsunami, wash it clear of all reason.

Veronica reaches out and takes his hand. He squeezes it tightly. There must be a way out. There has to be, for Veronica's sake; he got her into this mess, he has to get her out. This is a solvable problem, it has to be.

'Lake Victoria,' he says. 'Maybe we can charter a boat to Tanzania.'

'There are police at the port. They'll be looking for us.'

'Yeah. *Fuck*.'

'Maybe the Canadian embassy? Or the media?'

He considers. 'No. Embassies don't help you when you're wanted for murder. They'll just turn us over and promise to visit in jail. Media – by the time we convince anyone we're not crackpots it'll be too late. We have to get out of the country first.'

'At least we've got our passports.'

Think outside the box, he tells himself. But this box seems like an inescapable cage. 'OK. We have to get out of Uganda. We've got passports. Maybe five hundred dollars cash. Clothes. Cell phones we don't dare turn on. A car that will get us exactly as far as the next police checkpoint. Nobody we can trust.' He shakes his head and sags back in defeat. 'I'm sorry. We're fucked. There's no way out.'

Veronica says, 'Rukungu.'

Jacob blinks. They dropped Rukungu off at the Hotel Sun City this morning, just after arriving in Kampala. As far as Jacob was concerned the man then ceased to exist. 'What about him?'

'We can trust him. Lydia too.'

'Great. An *interahamwe* murderer and a refugee hooker dying of Aids. I'm sure they'll be a big help. What do you want to do, hide in that hotel for ever?'

'It beats sitting here.'

Jacob can't argue with that. A potential hiding place isn't much, but it's something. Maybe with time to concentrate he can think of a way out. They have until tomorrow morning at the latest. Then their faces will appear on the front page of all Kampala's newspapers. He puts the Toyota into drive, eases it into a U-turn and heads back towards Kampala.

Something moves in the corner of Veronica's vision, and she starts, but it's only a cockroach scuttling across the bathroom floor. Jacob lies on the bed next to her. His eyes are closed but she can tell by his breath that he's awake. She looks around the tiny room, at the holes in the wall, the shredded mosquito net dangling from the fan that doesn't work above the thin torn mattress on which they sit, the mattress beneath which they found Derek's notes and secret second cell phone less than a week ago. She starts breathing hard again, feels herself break out in sweat. This room is too small, too much like a coffin, she feels a desperate, fluttering need to escape, to get out by any means necessary; she feels a panicky scream begin to build up in her gut.

Veronica closes her eyes and tries to make herself breathe slowly and deeply, to think of anything but the tight confines of this room. It shouldn't be hard. There are so many other fears to focus on. It feels like they're up against some kind of enormous machine, a steamroller that will annihilate them for the sin of accidentally getting in its way. She tries to tell herself that the walls closing in are the least of her problems, but it doesn't help, her heart keeps thumping erratically, like a frightened bird in her ribcage.

'We should never have stayed,' she says angrily, trying to displace her fear with rage. 'We should have gone home like Prester told us, like everyone told us. Jesus, this is so crazy. We didn't do anything wrong. How did we wind up hiding in this shithole?'

Jacob doesn't answer.

'If they find us they'll kill us, won't they? They'll actually kill us. This is so fucking crazy. We were so stupid. We should have gone home.'

'Well, we didn't,' he says harshly, opening his eyes. 'Yes, we should have. Yes, it's my fault, is that what you're getting at? I don't know what to say. I'm sorry.'

'Your fault?' Veronica looks at him, astonished. 'What are you talking about? You didn't make me do anything.'

Jacob shrugs. 'It feels like my fault.'

She changes the subject. 'How long has it been?'

'Hours. Look. It's almost dark out.' He gestures to the single cracked window, covered with gunk, which faces a sheer concrete wall.

'We can trust them. They won't tell on us.'

'No. They'll just take our money and run.'

Lydia and Rukungu have taken Jacob and Veronica's ATM cards and gone to the downtown Barclays to withdraw as much money as possible. They didn't dare go themselves and risk discovery. Driving into Kampala, finding a place behind the Sun City to park and sneaking into the hotel had been terrifying enough.

'I don't think so,' Veronica says.

'I don't see why they wouldn't. She's a hooker. He's a sociopath.'

'He's not a sociopath. He saved my life. He didn't have to.'

'He's a mass murderer.'

'That was a long time ago. I'm sure he came to Kampala for Lydia. I wonder what their story is.'

Jacob smiles mordantly. 'Oh, you know. Same old cliché. Boy meets girl, boy commits genocide, boy loses girl.'

She winces. 'That's not funny.'

'That's Africa.'

'I don't think he's a sociopath. I think he's . . . he's repented.'

'I think he's using us, just like he was using Derek, and we'll never see him again.'

She shakes her head. 'What do we do if you're right?'

Jacob has no answer. Veronica lies back on the bed, closes her eyes and tries to think. Something has been bothering her since the embassy, a mental itch that won't go away, a vague but nagging notion that they have misunderstood something vital.

The idea that Danton, Strick and Dr Murray conspired to smuggle gold and coltan out of the Congo, and are now being blackmailed by al-Qaeda – the more she thinks about it, the less it makes sense. Veronica would have sworn that Danton would never have got involved in something as sordid as African smuggling. Prester was totally convinced that Strick was not corrupt. And the idea of Danton, Strick and Dr Murray, smart and cautious men, all being so careless as to leave evidence that could be used to blackmail them – it just seems unlikely.

She thinks of the expression on Danton's face when he said he came to Uganda to save lives. She was married to him for seven years, and she knows he meant it.

She thinks back to Rukungu telling them that the man who killed Derek wasn't al-Qaeda, wasn't even a Muslim, was one of Athanase's *interahamwe* thugs dressed up in a dishdasha, and furthermore that the only Arab among the *interahamwe* was a trader with no religion but money.

Veronica opens her eyes wide.

'Jacob,' she says.

He looks at her.

247

'Tell me something,' Veronica says slowly. 'How do we know, how do we actually *know*, that there were ever any terrorists?'

Jacob stares at her. 'What are you talking about? You mean in the Congo?'

'Yes.'

'But – we saw them.'

'No we didn't. We saw three black men in dishdashas. One of whom we now know was just one of Athanase's men. And one Arab guy who, if you think about it, never actually did anything except pose for the camera.'

Jacob considers, remembers. 'True. But why would Athanase pretend to be working with al-Qaeda?'

'Maybe because Strick and Danton and Dr Murray told him to.'

'*What?*'

'I don't know,' she admits. 'Maybe I'm wrong. But something about all this just doesn't seem to make any sense.'

'They don't benefit from a fake al-Qaeda scare. Nobody does.'

'No.' Veronica sighs. She should have known the idea was too crazy to be true.

Then Jacob says, thoughtfully, 'No, wait. That's not actually true. There is one guy who did very well off our abduction, isn't there?'

She looks at him.

'Our friend from Zimbabwe. General Gideon Gorokwe. Remember what Prester said? A couple weeks ago he was an evil general from a pariah state. Today he's getting weapons, meeting with American diplomats, he's a valuable ally in the War on Terror.'

'Right.' Veronica sits up. 'Maybe Gorokwe invented fake terrorists to get American support. Maybe he and Athanase were in cahoots.'

Jacob shakes his head. 'No. Sorry. If al-Qaeda aren't really in the Congo, then what's with the surface-to-air missiles?'

'Maybe they're for Gorokwe.'

'What does he need them for? More to the point, why did Strick want to get them to him? Why would Danton and Strick and Dr Murray get into bed with Gorokwe and Athanase?'

Veronica can't think of any answer. She tries to imagine what could bind her multimillionaire ex-husband, a senior American diplomat and a CIA agent to an *interahamwe* warlord and a Zimbabwean general, and fails.

'To save lives,' she says, repeating her ex-husband's words. 'That's why Danton said he was here. He actually said it like he meant it.'

'Yeah? Whose lives?'

She shrugs. 'He does donate a lot of money to Africa. Mostly to Zimbabwe, his mother was born there. Until last year, when Mugabe threw out most of the NGOs and stopped accepting money. So I guess that's one way Danton might be connected to Gorokwe. But I don't see how you save lives with surface-to-air missiles. I mean, he's deluded enough to believe you can, if you kill the right person.'

Jacob considers that for a moment. Then he stiffens.

Veronica looks at him curiously. 'What?'

'Holy fucking God.'

'*What?*'

'Kill the right person,' he repeats. 'Think about it. If you're right, if this was all a plot to get Gorokwe Western support. After you did that, who would you want to kill?'

She shrugs, uncomprehending.

'Mugabe,' he says. 'The president of Zimbabwe. They're going to shoot him down and have Gorokwe take over with American support.'

They stare wordlessly at one another for what feels like a long time.

Then Jacob half laughs. 'Jesus. You've got to give them credit for thinking big, don't you? And we thought this was about a few smugglers and terrorists. They're gunning for their own fucking *country*. The president of Zimbabwe dies in a mysterious plane crash, shot down by missiles. Russian missiles, smuggled in from Zanzibar, made to look like they're going to al-Qaeda in case they get intercepted en route. Nice touch. Good attention to detail. And then the USA, aided by nudges from Agent Strick and Dr Murray on the ground, plus rich Mr DeWitt and his paid lobbyists, naturally throws its support in the inevitable succession battle behind noble General Gorokwe, who they think so very highly of ever since he rescued American hostages from those nasty al-Qaeda terrorists. Nobody's going to care that those terrorists never existed, not after the fact. Saddam's weapons of mass destruction never existed either. It's elegant. It's fucking *brilliant*.'

'It makes sense,' Veronica says softly. 'It makes everything make sense.'

'And Derek was about to find out. So they abducted us, killed him and made it all look like the work of the terrorists whose non-existence Derek was about to discover.' Jacob laughs bitterly. 'And we thought Strick and Murray were corrupt. Oh no. It's much worse that that. They're fucking idealists. I bet this was never Gorokwe's idea. I bet they chose him. Danton's the money, he's involved so they don't have to sell arms to Iran or whatever. First they found their figurehead, then they rigged events to make sure the American government lined up behind him. And now that he's a staunch ally of course the USA will support Gorokwe once Mugabe's gone and he seizes power. This isn't even a coup. This is regime change.'

A long silence falls over the room.

There is a knock on the door. Both of them flinch.

'Who is it?' Veronica asks hoarsely.

Lydia's voice answers. 'It is us, Rukungu and I.'

Veronica sighs with relief, gets up and pulls open the loose, rusting bolt that holds the door shut. Lydia and Rukungu enter the room and she closes the door behind them.

'The machines gave us a million shillings,' Lydia says, as if she still can't quite believe their mechanical largesse.

Rukungu reaches into the black Adidas bag he carries and deposits a thick wad of Ugandan money on the bed beside Jacob. Veronica does a quick mental calculation. About five hundred US dollars. That leaves them with about a thousand in cash.

'You will give us a card?' Lydia asks nervously.

'One of them,' Jacob agrees. 'Mine. There's ten thousand dollars in that account, about twenty million shillings. You can take out maybe half a million a day. But they'll be tracking it. Make sure you never use it in the same bank twice in the same month, and if the machine eats the card, you turn around and walk away fast.'

Rukungu nods seriously. 'I understand.'

'Nobody followed you? You're sure?'

'No one followed us. You are safe here. We took great care.'

'And you're really going to drive us?' Jacob sounds like he can't quite believe this to be true.

'We have agreed. But we are refugees. We have no papers. The police will stop us.'

'That's fine.' Jacob pats the brick of money beside him. 'This is Africa. Who needs ID when you've got money? You better go get your things ready. We leave in fifteen minutes.'

Rukungu takes Lydia's arm and leads her out of the room. Veronica breathes a little more easily when they are gone. It was too crowded with four people crammed into this little space.

'This theory of ours,' Jacob says to her. 'It's testable.'

She blinks. 'Testable how?'

'We still have one phone we can use.' Jacob digs into his pocket and produces a candy-bar-sized Nokia. 'Derek's secret phone. The one he used here. The one he called Zimbabwe with. It's safe to use, nobody else knows its number, they can't track it to us. Or even if they can we'll be gone before they get here.'

'Who do you want to call?'

'Zimbabwe.'

Jacob puts the Nokia on speakerphone and dials a number from its memory. Three sets of doubled rings echo through the little room. Then a familiar voice replies. 'Yes?'

'Is this the man with no name?' Jacob asks.

'He and I might be connected in some way. Jacob Rockel, I presume?'

'Yes.'

'And is Veronica Kelly there?'

'Yes.'

'Fascinating. Forgive me, I don't normally try to ask awkward questions, but this time I just can't help my curiosity. Are you aware an Interpol alert went out earlier today calling for your arrest?'

After a moment Jacob says, 'We weren't aware, but we're not surprised.'

'We didn't do it,' Veronica says desperately. 'We've been set up. We've been framed.'

'Of course you have.'

'We're calling you for confirmation,' Jacob says.

'I see. Confirmation of what, precisely?'

'The information you had for Derek. The information he called you to get. Did it pertain to General Gideon Gorokwe?'

After a moment the voice says, 'You don't seriously expect me to answer that.'

'Derek called you to ask about Gorokwe, didn't he? Because he thought Gorokwe was involved with *interahamwe* smugglers. And then when you found out Gorokwe was helping the Americans chase the *interahamwe*, and their so-called terrorist allies, you thought this was strange, so you called to ask about it, didn't you? That was the real reason you called. You wanted to ask Prester because Derek had already let slip he wasn't a suspect any more.'

'It's an interesting supposition,' the man says carefully. 'Let's go back to your use of the words "so-called", if we may—'

Jacob says, 'We need to talk to Mugabe.'

'I beg your pardon?'

'Robert Mugabe. The president of Zimbabwe. We need to talk to him.'

252

'Right. As you do. You don't want much, do you? I'm sorry, Mr Rockel, but if you think I can put you in touch with our oh-so-esteemed president, you are barking up not just the wrong tree but frankly a rather poisonous one.'

'Can you tell us someone who *can* get us in contact?'

The British man says, acidly, 'Even if I could, to be perfectly honest I don't think I would. But it's a moot point. Mugabe's in China for some totalitarian tête-à-tête. He won't be back until next week.'

'Good,' Jacob says. 'Then there's time.'

'Time for what?'

Veronica opens her mouth to explain. Jacob shakes his head. She looks at him. He reaches out and covers the phone's mouth-piece.

'Getting out of Uganda isn't enough. Not with Interpol after us too. Kenya won't be any better. Nowhere will. Every customs officer and policeman in Africa is looking for us. You under-stand?'

Veronica just stares at him. She feels overwhelmed, as if she's been struck by a slow-motion tidal wave and has only just begun to tumble. 'Then what do we do?'

'This guy was a friend of Derek's. He might help us. But we have to meet him in person, show him what we've got. We can't convince him over the phone.'

She nods.

'I'm waiting,' the voice says drily.

Jacob removes his hand from the mouthpiece. 'We've been framed. If they catch us, if we get caught anywhere in Africa, they won't prosecute us, they'll *kill* us. These murder charges won't stick, they're just an excuse to grab us.'

'How tragic. And why exactly has this come to pass?'

'Because we've found out something about General Gorokwe. Something serious. Something that could affect, that will affect, the entire future of Zimbabwe.'

'How very melodramatic. What?'

Jacob says, 'We'll only tell you in person.'

After a moment the voice says, incredulously, 'I beg your pardon?'

'We've got evidence. You won't believe us without that. We need to show you.'

'Mr Rockel, I am not about to come to Uganda to visit a pair of wanted murderers.'

'Then we'll come to you. If you don't believe us then, you can do whatever you like, turn us over to Interpol, whatever.'

'You can't be serious.'

Jacob says, 'We're dead serious. We need to get to Zimbabwe as fast as we can.'

A long pause follows. Veronica is jittery. It feels like minutes are critical now, as if the Ugandan police or even military might track them down at any moment.

'*We didn't do it,*' she bursts out. 'Prester was our friend. They tortured him to death. That's what they'll do to us if they catch us. Please. You were Derek's friend. There's no one else. Help us. *Please.*'

When the man eventually speaks his voice is full of reluctance, but there's a tinge of curiosity as well. 'Tell you what. I'll do this much. If you actually do come here, I'll meet with you. I won't promise anything more than that. Get yourselves to Livingstone, in Zambia, on the Zimbabwe border. Give me an email address, one that can't be traced to you, and I'll send you details of what to do once you arrive. I promise I'll listen to you. No more than that.'

'Get to Zimbabwe?' Veronica asks. She feels betrayed. This sounds like the next worst thing to no help at all. 'How?'

'As to that,' the stranger says, 'I'm afraid you're on your own.'

Jacob has lost all track of time. It feels like it has stopped, like he and Veronica have been and will be forever crammed into this dark and ill-fitting pocket of space. The air stinks of gasoline, his head feels as if it is being crushed in a vice. Even with the spare tyre moved to the back seat there's barely room for them both in the trunk of the Toyota. Jacob lies curled in a painfully hunch-backed position, his left leg has gone half numb, and metal protrusions stab him every time they go over a bump, which means several times a minute on the good stretches of road. The trunk is open only a crack, enough to let in a little air. Veronica shudders in his arms and moans with every exhalation, as if experiencing a terrible nightmare, but she is awake. It took a visible effort of will for her to get into the trunk at all, and this journey will occupy five hours at least. Jacob has no idea how many of those hours have passed. Time has no meaning in this stinking darkness.

The timbre of the engine changes and the vehicle slows down. Jacob sees flashes of light outside. Another police checkpoint.

'Quiet,' he whispers into Veronica's ear. He isn't sure she can really hear him at all any more, her rational mind seems to have fled, leaving behind a terrified child – but then she stiffens, stops whimpering and starts breathing silently again. He squeezes her tightly. Her face is damp with tears.

'It's going to be OK,' he whispers.

He hears Rukungu's voice, and that of other men, the police. They hold each other closely, muscles tense with fear, breathing through their mouths, until the conversation finally ends and the Toyota accelerates forward again. A few minutes later they turn sharply to the left and begin to move along a bumpy dirt road. Jacob's head groans, he feels like his whole body is shaking apart, his bones and muscles are being unravelled by the endless, violent rattling. In one of the rare moments of calm that follow he wishes he could just hit his head and be knocked unconscious.

He is so dazed he doesn't realize the Toyota has come to a stop until the engine is switched off. A minute later the trunk lid yawns open, ushering in a blissful wave of cool night air. Rukungu has to bodily lift Veronica to freedom, and Jacob too needs his help to emerge from the trunk. He falls back against the vehicle, next to Veronica, both of them so shaken they can barely stand.

'Where are we?' Jacob manages.

'Suam,' Rukungu says. 'Near the border. It is almost dawn.'

Lydia offers them water. They drink greedily. Jacob looks around. One horizon is limned with light, outlining a huge mass to the south-east: Mount Elgon, on the Uganda–Kenya border. The Toyota has stopped beside a wide dirt road. In the distance, maybe a kilometre away, a single gas lamp illuminates a few wooden buildings and *bandas*. As Jacob's head clears and its ache fades away he slowly begins to realize they are on the brink of success. This border post is so remote there is no phone service, no way for the guards to know he and Veronica are fugitives. Not that Kenya is safe. They have to go overland all the way to Zimbabwe, across half of Africa, before they approach anything like safety. But this is a start.

'Is there anything to eat?' Veronica asks.

Lydia produces a packet of tasteless biscuits and a huge avocado that Jacob halves and sections with Derek's Leatherman. He has never eaten a finer breakfast in his life.

'We cannot cross with you,' Rukungu says. 'We have no papers.'

Jacob nods.

'Do you want us to stay?' Lydia asks.

Veronica shakes her head. 'No. You don't want to be seen with us.'

Rukungu says, 'Then we will go.'

Jacob looks at him. In the predawn light he can see Rukungu and Lydia only in silhouette, in outline. He has never felt so grateful to anyone. They didn't need to take the enormous risk of spiriting Jacob and Veronica out of the country. He supposes they did it for Derek, really, but he doesn't know why they are so loyal to the memory of his best friend. He doesn't really know anything about them: where they are from, how they met, how they were parted, what Rukungu did in Rwanda and in the Congo in the years after, how Lydia came to Kampala, why and how Rukungu came to betray Athanase to Derek – all these are mysteries. All

Jacob knows is that he owes them his life. He wishes there was time to enquire, to try to understand; he wishes he had cared and asked about their stories before. He had the opportunity. But they were just Africans, he didn't really care. And now it is too late.

'Thank you,' he says inadequately, and puts out his hand.

Rukungu and Lydia shake it, formally. Veronica hugs them both goodbye. Then Jacob shoulders the little pack that contains all the possessions he has left in this world, takes Veronica's hand in his and leads her towards the border, towards the dawn.

III   Zimbabwe

1

Veronica says, 'Where there's smoke there's fire.'

Jacob half smiles. 'Except here.'

The pale plume rising into the sky half a mile away, seen over the trees that line the road, looks exactly like smoke from a big fire. Even the distant noise sounds like something far away burning furiously. High above, the noon sun is surrounded by something Veronica has never seen before: a perfectly circular rainbow.

She pauses for a moment to appreciate the beauty, then takes a deep breath and looks back down to earth. No sense delaying any longer. 'All right. Let's go.'

The road that carried them the ten kilometres from Livingstone to the border ends at a chain-link gate. A series of other fences steers the small queue of pedestrians into a squat building labelled ZAMBIA EMIGRATION. Beyond this checkpoint, a metal bridge about three hundred feet long traverses a steep-walled gorge.

Jacob takes her hand as they wait, holding the small day packs that carry all their remaining worldly possessions. 'Almost there.'

Veronica forces a smile. This is their fourth border in four days. She knows in theory the line is good – busy officials are likely to hurry them along, bored ones are dangerous – but the anticipation is always worse than the crossing itself. Assuming, of course, that they don't get caught. A fate more likely to happen here than anywhere else. The tiny posts where they entered and exited Uganda, Kenya and Tanzania were so far from modern networked civilization it will likely take months for those immigration officers to learn that Jacob and Veronica were wanted fugitives, but this is a major transit nexus. When Veronica sees computers beyond the building's glass-fronted wickets, her stomach tenses and she starts to breathe fast.

'Those won't be connected to anything,' Jacob says quietly into her ear. His voice is reassuring, but his hand is clammy. 'They'll only know if they call in our names. They won't do that unless they get suspicious. And they won't get suspicious. There's nothing suspicious about us. Nobody's even dreaming that we'd come down here. Just stay cool and we'll be fine. If you're shaking, just pretend you're sick or something.'

The line edges forward. They begin to near the uniformed immigration officer. Veronica can't believe she's here, doing this, sneaking across a border, hoping to escape an Interpol warrant. It doesn't feel real. Nothing about their epic journey across half of Africa, in the hundred hours since they escaped Uganda, has felt particularly real.

Sunset at the Kenya–Tanzania border, watching clouds of winged termites erupt from a mound the size of a small house, with snowcapped Mount Kilimanjaro looming in the distance beyond. Their roller-coaster early-morning flight to Dar es Salaam, followed by a panicky taxi ride to the railway station, arriving only ten minutes before the departure of the weekly train to Zambia. A young woman moving along the length of the train at one of its many unscheduled stops, selling live locusts, a local delicacy, from a red plastic bowl. Ghostly stick-figure men and women, more like shadows than humans, standing beside the tracks and staring as the Tazara train rolled through the desiccated, drought-blasted hills of south-west Tanzania.

'Passport,' the immigration officer says.

Now that she is at the front of the line, in the moment of truth, she feels inexplicably calm and relaxed; her breath has slowed, her muscles have loosened. Maybe she has just run out of adrenalin. Veronica produces her passport and passes it over with steady hands. It seems strange that so much rests on that little blue booklet, that her ability to pass between nations is determined solely by the words and pictures within. The Zambian officer stamps it and hands it back without even looking at her name. Jacob receives the same treatment. Veronica's legs are weak with exhaustion and relief as they walk out of the immigration post. Only one more border post to go, and it should be the easiest of all.

When she steps on to the bridge she gasps aloud at the sudden sight of gargantuan Victoria Falls. The majestic curtain of water to her right, the source of that towering plume that is not smoke, tumbles over a four-hundred-foot cliff into a gorge that curves sharply before passing beneath this bridge. Amid the whitewater below she can see little inflatable blue-and-yellow rafts: tourists rafting the mighty Zambezi. They look like children's toys. More tourists, all white, some looking distinctly pale and nervous, cluster around the bungee-jumping booth midway across the bridge. Veronica half smiles as she passes. After her last few weeks, bungee jumping seems about as nerve-racking as a stroll through a flower garden. She wonders whether she's grown tough or just numb.

There is another line-up to enter Zimbabwe. Veronica is taken aback; she thought this was a pariah state. From the voices and accents most of these would-be adventure tourists are British, Australian and South African, with a sprinkling of Europeans. Two immigration officers are on duty. To Veronica's relief one is a woman. Yesterday's email from their only hope, their still-nameless contact in Zimbabwe, told them to go to the woman on duty.

They have to fill out forms before presenting their passports. Jacob's hands are now shaking from tension, it takes him three attempts to legibly complete a form, and this makes Veronica nervous too – surely this is exactly the kind of thing they look for. Jacob's face looks pinched and he is sweating heavily, he might as well be wearing a SUSPICIOUS CHARACTER T-shirt – but no one seems to notice. The woman takes Veronica's passport and thirty dollars cash, reads her name, hesitates for a moment, then gives her a knowing look through the glass. Veronica doesn't move. The woman smiles slightly, smooths a very modern visa sticker on to one of the passport's last virgin pages, stamps it, hands it back and waves her on. Jacob rejoins her as they walk into Zimbabwe.

'We made it,' she says giddily.

He does not share her euphoria. 'We have forty dollars cash left, and we can't use cards. If our man with no name doesn't show, we're finished.'

According to the email, they are meant to meet him outside the nearest Total gas station. A long road winds from the bridge up towards the town of Victoria Falls, past empty fields of dry bushes and grass. They pass little gaggles of white tourists, and a few men selling yogurt drinks, before they reach a remarkably modern strip mall that boasts a tourist information office, souvenir shops and the green-and-blue logo of Standard Chartered Bank. A massive and apparently brand-new hotel/casino complex built to First World standards is just opposite. Veronica is amazed: isn't Zimbabwe supposed to be a wretched, dangerous place?

'There,' Jacob says, pointing at a red sign. 'Total.' He pronounces it the French way, stressing the second syllable.

She looks. Like all gas stations, the Total has a big board that displays its prices. But this station's board says

PETROL	NO
DIESEL	NO
PARAFFIN	NO

No one is waiting for them outside. The little shop within the station is named La Boutique: its windows are cracked and the door hangs open as if broken. When they enter, the attendant, a young man reading some kind of photocopied book, stares at them as if customers are an unheard-of innovation. The shelves are covered with dusty containers of motor oil and spark plugs, and there are two large Coca-Cola fridges, both empty.

'No Coke?' Jacob asks, disappointed.

'No.'

'Do you know where I can get some?'

The young man shakes his head. 'No Coke anywhere.'

They retreat from this empty shell that was once a gas station. Veronica is more shocked by the absence of Coca-Cola than that of gasoline. She stops between the gas pumps, which are actually rusting from lack of use, digs into her cargo pants and produces her last pack of Marlboro Lights.

'What the hell,' she says to Jacob's questioning look. 'How often do you get to smoke in a gas station, right?'

He shrugs and takes a cigarette. She looks around. The elaborate casino complex is almost entirely deserted, weeds are growing in its lawns. Two of the souvenir shops are closed. There are no vehicles moving on the street.

A small boy approaches from across the street and asks, 'Change money?'

They shake their heads in unison.

The boy looks around furtively, then whispers, loudly, 'Are you Jacob and Veronica?'

They stare at him. Eventually Jacob says, 'What if we were?'

'You go down to Vic Falls Park. You go to jungle there.'

The boy scurries away before they can interrogate him.

'I guess he wants to meet in private,' Veronica says.

Jacob nods. 'There was a sign for Victoria Falls Park just after the bridge.'

They retrace their steps to this sign and follow a narrow concrete path away from the road, towards the falls. Veronica wonders what the boy meant by *jungle*. It is already apparent that Zimbabwe, like southern Zambia, is a dry country of brown grasses, wiry bushes, termite mounds and thorny trees, nothing like verdant central Africa.

A fat ranger at a guardpost informs them that admittance to the park will cost twenty of their last forty US dollars. Veronica tries to negotiate, but the ranger just stares at them stonily. Eventually she shrugs and pays; what choice do they have?

'I guess we can get money from the ATMs here if we really have to,' she says as they advance through the turnstile. 'Or a credit card advance.'

'I think Zimbabwe's been cut off from the global banking networks. Hyperinflation and failure to make payments, or something.'

Veronica winces. If this meeting with their mysterious stranger doesn't pan out they will be out of both money and options. 'We should have gotten money in Livingstone.'

'Then they'd know we were there, and they'd figure out we were coming here. We have to stay completely off the grid. No cards, no phone calls, no international flights.'

They advance into forested parkland along a path of cracked and broken concrete slabs. The roar of water grows as they advance, until suddenly the forest opens and they see the falls' entire length edge-on. They are a full half-mile across. A rainbow shimmers amid the whitewater as the Zambezi plunges endlessly over a sheer cliff. In the distance, the gorge bends sharply to the right, towards the bridge. The air is thick with ambient water.

'Look,' Jacob says, pointing to the right, to the lip of the gorge opposite the falls. There is a small patch of deep green vegetation where the spray is densest. Surrounded by dry grasses, it looks like an oasis in the desert.

They follow the paths along the dry side of the gorge and into a whole new ecosystem: palm trees, huge ferns, intertwining vines, leaves so dense they block out the sun. It reminds Veronica uncomfortably of the Impenetrable Forest. The concrete slabs in this bizarre patch of jungle are drenched with the perpetual spray; they have to pick their way carefully past mud and puddles.

The man waiting for them is tall and athletic, mid-twenties. His arms are ropy with muscle, his high cheekbones are carved into a statuesque face. His head is so closely cropped it is almost shaved, and his skin is very dark. His movie-star looks are marred by a sickle-shaped scar on his left cheek. He wears jeans, a red T-shirt and a denim jacket. Something about him, his watchful readiness, reminds Veronica of both Derek and Rukungu.

'Jacob Rockel, Veronica Kelly,' he greets them. His accent is African; this is not the nameless man on the phone. 'Are you alone?'

After a nervous moment Veronica admits, 'Yes.'

'My name is Lovemore. Please, wait.'

Moments later another man, short and white and tubby, emerges from the path that brought them here. He wears jeans, a T-shirt, muddy boots and a battered leather rucksack, and walks with a slight limp. A shock of brown hair and a dense pepper-and-salt beard adorn a shrewd, professorial face that has seen maybe fifty years.

'Terribly sorry for all this cloak-and-dagger guff,' he says with a self-deprecating grin, shaking their hands casually. 'Mostly childish nonsense, if you ask me. But we're living in interesting times here in Zimbabwe, have to dust off a few of the old tricks. Our esteemed government seems to feel the need to keep an eye on harmless old me.'

'You're who we talked to on the phone?' Veronica asks warily.

'The very same. Lysander Tennant, at your service, in the flesh. You've met my driver and minister without portfolio.' He nods towards Lovemore. Then his face hardens, and his voice, while remaining courteous, turns curt. 'Now then. I don't mean to be unwelcoming, but you'll understand I can't be found harbouring international fugitives without bloody good reason. I really shouldn't be talking to you at all. I'm here only out of that which killed the cat, and a certain morbid loyalty to our dear departed Derek. So you'd best think of this as a job interview. I'll give you five minutes. What happened in Uganda? What do you have for me?'

Jacob looks at Veronica.

She shrugs – what choice do they have? – and says, curtly, 'General Gorokwe is going to assassinate Mugabe with surface-to-air missiles.'

Lysander's stony face is wiped away for a moment by sheer amazement. Then it returns and he says, sceptically, 'Really. And why would he do a silly thing like that? He wouldn't have a hope in hell of taking charge afterwards.'

Jacob says, 'He thinks he does. He has American support. This whole thing was an American plan from the start. Gorokwe is just their instrument.'

'An *American* plan?' It takes a few seconds for Lysander to digest those words. He looks at Lovemore, who is listening intently. 'That's . . . no. That's ridiculous. They wouldn't, nobody could be that stupid. That would be madness. Sheer bloody madness.'

But this time he doesn't sound dismissive. He sounds worried.

'Maybe so,' Veronica says, 'but that's what they're doing.'

'They who? The White House? You can't possibly expect me to believe—'

'No. A few diplomats and CIA agents who faked that al-Qaeda scare in the Congo so that the US government would line up behind Gorokwe. Now that he's a friend of America, they'll back him to take over when Mugabe dies. I know it sounds crazy. But that's why Derek died, that's why Prester died, that's why we got kidnapped in the first place, that's why they're after us now. They're going to shoot down Mugabe first chance they get and try to install Gorokwe as president.'

Jacob adds, 'We have evidence.'

Lysander looks from one of them to the other for what feels like a long time. Then he looks at Lovemore, who nods, slowly.

Lysander says, reluctantly, 'I suppose you'd better show me.'

2

Entering the grounds of the Victoria Falls Hotel feels like walking into the nineteenth century. This elegant relic of colonialism boasts musty hallways, mahogany doors, faded paintings of great

British explorers, ancient maps of BOAC air services to Africa, a smoking room walled with books, and high-tea service. Even the furniture in Lysander's room looks like something from the set of a Jane Austen movie. His modern Toshiba laptop looks terribly out of place on a rolltop mahogany desk.

Jacob and Veronica wait tensely as Lysander and Lovemore go through the contents of Jacob's CD for the third time, watching the Toshiba's screen intently, as if there might be a hidden message within. Veronica realizes for the first time that actually they have very little evidence. Incomprehensible matrices of telephone and GPS records; some blurry, night-time photos from Jacob's camera; a few more from Prester's Razr phone; and their own testimony – all of which could easily have been faked.

Lysander turns from one of the night shots to Veronica. She braces herself for an interrogation: but instead he says, wonderingly, 'He was the one who held you down. I saw it on YouTube.'

Veronica blinks and looks more closely. It is the photo of Casimir, the muscle-bound *interahamwe* who murdered Derek. She remembers how he pulled her choking to the ground, and held her while the Arab put the machete to her throat. 'Yes.'

Jacob says, 'He killed Derek.'

Lysander frowns. 'I never saw that. YouTube didn't host that, it was on more prurient sites. Easy enough to find if you wanted, and apparently millions did, but not I.'

Veronica doesn't have anything to say to that.

'If what you're telling me is actually true, and please note I'm not saying I'm fully convinced yet, but if it is, then . . .' Lysander shakes his head, appalled. 'Then this is one of the most horrifically stupid ideas in history. I want Mugabe gone as much as the next rational man, but Christ almighty, there's not a lot of happy precedent for shooting down aeroplanes carrying African presidents. The Rwandan genocide was sparked when President Habyarimana was shot down. That's a million dead. The president of Burundi was with him, and that civil war *still* hasn't

269

ended. There's another quarter-million. Mobutu was supposed to be dead dictator number three on that flight. God knows what would have happened if the paranoid bastard hadn't changed his plans, but we know the wars after he finally did buy the farm killed three million more, and counting. You've seen what happened to eastern Congo. Then there's Mozambique, Samora Machel shot down by the South Africans, deny it though they try. I don't know how many people died, nobody does, but I do know that civil war took them back to the bloody Stone Age, they didn't even have matches or soap by the time it finally ended. You only blow up the big man if you don't have enough support for a proper coup. Because once he's gone all his jackals start fighting for the scraps. There's an old African proverb – when the elephants fight, the grass gets trampled. Well, I know Zimbabwe a good deal better than any starry-eyed American, and I'm telling you, never mind trampled, an assassination right now could start off a bushfire that would burn the whole bloody country.'

After a moment Jacob says, cautiously, 'You sound like you believe us.'

'No. I sound like I think I can't afford not to. But this isn't proof, what you have here, it isn't even evidence, it's barely circumstantial. I was wondering why you hadn't gone to the media if you were for real. Now I know. If I take this to my superiors they'll laugh me out of the room.'

Veronica says, 'I don't mean to pry, but who exactly are your superiors? The British?'

'If you don't mean to,' Lysander says curtly, 'then don't.'

Veronica falls silent, her face reddens, she feels like she's committed some unforgivable faux pas.

'If you're here to mislead me, if you're really part of that smuggling ring like Interpol says, believe me, you have come to the wrong place,' he continues. 'This has become a country where people disappear. Especially this last month. Important people, powerful people, have begun to disappear. People have started whispering about death squads working for Mugabe. Make no mistake, you'd do far better to turn yourselves in than to come here and try to deceive me.'

Jacob says, 'We're not lying, and you know it.'

'What I think I know or don't know doesn't matter right now. The question is, what can I prove?'

Jacob looks as if he wants to say something, but Veronica, sensing that this is the key moment, shoots him a look, and he shuts up. Lysander looks at Lovemore.

'I certainly understand the appeal of assassination,' Lysander mutters. 'It's not as if anyone supports Mugabe but his cronies. He's lost the plot, his wife's a hyena, and his government's a kleptocracy. But consider Amin, consider Bokassa, consider Mobutu. Consider the fact that our fine upstanding General Gorokwe is happy to conspire with the likes of Athanase. Then consider what I found out for Derek. That the general was profoundly involved in the Gukurahundi massacres of the early eighties. Zimbabwe's own little micro-genocide, twenty thousand dead. There's no actual surviving proof, but the men who told me are reliable sources. He's a genocidist himself. Gorokwe could easily be ten times worse than Mugabe.'

'And that's if it's a bloodless coup,' Lovemore says grimly.

Lysander nods. 'Exactly. If this does happen, if Gorokwe actually pulls the trigger, then love him or hate him, we'd best all start praying everything goes exactly according to his plan. Because God only knows how big a bloodbath this will set off if it goes wrong.'

After a second Veronica asks, 'So what do we do?'

Lysander's frown deepens. 'We, is it? I suppose it is. Very temporarily. Very well. We go back to Harare tonight. That's the capital, the big city. I'll report from there, ask Vauxhall for assistance, call in all my favours. Mugabe's due to fly back from China in four days. We've got that long to try to find out where they are, what their plan is, and how to stop them.' He shakes his head. 'Interpol fugitives. Surface-to-air missiles. Bloody hell. I need a drink.'

*   *   *

'I'm afraid we're going to have to take the train,' Lysander says, as they sit in the hotel's gardens, eating scones, sipping Earl Grey and watching the glorious view of sunset over Victoria Falls. 'We can't take the chance of your names on flight records, they might be keeping an eye out for you, and I don't have any friends in the local airport. In Harare or Bulawayo I could get you documents, but not here. No choice but the overnight train.'

'That sounds fine,' Jacob says. 'We took the train from Dar es Salaam to Zambia.'

Lysander smiles wryly. 'I think you'll find today's Zimbabwe Railways to be considerably less luxurious.'

Veronica winces. The Tazara train that took them into Zambia was anything but luxury. 'Aren't there any buses?'

'Good heavens, no. Nobody's going to waste petrol on a ten-hour drive, not in this country. You do realize petrol – I'm sorry, gasoline – is not legally available for sale anywhere in this country?'

'Why's that?' Jacob asks, amazed.

'Various reasons. One is that the government has no foreign exchange with which to buy it. Another is that they fix petrol's price so low that stations can't afford to sell it. But the real reason is that there's big money in the black market, and most of it goes to government cronies. Unfortunately their distribution networks are as dubious as they are. Here in Vic Falls we're right near the border, there's plenty of supply. And Harare's black market is apparently inexhaustible. But in much of the country right now there's no petrol available no matter how many US dollars you wave in the air. They simply don't have it.'

'So what do they do?' Veronica asks.

Lysander shrugs.

'We use ox carts as ambulances,' Lovemore says unexpectedly. 'We travel from Harare to our home village to attend a funeral, and we must remain for weeks because there is no petrol to carry us home. In the countryside now, in the bush, we no longer live in this twenty-first century. We have returned to the nineteenth.'

A plump bow-tied waiter brings them the bill. At first Veronica thinks it must be some kind of misprint: the total scrawled on the bottom of the slip of paper is more than a million dollars. But Lysander nods absently, digs into his pack, comes up with two wads of pink notes as thick as a deck of cards, each wrapped in a rubber band. He drops one wad on the table and adds a handful from the other. Each note is labelled *20,000*.

'What's the exchange rate?' Jacob asks, equally stunned.

Lysander smiles thinly. 'At the government rate, which nobody uses, about twenty-five thousand Zim dollars to one US. At the black-market rate, more like a hundred thousand. Seven years ago it was twenty to one.'

Jacob whistles.

'In Zimbabwe the last seven years have been very educational,' Lovemore says. His voice still sounds completely serious, but Veronica sees a hint of a sardonic smile. 'Every man on the street has become an economics master. Every housewife can give lectures on the perils of hyperinflation and the importance of foreign exchange. We have become so knowledgeable, and so hard working. Every day we hustle, we work so hard. We have no choice. Because every day we wake up knowing all the money we have will soon be worth nothing.'

'Half the adult population's fled the country,' Lysander says. 'To South Africa, Botswana, Zambia. The money they send home is the only thing that keeps half this country alive. And the other half is starving, or dying of Aids, or both. And we used to be the breadbasket of Africa, we used to feed our neighbours.'

'What happened?' Veronica asks.

He sighs. 'Mugabe went mad is what happened. He was a perfectly good leader for a long time, by African standards. He was practically enlightened. Then seven years ago he and his thugs, his so-called war vets, most of them weren't even born during the civil war here, they started to invade all the white-owned farms and drive out the whites. That violence erased the tourism industry overnight, the expulsion of most of the good farmers wiped out all the crops, and the Zim dollar collapsed. We've been lurching from crisis to crisis ever since. Bad to worse. Aids, corruption, drought. This country's like a rock rolling downhill towards a cliff. And if you're right, we're in danger of going into the abyss as soon as this week.' Lysander stands. 'Come on. Let's get to the station in case tonight is a night of miracles and the train actually departs on time.'

It is fully dark by the time a rusting train wheezes to a halt and its doors open to accept the hundreds of passengers that clog the Victoria Falls railway platform. A few are middle-aged business-men with enormous amounts of luggage in tow, but most are dressed in ragged clothing and carry very little. There are no other white people: it seems those tourists who dare to enter Zimbabwe at all go no farther than Victoria Falls.

Lovemore leads Veronica and Jacob through the crowd and on to the train. Its interior is stained grey linoleum and tarnished metal. Naked wires protrude from holes in walls, and the cracked windows are jammed permanently open or shut. They pass a rusted, filthy bathroom. Their first-class berth has four bunks covered with torn blue upholstery, a rusting fold-out table and a sink that doesn't work. One of the two fluorescent lights overhead is dead; the other flickers like a strobe light. Cockroaches crawl in the dark corners. Lysander was right, this makes the battered Tazara rolling stock that carried them to Zambia look like the Orient Express.

'Well,' Veronica says gamely, 'at least it's cheap.'

Their tickets cost the equivalent of three US dollars apiece, at the black-market rate. The cramped size of the berth makes her a little uncomfortable, but its window is stuck half open, that helps, and compared to the five harrowing, endless hours she spent trapped in the trunk of a car, on their way to the Ugandan border, this is the Taj Mahal.

'Where's Lysander?' Jacob asks.

'Seeing Innocent,' Lovemore says. 'The train conductor. He's a friend.'

Lysander appears shortly after, along with a middle-aged black man wearing glasses and a cheerful smile. Innocent shakes hands briefly with Veronica and Jacob, then speaks briefly with Lysander and Lovemore in an African language. After another round of handshakes he disappears down the corridor.

'Happy coincidence he's on duty,' Lysander says with a satisfied smile. 'Foreigners are supposed to show passports to get tickets, and I'd rather not have your names on record. For the purpose of this journey you two are honorary Zimbabwe residents.'

'You speak the language,' Veronica says. 'I'm impressed.'

Lysander waves self-deprecatingly. 'Not really. I grew up speaking Shona, that's the majority language here, but Innocent speaks Ndebele. Lovemore's fluent but I can barely get by.'

She looks at him. 'Grew up speaking Shona?'

'Oh, I was born here. Zimbabwe passport, quite useful, I can't be expelled. British passport too, of course. We moved to the UK when I was young, because of the civil war, and I didn't come back until the nineties. To study wild dogs, of all things. Then I started buying and selling art around the country, mostly just as a sideline, to help finance my research. There's wonderful art here. Then when it all started to go wrong the embassy chaps realized I might be useful. A few heartstring-tugging appeals to God and Queen and country, and here I am, on Her Majesty's secret service, in a very quiet and unofficial way.'

Veronica smiles, mostly with relief. Obviously he has decided to trust them.

Lysander looks around. 'Back when it was Rhodesian Railways, or even ten years ago, these were proper trains, first class meant wood panels and luxury, they brought you food and bedding, they departed on time. Now you count yourself lucky to leave at all.'

'What happens if the train doesn't go?' Jacob asks.

Lysander shrugs. 'Usually it eventually does. But if there's a breakdown here tonight, we'll have to try to fly tomorrow. It'll be a big risk, but we'll have to take it, no time for anything else.'

They wait anxiously. Almost an hour passes before the train finally lurches into motion. After a bumpy first few minutes the lurching and shuddering smooths into a kind of soothing rattling, and they celebrate departure with beer and cigarettes.

Then Jacob and Lysander climb into their upper bunks. Lovemore simply lies down on the bunk opposite Veronica, closes his eyes and is asleep in less than a minute; he doesn't seem to even notice the cold breeze from the open window. Veronica puts on three layers of shirts and two of socks, and folds her small pile of remaining clothes into a pillow. Jacob leans down and switches out the light. She takes his outstretched hand for a moment. Then she leans back and closes her eyes. She is very tired, and for the first time in longer than she wants to remember she feels safe. It takes only moments for the train's rocking motion and white noise to lull her too into deep sleep.

There is a hard hand on her shoulder, shaking her awake. Veronica comes halfway out of her deep sleep and opens her eyes to flickering fluorescent light. For a bad moment she doesn't know where she is or why, she doesn't recognize the bearded man standing over her, or the two black men flanking him. She pushes his hand away violently. Then her mind's gears stop grinding and begin to mesh. Lysander, the British spy. She is in Zimbabwe, on a train. The other men are Lovemore and Innocent the train conductor. They can't have reached Bulawayo, the train is still moving, and it is still night.

'What's going on?' she asks, in a ragged voice.

'I'm afraid it seems we've got a bit of a problem,' Lysander says, but she knows immediately from his voice that it's a great deal worse than that. 'There are soldiers on the train. I'm afraid they're looking for you two.'

3

'This is crazy,' Jacob mutters. 'How can they possibly know we're here?'

'They must have had someone watching in Victoria Falls,' Lovemore says.

Innocent says something in a husky voice.

'The train stopped at an army base, just now,' Lovemore translates. 'Other nights it passes through without stopping, he has never before seen them signal for a stop. The soldiers embarked there.'

'Is it so bad if the army gets us?' Jacob asks. 'I mean, we're trying to save their president's life. If we can just convince them—'

'No,' Lysander says. 'Not just any army base. The Fifth Brigade. The same unit I'm told Gorokwe served in, during the Gukurahundi. The Matabeleland massacres.'

Jacob groans. 'Shit. His old army buddies. And we walked right into it.'

'We have to hide,' Veronica says. She looks around for a suitable place. Beneath the berths? The luggage compartment above? Both are too obvious, they'll be found in seconds. But there is nowhere else. Do they have time to flee down the corridor and try to find some hiding spot elsewhere on the train?

The question is answered before she can ask it. A metal door slams and loud voices fill the corridor outside, only two or three berths away, barking orders. The soldiers are in their car. Veronica's heart begins to pound, she feels her breath begin to quicken, her lungs seem squeezed half shut, she feels cold, her skin feels stretched too tight – but she has now grown almost accustomed to her body's fight-or-flight reaction, and this time her mind does not shut down, she can still think clearly. She never imagined that fear for her life might grow so terribly familiar.

'Only one way out,' she says quietly.

All eyes turn to the open window.

*   *   *

There is a little table set into the wall immediately beneath the window. Lovemore crouches on that table, facing into the car, grabs the top of the window frame, extends his head and shoulders into the night – then ducks them back in as a wooden pole goes past, less than a foot from the window. To Veronica's relief it does not go past particularly quickly. The train's locomotive is old and slow, they probably aren't moving at more than twenty miles an hour. But that's plenty fast enough to break your neck if you hit the ground the wrong way.

The soldiers' voices are closer now, the next berth over. Innocent went out to try to stall them, but it doesn't sound as if he's having much luck, their voices sound hostile, angry. Veronica checks to see that their door is still locked by its single metal bolt. Lovemore tries again. His hands leave the window frame and find some purchase above, his legs straighten and levitate away from the table, and then he is gone. Jacob climbs awkwardly up on to the table.

A fist hammers on their door and a voice shouts a demand.

'Hurry,' Lysander says, so quietly Veronica can barely hear him.

Jacob, clumsier and less athletic than Lovemore, manages to contort himself so his gangly body extends out of the window. Then he slips, his foot gives way and he starts to fall; it seems to be happening in slow motion, Veronica's heart convulses as Jacob begins to topple away from the window – and a muscular, dark-skinned hand reaches down as if from the heavens, catches a flailing wrist, steadies him.

The soldiers at their door resume their hammering and shouting, and this time they don't stop.

'They say they're going to break it down,' Lysander murmurs urgently into Veronica's ear as Jacob pulls himself or is pulled up and out of the window. 'You go. I'll stay.'

She looks at him, alarmed.

'They'll be awfully suspicious if they find an empty berth locked from the inside. Fear not. I know how to handle these people. I'll be fine.' He tries to smile.

278

Something hits the door so hard that the bolt that holds it bends backwards slightly.

'All right, all right!' Lysander shouts, and the cacophony on the other side of the door falls silent for a moment. 'Just give me a moment to get dressed.'

He nods to her. Veronica realizes she doesn't have time to argue. She steps up on to the table, trying to be quiet, holds the side of the window frame and sticks her head outside. No oncoming poles are evident. She looks up and sees the heads and arms of Jacob and Lovemore, on top of the train only a few feet above her. She reaches up towards them, each takes an arm and the two men lift her up like a rag doll. Jacob's contribution is almost irrelevant; Lovemore is phenomenally strong and all but single-handedly pulls her up and on to the roof.

For a moment she lies on her belly, breathing hard, cold iron against her face as the train rattles and vibrates beneath her. Then she carefully pulls herself up to her knees and looks around. The roof of the train is trapezoidal in cross-section, two slight slopes on either side rising to a flat walkway down the middle. They are moving through a vast field of dry grasses lit by the hanging crescent moon. The stiff wind and the rocking, lurching motion make it hard to keep her balance even on her knees, she has to reach out frequently to steady herself. The wind and the churning train-sounds drown out all else, she can't hear what if anything is happening to Lysander in the berth below.

Veronica wishes she had taken the thirty extra seconds to collect her day pack and its contents. She has nothing left but her clothes, her shoes, her passport in her money belt, cigarettes and lighter in one of her cargo pants' side pockets, useless cell phone and Leatherman in the other, and her empty wallet in her back pocket. She supposes it's better than nothing. She pulls out her phone, intending to turn it on and check the time.

Jacob grabs her. 'Don't,' he says. 'No phones, never, not in this country.'

She understands and replaces it in her pocket. She supposes it doesn't matter what time it is. They have to wait up here until they are safe, however long it takes. Maybe all the way to Bulawayo.

Veronica is freezing, the icy wind is relentless, she can't stop shivering. Jacob kneels behind her, his arms wrapped around her, but his limbs too are cold and she can hear his teeth chatter. Lovemore, apparently insensate to the frigid wind, stands like a surfer atop the moving train, peering down its length.

Veronica wonders whether the soldiers have fully searched the train by now, whether it might be safe to go back in and hide in a warm corner. But of course they can't. Better to risk hypothermia than a firing squad.

Lovemore crouches back down and says, conversationally, 'Once I was on a train that struck an elephant near here. We are not far from Hwange park. The elephants have grown too many for the park, there is not enough food there, so many forage outside. Perhaps this one was old and did not hear the train. Or perhaps it was curious. Nothing troubles an elephant. They are slow to learn fear.'

Veronica stares at him. That is a potential hazard she had not even considered. 'Really? What happened?'

'It died.'

'I mean to the train.'

Lovemore shrugs as if that hardly matters. 'The lead car derailed. There were many injuries.'

After a silent minute Lovemore stands back up and sights down the train again – but this time he drops immediately back into a crouch, one hand on the slippery metal beneath him. He looks like an NFL lineman waiting for the ball to be snapped, peering forward, muscles taut, ready for action.

'What is it?' Jacob asks.

'Someone else on the train. On the engine car.'

280

Veronica stiffens and turns to look. The high moon sheds enough light that she can see motion at the end of the train, near the engine. Oncoming motion. She can't tell how many.

'Soldiers,' Lovemore says grimly. 'They have seen us.'

Veronica looks back down the length of the train. The gaps between the cars are narrow enough for the sure footed to step across. The several men in the distance make their way slowly but inexorably along the train, towards their quarry. Their attempt to hide has failed.

She looks out at the field of darkness through which they move, and takes a deep breath. She can't stop shivering. 'I guess we've got no choice.'

There's a little ridge at the rim of the roof, maybe an inch high, just enough for Jacob to hold on to as he worms his way sideways over the edge, half slipping, half dangling, until he is literally holding on by his fingertips. Veronica gasps as a wooden pole flashes past the train, but it isn't quite close enough to knock Jacob off.

The soldiers are only three cars away now, and closing fast; they seem to have gotten the knack of leaping over the gaps between cars.

'Don't think about it,' Jacob says. She can barely hear him, she isn't sure whether he's talking to himself or giving her advice. 'Just go. Try to land on your butt and roll.'

Then his hands vanish and he disappears into the night. The rattling train drowns out any sound of impact. Veronica stares at the space Jacob's hands just occupied. He might already be dead.

'Hurry!' Lovemore says urgently.

She nods, drops to her hands and knees and begins crawling towards the edge of the train. The slippery metal is rocking precariously beneath her and when she nears the edge she switches to belly-crawling. She grabs the ridge and slowly, agonizingly, works herself over the edge of the train; it isn't easy to do without falling, especially when the train itself is shaking violently back and forth, and wooden posts keep flashing past.

She hears shouts over the grinding noise of the train, and when she looks up she sees that the half-dozen soldiers are now only one car away, and running towards them. Sudden desperation lends Veronica a gymnast's speed and grace. She swings her whole body down at once, catches herself by her fingers as her legs and torso fall down the outer wall of the train. Her shoulders squawk with pain but she manages to hold on. Lovemore is already sliding and scrambling to the edge beside her. Veronica lifts her feet so they are flat against the wall of the train, then uses her legs to propel herself back, away from the train, into the darkness. For a moment she hangs weightless in the air. It feels like flying.

4

'Jacob,' Veronica says, her voice frantic. 'Jacob, wake up, please. Please, you have to wake up. Jacob, *please*!'

Jacob's world is pain. He is shaking. No, he is being shaken, someone's hands are on his shoulders, pushing and pulling. Veronica's hands. He opens his eyes, and his mouth too, to complain. It is night and he can barely make out Veronica's face as she kneels over him. There are tears in her eyes. A glittering curtain of stars hangs above her. He lies on a bed of rough earth and jagged stones, poorly cushioned by grass as dry as sandpaper. He can't remember why.

'Wha's going on?' Jacob manages.

Veronica takes a deep, relieved breath, then says, 'They've stopped the train down the track, I don't know how exactly, but we heard shots. They're coming. We have to go.'

There is a black man standing beside her, a man with a gun in his hand, watching silently, a man Jacob feels he knows. He searches his mind and finds a dim memory of a train, a vague notion that they are being chased. He gets up. He feels like he is watching himself stand, a witness rather than a participant; he observes with admiration as his limbs coordinate to draw his

282

battered body up into a gravity-defying bipedal configuration, and his muscles fight to keep him there. He has new bruises aplenty, but nothing seems torn or broken. His head has taken at least some of the impact of the fall. He takes a single step and suddenly comes back to himself. It feels like imploding. He falls to his knees and throws up, his abdominal muscles cramp with agony as he retches and shudders. Veronica kneels and hovers over him, holding his shoulders lightly with nervous hands.

'I'm fine,' he manages to say. 'It's OK. I'm back.' Then he is throwing up again. But when it is finally over he does feel stronger, as if he has purged himself of some weakness, left nothing but animal vitality. He can feel pain across a frightening amount of his body, but it is as if he feels it through a cushion, he is aware of it but unaffected. Jacob staggers back to his feet and looks around. The lights of the train are dimly visible about a kilometre down the track. They are in a field of dry waist-high grass. About a hundred feet from the railway track he can see a sparse forest of withered, leafless trees silhouetted by moonlight.

'What do we do?' he asks Veronica and Lovemore. He re-members Lovemore again, remembers dangling from the edge of the train and letting go. He supposes he suffered a concussion in the fall. He feels physically capable again but his mind is like scrambled eggs, he is in no shape to make any decisions. At least they were right that the soldiers would not follow; the train wasn't moving too fast but nobody would throw themselves from it who didn't actually have to.

She says, 'We run.'

'I'm sick of running,' he says petulantly.

'If you have a better idea I'd love to hear it.'

Jacob looks back to the train and tries to make his brain work. He can see motion in the dry grass beside the tracks. Soldiers coming after them. If he can see them, beneath this hatefully bright moon, then they can see him, and hiding in this drought-shrivelled grass will never work.

'OK,' he says. 'Maybe we can lose them in the trees.'

But either their motion stands out too sharply in the moonlight, or one of the soldiers has preternaturally good night vision. They can't have night vision goggles, Jacob thinks loopily, they don't have any money for that, it would take a whole backpack full of Zimbabwe dollars to buy a single pair, and besides, the country is under sanctions, no military technology sales allowed, that's why Gorokwe has to smuggle his missiles in from Russia – but whatever the reason, every time he looks over his shoulder, the rustling motion of the soldiers is a little closer.

Jacob is too unsteady on his feet to sprint, Lovemore is now moving with a definite limp, and Veronica is bruised too; the best they can do is jog. Their heavy footsteps rustle loudly, cutting through the slight whispers of the dry grass in the night wind. Even in pitch black the soldiers might be able to track them by sound. Ahead of them an open savannah of arid grass and trees stretches on to the moonlit horizon. Behind them, the soldiers are less than half a kilometre away and closing fast.

'I think we're fucked,' Jacob gasps.

Veronica says, 'Do you have any money? Zim dollars?'

Jacob finds the question so bizarre he almost stops in his tracks. 'What do you want to do, bribe them?'

'Just tell me!'

'Yes. A million.' He changed ten US dollars yesterday, at the hotel.

'Give me.'

She stops. He follows suit, and, unable to imagine what she wants with it, pulls out his wallet and passes over the fifty pink twenty-thousand-dollar bills, cheap paper printed only on one side. Veronica has something metal in her hand. Her Zippo lighter. She touches its flame to the wad of money.

'No, they'll see it,' Jacob says, still utterly baffled.

'Let them.' When the flame has taken a secure hold of the wedge of bills, Veronica simply stoops and puts them down on the ground. There is a thick mesh of dead grass beneath those arid blades still waving in the air. This carpet of dry vegetation catches fire almost immediately. Jacob's eyes widen as he understands. Drought as a weapon.

The heat of the surging flames begins to warm him. Over the crackling sounds of the fire he hears dim cries of dismay from the pursuing soldiers.

'We must run faster,' Lovemore says.

Jacob doesn't need to be told twice. The night wind is coming from the train tracks, the fire will follow them. He turns and sprints. Veronica and Lovemore run behind him. A bright glow is already emanating from behind them.

When Jacob next looks over his shoulder the burgeoning bushfire is already several metres across, growing towards them in a wedge shape, fanned by the wind. Two anorexic trees are already aflame. He can't see the soldiers through the firelight and thick smoke. Jacob supposes that's a good thing. He just hopes they can outrun the bushfire.

Lovemore soon passes him, running fast despite his awkward, painful limp. Veronica follows behind. Jacob is gasping for breath with every step, and both his legs and lungs are cramping when they unexpectedly run across a dirt track that cuts across this desolate grassland. It is only a few feet wide, but it is a sign of civilization, and more importantly it could act as a firebreak.

He stops on the road and doubles over. It takes him a few seconds before he can even manage to gasp, 'I need to rest.'

'All right,' Veronica says.

Lovemore advises, 'Keep on walking.'

'Who are you, Johnnie Walker?' Jacob grunts, but he obeys.

A minute later he has recovered enough to take in their surroundings. The dirt track runs east and west as far as he can see. To the north, towards the train tracks, the approaching red-and-yellow glow has devoured almost the entire horizon. To the south, barely visible on the horizon, the ground leads up to odd rounded silhouettes protruding from the earth.

'What are those?' Jacob asks.

Lovemore glances. 'Koppies.'

'Excuse me?'

'Big rocks, granite boulders. Very common in Zimbabwe.'

Veronica says, 'Should we take the road?'

Jacob takes a deep breath. He wants to, it would be so much easier than crossing the rough and grassy ground, but – 'No. The fire will burn right up to it. If it doesn't cross. And they'll come looking for us in the morning. We have to keep running as long as we can.'

They set out again. Jacob makes it as far as the looming koppies before he collapses and can go no farther. Veronica and Lovemore too are near the end of their strength. They pass a wordless and delirious night on the hard, cold ground between two of the massive boulders, all three of them clinging tightly to one another for warmth, lapsing only occasionally into sleep, as the bushfire rages and burns in the distance, much too far away to warm their shivering bodies.

'I feel like the Tin Woodsman,' Jacob croaks, as Veronica and Lovemore help him to his feet. They have to support almost all his weight. His muscles are powerless. His joints feel as if they have rusted into place. If it was warmer he would try to insist on sleeping longer, but the unforgiving cold of the hard ground and predawn air has seeped into his whole shivering body, invaded every aperture in his clothing, and made the suffering of motion seem less awful than the suffering of inaction. The cold night makes him irrationally angry. Africa is supposed to be warm, everyone knows that. But Zimbabwe is two thousand kilometres south of the equator, and its vast central plateau a thousand metres above sea level.

'You'll feel better when we start moving,' Veronica says.

She doesn't sound confident. He can't blame her. Standing makes him dizzy, he has to lean on Lovemore or fall. His hands are covered by a mixture of dirt and his own dried blood, he half skinned them when he fell from the train. He looks around. The dawn illuminates a few trees growing at unnatural angles from clefts in the smoothly rounded koppies. Beyond this bizarre cluster of house-sized boulders, which look as if they have been dropped on to this grassland from outer space, the ground climbs southwards through more grassland. To the north, the kilometre-wide belt demarcated by the railway and the dirt cart track has been reduced to a still-smoking plain of black ash that continues east and west as far as Jacob can see.

They start south. Walking is a struggle. At first he has to lean on Lovemore. But after a few minutes, despite or perhaps because of the pain in his blistered feet, Jacob's head begins to clear and unexpected reservoirs of strength reopen. He thinks he might even be able to run again. For a short distance.

'Do you think they'll come after us?' he asks.

'Yes,' Lovemore says.

'They haven't yet.'

'Perhaps they were also waiting for dawn. Perhaps they went to get new orders. But they will come after us.'

'Where can we go?' Veronica asks.

Lovemore says, simply, 'Forward.'

They walk on in silence. Lovemore moves steadily forward, and makes no complaint, but Jacob sees than his face is taut with pain and realizes his limping leg is badly injured. At least Veronica seems to have survived the fall from the moving train relatively unscathed.

He imagines himself far away, in his favourite bar, the Duke of Gloucester on Yonge Street back in Toronto, telling his story to a rapt audience. Maybe then it will all seem worth it. What Jacob has learned about adventure is that it is wonderful only in retrospect; at the time, it's unspeakably awful. He never wants to have another adventure again. All he wants is to be back home. He limps onward, propelled by that vision. If they can just get out of Africa they will be safe, the Interpol charges will never stick.

The sun rises and warms them. They follow a shallow dry watercourse for a while, as it snakes its way up and south.

287

Around them the world is a vast tawny field of dried grass dotted with koppies and clumps of trees. It is bleak but starkly beautiful. Here the trees at least are green, there must be some subsurface water left. Jacob wonders whether they can somehow dig for it. His throat feels as if it is cracking with thirst. But whatever water is left beneath this parched soil must be buried deep.

'All Zimbabwe prays for rain,' Lovemore says, in a rasping voice. 'Last year's rainy season did not even begin. If the drought continues . . .' He leaves the sentence unfinished. 'These are hard times.'

About an hour past dawn they come across what was once a fence. The posts still stand in the ground, stretching towards the horizon to their left and right, but the three strands of rusted barbed wire that once connected them have fallen in so many places that what remains is more the idea of a fence than an actual barrier. The dried grass beyond has a different character, more geometric, and there are ragged patches of ground covered by the withered remains of different vegetation.

'Tobacco. This was a farm, once.' Lovemore sounds worried. He stops walking and looks around warily.

Jacob looks at him, confused. 'What's wrong?'

'An abandoned farm means war vets. War vets mean trouble.'

Veronica shrugs helplessly. 'You got somewhere else to go?'

She keeps walking forward. After a moment Jacob joins her. They have nowhere else to go, and little strength left, and his thirst has turned from an ache into a fiery need. Eventually Lovemore follows too.

They keep going, crossing rolling hills for about twenty minutes before coming across the remains of a tractor trail. The tread marks in the dried dirt look like a palaeontological discovery.

'It feels like the end of the world,' Veronica says in a near-whisper, 'like there's no one else alive.'

They follow the trail past a few rusted pipes that are all that remain of what was once an advanced irrigation system. After the withered fields they pass into a huge orchard of dead orange trees, where branches flutter and whisper eerily in the light wind. When they crest a ridge on the other side they see a copse of silver-leafed eucalyptus trees, and in their midst, buildings: a big house and two barns, near a pool of muddy sludge created by the damming of a local stream.

There are a dozen other shelters, round mud huts with wooden skeletons and raggedly thatched roofs, along the gravel road that runs between the barns and up to the house. Smoke rises from several of them. Clothes hang from a line stretched between two eucalyptus trees. Jacob sees sudden darting motions near the back of the house; children, running through the weed-strewn garden decorated with faded old lawn furniture. Plots of hand-tilled land surround the two barns. The gravel road runs from the house down through a kilometre more of dead farmland, in which a few dangerously lean cattle and maybe fifty goats graze, before it merges with a road that is dirt but for two paved strips barely wide enough for tyres. The road is lined by fallen power and telephone wires.

'War vets,' Lovemore says, in the same way he might say *crocodiles*.

They stand watching for a moment. Then Jacob says, his voice rattling in his parched throat, 'I guess we go say hi.'

5

The children see them as they descend the gentle slope, and by the time they reach the house the unexpected visitors have attracted a crowd of more than fifty people. About a dozen are adults. Their once-bright clothes are ragged and faded; several of the smaller children wear no clothes at all. A few of the adults look dangerously thin. Some of the men carry hoes and big sticks, but Veronica is almost too exhausted to be afraid. If these people attack them, so be it. But she doesn't think they will. They look more to be pitied than feared.

'Hello,' she says, as loudly as she can manage, and holds her hands up in the universal we-come-in-peace gesture.

Lovemore greets the crowd that faces them in an African language. Shona, Veronica supposes. After a brief pause the eldest man answers. His voice is clear, but he is so thin and weak that he has to lean on another man, and there are visible sores on his face. He and the several other gaunt adults are dying of Aids. Veronica guesses there are more in the house and the shelters, too weak to come see their visitors.

Lovemore pauses in conversation with the eldest man to update Jacob and Veronica. 'I told him we got off the train to look around when it stopped, and it left without us.'

'Are you sure that was a good idea?' Jacob asks, keeping his voice very low. Veronica supposes on one level that's sensible, English is the country's official language and some of them might speak it, but it also makes them look suspicious. 'If they hear the army's looking for people from the train—'

'Where else would we have come from?' Veronica asks, making a point of speaking normally. 'I don't think it matters. I don't think they exactly keep up with current events out here.'

'She's right,' Lovemore says. 'That road no longer goes anywhere, it leads to a bridge that broke two years ago. They say they must take an ox cart twenty kilometres to reach the nearest taxi stop. He says they'll take us if we pay a good price.'

Veronica winces. 'And we burned all our Zim dollars.'

Jacob says, 'I'm sure even here they understand US dollars. But we're down to our last ten bucks.'

Lovemore says, 'I have American dollars. Not many, but enough.'

The elderly man declaims something loud and rhythmic.

'What was that?' Veronica asks.

'He invited us to eat with them.'

Veronica's throat is aflame with thirst, and her stomach quickens at the thought of food.

Jacob hesitates. 'Can we trust them? They're war vets. What if they . . .'

'What? Poison us? Don't be ridiculous,' Veronica snaps, exasperated. 'They're not the enemy. They're just people. If they wanted to come after us they'd just do it now. And I don't think I can talk much longer if I don't get something to drink. Tell him we accept.'

Lovemore nods and speaks to the old man in Shona.

A crowd of children follow them as they continue to the house, which is in a half-rotted state, almost devoid of furniture and used largely for storage. The large ground-floor room off the entrance is inhabited by rusting tools and half-deflated cornmeal sacks marked by the depredations of vermin. There is obviously no power or running water any more, and without those, Veronica supposes African shelters are preferable to a big European-style house. Food is still prepared and washed on the kitchen's counters and in the sinks, but the cooking is done on an open fire in the back garden outside the kitchen. The dining room is dominated by a magnificent mahogany table, probably too big to have been removed from the house. The home-made wooden stools that now surround the table are crude but sturdy. Veronica wonders what the upstairs is like, whether the bedrooms are used for anything or have simply been abandoned.

She greedily accepts a pot of tea and metal cup and promptly burns her tongue, unable to wait to quench the edge of her thirst. She drinks four more cups before her body's sharp need for water begins to dull and awareness of her surroundings returns.

The room is full of people, most of them children, sitting on the stools and the floor, or leaning against the walls. Women bustle in the kitchen. Lovemore talks in laconic Shona with the war vets' patriarch and two other men. The children surround Veronica and Jacob, cluster around and under the table. A few of the more daring reach out to touch them before jumping back and giggling. Veronica smiles at them awkwardly. At least they do not have the distended bellies of the ill fed, and their eyes are bright and lively.

She wonders how many of them were born with HIV. According to Lysander more than one in three adult Zimbabweans has the virus.

The meal is preceded by a woman who circles among the diners with a bar of soap and a pitcher of water; Veronica uses most of a pitcher to wash her hands. The food, which Lovemore calls sadza, is ground cornmeal garnished with tomato sauce and salt; a little like pocho, only better. It is brought in from outside in a huge serving bowl, dished out on to metal pans and eaten with one's right hand. It isn't much, but Veronica devours two platefuls and is ready to give the house three Michelin stars when she is done.

'When do you think the army will get here?' Jacob asks.

Lovemore frowns. 'It depends on how they search. Perhaps this afternoon. Perhaps as late as tomorrow, with the broken bridge.'

'And then they'll know where we're going.'

Lovemore considers. 'These people may not speak. They too have been betrayed by the government. When they came here and took the property from the whites, Mugabe and the war-vet leaders promised them they would keep the power running, they would build schools and clinics, there would be taxi services every day, they would be given seeds and farming tools. Then the leaders went away and nothing happened. Now they have been abandoned. They say they don't want to stay. But they don't have any money or anywhere else to go. They are victims as much as anyone else.'

A very bold little girl, about six years old, leaps up into Jacob's lap. For a second he freezes, he doesn't know what to do, and Veronica suppresses a chuckle. The girl puts her arms around Jacob and her face against his chest. After a moment he drapes an awkward arm around her shoulders. The girl says something Veronica doesn't understand, and much of the room laughs, including Lovemore.

'She said you smell funny and you should take a bath,' Lovemore says, smiling.

Jacob chuckles. 'Not a bad idea.'

'I don't think we should use their water,' Veronica objects. 'They don't have much. They've already done a lot for us. And we don't have time.'

Jacob nods. 'Ask him when we can take the ox cart.'

Lovemore and the old man bargain in a good-natured way, as the rest of the room chuckles and catcalls along, until Lovemore puts his hands up in mock-surrender and speaks a word of agreement. Veronica has noticed that Lovemore seems much more at ease speaking Shona than he does when he speaks English: it's almost as if he has two different personalities, one relaxed and amused, the other serious and intense. The old man, who looks pleased, speaks to a man in his thirties, who gets up and leaves. Lovemore turns to Jacob and Veronica and says, 'We will pay them thirty dollars. His son is going now to ready the cart.'

A woman enters with a chipped bowl full of some small yellow fruit. Its taste is tart and sweet and it serves as a perfect dessert. Lovemore's eyes light up and he grabs an entire handful. The girl on Jacob's lap is obviously also an aficionado; Jacob and Veronica slip her a few extra and are rewarded by a gap-toothed smile.

'How many of them are sick?' Veronica asks, wondering whether this girl contracted HIV from her mother at birth. Or even by other means. She has heard that a widespread African belief that sex with a virgin cures Aids has led to a horrific rise in child rape.

Lovemore shakes his head. 'I can't ask. No one speaks of it. Even in the cities we don't speak of it, we don't get tested, we don't want to know. But in the cities at least we have food. Here it is worst of all. The sick cannot work the fields, so then there is hunger, and hunger makes the sickness even worse.'

Veronica winces. A vicious-circle death spiral.

Jacob asks Lovemore, 'Have you been tested?'

He frowns and admits, 'No.'

The patriarch's son returns to the dining room. Their ride is ready.

The whole community follows them out to the gravel road. The cart creaks, and rusty nails protrude from its wood, but it looks solid enough. The bull attached to it is another matter; old, so gaunt that its ribs are visible, walking with slow, fragile steps. Incentive will clearly not be a problem – the driver holds one end of a cord lashed into a miniature noose around the bull's testicles – but Veronica wonders how much longer the beast can work before it simply falls over dead.

Lovemore produces thirty US dollars from an inner pocket. The old man examines the bills closely, smelling them and rubbing them between his fingers, before declaring them acceptable. Veronica, Jacob and Lovemore take their positions behind the driver, the same man who readied the cart. There is a moment of heartbreaking comedy when the girl who sat on Jacob's lap climbs up with them. She is pulled away dejected by a teenager who explains something apologetically to Lovemore before taking the little girl away.

'Her father died last year,' Lovemore translates.

Veronica nods wordlessly. Jacob looks stricken. The driver flicks the reins, the gaunt bull begins to walk and the cart starts to creak and jostle forward. Veronica turns around and looks at the little girl with the gap-toothed smile. She isn't smiling now. Her eyes are big and full of tears. She watches Jacob depart as if he was her last hope in all the world. Veronica tries to stop herself from wondering what will happen to the little girl. Nothing good will come of that.

The old bull trudges across Zimbabwe's sunburnt fields, past ruined fences and clusters of koppies. The dirt track is a thin line stitched into a canvas of golden hills. Occasionally they rattle across dry watercourses on bridges made of planks. Dark morning clouds cluster in the sky, but dissipate as noon approaches. The cart bumps and wobbles uncomfortably, and the planks they sit on are old and splintering. The sun is intense. Veronica wishes they had some sunscreen, especially for Jacob, his skin is very pale and he's already in rough shape, victim of concussion and exhaustion. Their driver, whose name they do not know, does not speak, seems almost to be in a trance. Veronica tries to follow his example.

Out of nowhere Lovemore says, contemplatively, 'My father was born near here.'

Veronica looks at him. He does not seem particularly inclined to add to the statement, so she asks, 'But not you?'

'No. I grew up in the east, the Vumba, the highlands near Mozambique. The country is different there, very green. My father went east to work in the mines, and met my mother there.'

'Where are they now?'

'Dead,' he says. 'My father in the civil war, he fought for Mugabe, he was a true war vet. My mother of sickness, last year.'

Veronica doesn't ask which sickness. 'I'm sorry.'

He shrugs. 'We all die. They had good lives.'

'So you grew up out east?'

He hesitates. 'When I was twelve I came to Bulawayo to live with an uncle. Then to Harare for university. I met Lysander there. After university I went back to the Vumba. I worked at a tourist lodge there. Then the crisis began, and there were no more tourists, no more work anywhere. I left the country. Many of us have, hundreds of thousands. Most to South Africa. I went to Botswana.' Lovemore smiles wistfully, the first flicker of real emotion Veronica has seen on his face. 'Into the desert, the Kalahari. I lived with the Bushmen there, the San, for two years. I learned from them how to hunt, how to live off the land. I wanted to become a licensed guide, to make money from tourists. Rich tourists leave big tips in hard currency, they give you gifts, they invite you back to their homes in Britain and America. And you are outside, in the bush, among the animals, doing the things I love. Guiding is the best job a man can have, for me. But they do not like Zimbabwe men in Botswana. Not at all. There were problems. There was a woman.'

'There always is,' Jacob interjects, smiling.

'There was terrible trouble.' Lovemore reaches up unconsciously and touches the scar on his cheek. 'Two men died. I was nearly killed. I cannot go back to Botswana. I had to return to my country. I was lucky I found Lysander. In Zimbabwe today, even someone like me, a university graduate, must have a second job, a hard-currency job, or a relative who sends forex from abroad, only to survive. You have seen.'

Veronica nods. 'We have seen.'

Their conversation lapses. Veronica tries to picture what Zimbabwe was like ten years ago, when it was one of the most advanced countries in Africa, full of hope for the future. It's difficult to imagine.

The sun is directly overhead when she sees power lines about a mile away. A road; and a chance that soldiers will be there waiting for them. Not much they can do if so. Veronica hopes their long detour has taken them away from the army's search zone.

There is a single building where the dirt trail, deeply furrowed with many cart tracks, meets the paved one-lane road. There are no soldiers in sight. In fact there is nothing else in sight; no other buildings or vehicles, no people. It reminds Veronica a little of Hopper's famous Mobilgas painting.

The building is a combination general store, post office and taxi shelter. It has a neon sign in its window, and just inside its door there stands a gleaming fridge adorned with the Coca-Cola logo. The fridge holds plenty of Fanta but no Coke. No one is inside but the store's proprietor, a paunchy man sitting on a stool behind his modern cash register. He looks suspiciously at Lovemore, Jacob and Veronica as they enter. Bright posters advertising Peter Stuyvesant and Madison cigarettes hang on the walls, as does, surreally, a surfing poster from South Africa. A paper sign taped above an empty desk indicates that the post office is open Mondays and Fridays. The shelves are barren in patches, but still sell a wide assortment of crisps, chocolates, toiletries, canned foods, bread and sacks of rice and cornmeal.

The man behind the counter frowns at Lovemore's offer of US dollars. Eventually he agrees to exchange Zim dollars, but only at the official government rate printed in the week-old *Zimbabwe Herald* he digs out from beneath his desk. They buy chocolate and Fantas, for themselves and for their driver, but when they emerge from the store the cart is already gone. If Veronica squints she can see a disappearing dark smudge where the cart track climbs back into the fields.

'No Milo chocolate.' Lovemore looks with some disappointment at the Snickers in his hand.

'Is that good?' Jacob asks.

Lovemore looks at him as if he has just asked whether water is wet. 'Don't you have Milo chocolate in Canada and America?'

Jacob and Veronica admit they don't. Lovemore shakes his head sadly at their deprivation and bites gloomily into his Snickers. They sit down outside, in an open-walled shade structure made of metal legs and a canvas top. Between bites, Lovemore explains that the store owner said a taxi – the word means here what *matatu* does in Uganda – to Bulawayo will soon arrive. From Bulawayo there is a bus to Chitungwiza, a township only miles from Harare. There they should be safe, at least for now.

The taxi will come from the east, but they watch the west. Not that there is anything they can do if they see soldiers approaching. Veronica feels much stronger than she did at dawn, but she knows she has no more long pursuits left in her, and Jacob and Lovemore are in worse shape yet.

The taxi comes before the army. Its white exterior is mottled with rust, its windshield is covered with spiderweb cracks, and its roof supports a toppling pyramid of baskets, boxes and sacks, all secured with fraying yellow rope. Lovemore is prepared to pay twenty American dollars apiece for their seats, but there is no need, only twelve of its sixteen spaces are inhabited.

Veronica squeezes herself into the back row, which she shares with a tall man in a shirt and tie, a gaunt teenage mother with two infants, and a fat woman in bright robes, all of whom seem

297

entirely incurious about their new fellow-travellers. Jacob takes the seat in front of her, which folds into the minibus's single aisle. Its mechanism is broken and he has to sit at an angle, crammed next to three lean men in dirty clothes. Veronica can smell gasoline. The tiny storage area behind the back seat contains two full yellow jerrycans. She hopes they don't crash.

They drive for an hour, dropping off and picking up a few passengers in empty fields en route, before merging on to a heavily trafficked and potholed two-lane road. Here their driver accelerates until he is driving as if on speed and pursued by the devil, overtaking slower traffic from both sides. They zoom past roadside vendors selling jars of wild honey and bowls of bushfruit. They pass through small towns whose brick houses and smartly painted stores are beginning to sag and peel. The one police roadblock is so unexpected that Veronica doesn't even have time to be frightened; they are waved through by the time she sees the uniforms. She supposes no one was expecting them, or indeed any whites, to come via taxi.

Her brief impression of Bulawayo is of a city of wide boulevards, department stores and green parks. The streets are bustling with pedestrians but almost empty of vehicular traffic. The bus station is big and bustling, and the bus they transfer on to creaky but comfortable. It leaves when full, including a good thirty people standing in the aisle; Veronica is relieved they came early enough to get seats. She sits beside a window, next to Jacob, just behind Lovemore. By the time it rolls out of Bulawayo and on to the Harare road, twilight is dissipating into night.

'I thought they'd catch us,' Veronica says wonderingly.

Jacob nods. 'We got lucky with that cart ride. And it's not the whole Zimbabwe army looking for us, just Gorokwe's troops, unofficially. Lovemore says his supporters are mostly here and in the east of the country, he doesn't have much influence in Harare. If we get to Harare we should be OK.'

'I hope Lysander got out.'

'I'm sure he did. He knows what he's doing. He's been here for ever, he has lots of friends here.'

Veronica frowns. She doesn't think that counts for much here and now, not with so much at stake. And if Lysander is gone their only friend is Lovemore. 'Let's hope so.'

Jacob shrugs. 'Que sera sera. I'm beginning to understand the famous African fatalism, you know?'

Veronica does. It feels less and less as if she has any influence on the direction her life will take. She will find out tomorrow whether she will live another day, whether she will ever escape home, and those answers will depend on chance and on others, not on herself. But at least she is still here, battered and exhausted but also alive and free, at least for now. She closes her eyes and lets the swaying motion of the bus rock her to sleep.

Veronica opens her eyes to the dawn sun through the dew-streaked window. The first thing she sees is a hand-painted CHITUNGWIZA NO. 1 BUTCHER sign above a dozen bloody carcasses hanging on hooks. As she watches, civilization slowly grows denser: filthy shanty towns, busy shopping streets, long rows of tiny brick houses, warehouses and workshops, open-air markets, all jumbled together like a madman's jigsaw puzzle. Ditches full of plastic bags and rotting trash cut through muddy vacant lots cratered like First World War no man's land. Pools of dirty water, obviously sewage leaks, moulder in culverts and trenches crossed by improvised bridges made of planks or rusting pipes.

Chitungwiza's taxi park is a huge dirt field surrounded by barbed wire. Lovemore, Jacob and Veronica emerge from their taxi, admit they are going to Harare and are immediately and not quite forcibly hustled to another vehicle which then hangs about for forty minutes, waiting to fill, before embarking on the thirty-minute ride to Harare.

En route, Lovemore says, 'Look over there. That is Zimbabwe.'

Veronica looks over and sees a mostly flat field, studded with granite boulders, strewn with trash, rubble, tufts of grass and occasional one-room tin-roofed shacks.

'That was a big commercial farm, maize and potatoes, some tobacco. A white farmer. Five years ago the war vets came and stole it from him. After they took the land they started putting up buildings. Little houses, vegetable gardens, there was a market, all this land was covered with them, people everywhere. And then, earlier this year, the government, the same government that put them there, sent in bulldozers and flattened everything, destroyed everything, threw them all off the land. Operation Murambatsvina. That means "clean up the trash". Thousands of houses, whole little towns, trading stalls, markets, all over the country, all destroyed. Because the war vets were becoming powerful. No one is allowed to be powerful. No one but Mugabe.'

Harare proper is a strikingly pretty city, well watered and full of greenery, its major streets lined by flowering trees that turn them into purple- and orange-latticed tunnels. The downtown towers are skyscrapers, by African standards. The city buzzes with traffic. They reach Harare's downtown taxi park at mid-morning.

'We made it,' Veronica says, not quite believing her own words, as they stand and stretch their cramped and battered limbs. Around them pedestrians hustle through the taxi park. Denizens of Harare, in the way of big-city people everywhere, move much faster than their rural cousins.

'Where now?' Jacob asks, yawning.

'Avondale,' Lovemore says, which means nothing to them. 'You will wait. I will seek out Lysander.'

Avondale appears to be a mall full of white people. Veronica finds being among a white majority, for the first time since she came to Africa, a little shocking and disturbing. Lovemore leaves them at an Italian coffee shop that would not look out of place in San Francisco.

'Stay here,' he says. 'I will try to find Lysander. If he is gone I will find his friend Duncan. I will come back and we will take care of you. You will be safe.'

300

'How long do you think you'll be?' Veronica asks.

Lovemore hesitates. 'One hour. Not more.'

He limps away.

One hour falls past, and then a second, and then a third.

The cappuccino is excellent. The people-watching is interesting. The movie theatre, supermarket, fast-food restaurant, ice-cream stall and Internet café in the mall are refreshing and enticing. But as time trickles onwards, and Lovemore fails to reappear, a numb dread begins to take root in Veronica's gut and then to spread.

After the fourth hour she can no longer tell herself and Jacob that Lovemore has merely been delayed, that everything in Africa takes longer than you think, that he has just been held up. She is forced to begin to wonder what they can possibly do if he does not come back at all. They have ten US dollars and nowhere else to go.

As the fifth hour begins, she dares to say it: 'He's not coming back. They got him.'

Jacob nods wordlessly.

'What do we do now?'

He shakes his head ruefully. 'I've only got one idea left.'

6

Harare International Airport is a gleaming white elephant, an empty edifice of marble floors overseen by fading posters of Zimbabwe's various tourist destinations and the Big Five safari animals. The woman at the British Airways ticket window looks very bored. Jacob waits nervously while his Bank of Montreal MasterCard is processed, but to his great relief the woman returns to the window with two airline tickets.

Their plan is almost pathetically simple. Their last ten dollars bought them a taxi ride to the airport. British Airways flies overnight to Heathrow. Their status as Interpol fugitives will doubtless lead to detainment by British immigration, but at least they'll be out of Africa and back in civilization. Arrest might even be a good thing; the light of publicity will shine on their trumped-up accusations of homicide, and may even reveal the truth. Their notoriety as former Congo hostages won't hurt either.

All they have to do is get past Zimbabwe immigration and on to the plane. It's possible that their names have already been flagged, that they will be arrested on Interpol's behalf – but the more Jacob thinks about it, the less likely that seems. Zimbabwe isn't exactly a poster-child member of the international community. There's a good chance they don't even receive Interpol alerts. And even if they are arrested by Mugabe's police, even that isn't worst-case; they are, after all, bizarre as it still seems, trying to save Mugabe's life.

Armed with their tickets, they walk through the cavernous arrivals hall to a small outdoor observation platform above the runway. There is no one else sitting at the wrought-iron tables and chairs. They have just enough money left to order a single Coke from the girl behind the small snack bar. Jacob hopes there isn't a departure tax.

They sit and look out on the runway. Jacob's heart convulses when he sees a black army helicopter in the distance – but it is flying away from them. He supposes its presence is normal, this is a military airbase too. It occurs to him that back in Canada today is Remembrance Day.

The only other craft in sight is a narrow white 727 parked next to the runway. After a moment a slow smile spreads across Jacob's face. He knows this legendary airplane, he remembers reading about its story with great interest: it once carried sixty South African mercenaries who stopped here a few years ago to pick up weapons from Zimbabwean co-conspirators, en route to foment a coup in oil-rich Equatorial Guinea. The mercenaries were captured, arrested, jailed and eventually deported; the airplane remains in legal limbo. Jacob is oddly comforted by this reminder that he and Veronica aren't the only Harare airport passengers to have been in dire and melodramatic straits.

The glass doors that lead into the airport open. When Jacob sees the man who murdered Derek step out of those doors, followed by several armed and uniformed soldiers and then Athanase the *interahamwe* leader himself, he thinks at first that this has to be some kind of nightmare, a terrible dream-vision, can't possibly be reality. He and Veronica stay seated, frozen by the sheer impossibility of this horror, as the soldiers and casually dressed *interahamwe* surround them.

'Jacob Rockel,' Athanase says, smiling thinly. 'Veronica Kelly. We meet again. *Enchanté pour la deuxième fois.*'

There is nowhere to go. Even if there were, Jacob is too stunned to move. One of the soldiers goes behind him, grabs his arms and pulls them behind his back. Jacob does not resist as his wrists are handcuffed. All he can do is grunt with disbelief. Beside him Veronica too is shackled. Both are grabbed by their throats and dragged to their feet. The snack-bar girl watches with appalled fascination.

The world goes dark and Jacob feels fabric against his face. A hood, his head has been covered. Blind and handcuffed and helpless, he is dragged along the airport's smooth marble floors, then out into the open air again.

'Up,' a soft voice commands, pushing him forwards. Jacob barks his shin against the vehicle in front of him before he understands and steps upwards. Once inside he is shoved down on to some kind of bench. A van, he guesses, with facing benches in the back. The engine is already running. He doesn't know where Veronica is. The doors clank shut and the van begins to move. They don't go far. Jacob's handcuffs are very tight and by the time the van comes to a halt his hands and fingers are already beginning to prickle.

'Veronica,' he gasps.

'I'm here.' Her voice too is weak and quavering.

'No talking!' someone orders.

Jacob doesn't doubt that rule will be brutally enforced. He remains silent as the van doors open. A soldier grabs a fistful of his shirt and drags him outside, down on to concrete again. He is walked for a short distance to a wobbly set of steps. Jacob nearly overbalances and falls as he climbs them. He smells oil and metal. Then he is shoved on to another bench and straps are fastened around his waist and belt.

'Now you are mine,' Athanase croons into Jacob's ear. 'This time we will not let you go.'

An engine starts up, a very loud engine, and the bench he sits on begins to shake and vibrate as the noise around him grows to ear-splitting levels, and a huge wind begins to blow. He understands what is happening, it has happened to him before, to him and Veronica both, in the Congo. They are in a helicopter. His stomach lurches as they lift off.

Then a strong and wiry hand is on Jacob's throat, squeezing it shut. He fights for air, struggles to escape the fingers that grip like a vice, but he can't move, the handcuffs and safety straps hold him securely. His lungs sour and burn until it feels as if they are filled with acid, he needs to breathe more than he has ever needed anything before, but it is still impossible. Jacob feels himself beginning to slip away from the world. Then the hand relaxes and Jacob begins to suck in air again, in long, choking, rattling gasps.

'Only *imagine* what we will do to you now,' Athanase shouts into Jacob's ear. 'Only *anticipate*.'

Jacob breathes deeply, tries to steady himself, tries to seal off all his fear, all emotion, and cage it deep inside his skull, bury it like radioactive waste and face their coming doom with cold resolve. It doesn't work. He's so frightened he's nauseous. He finds himself hoping for the helicopter to crash. A fiery death would surely be miles better than whatever awaits them at their destination. At least it would be quick and painless, and would consume Athanase and the man who killed Derek as well.

The tone of the helicopter's engine changes. Jacob's stomach lurches with trepidation, and then with sickening motion, as the helicopter sinks from the sky. Its skids suddenly re-encounter the ground, and after a few dancing thumps they are earthbound again.

The engine is switched off. Someone undoes Jacob's safety straps and pulls off his hood. The sudden light is blinding and Jacob has to squint. At first all he can see is the black interior of the aircraft, and Veronica's pale face as she steps off it into the grass that surrounds them. Then he registers the building looming above the grassy helipad.

It's no military base: it is some kind of elegant hotel, reminiscent of the one in Victoria Falls. The main building, two wings in the shape of a shallow V with a circular hub between, nestles in the shadow of a huge overhanging cliff. The circular driveway leading up to the main entrance encompasses a swimming pool and croquet field. A few other buildings are scattered around like satellites.

Jacob expected some kind of secret military prison, not a luxury hotel. Maybe Gorokwe can't be sure of his support on a base. Meaning he doesn't have much popular support among the military, which in turn explains why he is shooting down Mugabe rather than storming his presidential abode. But it doesn't really matter where they have been taken. The outcome will be the same. Jacob can't imagine any plausible future in which he escapes Gorokwe's custody alive.

He is pulled from the bench and propelled out of the helicopter, on to the grass, towards the hotel. His hands, constricted by the too-tight handcuffs, have gone almost completely numb, are little more than dead lumps of flesh attached to the rest of his body. Athanase and Veronica climb to a stone-floored patio, and then inside through a set of double glass doors, to wide red-carpeted stairs. Jacob follows, pushed along by the man who killed Derek. The uniformed soldiers stay by the helipad.

He feels like a death row prisoner marching towards the electric chair. Every step, every sight, is a major event as they climb the stairs and walk along a plushly decorated hallway, to a doorway with a plaque that announces, surreally, that the Queen Mother once stayed in this room.

When Jacob sees who is waiting for them within he wonders for a moment whether he is dreaming.

The high-ceilinged room is decorated with spindly wooden furniture, expensive but old. A huge window opens on to a stone balcony, beyond which lies a glorious view of a golf course nestled amid rolling hills and shining rivers. Jacob doesn't know the big, powerfully built black man in a suit standing restless by the window, nor the short, barrel-chested white man with thinning hair lounging uncomfortably on the sofa in khaki slacks and vest. But he knows the young, pretty blonde woman in jeans sitting between them.

'*Susan?*' he blurts, startled out of paralysing fear by sheer amazement.

She looks sadly at him and Veronica, and slowly Jacob begins to understand.

'This wasn't supposed to happen,' Susan says. 'None of it was. I'm sorry.' She pauses. 'No, I'm not. I *regret* it. Nobody was supposed to get hurt except Michael and Diane, and they deserved it. I regret anybody else got hurt. But I'm not sorry. We're trying to save lives here, millions of lives, two whole countries. I regret that people like you keep getting in the way. But we can't let you stop us.'

Jacob looks over to Veronica. She does not even seem to be listening. Instead her gaze is fixed on the man on the couch. Jacob deduces that must be her ex-husband. Danton DeWitt. And the man by the window who looks like a heavyweight boxer—

'General Gorokwe, I presume?' Jacob guesses.

He smiles absently, as if addressed by a child. 'Very good.'

Jacob shakes his head, as if to dislodge loose pieces of thought within. He looks back to Susan. 'What did Michael and Diane do?'

'The so-called philanthropists?' Her voice drips sarcastic rage. 'Where to begin? Those *orphanages* they funded were like fundamentalist slave camps. They were such good Christians that they bribed officials to destroy whole shipping containers of condoms that had already gone to Uganda. God knows how many thousand people got Aids as a result. What happened to them was too good for them.'

'Right. And how about what happened to Derek?' Jacob feels a futile fury begin to burn within him. 'Let me guess. He came to you at the camp and started asking questions about the smuggling going on there. Not knowing you were part of it, because who would ever guess that looking at a pretty blonde girl like you, right? And then, what, you invited him to come to Bwindi? Or just planted the idea? And you made sure there were slots available in Michael and Diane's gorilla group. Then when you grabbed us you made it look like they were going to rape you, just so we wouldn't suspect anything.'

Susan smiles thinly. 'Actually Patrice was taking me outside to give me better food. I was quite annoyed with you all for saving me.'

'Yeah? You hid it well. But of course you're an actress, aren't you. And a lot better than you admitted. Shit, you deserve an Oscar. No wonder we got out so easy, with you to lead the way. Then we show up at the refugee camp and say hi, we take a few pictures of buddy here,' he indicates Derek's muscled killer Casimir, 'taking custody of your shiny new missiles, and the very next day Prester is tortured to death and we're fugitives from justice. I should have fucking known.'

'Like she says, we regret it,' Danton says. He sounds angry. 'But you were warned often enough to leave well enough alone.'

'Listen to yourself,' Veronica spits out. ' "Leave well enough alone". How many people have you killed already? How many? Elijah and the guards, Michael, Diane, Derek, Prester. How many more we don't know about? How many murdered?'

Danton shakes his head. 'Wrong question. How many more will die here if Mugabe doesn't go? Haven't you seen what's happened to this country? It's starving. It's dying. We're saving it. And I'm sorry, but you can't change the world without hurting someone. I wish you could, but that's the choice you have to make, to make a real difference. Someone always suffers from change. You have to choose to shed a little blood in order to save a lot.'

'Right,' Jacob says. He nods at Athanase and Casimir. 'And that's why you're working with these two. Because they're the experts on blood. On fucking genocide.'

'What would you rather have?' Susan asks. 'Them in the Congo, killing and destabilizing, where there's already four million dead in the civil war, or in quiet exile here in Zimbabwe after Gorokwe takes over?'

'Oh. Oh, I see. Of course. That's what's in it for them. You're their retirement package. Athanase here is wanted for crimes against humanity and you're his fucking pension plan. You have to play nice with him or he'll tell the whole world everything about you, so if you win, you'll put him and his people up in a nice little villa here for as long as he wants. He committed a fucking holocaust and you're putting him out to pasture.'

'What now?' Veronica asks, looking directly at Danton. 'What are you going to do to us?'

A long silence hangs over the room; long enough for Jacob's rage to begin to dissipate.

'Nobody's going to touch you. I promise you that,' Danton says to Veronica. 'But I can't say the same about your boyfriend.'

Jacob swallows. He feels very cold.

Danton stands and walks over to Jacob. 'You need to tell us where your evidence is.'

'I don't have any.'

'Not on you, no. You gave your CD to Lysander, and he gave it to us.' Jacob winces. 'But you have more, don't you? Backed up online. I'm sure you do, you must, you're a technical professional.

Ready to be sent out automatically if you don't log in to a certain website, maybe? A dead man's switch?'

'No,' Jacob lies. 'Nothing like that.'

'You really need to tell us the truth now,' Danton warns. 'We're not playing games. We can't afford to. You're going to tell us. The easy way or the hard. Up to you.'

Jacob stares into Danton's face, then looks at their other enemies, at Gorokwe, Susan, Athanase, Casimir. He thinks of the little girl at the ruined farm. He thinks of Derek on that airstrip in the Congo, remembers how his best friend's head rolled forward from his body after Casimir's third and final stroke of the panga. He remembers holding Veronica close in the Ruwenzori Travellers' Inn.

Jacob makes a decision, takes a deep breath. 'There's nothing to tell.'

Danton and Susan look dismayed. Gorokwe and Casimir look indifferent.

Athanase smiles, showing his teeth, and croons, '*On va voir.*' Meaning, *we shall see.*

The last Jacob sees of Veronica is her stricken, alarmed face as Athanase and Casimir drag him out of the room where the Queen Mother once slept.

Jacob is shivering as if with malaria, he feels as if he is about to lose control of all his body, too weak from fear to struggle as they half drag him to the end of a long corridor. He knows what's going to happen. But he also knows that the result will be the same regardless. They will kill him. Probably Veronica too, but definitely him. He knows too much. He will die here in this hotel. The only thing left is to not tell them anything – because Danton is right about his dead man's switch.

He tries to tell himself it doesn't matter how he dies.

The room at the end of the hall smells vile. There is something big and bloody hanging from its ceiling. It takes Jacob a moment to recognize it as a human form. The man's wrists are tied to a rope dangling from a hook in the ceiling originally intended for a light. The ankles are attached to a similar but longer rope, so that the man hangs diagonally over the bed, at something like a forty-five-degree angle. Blood oozes from burn-blackened flesh all over the body, a Rorschach-like stain has formed on the beige carpet beneath. The man's face and genitals have been almost entirely burnt away. Jacob can see the bone of the eye sockets.

Athanase picks up a bloodstained steak knife from the bed and sticks it into the body, as if impaling a piece of meat on his plate. It is not until the man wriggles a little, and a rattling breath emerges from his throat, that Jacob realizes he is still alive. Then he sees, and recognizes, the clothes piled in the corner of the room. Jacob wants to scream but can't breathe, can't move, can barely stand.

'*Tu le connais, je crois,*' Athanase says conversationally. '*Ici c'est Lysander.*'

'No,' Jacob moans.

Athanase produces a Zippo lighter much like Veronica's, idly flicks open and ignites it, then claps it shut again. He smiles. 'He was a strong man, but he told me everything. You are not strong. Perhaps you would like now to reconsider your silence.'

Jacob closes his eyes. 'There's nothing to tell.'

'*Bon,*' Athanase says. He sounds genuinely pleased. '*Casimir, tue-le et descend-le. On va recommencer avec le Canadien.*'

Jacob opens his eyes and watches Casimir strangle Lysander, or what is left of Lysander, with his own belt. It seems a mercy. The dead man is lowered to the ground, and removed from his bonds. Then Casimir turns to Jacob.

He tries to fight, but he is weak and handcuffed, and Casimir is incredibly strong. One punch to his solar plexus, followed by a kick to his testicles, and by the time Jacob can think of anything other than breath and agony, he is bound to the same ropes that held Lysander, and Casimir is hoisting him up. The hook that holds him doesn't even wobble as his feet leave the ground. Casimir ties the rope off around the leg of the bed, anchoring Jacob, leaving him hanging diagonally in midair.

Athanase takes the steak knife and begins to cut Jacob's clothes away. Jacob closes his eyes and tries to pretend he isn't there. As Athanase works he makes a point of cutting his victim, the knife rips into Jacob's skin, tearing into his ankles, the insides of his legs, his stomach, his armpits, and despite his best attempts he jerks and moans. Soon he is dangling naked and bleeding from the ceiling.

Then he hears the Zippo flick open again.

'Please,' Jacob begs, opening his eyes, abandoning all hope and all stoicism. He begins to weep. It is hard to breathe, his voice is so weak he can hardly hear himself. His shoulders already feel as if they're slowly being pulled out of their sockets, and blood drips from a dozen shallow but agonizing cuts on to the floor below him. 'Please, no, please.'

'Tell me everything.'

'Please. There's nothing to tell. Please, God, no, please.' He is no longer addressing Athanase, but there is no God, no merciful God would allow a life to come to this, would ever have created beings capable of suffering so much physical pain. It already feels like almost more than he can bear, just from his shoulders and the cuts, and he knows it has really not yet even begun.

'*Alors.*' Athanase smiles and ignites the Zippo. '*On va voir.*'

7

'And what do you intend to do with her?' General Gorokwe asks.

His voice is low, powerful, accustomed to command. Veronica looks at Danton, wide eyed, awaiting the answer, trying to look as pitiful as possible. She hates him with every cell of her being, but right now her only hope is his forbearance.

'Nobody touches her,' Danton orders. 'She was my wife.'

Susan says, 'We can't let her go.'

'I'm not talking about letting her go.'

'We can't *ever* let her go. Even after it's over.'

Danton says, 'We'll worry about that when it's over. She won't be a problem until then.'

'She doesn't have to be a problem at all,' Gorokwe says.

'No. She was my wife. You're not giving her to those monsters.'

'It doesn't have to be Athanase. It can be quick and painless. Only say the word and you will never see her again, it is as simple as that.'

But Veronica isn't worried. She knows what Danton is like when someone tries to argue with him after he has made up his mind.

'I said *no*,' he repeats, in a tone of voice all too familiar to her, petulance more than anger, as if perhaps the problem is just that he has not been heard correctly until now.

'We don't even know what she knows,' Susan says.

'Rockel will tell us.' Danton considers Veronica. 'But I'll talk to her.'

Veronica looks meekly at the floor rather than aim her venomous gaze at him.

'In private,' Danton says archly.

Susan and Gorokwe look at one another. Eventually Gorokwe nods. Both of them stand and leave the room. As they reach the door Veronica sees Susan put a familiar hand on Gorokwe's back. It is the touch of an intimate, a lover. She remembers Susan saying that she lived in Zimbabwe before she came to Uganda.

'I told you to go home,' Danton says, when there is no one in the room but the two of them. 'I gave you a second chance.'

Veronica looks around for a weapon. He is a strong man and her arms are cuffed behind her, but this is the only chance she has. Maybe he has handcuff keys on him. Maybe she can kill him, free herself, burn down the hotel or something, liberate Jacob and escape. It doesn't seem particularly likely but it's apparently the only hope she's got.

'Who else did you talk to?' Danton asks. 'We know Prester. Who else? Who got you to the Uganda border?'

'What are you doing?' she bursts out. 'You stupid asshole. What the fuck are you doing? Trying to prove yourself? Trying to show the world you're not just some useless rich kid, you're as good as your daddy? What the fuck are you *doing*, Danton?'

He is so taken aback by her unexpected verbal assault that he actually recoils. Then he says, 'Don't you understand? Do you still not understand? We're saving Zimbabwe. And half the Congo. We're doing a great thing here. You're getting in the way of something wonderful.'

'Something wonderful. Murder, civil war, you're in bed with a man who committed genocide. What's going to happen to Jacob? What are they doing to him right now?'

'I'd worry about yourself, if I were you, not your new boyfriend.'

'I'd worry about yourself if I were you too. You think I'm the only one who knows too much? You really think you're going to get out of this country alive after they shoot down Mugabe? Don't you see? Once they've gone and spent your daddy's money you'll be totally fucking expendable.'

Danton's face flickers, and she realizes she has just given away how much she knows – but she almost doesn't care, it's worth it to have scored a point.

'We know they're not trustworthy,' he says quietly. 'We know Gorokwe is volatile, he's a good man but he needs a short leash. We know Athanase and his men are monsters. We've made arrangements. They'll be taken care of when it's over. And in turn they know that if I disappear, certain revelations will come to light all around the world. I've made video recordings, copied documents, everyone will be exposed. I'm the opposite of ex-pendable. They know that.'

'A short leash, huh. Looks to me like you're the one on it.'

'No. And don't judge the general. You don't know him. He's a good man. Brilliant, too. Unpredictable, volatile, but he wants an African renaissance more than anyone, and he's the one man who might actually make it happen.'

'Or so he's convinced you.'

'This isn't about me,' Danton snaps. 'Or the general. This is about what we do with you. And about trying to save your boyfriend's life before it's too late. If you tell me right now everything there is to know about his evidence, his back-ups, I'll go down that hall and stop what's happening.'

'I don't know anything, he never told me,' Veronica says, and she sees as she says it that Danton knows it is the truth.

'So. Too bad for him.'

Danton picks up the phone. Veronica knows this is her last chance, she has to rush him now – but she has no weapon, no chance of victory, the idea is too ridiculous, too pathetic. She just sags into a chair and listens as he orders soldiers to the room to escort her away.

In the distance she hears a scream, muffled but soul-curdling. Veronica moans loudly in response, she can't help it. She knows it is Jacob. She knows they are torturing him. When they are finished they will kill him. There's nothing she can do, no way to stop it. He shrieks again, several times in quick succession; they're like sounds from a nightmare, animal and desperate. But she can't even try to convince herself that this might be a nightmare. Nothing has ever felt so awful and so real.

Danton winces. 'He has to just tell them. He will. He has to do it now.'

She stares at her ex-husband with genuine horror. 'Look at yourself. Listen. How can you do this? What are you doing?'

He looks at her for a long moment. In the distance Jacob screams like a child.

Danton lowers his eyes to the floor and says, softly, in the boy's voice he used when they murmured in bed together, when they were married, 'I don't even know any more. I swear, I never knew it was going to be like this. It wasn't supposed to be like this. I'm sorry. But it's too late now.'

She can't think of anything to say.

Danton says, 'I'm going to get you out of here. Eventually. I promise. Nobody's going to touch you.'

*　　*　　*

Two burly men in plain clothes march Veronica down the velvet-carpeted stairs to the huge, vaulted main entrance, where she learns that this is the Leopard Rock Hotel. Behind her Jacob has gone silent. She hopes he just told them everything. It doesn't even matter whether their evidence gets out. There wasn't much to it anyways. She should have tried to explain that to Danton.

Two soldiers wait behind the reception desk. Gorokwe's troops have obviously taken over the whole property. After a brief Shona conversation she is propelled outside, down the circular driveway and into a parking lot crowded with military jeeps and black Mercedes and BMWs with opaque windows and no licence plates. She is still handcuffed. The hands on her arms are firm but not crushing. Danton told the men who have taken her into custody several times that nobody was to touch her, no matter what. She supposes she should feel grateful.

She is hustled into the back of a black Mercedes. One man drives, the other sits beside her, the doors are locked. The road out of the Leopard Rock climbs upward, winding around the huge cliff that looms above the hotel, through dense forest on either side, very different from the dry plains of central Zimbabwe. These must be the eastern highlands near Mozambique that Lovemore described.

The route they take snakes through rippling ridges of steep, folded hills and valleys, covered by grassy plains and rainforest and shot through by tumbling rivers. The only signs of life come from clusters of crude wooden shelters whose denizens stare sullenly at the passing vehicle. Countless red-dirt tributaries extend from the main road into the hills.

After a long descent they skirt a busy city, Mutare from the signs, climb around a huge koppie and back up into hills that seem more raw and rugged. Several times the road winds along the base of sheer forty-foot precipices. They pass a few slopes covered by burnt bare ground and sparse trees, with fire-blackened trunks jutting from the ground like fence stakes. They pass through a military checkpoint, and then another. Veronica supposes they're going to some kind of military base where she will be imprisoned.

She doesn't really believe she will ever be released. Maybe that's what Danton intends right now, in a sudden burst of guilty morality, but he will eventually come to realize that his own interests are best served by Veronica's death. And it seems likely that Gorokwe will take matters into his own hands if necessary. Either way her imminent death feels as good as foreordained. She supposes she will probably at least outlive Mugabe, they have bigger things to worry about than her right now. She will live long enough to be a loose end, and then she will be tied up. She almost wishes they would just get it over with now.

The faded sign on the fence topped with barbed wire says REZENDE. The gate is guarded by two bored-looking soldiers. The gravel parking lot is occupied by jeeps, white vans and a few yellow Caterpillar industrial vehicles. Beyond, a complex of low and battered buildings is set into the side of a steep and rocky hill. Outside the fence, a dozen gargantuan heaps of yellow dirt, like termite mounds fifty metres high, loom above the scrub brush and trees.

The car doors open. Veronica emerges willingly, no sense in resisting now, and is led past broken windows to a kind of courtyard where weeds grow through cracked concrete and patches of gravel. A generator buzzes somewhere inside the largest nearby building. Here a half-dozen armed soldiers guard what looks at first like some bizarre Rube Goldberg contraption. Four metal legs support a roof of corrugated tin over a massive piece of machinery festooned with gears, wheels and pulleys. This machinery in turn holds a big metal cage directly above a hole in the ground. The cage is about three metres by two, the hole slightly larger. Four rusting chains dangle into the corners of the abyss. It takes Veronica most of the walk across the parking lot to figure out that the hole is a mineshaft, the contraption above an elevator, and the huge piles of yellow dirt are heaps of processed and discarded ore. This is a semi-abandoned mining complex. She thinks of the open-pit coltan mine in the Congo.

The men lead her to the cage and pause long enough to chat a little with the soldiers; she can't understand the words but can tell that they are asking about her, and are amused by the answers. Eventually the conversation ceases and the cage is opened, its whole wall hinges inwards, and Veronica begins to understand exactly where she will be imprisoned.

'No,' she says weakly, staring at the cage door as if it is a fanged jaw that might devour her. Her heart begins to pound. Being buried alive has always been her greatest fear. 'No, please. Put me somewhere else. Not down there. Please.'

The men exchange amused smiles as they pull Veronica inside. She groans weakly. The cage is just high enough for her to stand upright. Its floor is rusted sheet metal. A strong, hot updraught rises from the pit beneath.

The door clangs shut. One man lights the paraffin lamps that dangle from hooks on the ceiling. Veronica feels dizzy, her skin is damp with sweat, it takes all her will to keep the trembling seed of terror within her from burgeoning and conquering her mind and body. Then the generator noise hits a new register and the cage lurches suddenly downwards. Veronica almost falls to her knees.

They continue to descend, a little more smoothly. The chains at the corners clank loudly as they rise. They fall into darkness, lit only by lamplight. The air grows steadily warmer. It feels like sinking into hell. Like being buried alive.

'No,' Veronica moans. There is a roaring sound in her ears and her whole body fills with an electric tingling. She can't get enough air, there is a painful tightness in her chest as if her lungs have been squeezed shut. She closes her eyes, sags down the cage walls to a sitting position with her arms wrapped around her knees, and tries to forget where she is, to just focus on breathing, on not passing out.

An eternity seems to pass before the panic attack subsides. When it does Veronica feels completely exhausted, but at least she can think and breathe again – although she can still feel the panic lurking darkly in her mind, a crouching, howling beast ready to spring and savage her again.

Warm air blows up the mineshaft past them, wind from the centre of the earth. Veronica opens her eyes. They fall past a dark opening in the sheer stone walls, an abandoned corridor like an open mouth. There is a faint glow from below. Veronica looks up. The mouth of the mineshaft has shrunk to a tiny dot, like a single pixel on a computer screen. The sight nearly triggers another attack.

One of her escorts pulls a cord that dangles from a corner of the roof. A cable runs up one of the chains that holds the cage, some kind of signalling mechanism. Their descent slows to a crawl as they approach an opening in the stone walls around them, lit by flickering lamplight. The man pulls the cord twice as the cage grows level with the opening. They come to a halt about two inches below the lip of the opening. Gaps around the edge of the sheet-metal floor reveal that the mineshaft continues below.

The corridor is about as big as the cage itself, eight feet wide and six high. Its walls and ceiling are sheer whitewashed stone. Narrow rail tracks begin at the edge of the mineshaft and continue down the corridor into darkness.

'He says we must not touch you,' one of her escorts says, the first words that have been directed to her. He sounds darkly amused. 'Very well. We follow orders. None of us will touch you.'

The other pushes her in the back, ungently. 'Go.'

Veronica has no choice, she starts down the corridor. The two men follow. One carries a paraffin lamp. The stone ceiling grows lower, and Veronica has to stoop to keep her head clear. Pipes and cables run along the ceiling, rusted and in several places severed. She hears murmuring voices. They reach a little alcove where an old wooden desk stands beneath a dust-covered sign warning that SAFETY IS EVERYONE'S JOB. A half-dozen soldiers with rifles are here, seated on crude wooden stools, chatting quietly. After a brief conversation four of them stand to join the procession.

318

They continue into the mine, soldiers in front, then Veronica, then the two men in street clothes. The soldiers' boots echo hollowly on the stone floors. Other, smaller passages intersect this one, and connecting shafts run diagonally upwards and downwards, covered by grids of old wood, presumably to stop rockfalls. They pass two small passages entirely blocked by rubble. In several places the ceiling is supported by wooden pillars with bases carved into sharp points.

The faintly draughty air is dense, hot and dusty. The lamplight is dim and flickering. At first the only sounds are occasional drips of water, distant *tik-tik-tik* noises, which she takes to be miners working with hammer and chisel. Then Veronica begins to hear voices, so distant that she wonders at first if they are her imagination. They pass a large chamber with whitewashed walls, where two more armed soldiers sit on a wooden bench.

Veronica turns her head to look, then suddenly stops walking and stares. She knows the two gleaming coffin-shaped boxes stacked behind those soldiers, close enough that she can read their etched Cyrillic letters. The Iglas, the missiles, the weapons that will assassinate Mugabe.

Her guards shove her onwards hard enough that she stumbles. When she looks back she sees them glance curiously into that chamber themselves. Her mind whirls as she continues on and the voices grow louder. It makes sense that they're here, it's hard to imagine a more secret or secure hiding spot than half a mile underground, and probably very few of Gorokwe's men know what is in those boxes and why. Maybe even her two escorts don't know that Mugabe will be shot down the day after tomorrow. Maybe she should tell them, maybe they will find a burning patriotism within and try to save their country from bloody ruin – but that doesn't seem likely, and anyways it's too late, they have stopped in front of a wall of rusted iron bars.

The metal grille is set into the walls and ceiling, blocking the corridor completely. It has been crudely but firmly welded together, blobs and seams are visible. The door in the middle of the cage is chained securely shut. An unsettling chorus of dull, hoarse voices emanates from behind the iron bars: dozens of voices, maybe more. The air stinks of filth and sweat.

A man grabs her wrists and unlocks her handcuffs. The guards turn to the bars. Two of them point their rifles inside; the other two activate flashlights and aim them inside. Veronica gasps with horror. Her first impression is of a solid mass of naked human misery. There are maybe sixty men inside, crammed into a space maybe thirty feet square. When the lights come on they fall silent and shrink back from the guns, press themselves against what look like metal walls in the middle of the chamber. All are black, naked or stripped to their underwear, covered in dust and filth, many with bleeding or swollen faces.

'None of *us* will touch you,' murmurs the man behind her. She knows by his voice that he is smiling.

Each of the soldiers with flashlights opens one of the cell door's two padlocks. She is thrust forward into the black hole, surrounded by scores of other prisoners who stare at her with slack, unreadable expressions as the door is resecured behind her. She tries not to hyperventilate, she can't afford to, there isn't much oxygen in this air, and it might set off another panic attack, she's close enough already.

The floor is flat cracked concrete. The jagged walls and ceiling are marked with odd striations. The metal wall-thing in the middle of the chamber is a row of metal lockers that barely fit under the low ceiling. Their familiar appearance is surreal. A water pipe runs from the corridor ceiling into and along the other side of the room, where it feeds several head-high nozzles, all dark with rust. She sees and feels a ventilation shaft, a sighing draught carrying hot air from a metal grille in the floor directly in front of her to another in the ceiling.

The flashlights are switched off.

'Have a nice day,' a guard advises her mockingly. The men who brought her here walk away. Their boot-sounds and lamplight diminish down the corridor, leaving Veronica in darkness.

8

The air is so hot and stuffy, the stench so vile, that at first it is almost impossible to breathe. Veronica just stands gasping in the darkness as a surprised and speculative murmuring arises all around her. There is nothing she can do. Obviously the men who brought her expect her to be attacked by her fellow-prisoners. Maybe she should beg for mercy, or maybe that will show weakness; maybe she should try to act the haughty untouchable white woman, or maybe that will just provoke them. She reaches into the pocket of her cargo pants for her Leatherman; at least they didn't search her, at least she can try to defend herself, not that that will mean anything if they all rush her—

'Veronica?' a loud voice says, a familiar voice. 'Veronica Kelly?'

She gasps. 'Lovemore?'

A babble of Shona conversation breaks out. Then suddenly there is a strong hand on her arm. She flinches, but Lovemore's voice says, 'It's me. It's all right.'

She doubts that very much. 'What are you doing here?'

He speaks in a low voice, into her ear. 'We must be quiet. The guards speak English. Sometimes they listen in the dark. They captured me in Harare. They don't know I was with you, or they would have killed me. They only know I was a friend of Lysander's. They said they captured him. Have you seen him?'

She shakes her head, then remembers he can't see her even though their faces are almost close enough to touch. There are men all around her now, using all the available space, she feels limbs pressed against hers, it is weirdly like being at a rock concert. 'No. But I saw the missiles. They're just down the hall from here.'

'Izzit?' Lovemore considers. 'So close.'

'Who are all these other men?'

'Hostages. These are sons, brothers, uncles of powerful men. The women and children are in another cell. When Mugabe is gone Gorokwe will try to use them in negotiations to take power.

I don't believe it will work. I don't believe men in power care more for their sons and brothers than their power. I think there will be war. And it will happen as soon as Mugabe returns, before word of these kidnappings reaches him.'

Veronica remembers Lysander's warning: *Important people, powerful people, have begun to disappear. People have started whispering about death squads.*

'The day after tomorrow,' Veronica says. 'If Lysander was right. We have to try to get out of here.'

Lovemore grunts. 'The mice voted to bell the cat.'

Veronica leans towards Lovemore and whispers into his ear, 'They didn't search me. I've got tools.'

He stiffens. 'What tools?'

'A Leatherman. A phone. A lighter. Some cigarettes. My wallet, my money belt, they even left me my passport.'

'Izzit,' he breathes. 'Then maybe this ventilation shaft—'

He takes her hand and raises it upwards. The ceiling is low enough that she can easily touch its uneven surface. She feels her way along it, guided by the wispy air currents from below, until she finds the place where they disappear, a two-foot-square rusty grate in the ceiling. It is set solidly into the rock that surrounds it, appears to have been welded in place like the iron bars that blocked the main entrance. They'll clearly never get through that.

The shaft slopes down at about a thirty-degree angle; the grille in the concrete floor is three feet over from its counterpart on the ceiling. Lovemore has to talk men into moving off it. Veronica kneels on the ground. She can feel the hot air rising; looking into the shaft is like facing into a weak hairdryer. She grabs the metal bars and pulls. This grille is as solidly set in the concrete floor as its counterpart in the stone ceiling. She would need a real hack-saw, not the Leatherman. Brass padlocks are one thing; inch-thick metal bars are entirely another.

'Sorry,' she says. 'No good.' She casts about for ideas. 'Maybe we can rush them, next time someone comes in. There're like sixty of us, just four of them.'

'No,' Lovemore says, and he sounds alarmed. 'Four men with Kalashnikovs? They will not hesitate to shoot.'

'Then what?'

'They don't plan to kill us. Not all of us. They bring us water sometimes, enough to live. We must wait for opportunity.'

Veronica frowns. She feels certain they'll be waiting for ever. But he's right, there's no breaking out of this prison, not with what they have. 'Will these other men help? Have you told them what's going on?'

He hesitates. 'No. I fear one might be a spy. And they may help, but not with violence. These men are wealthy, educated. They have been beaten and tortured, they are weak and frightened. They will not risk themselves.'

'What—' Veronica swallows. 'What did they do to you?'

'I have suffered worse.'

'They're torturing Jacob.'

After a moment Lovemore says, 'If they will torture a white man, then they will kill him.'

'I know.'

Veronica sits beside Lovemore with her back to the uneven rock wall. She feels rubber limbed, overpowered by lassitude and despair. She vaguely wonders just how little oxygen there is in this air. The cell is sardine-packed but the rest of the men find a way to give her a little extra space. She is ashamed, now, that she thought they would attack her. Most seem to speak good English, and several have asked in halting voices who she is and why she is here. Her terse answer – that she is American, and she made an enemy of General Gorokwe – seems enough to satisfy their curiosity. Most of the cell's inhabitants seem too enervated for conversation. The absolute darkness is matched now by eerie silence.

It occurs to Veronica that, in a perverse and bloody way, she has almost succeeded at what they set out to do when they left Victoria Falls. She knows where the conspiracy is based, she

knows where the missiles are, she knows the details of Gorokwe's plan, that he almost certainly intends to shoot down
Mugabe when he lands in Harare the day after tomorrow.
There's only one small problem. It's almost funny, but she can't
laugh.

The longer she sits the more she feels acutely aware of the half-
mile of solid rock above her, as if she can feel its gravitational
pull. This cell feels more and more like a mass coffin. She starts to
tremble, and her breathing grows strained again, her heart begins
to lurch, she can feel another panic attack on the verge of
eruption, there is a faint humming in her ears—

No, not just in her ears, not just an artefact of her brain.
Veronica can actually feel the air throbbing with a low hum on
the edge of human hearing. Her panic is dissuaded for a moment
by surprised curiosity.

'What's that?' she whispers.

Lovemore sits up a little straighter, then says, 'The lift. Some
trick of acoustics. They are coming.'

They wait, listening intently. Soon they hear the dim rhythmic
slapping of rubber boots on stone. Lamplight flickers in the tunnel
outside, and the iron grid of bars begins to gleam. The sight of the
cell makes Veronica moan, it's easier coping in the darkness, but
she steels herself, makes herself sit up, pay attention and ignore
the gibbering panic in the back of her mind. This might be
important. The guards are coming, and a new man not in uniform
is with them.

As the guards aim their weapons at the crowd, and unlock the
doors, the newcomer begins to shout out a short phrase. He
repeats it several times before Veronica realizes it is a name.
Slowly a man emerges from the mass of prisoners and, shivering
with fear, approaches the door. He is escorted outside. Gorokwe's
man says something in Shona and a ripple passes through the
crowd.

'He says this man's father has agreed to the general's terms,'
Lovemore whispers, 'and so he is being released.'

Another name is called out. This time half a dozen men step forward. Veronica smiles despite herself. Gorokwe's man calls out a question, and apparently only one man answers it correctly. The others slink back into the mass. The selected man steps towards the open doorway, to freedom.

Gorokwe's man issues a curt command. The guards don't hesitate. The guns' muzzle flashes are much brighter than the lamplight, and in that enclosed space the gunshots are incredible, deafening. Veronica sees dark blotches appear as if by magic on the body of the man at the door, sees him twitch as if dancing, then collapse to the concrete floor like a shop-window dummy. He scrapes spastically at the ground for a few seconds, and then he is still. The floor beside him is badly scarred; one of the bullets struck the concrete floor and gouged a deep rut surrounded by a web of cracks and chips of concrete.

Veronica can barely hear Lovemore's translation of the words that follow. 'This man's family would not negotiate.'

Nobody makes any sound at all, it is as if everyone has gone mute. Gorokwe's man walks away, bearing the light with him. In the dwindling lamplight Veronica sees blood seeping from the body in the corner, filling and flowing down the cracks in the concrete floor.

Veronica is shocked, numb, half deaf, utterly drained, and so overwhelmed with terror and desperation that she can barely feel anything else at all; but as she stares at the cratered floor beside the dead man, an idea flickers to life in her mind.

She forces her way through the silent crowd of prisoners to the grid of bars that cover the ventilation shaft in the floor, kneels down and feels with her fingers. It's true that these bars are set in concrete. But that stray bullet revealed something about this concrete: it is weak, old and flaking. And only about an inch of it grips the grille.

Veronica draws out her Leatherman, unfolds its hardened steel, selects its sharp awl, grabs the tool in her fist and stabs it hard into the ground at the edge of the metal grate. There is a loud *chink*. She feels the concrete with her finger. A chip as big as her thumbnail has broken free.

'Lovemore,' she says, suddenly feeling strong again, rejuvenated by sudden hope. 'I think I've got something here.'

The other prisoners are playing their part almost too well: their loud babble is giving Veronica a headache. She can barely hear the sounds as Lovemore stabs the Leatherman again and again at the floor between the two of them. The noise and utter darkness are dizzying, disorienting. It takes her a few seconds to realize he's stopped.

She reaches out to survey the damage. The concrete around the edges of the grille has been reduced to less than half its initial depth, and flakes cover the nearby floor. Her hands encounter Lovemore's fists, wrapped around the iron bars, pulling as hard as he can. Veronica adds her strength to the effort. They gasp for air, but the grille doesn't move.

'Not yet,' Veronica groans.

'Harder,' Lovemore insists. 'Use your legs.'

She does, she pulls with all her might, as he does the same – and with a *crack* so loud Veronica fears the guards might have heard, the grate pulls free. The high-volume conversation around them dwindles for a moment as the prisoners realize what has happened; then the noise swells up again, this time with a jubilant tone.

Veronica feels around inside the now open shaft. It is walled by uneven rocks, and its thirty-degree angle will make it difficult to descend, but they have no choice. She takes a deep breath. She has never wanted to do anything less than to descend into this dark, narrow, slanted pit with no known bottom.

'We can't all go,' she says.

'They know. I have spoken with them. We will go first. Perhaps some of them will follow later, but they are not eager to go deeper into the mine.'

Veronica certainly understands that: she's not exactly eager herself. But it's that or throw herself on Danton's eventual mercy. If she can just get out of this mine, according to Lovemore they're near the Mozambique border, she can get out to there and seek help from someone, maybe get to South Africa, to the civilized world. Even being captured on an Interpol warrant will be better than this.

It occurs to her that maybe, just maybe, if they do somehow manage to escape this abandoned mine, it might not be too late to stop Gorokwe, to blow the whistle before Mugabe is murdered. Maybe she can turn Danton's weakness into a fatal error. By imprisoning her instead of killing her they have brought her into the vulnerable belly of the beast. Now she knows where the missiles are, and when the assassination will happen. If only that when was not too soon – but it is. Less than forty-eight hours. She'll be lucky to even get to a phone in that time, much less make somebody believe her. But she has to try. If they assassinate Mugabe, if Lysander was right, soon afterwards all Zimbabwe will erupt in a civil war that might kill hundreds of thousands. She can't really wrap her head around what that means, the sheer scale of the disaster beggars the mind; but Veronica thinks of that little girl who tried to ride with them on the ox cart, and tries to imagine a city full of little girls like that, all of them dead.

Descent into the slender ventilation shaft is awkward. The walls of rough-hewn rock are full of sharp stony protrusions; they serve as ledges and handles, but also jab and scrape. It is steep enough that initially Veronica props herself up with a foothold or handhold at all times, rather than risk sliding down the sharp rocks into Lovemore beneath her, and maybe sending them both tumbling to their deaths. She eventually settles on lying on her belly, allowing the grip of her body on the stones to keep herself from falling, and worming her way down in reverse. At least the ongoing physical effort helps to keep panic at bay. The air is thick with dust dislodged by their passage, and she has to breathe through her shirt. She seems to be moving faster than Lovemore, her feet keep connecting with his hands. Of course he is weaker: he was beaten and tortured before being left to languish in that nightmarish cell.

They have the Leatherman, her phone, her money belt and wallet, her cigarettes and lighter. It isn't much. Veronica turns on the phone only once while down-climbing, after half an hour, when the voices above are no longer audible. Green light blooms from its screen, enough to illuminate a narrow shaft continuing both up and down without any visible end. The sight is so horrifying she immediately switches the phone off and has to bite her lip until it bleeds to forestall another panic attack.

Veronica decides not to think about where she is, or about the future, near or distant. The present is all that matters, and in it she is climbing down. The future does not exist.

It gets steadily warmer as they descend, and her sweat-soaked hands begin to slip off the rocks. She is already desperately thirsty. At least there is a draught, hot air rising past them. She can't imagine where that air is coming from.

A small eternity seems to pass before Lovemore grunts, 'Floor.'

She follows him down to a flat surface that seems unnatural after their long descent. Lovemore is doubled over, panting for breath. This worries Veronica more than she lets on. Going down is easy compared to climbing up, and they may have descended as much as a kilometre below ground level. At least they haven't been intercepted.

She checks her phone. Nine p.m. Somewhere up above, night has fallen. They have thirty-six hours to try to avert a bloody civil war, and all they've succeeded in doing is going deeper into this mine with no idea how to get out. It's not going to happen, Veronica realizes, they're not going to be able to get the word out and save Mugabe, she doesn't even know who to call. She and Lovemore have to focus on saving themselves.

The phone's LCD seems incredibly bright in the absolute darkness of the mine. Its pale green glow illuminates another corridor with inset rail tracks, almost exactly like the level above. Veronica supposes there isn't a whole lot of room for originality in mine design.

'No signal?' Lovemore asks, with the ghost of a smile.

'Very funny.'

Veronica realizes she can look around at this corridor's low ceiling and narrow walls with something like equilibrium. Maybe her body has run out of the enzymes and chemicals required to manufacture a panic attack. Maybe this mine has served as involuntary exposure therapy. After the ventilation shaft this tight corridor seems almost spacious.

Lovemore's face and body are streaked with blood. He is wider and thicker than her, was less able to keep clear of the sharp stones of the shaft walls. None of the cuts is serious, but they worry her all the same; the opening and descent of the shaft seem to have consumed all his strength reserves, he looks worryingly frail and feeble.

'What do we do now?' she asks, and her voice is more frightened than she had intended.

Lovemore says, 'We must walk into the wind.'

She blinks. 'But . . . no, the wind's coming from below. We have to go up now.'

'I know something about mines. My father was a miner. They are built with ventilation circuits. As we go deeper, it becomes hotter.' She nods, wondering how deep they are right now, how close to the earth's molten mantle. 'Hot air rises, any schoolboy will tell you. This creates a pressure imbalance that brings cooler air down from somewhere else, somewhere outside. All we must do is keep walking into the wind, to the source of that air.'

It sounds good. As long as their escape isn't discovered, or the air doesn't get unbreathable, or the heat unbearable, or the climb up to the surface isn't too much for them or the exit isn't blocked. There are so many ways to fail. But at least they have a plan.

'How are you feeling?' she asks.

She sees his teeth but can't tell whether he's smiling or grim-
acing. 'I will be fine.'

Veronica isn't at all sure of that. 'Let's rest a little longer.'

'We have no time.'

'Five minutes won't make any difference.'

'With this air perhaps it will.'

He has a point. The air is now so thick and hot it feels like
breathing through a cigarette. If they stay too long at this level
oxygen deprivation might become a real issue, like altitude
sickness in reverse. And heat exhaustion is unquestionably a
danger.

'All right,' she says. 'Let's get going.'

They advance into the draught, much fainter in this wide
corridor than it was in the shaft, but still noticeable. Everything
looks green in the phone's LCD light. Walking fast is a relief after
slowly worming their way down the endless shaft in darkness, but
she has to slow down for Lovemore, who is limping. At one point
he bumps his head painfully on the ceiling; afterwards he walks
on exaggeratedly bent knees. They reach an intersection with an
equally wide and high corridor, but one without rail tracks. They
stand there for a moment, unable to determine from which
direction the stronger draught comes.

'The tracks must go to the main elevator shaft,' Veronica says.
'We can't go up there. Let's try the other way.'

Lovemore nods. He is now panting after every few steps he
takes, as if running rather than walking. They continue down this
corridor, moving with new hope; the wind is stronger here, and
noticeably cooler.

The corridor ends at a metal grille set in stone. Beyond the
grille, a circular shaft six feet across rises at a forty-five-degree
angle towards the sky. Cool air hurtles down into the mine.
Veronica thinks she tastes water in the air. It's a way out – except
for the solid metal grate that bars their way.

She examines this obstacle. It is not welded in place like the
ones up above. This one has two halves separately seated in the

stone walls; in the middle, their flat metal edges overlap and are bolted together. She unfolds her Leatherman and sets to work. Lovemore sits with his back to the corridor wall and concentrates on breathing.

There are only four narrow bolts. Two come out easily once she scrapes the rust off. The third requires a great deal more effort. But the fourth, near the bottom, will not budge, despite Veronica's increasingly frantic efforts. It appears to have rusted in place.

'Mother*fucker*,' she pants, staring at the grate. One rusted nut. That is all that stands between them and the path to freedom. But it will not move.

'There must be stairs,' Lovemore says hoarsely. 'In case of some disaster. There must be stairs.'

'If we can find them. Maybe they've been blocked. Or that exit's locked. And they'll probably take us right to Gorokwe's troops. Fuck. One fucking nut.'

'The top of this shaft may also be walled off.'

She winces. He's right. She stares venomously at the offending hexagonal hunk of metal. Then she reaches up to the top of the grate. Her previous removal of three bolts allows the two halves to pull away from each other and create a little V of space, just enough to wedge her fingers into. She pulls as hard as she can. Even with this leverage it doesn't feel much different from trying to rip an iron bar apart with her bare hands.

Veronica threads the fingers of her other hand into the grate, and then climbs up on to it, placing both her feet flat against the metal bars, supporting herself with her hands. She pushes with all the strength of her legs. At first nothing happens. Then there is a groaning sound – and then an unexpected *crack* – and suddenly the grate is open and Veronica has to flail about to avoid falling off as metal rattles on the floor. She hoped she might loosen the rusted nut; instead she has torn it right off its bolt.

'Marvellous,' Lovemore wheezes.

She drops back to the ground and pulls the two halves of the grate apart wide enough that she can squeeze between them. Then she looks up the wide ventilation intake shaft and wishes it wasn't so steep. They could maybe walk up a thirty-degree incline, like that they descended. This forty-five-degree shaft will have to be climbed with both hands. It will take them hours to reach the surface.

She says, 'Maybe there's another way out, but I'm thinking this is the only way we might actually escape.'

'Yes.'

'It's a long way up.'

'Yes.'

'Do you think you can climb all the way?'

Lovemore looks at her for a moment, then says, softly, 'If I must, I will.'

'I'm sorry,' Veronica says. 'I think you must.'

9

'Lovemore,' Veronica croaks. 'Look.'

He doesn't react.

'Look.' She grabs at him clumsily. 'Up.'

His head slowly turns upward, towards the distant blotch of . . . not light, exactly, but a different shade of darkness to what they have been moving through for hours.

'What is it?' he asks dully.

'I think it's the outside.'

At least the air is clean up here. That has been the only good thing about the climb. Their ascent has been far longer and more gruelling than Veronica expected. Her muscles are near collapse, her toes are covered in blisters, the skin on her hands has been ribboned by sharp rocks. Her blood- and sweat-wet fingers keep skidding away from handholds. This slanted six-foot-square shaft is far more dangerous than the smaller one they descended. Veronica's feet have slipped off footholds once, and Lovemore's twice. All three times they barely avoided tumbling to their deaths, and survival cost them several deep cuts. Her thirst is burning, ravenous, and the pebble she sucks on has ceased to help, the inside of her mouth feels as dry as paper. Lovemore seems in even worse condition. He has almost ceased to engage with the world.

'We're almost there,' she promises him. 'Just a little farther.'

'You go.'

'You first.' She wants to be below him in case he faints.

He sighs, takes two shivering breaths, then forces himself to resume his upward progress. Veronica climbs behind him. She is only dimly aware of her external pain. It pales next to her all-consuming thirst.

When she looks up next the blotch seems hardly larger. She wants to cry. *You can't spare the moisture*, she tells herself firmly. *Just climb. This will be over soon and you will forget this nightmare ever happened.*

Climbing a forty-five-degree slope is equally unlike rock climbing and walking erect; it requires locomotion on all fours, like an animal. Veronica tries to climb like a monkey. It actually seems to help a little. When she looks up next the blotch is noticeably larger, and definitely a paler shade of black than its surroundings. She remembers with something like despair that the exit is probably blocked by a grate, as at the other end of the shaft. If it has been welded in place she doesn't know what they will do. Lovemore certainly doesn't have enough strength to climb back down. Veronica doubts she does either.

Nothing they can do about it now. Above her, Lovemore is moving faster; proximity to the surface seems to have lent him new strength.

'It's open,' he grunts when they are only a hundred feet away.

She refuses to believe him, refuses to hope. But it's true. The shaft leads straight into open air. It isn't until they reach the edge that they realize why; the exit is in the middle of a sheer rock wall, directly above a wide river. The moon is clouded but there is enough light to see the boundary where the cliff meets the river twenty feet below. They can hear and smell the rushing water beneath them. Water. She has to hold herself back from simply throwing herself into the river and drinking deep.

'What do we do now?' Lovemore asks.

Veronica thinks. There aren't a whole lot of options.

'We rest, get some strength back,' she says. 'Then we jump. It doesn't look shallow.' She has no idea what shallow water looks like in darkness, but saying it makes her feel better. Then a horrible idea occurs to her. 'Wait. Are there crocodiles?'

'No,' Lovemore says. 'In the Zambezi, the Limpopo, yes. But not here.'

She sighs with relief.

'But I cannot swim.'

She stares at him. 'Really?'

'I'm sorry. I never learned.'

'Well, we can't climb back down. I was a lifeguard once.' She thinks back to when she watched children in the neighbourhood pool when she was sixteen. Not exactly the same as supporting a full-grown man in a powerful river at night. But she has no choice. 'Just trust me and don't panic, and I'll keep you up.'

After a second Lovemore says, 'I trust you.'

'Good.' Veronica looks at the water. She knows she should wait, gather her strength. But she doesn't think there's much left to gather, and she is overcome by a blinding urge to just get this over with. 'Fuck it. Follow me.'

She steps back down the shaft, lowers herself like a sprinter on blocks, then takes a stumbling running jump into the river. The fall is so terrifying she almost screams.

But the water is deep and cool and deliriously refreshing. Veronica is drinking from it even before her head breaks the surface. She has to pull away and remind herself not to drink too much too fast.

'Hurry!' she cries, floating in the strong current, trying to stay near the shaft entrance.

She is almost too successful; Lovemore nearly falls directly on to her. He comes up spluttering and thrashing, panicked despite her warnings, grabs Veronica's arm with a vice grip and drags her head down below the water. His body is convulsing like a landed fish, pulling them both deeper into the river. Veronica kicks as hard as she can but barely manages to get her head above water for another breath.

She fights to free herself but he is far too strong. Veronica gives up the struggle and allows him to pull her closer, wraps her other arm around him so she holds him from behind, and kicks again, with all the strength left in her legs. Their heads emerge from the river again for a few seconds. Lovemore is still thrashing uncontrollably.

'Calm down!' she orders him.

They fall back into the water. Then Lovemore goes limp, and his grip on her arm loosens. Veronica grabs him in a bear hug and pulls them back up above the water. It isn't easy treading water for two, Lovemore is dense with muscle, but she manages.

'Sorry, sorry,' he coughs.

'It's OK. Just hang loose.'

She can't tell whether the rushing sound ahead indicates rapids or a waterfall, but she knows they don't want to find out. They make clumsily for the shore opposite the mine. The river shallows into a pebbly bed, and they stumble on to rocky land. Above them she can see the outlines of trees against the clouds; thick, untracked African bush.

'Free,' Veronica says, almost disbelievingly, and collapses to the ground.

Now that her thirst is gone Veronica is bitterly aware of her hunger, and of the blisters, cuts and scrapes that cover seemingly her entire body. She tries to imagine what it would be like to be safe, well fed and pain free. It seems like an impossible dream.

Ahead of her Lovemore fights his way through the trackless bush. He staggers with every step, but Veronica isn't worried about him as she was in the mine. Freedom and water seem to have given him back some strength. She follows wearily in his

335

steps. Branches slap at her face, her soaked shoes squelch noisily on the slippery underbrush. To their left the sky is just beginning to shine with the dawn.

'What is it?' she asks, when he stops.

'A footpath.'

She has to squint to see it in the moonlight, a thin dirt path.

'There are many who live now in these hills,' Lovemore says. 'They come from the cities, they lose their homes to sickness or Operation Murambatsvina and they come here to live in the bush, as their grandparents did.'

'Do we follow it?'

'Yes.'

The trail is narrow, uneven and often impeded by roots and branches, but it's much better than fighting their way through dense forest. Veronica's breath grows ragged and her mind fogs with exhaustion, but she doesn't let herself stop, until Lovemore comes to a halt so suddenly she almost collides with him.

'What is it?' she asks.

'Be silent,' he whispers. 'Look. Up that *msasa* tree.'

Veronica follows Lovemore's gaze up to a tall, leafy tree that overhangs the path. There is something on one of its uppermost branches, she can't quite make it out in the dappled shadows, but she knows immediately, on some instinctive level, that she doesn't want to be any closer to it.

'Leopard,' Lovemore says softly. 'They leap on their prey from above.'

The tawny shape is immediately above the path. 'You mean if we kept walking—'

'More likely it is just sunning itself. It is very rare for them to attack humans.'

His actions are not nearly as confident as his words; he takes her hand and leads her in a wide semicircle around the predator. Veronica looks over her shoulder as they return to the trail, just in time to see the leopard stand and stretch with malevolent grace, and her breath freezes in her throat, but after stretching it lies back down again.

They continue, fuelled by adrenalin. The path leads upwards and then opens without warning on to a wide dirt road. To their right, the road crosses a wooden bridge, leading back towards the mine.

'That way to Mozambique,' Lovemore says, looking east, to where the road skirts a sheer ten-foot cliff.

'Does this road go to the border?' she asks.

'It goes near. Afterwards there are trails.'

'Let me guess. It's like this all the way. Steep hills and cliffs.'

'Yes.'

She sighs. 'Can we get there before they follow us? Do you think they'll track us?'

'Is Mozambique where you want to go?'

She is taken aback by the question. 'Where else?'

Lovemore considers. Then he says, 'Yes. You must go east. You must escape. But I will go back to the mine.'

'To the *mine*? Are you crazy? What for?'

'To try to stop them.'

'What? How?'

'I don't know,' Lovemore says. 'But I know they have made a mistake in bringing us here. They have brought us like vipers into their heart. We know they will attack tomorrow, we know their missiles are in that mine. Maybe I can find a weapon, and find the stairs into the mine. I must try. There will be war. Mugabe must go, but not like this. So many will die. I must at least try.'

Veronica tries to find the right words. 'I understand. I know what you mean, I'd want to try too if we had any chance at all. But please, don't be crazy. They've got guns, we've got nothing, we're on our last legs here. We can't stop them. It's too late, we don't have time. Mugabe's flight is probably already in the air.'

'You go to Mozambique,' he says. 'Escape. Tell the world.'

'I don't think I can get there without you.'

'I'm sorry. I can't leave my people.'

337

Veronica looks east, along the road that has been blasted through the hillside and curls beneath a sheer granite cliff. Then she looks west, towards the mine.

'We'll go and see,' she offers. 'If it looks like we can do something, we will. Maybe I can help. If not, if it just looks useless, we go to Mozambique.'

Lovemore looks at her for a long moment before he acquiesces.

The intersection where the dirt road meets the paved road seems deserted. A faint mist has risen here, making the hills around them seem ghostly, unearthly. Down the main road, they can see, half lost in the mist, the edge of the chain-link fence surrounded by the yellow mounds of discarded ore. They make their way cautiously, staying to the shoulder of the road, ready to leap into the bush at the slightest sound, but the hills are silent, not even a bird sings.

From the base of one of the great heaps of dirt they can see the low buildings and gravel parking lot of the mine. Four men guard the main entrance. Veronica and Lovemore are as far away from them as possible, and it's too misty to see well, but she thinks they are all carrying rifles. Otherwise the complex is deserted. The fence seems to be in good repair and surrounded by barbed wire everywhere.

'Your Leatherman,' Lovemore says to her.

She looks at him. His breath is still ragged. 'What are you going to do? Climb the fence, cut the wire, walk in and challenge Gorokwe to a duel?'

'The mineshaft. If we can destroy the elevator—'

'It's guarded,' she says. 'Even if you do, there'll be stairs out somewhere, and they'll be guarded too. You can't stop them.'

'I must try.'

She shakes her head. 'No. I won't let you do it.'

'Please. Give me the Leatherman. You go to Mozambique and tell the world everything that has happened. Please, Veronica. So many could die. Think of Rwanda. Imagine if it was your country. I must *try*.'

After a moment she swallows, nods, surrenders the Leatherman. He limps to the fence, and begins to climb. Veronica doesn't move. She looks out at the gate guards. They haven't noticed anything yet. Lovemore sways and almost falls as he climbs the fence, and its rattle as he rights himself seems to carry a terrifyingly long way, but the guards do not react. Once at the barbed wire he hangs on with one hand and begins to saw with the other. It looks awkward and incredibly difficult.

After only a short time he stops to rest. When he looks around and sees Veronica his eyes widen and he makes a shooing gesture. She stands up reluctantly. Then she looks past Lovemore and quickly drops back down to her belly. He turns and sees: the guards have noticed him. Two of them are coming.

Lovemore drops down from the fence, doubles over, assumes a hunched posture with his arms dangling right down to the ground, and runs away with a strange leaping gait. Veronica thinks he must be hurt, but once the mound of dirt is between him and the guards, he straightens back up, motions to her to follow, and rushes into the bush.

She runs after him, but not for long – he stops just far enough into the bush to be invisible, then moves along the bush line. His whole body is glistening with sweat, his breath is ragged, but he moves with grace. Veronica follows. He stops when they can see the guards again, walking across the parking lot. Their rifles are at the ready but they seem more suspicious than hostile.

Lovemore drops to his knees, takes a few deep breaths, opens his mouth and emits a loud, nasal hooting that echoes across the misty hillside. Veronica is so startled she nearly cries out. It does not sound like a human noise. Then he beats the bush around him with a kind of epileptic rhythm, and hoots again.

The guards stop walking, and peer carefully in their direction. After a brief discussion, they turn back to the gate.

'Baboon,' Lovemore explains. 'Very common.'

She nods.

339

'We can't enter the mine now.' His voice is grim, defeated. 'They will be watching carefully, to shoot and kill the baboons.'

She nods again. 'I'm sorry. We have to go to Mozambique. At least we can escape, and get the truth out.'

He doesn't argue. They stand and begin to walk again, moving back through the bush.

'Do you all know how to make perfect animal noises?' Veronica asks as they emerge on to the dirt road, thinking of Rukungu at the refugee camp. 'Is it part of the standard African grade-school curriculum or something?'

'No. I learned in Botswana, from the San. They live in the wild.'

She supposes Rukungu too has lived in the wild, in the untamed Africa she has hardly seen at all herself. Veronica suddenly wishes she had at least seen the gorillas in Bwindi before she was kidnapped. Living in Kampala it was easy to forget just how wild Africa is, full of baboons, crocodiles, elephants, leopards like the one they saw just now, perched on that tree branch above the path, waiting for prey to pass beneath—

Veronica's eyes widen. She stops, turns and looks back to the paved road that snakes its way through steep hills.

'Wait,' she says. 'I have an idea.'

Veronica stands shivering beside the paved road that winds its way up to the mine. The sun has risen, but it does not penetrate the thick mist that seems to have emanated from these hills. She tries to breathe hard, to warm herself up, but all her reservoirs of inner strength seem exhausted, the cool damp air seems to be sucking the heat directly from her blood. It isn't even that cold but her teeth begin to chatter. She looks around for Lovemore, but he has disappeared into the bush. She suddenly wants a cigarette, but they were soaked by the river. Her Zippo will still work; she considers trying to warm herself with it, but rejects the idea as futile.

Then she hears an engine in the distance. She straightens up. Her heart begins to pound, and her teeth cease to chatter. The vehicle is coming from below, moving towards the mine. She waits to see what it is. In the mist she can see only a few hundred feet, down to where the road meets a dirt tributary and then bends around the base of a sheer forty-foot cliff. If it's a jeep full of soldiers, then that does them no good – but no, it's a white hatchback, and the driver is unaccompanied by any passengers, it's almost perfect. A 4WD would be better, but this is hopefully good enough, and it's probably the best chance they're going to get.

Veronica takes a deep breath. Then she walks out into the middle of the road and begins to wave her arms at the driver, hopefully signalling him to stop. She feels a little ridiculous.

The hatchback, a Suzuki, stops in front of her. Veronica stays where she is for a moment, then sinks down to the ground, feigning a dramatic swoon worthy of a nineteenth-century novel. In her current state physical collapse is not hard to fake. After a moment the door opens and the driver steps out to investigate, amazed by the sight of a filthy and blood-streaked white woman lying in the middle of the road. Veronica moans loudly, hoping to cover any sound, as Lovemore steps out of the roadside foliage behind the man.

Despite his injuries and exhaustion Lovemore moves fast and catlike, the Leatherman gleaming in his hand. The driver senses something and turns to face him, but too late. The multi-tool's metal blade sinks into the man's gut. The man gasps with amazed shock. So does Veronica; this wasn't part of the plan. Lovemore withdraws the blade. The driver lifts his arms pathetically to protect his face, and opens his mouth to cry out, but as he does so Lovemore takes a quick step forward, ducking underneath and then into the man's upraised arms, and as their bodies press together, Lovemore finishes his motion by reaching the blade up and into the other man's throat.

For a moment the two of them seem frozen together, locked in place. Then Lovemore steps calmly away, and the driver claps his hands to his neck to try to staunch the pulsing fountain of blood.

Veronica thinks with distant horror of Derek's murder. Lovemore grabs the man and pulls him off the road and into the woods as he topples to the ground. There is blood everywhere, so much blood Veronica can almost taste its rich iron scent.

'Hide the blood,' Lovemore snaps at her. 'Cover it with dirt.'

She numbly follows the command while he hides the body in the bush. A minute later he is back on the road, wearing the man's trousers. They are too short for him.

'You said you weren't going to hurt them,' she says helplessly.

'We can't afford the danger. He went through the checkpoints. He must have been going to the mine.'

'How can you know that? The road goes past the mine too. How can you be sure?'

'Get in. Please. We have no time.'

Getting the Suzuki hatchback up the steep dirt road is easy enough. Getting it through the twenty feet of bush that leads up to the cliff is surprisingly not too difficult either. The ground is rocky enough that the vegetation here is mostly bush, trees big enough to stop its progress are few and far, and in first gear the Suzuki's tyres are more than equal to the uneven dirt and underbrush. All the same Veronica is glad Lovemore is driving.

As they pass through the bush there is a sudden rustle of motion up above them, and Veronica leaps with alarm as a series of loud nasal snorts echo through the air – but it is only a small family of monkeys, expressing their displeasure at this human invasion before they move away. Veronica smiles ruefully.

When they reach the top of the overlook, about fifty metres square of cracked but flattish rock, the seething sun in the eastern sky is beginning to burn away the early morning mist. Lovemore halts the Suzuki at a suitable-seeming location, hidden from where the asphalt road curves directly beneath the cliff.

'You really think this might work?' Veronica asks, breathless.

Lovemore says, simply, 'I don't know.'

The more she thinks about it the more she dares to think that they actually have a chance. A single and desperate chance, but that's much better than none at all. Their capture has brought them into the heart of the conspiracy, and because of that, because of Danton's mercy, they know enough to be dangerous. They know where the missiles are, and they know they will leave today and be taken west, to Harare airport, where Mugabe will touch down in less than twenty-four hours.

But most of all, their enemies are hamstrung by their secrecy. General Gorokwe may command hundreds or even thousands of troops, but Veronica is certain that the number of people who know exactly what is meant to happen to President Mugabe today is very small. Gorokwe, Susan, Danton, Athanase, Casimir, a handful of faraway Americans; perhaps a few more trusted lieutenants; and no one else. No one but herself and Lovemore. And Jacob and Lysander, if they are alive. In her secret heart she doubts it.

Veronica is no longer cold. She is burning with rage and anticipation. Maybe their escape has already been discovered, maybe they are already being hunted, maybe they will soon be recaptured and killed, but right now she doesn't care. Right now this solitary hope of vengeance or justice, or both, seems worth any price.

The road beneath describes a U-shape around the cliff face. From one end of the U, they can see for a few hundred metres to the east, towards the mine. At the other end, the cliff is sheerest, and the road runs closest to the wall of rock. Lovemore watches from the cliff edge while Veronica waits beside the Suzuki.

She hears an engine, and tenses – but it is coming from the other direction. She looks down on the road and sees a share-taxi, a pale minivan stuffed with people, climb laboriously up the road beneath them, then round the U and disappear. Moments later Lovemore stands up – but then shakes his head and drops back

343

down again, and a nondescript gunmetal Toyota, not nearly big enough to hold the missiles, drives past.

Then Lovemore stands up again, and this time he starts back towards the Suzuki; and as he steps away from the cliff, he nods meaningfully. Veronica hears an engine. No, two engines. And Lovemore is holding up two fingers.

'Shit,' she mutters under her breath. She had hoped for only one car. That would make sense. They are on a clandestine mission to assassinate a president, what are they doing driving in a convoy, have they never heard the phrase *covert operation*? But apparently there are two vehicles.

Veronica takes a deep breath. Her stomach is suddenly tight and squirming. The Suzuki's engine is already purring, and its gear-shift rests in neutral. She kneels next to its open door, reaches inside, pushes the clutch down with one hand and guides the stick into first gear with the other. Lovemore comes around the car and crouches in front of her, peering over the cliff edge.

'Say when,' Veronica hisses.

The approaching engines grow louder and clearer as they round the bend. Surely she has to do it now, now, any longer will be too late, they will get away, and this is their only chance. Every instinct screams at her to go, tells her that Lovemore doesn't know, he's waiting too long, he can't judge how much time it will take, she has to trust her own gut, not his—

Veronica makes herself wait for Lovemore's signal. He can see and she can't.

'Now,' he breathes.

She releases the clutch as smoothly as she can. The Suzuki shudders but lurches successfully into first gear, leaves Veronica and Lovemore behind as it crosses the few feet to the edge, then noses over the cliff and unceremoniously disappears.

A half-second later an almighty *crash* erupts from the road, followed by the ear-torturing scraping sounds of metal and concrete; a less loud, but somehow satisfying, crumpling *thud*; and then another; and then a short, oddly rhythmic series of

344

bumping noises. It is all over by the time Veronica and Lovemore poke their heads over the cliff edge to see.

It is immediately apparent that their four-wheeled missile has missed its target.

10

As far as Veronica can tell from the skid marks and trail of debris, the falling Suzuki smashed nose first into the road about ten feet in front of the black Land Rover. The Land Rover hit the carcass of the Suzuki, then skidded across the road and away from the cliff, taking the Suzuki with it, until both collided with a big tree and their intermingled remains bounced halfway back on to the road again. Whatever vehicle was following the Land Rover collided with this mangled wreckage, spun off the road and tumbled down the steep slope, scraping and flattening a rough trail through the vegetation and small trees beneath the road before disappearing into denser bush. The third collision knocked the Suzuki and Land Rover back to the edge of the road, which, amazingly, is still navigable, although dusted with shards of twisted metal and broken glass. The air above this debris is warped with sizzling heat.

Veronica stares amazed and triumphant at this field of wreckage and fragments. It reminds her a little of the scrapyard in Kampala. She can smell oil and seared metal. It's hard to believe that she and Lovemore caused all this destruction themselves, just by sending a small car over a forty-foot cliff. It looks like a bomb has gone off. There is something beautiful about it. She has a new and sudden understanding of the allure of wanton destruction.

'We must go down,' Lovemore says. 'We must be certain.'

Veronica knows it is dangerous, but part of her actually wants to inspect her demolition handiwork in greater detail. They scrabble back through the bush to the dirt road and down to the asphalt. The naked blade of the Leatherman glints in

Lovemore's fist. He cleaned it after killing the Suzuki's driver, but it is still spotted with blood.

The Land Rover is upside down, and crumpled on all sides, but surprisingly intact. She doesn't recognize the driver, or the uniformed man in the passenger seat, both of whom lie motionless. But the two men in the back are Casimir and Athanase. They were not wearing seat belts. Blood flows freely from their heads, jagged bone protrudes from Athanase's arm, and they lie slumped together on the ceiling of the inverted Land Rover, but Veronica can tell by the movement of their chests that both are still alive.

She walks around the vehicle. The tank has ruptured, and gasoline is trickling out from the Land Rover and down the slope, forming little pools and rivulets. Its occupants are lucky nothing has struck a spark. The smell of oil is intense. The back window is intact, and Veronica sees two shining metal containers within, etched with Cyrillic inscriptions. She looks up at Lovemore. Then, almost in slow motion, her hand dips into a side pocket of her cargo pants and emerges holding her Zippo lighter.

He nods. They back away from the ruins of the Land Rover to the shelter of a nearby tree. She sees Casimir, the man who murdered Derek, begin to stir within, to disentangle himself from Athanase. Veronica ignites the flame of her Zippo and tosses it gently, underhand, towards the shimmering pool of gasoline just outside the Land Rover's ruptured gas tank.

It's not like Hollywood, the vehicle does not explode, but the gas goes up immediately with a loud *whoosh*. Heavy, black smoke billows up, quickly obscuring the Land Rover. Even at this distance the fire is searingly hot and after only a few seconds they have to move farther away. It occurs to Veronica that there are missiles full of high explosive within the Land Rover. She wonders whether fire alone will be enough to set them off.

'We have to hurry,' she says. 'Come on.'

She leads Lovemore through the bush, following the trail of flattened bushes and broken trees. The vehicle is a black BMW, and it lies propped at a forty-five-degree angle against a big tree with its tyres in the air. It is not as battered as the Land Rover, and all its windows are intact. Veronica supposes they're bullet-proof. All its air bags have deployed. Again she doesn't know the driver, but she recognizes Susan in the passenger seat by her long blonde hair, now blood streaked. The passenger door is a dented concavity. There is no one else in the car. One of the back doors has crumpled shut, but the other has been opened.

'Gorokwe,' Lovemore says.

Veronica says, 'Danton.'

'They will have weapons.'

'Do you want to go?'

'No. We will never have another opportunity like this.'

He opens the driver's door. The driver twitches and groans. Lovemore thrusts the Leatherman up through the driver's ribcage, into his heart. This time Veronica doesn't protest; she just watches as Lovemore draws a gleaming pistol from the driver's belt and turns to look at her. She nods and wonders where he learned to kill.

There are no trails apparent anywhere in this bush, just thick bushes, tangled branches, tall grass and trickling rivulets. Perfect territory for hiding. Impossible territory for finding anyone. But Danton and Gorokwe don't have much of a head start, and they must still be dazed from the collision. Veronica and Lovemore stop and listen. They hear nothing but the morning wind through the branches.

'I learned tracking from the San, but that was in desert,' Lovemore says in a low voice. 'I don't know if I can follow them in this bush.'

'We don't need to,' Veronica says, as understanding dawns. 'We just need to think like them.'

He looks at her. 'What do you mean?'

'They're not bush people. They won't try and escape through the forest. They know they've been attacked, so they'll run away for a few minutes to get away from the car, but then they'll go back up to the road and carjack the next vehicle that comes along. Just like we did.'

'Yes,' Lovemore says.

He gives her the Leatherman. Veronica is amazed by how steady her own hands are as she takes it. She looks over at Susan's slumped form; abandoned by Danton and her lover the general, left here to die. Veronica considers for a moment. Then she turns and follows Lovemore.

They climb diagonally through the thick bush, moving towards the road and away from the fiercely burning Land Rover. Veronica supposes the missiles aren't going to explode, or they would have by now. Military explosives probably need some kind of electronic trigger or something to blow up. Her adrenalin rush is beginning to wane, and she is weak, exhausted, and covered with cuts and blisters. Lovemore is limping slowly again, and twice he slips and staggers, but she is moving more slowly still, he is a good thirty feet ahead, almost out of sight. Veronica opens her mouth to call on him to slow down.

Then a loud *crack* echoes through the bush. For an instant Veronica is taken back to that moment in the Bwindi Impenetrable Forest. But this time she knows what the sound is: a gunshot, very near. Lovemore jerks forward, and droplets of blood fly through the air as he falls to the ground – but he hits rolling, and as the second shot is fired, from just behind and to the left of Veronica, he disappears behind a thick bush.

In her dazed weakness she is too slow to react. A long, strong arm wraps around her neck from behind. She whimpers as searing metal is pressed up against her head, a gun barrel hot from recent use. An African voice, General Gorokwe's voice, orders her, 'You drop the knife or you die.'

Veronica struggles for air, tries to look around. Gorokwe's forearm across her throat is so tight that she can barely move her head, but out of the corner of her eye she sees Danton, crouched behind a tree. His eyes are wild, he is panting like a dog, and one side of his face is covered with rivulets of blood; he suffered a head injury in the crash.

348

'*Drop it*,' Gorokwe orders.

She briefly considers trying to stab him, but he'll shoot her, her only value right now is as a human shield. She lowers her arms – then lobs the Leatherman into the bush towards Lovemore, rather than drop it for Danton to use.

Gorokwe grunts with anger and slams the base of his gun into the side of Veronica's head. She actually sees stars, her knees buckle, only his arm tight around her throat keeps her upright. She can't breathe, he's crushing her windpipe, the world around her is going hazy. She doesn't even have the strength to struggle. When he loosens his grip long enough for her to draw a single rattling breath she slumps halfway to the ground before he catches her and draws her back up, this time holding her under her arms instead of around her neck.

Gorokwe shouts out something in Shona. Veronica suspects it is a threat to kill her if Lovemore does not show himself. Lovemore does not respond. Her head hurts like fire. Gorokwe's legs are both between hers, she can't kick backwards at his groin. She could try stamping on his feet, but he will just kill her if she becomes too much of a problem. Instead she just lets herself go limp and closes her eyes to slits, pretending to have been knocked out by that blow.

Gorokwe grunts and moves forward towards where Lovemore disappeared, muscling Veronica's dead weight along with him, keeping her body before him. The general advances slowly into the bushes, following Lovemore's blood trail, keeping Veronica before him, holding her easily with one arm; his strength is incredible.

There is no sound except for Gorokwe's footsteps on the slippery undergrowth. Veronica hopes Lovemore had the presence of mind to set some kind of ambush, to double back on his trail – but it doesn't seem likely, he is clearly bleeding badly, and he was already weak.

Something rustles in the bush not far ahead. Veronica manages to keep herself from tensing. The concussion makes it very easy to feign unconsciousness. She looks at the noise, hoping it is a bird or a monkey, but she can't see anything move, and that means it must be Lovemore. He's maybe twenty feet away. If he shoots, he'll almost certainly hit Veronica and give away his location; maybe he's a crack shot but he's badly wounded, he won't hit Gorokwe except by freak chance.

Veronica, still hanging like a rag doll, gives the thumbs-up sign in what she hopes is a surreptitious way, and hopes Lovemore understands.

Two shots blast out from the forest, two flashes from only about twenty feet away. The sounds are overwhelming but Veronica was half hoping for them; she manages to keep hanging limp. Nothing happens. Either Lovemore missed entirely or he never intended to hit.

Then Gorokwe reaches his gun out over Veronica's shoulder, aiming at Lovemore, and Veronica finally goes into action.

She grabs his gun arm with both hands, shoving it upwards as he fires. The recoil ripples through her as she bites into his bicep as hard as she can and twists her own body towards him. She feels herself snarling like an animal. As his blood fills her mouth she manages to rotate her body further so her legs are between his, and as he fires again, again into the air, Veronica brings her knee up as hard as she can. Gorokwe grunts and folds forward into her. She doesn't resist, she falls backwards and pulls him with her, so they both topple into the bush, and the gun goes off a third time right next to her head. Then he punches her with his free arm so hard that she can't help but let him go. He is kneeling on top of her, aiming the gun at her face, and she is stunned, she can't move.

Then the general's whole head snaps hard to the side, and blood begins to gout from it, and he goes limp and falls off her.

Lovemore lurches into view, holding his gun with one hand. The other, soaked in blood, is clamped over his stomach. He keeps the gun aimed at Gorokwe's fallen body.

'It's OK,' Veronica manages. 'It's over. He's dead.'

She doesn't need to check for the absence of a pulse. There is a gaping, dripping exit wound in the side of Gorokwe's head.

Lovemore drops to his knees. Veronica sits up. She is almost deaf in one ear, and her head hurts. She gingerly disentangles Gorokwe's weapon from his fingers, thinking of Danton; they can't leave it lying around. Then she turns to Lovemore. 'Keep pressure on it. Let me see.'

She reaches around behind him and feels with her fingers. He stiffens and groans as she touches the ragged edge of the exit wound. Of course she shouldn't have done that, her hands aren't clean, but it hardly matters now, his wounds are already filthy. She puts down Gorokwe's gun, pulls the general's shirt off and ties the bloody rag around Lovemore's waist. It isn't much but it will have to do.

'Keep pressure on,' she instructs him. 'Both front and back. If you don't lose too much blood you're going to be fine. It'll hurt like hell but you'll be OK, we should have time to get you to a hospital.'

He nods weakly.

'Can you get up to the road?'

'If I must.'

She picks up Gorokwe's gun again and walks back into the bush.

Danton is where she left him. He stares at Veronica wide eyed as she approaches.

She smiles thinly, keeps the gun trained on him, keeps her distance. 'Expecting someone else?'

His jaw works but no words come out.

'What's the matter, Danton? Everything not going according to plan? Does it seem like all of a sudden your daddy's money really doesn't matter so much?'

'Please,' he manages.

'Please what?'

'Please don't shoot me. I let you go. I told them not to touch you. All I wanted was to save lives.'

'That's such a lie,' she says, furious. 'Being rich wasn't good enough, you wanted to be powerful, you wanted to be a big man. That's all this was ever about.'

'Maybe you're right. But I wanted to help people, I really did. I thought we would help people. It just all started going wrong somehow. I didn't know how. I wanted to get out but it was too late, don't you understand? I couldn't get out. They would have killed me. I was a prisoner just like you.'

'Where's Jacob?' she asks.

'I'll talk. I'll talk to CNN, the *New York Times*, whoever, I'll tell everyone everything. I've got names, dates, Veronica, you won't believe who's involved in this. It wasn't just me, it was never my idea, they came to me for help. I'll testify against them all.'

'We don't need your testimony,' Veronica says. 'Remember what you told me? "Certain revelations will come to light. Everyone will be exposed. I'm the opposite of expendable." You remember saying that, when you were fucking gloating?'

'Please,' he begs. 'Don't do this.'

'Where's Jacob?'

'Please. I'm sorry. He didn't talk. Not until it was too late. I didn't want to, I said we should let him go. I'm sorry, Veronica, I'm so sorry. Please. You won't do this. I know you won't do this. You're a good person.'

'That was before I met you,' Veronica says bitterly.

She aims the gun at her ex-husband's heart and pulls the trigger.

11

'She's awake,' a woman says.

'Ms Kelly?' a man's voice asks.

She opens her dazed eyes to a well-kept hospital room. Everything is clean and white. She is connected to an IV and a vital-signs monitor, one she recognizes, an old DRE model she used to work with in San Francisco General. There are two black women in nurse's uniforms standing attentively near the bed, and a tall, handsome, white-haired white man in a sharp suit.

Veronica struggles for some memory to connect her to this scene and fails. 'Where am I?'

'Johannesburg,' the man says. 'Milpark Hospital. You were medevacced here last night from Mutare. You probably don't remember that, I'm told you were under sedation for the better part of three days.'

'What . . . what happened?'

He gives the nurses a look. They reluctantly depart.

Veronica lifts her head, almost all she can manage right now, and looks around. 'Wait. Where's Lovemore? What happened to Lovemore?'

'He's next door.' The man grimaces. 'They threw him in as a kind of sweetener, I suppose. It took no end of negotiation to get the two of you out of there. At first they were going to hang you.'

'Hang me? For . . . for *what*?'

'Attempted assassination. But then, luckily for you, a series of rather embarrassing files began to turn up at BBC and CNN and al-Jazeera, it's been the lead story for a good two days now and shows no signs of stopping. You can see it for yourself after I leave. Although I suppose you already know the whole story, don't you?'

She starts to shake her head and quickly thinks better of it. 'Not all of it.'

'We're still amazed ourselves. After that, I guess Mugabe decided you didn't quite fit into all the international outrage, and it was in his best interests to jump on that bandwagon rather than keep pointing the finger at you. Or maybe he's just grateful you saved his life. It still wasn't easy to get you out of there. Back-channel negotiations and briefcases full of money, not that you ever heard me say that, because of course we don't negotiate with fascist dictators.'

Veronica tries to remember what happened. She remembers shooting Danton, that actually happened, it wasn't a dream. She remembers waiting by the side of the road with Lovemore, both of them shivering in the warm sun, barely conscious. She remembers the pick-up truck that appeared on the road, full of sturdy labourers with picks and shovels, and the way they lifted her so gently into the back of the truck, as if she might break. After that, nothing. They must have taken her to hospital in Mutare. She hopes they took Danton's wallet from her, there were hundreds of US dollars in it.

'Who are you?' she asks.

'Stanton. Deputy chief of mission at the embassy here.'

'OK. What's going to . . . what happens next?'

'Nothing, until they're ready to discharge you. Doctors say that won't be for a few days yet. You don't need to make any decisions until then.'

'Veronica,' Lovemore says.

His voice is weak but clear. His torso is swaddled in bandages but otherwise he looks fine. Veronica still feels weak and dizzy when she walks, and she's still recovering from exhaustion, the concussive blow to her head, and the multitudinous little wounds she suffered during their escape from the mine, but she can feel herself regaining strength with every passing hour.

'Lovemore. Good to see you. How are you?'

'The doctors here are excellent.'

'They should be. Johannesburg, world capital of gun violence, they must have plenty of practice. Maybe I should try to get a job here. I've gotten some good gunshot experience in the last' – she calculates, and is amazed by how little time has passed since that day in Bwindi – 'few weeks.'

Lovemore doesn't answer.

'What are you going to do when you get out?' she asks.

'I have no passport. I expect they will send me back to Zimbabwe.'

'Do you want to go back?'

His face clouds. 'No. I would stay in South Africa if I could. There is hope here.'

'Is that so. How about Uganda?'

'Uganda?'

'I'm going to go back to Uganda.' Veronica had not been certain of this until this moment. 'I'm going back to Kampala. I'm going to start a school. A nursing college. I bet I could work something out where you could come with me.'

'I don't know anything about Uganda.'

'It's a good place. Or it can be. There's hope there, anyways, definitely. And I'm sure I can scare up enough money to start up a school. I bet the US government will be willing to help. And anyways a certain notoriety never hurt any fund-raising. Heck, I can sell my story to the British tabloids. Whatever. It won't be easy, I'll need help, but after this last month, you know what, I bet it'll seem like a piece of cake.'

After a moment Lovemore says thoughtfully, 'Pygmies.'

Veronica blinks, caught off guard. 'What?'

'That's what I know of Uganda. There are pygmies there. I've heard they know the jungle as the San know the desert.'

'Yes, I guess so.'

He says, 'I would like to see them.'

She smiles. 'Well, I think that can be arranged. Is it a deal?'

'Yes.'

They shake hands very seriously.

'You don't want to go back to America?' Lovemore asks. 'In Zimbabwe there is nothing for me. There is no hope. But I thought there was everything in America.'

Veronica hesitates. She imagines going back home, back to a world of shopping malls, freeway traffic, Internet dating, air conditioning, office jobs, mortgage payments and parking meters.

The idea repels her. If she goes back the rest of her life will seem hollow and plastic, a vacant shadow.

How ironic that Africa is called the dark continent. Even the sun here is so much brighter.

'Not for me,' Veronica says thoughtfully. 'Not any more. I think what I want is here.'

Epilogue

'There you go,' Veronica says. 'Home sweet shipping container. But you can't beat the view.'

'You certainly can't,' Tom says, amazed. 'That's the bloody Nile down there, isn't it?'

'It is indeed. You can swim in it, there's a trail that goes down, but watch the currents. There's a Class Five rapid around the bend.'

'Worse than the one you went through at the mine?' Judy asks.

Veronica chuckles. 'I don't know and I have no desire to find out.'

'And this is your school?' The British woman looks around at the cleared half-acre plot surrounded by thick greenery. A dozen metal shipping containers surround a single one-storey wooden building. A Land Cruiser and a Pajero are parked by the red dirt road that leads south to Jinja proper.

'Welcome to the Jinja School for Nurses,' Veronica says. 'You wouldn't believe how much cheaper it is to have a shipping container delivered than a classroom built, and really, they're almost as good. One real building for headquarters, five classrooms, three students' quarters, one staff quarters, the ablution block next to the well there, one for storage, and our house.' She points out each in turn. 'We've got thirteen students enrolled already, but only four staying here, handy for you, leaves one container free as a guest house. Five of them actually live in Kampala and commute here every day, ninety minutes each way. They get Sundays off but you'll see them all tomorrow.'

'You've built all this in one year,' Judy says, impressed. 'No, less, it was one year today we were rescued, and I gather you were quite busy foiling dastardly plots for the first month of that!'

Veronica smiles sheepishly as Tom and Judy laugh.

'We were so sorry to hear about Jacob,' Judy says, suddenly serious. 'And such a pity about Susan too. So hard to believe.'

Veronica can't find it in herself to feel any sympathy for Susan. 'More of a pity about Dr Murray. You know he came back to Africa after he was acquitted? He's in Nairobi now? It was all his plan, I think. And Strick only got ten years. They let him plea-bargain so he wouldn't tell secrets in public. They both should have gotten death.'

A brief, awkward silence falls.

'But what you've done here,' Tom says, looking around, 'it's bloody amazing, it really is. Can't have been easy.'

Veronica sighs. 'It's a lot of work. There's so much left to do. The well isn't up to much, we need to start piping water up from the river, but for that we need more power, and the solar panels barely keep us going. Jinja has good reliable power, there's a hydro station just south where the Nile meets Lake Victoria, but you wouldn't believe the hoops you have to jump through to get connected. Then the Internet, we've got it over a mobile-phone card right now, it works but it's so slow, almost useless for classes, we have to get a satellite dish. And we want to paint all the containers with different murals, start a garden, get more medical equipment, we've got barely enough, get more teachers, we've only got two right now, so I'm teaching classes even though I haven't practised in eight years, the students keep catching me making embarrassing mistakes, and of course fund-raising, we've gotten some good publicity but we still spend half the time not knowing where our next shilling is coming from, and then the government wants to *tax* us—' She stops. Tom and Judy are laughing again. 'What?'

'It's just all so familiar,' Judy manages. 'You sound just like we did when we were starting the business.'

'Bollocks,' Tom says cheerfully. 'She sounds like we did just last week. It's good to be busy, isn't it?'

Veronica blinks, a little surprised, she hasn't really had time to think about it. 'I suppose it is. But listen, drop your bags off, take a shower, it's a solar heater so the water's really only warm in the day, we'll go down to the river and have a beer, then after lunch we'll take you into Jinja, it's a lovely little town, much nicer than Kampala.'

'That sounds like a cunning plan.' Tom picks up their bags.

'To the honeymoon suite, husband!' Judy orders.

'Bloody hell,' he mutters with mock frustration. 'I knew I shouldn't have married you.'

'Too late now, innit? Get those bags inside, husband. Chop chop!'

Chuckling, they disappear into the shipping container.

Veronica walks over to the ablution block. 'Is the shower working again?' she calls out.

Rukungu appears in the door. 'Yes.'

Both his voice and his face are devoid of all expression. Veronica pauses. She doesn't know what to do about Rukungu. Since Lydia's death he has seemed more automaton than man. She feels guilty for making him work, the more so since he works like a horse without complaint. But it's probably best for him to keep busy. 'Maybe you could start digging out the garden, then?'

She expects a dull yes, but Rukungu hesitates, looks thoughtful.

'What is it?' she asks hopefully. This is more life than he's shown in weeks.

'The place you chose for the garden,' he says eventually. 'It is not a good place. The soil is bad. The sun is wrong.'

'Well – yes, maybe so. I'm not a farmer. Where do you think?'

He glances to the south-east corner of their property.

'Wherever you think is best,' she says. 'Were you a farmer?'

'When I was young,' Rukungu says quietly.

He walks away to the south-east. Veronica watches as he kneels and begins to dig with his hands, crumble the dirt between his fingers, inspect the soil. She still knows very little about

359

Rukungu's past; she hasn't wanted to ask, and he hasn't wanted to tell. Maybe one day.

She enters the ablution block to wash her hands, and catches sight of herself in the mirror above the sink. She sees lines on her face around the corners of her mouth, the beginnings of wrinkles. Well, at least they're smile lines. There are far worse fates. She of all people ought to know.

Veronica walks outside and sees a familiar figure appear on one of the several bush trails that lead on to their property. He holds a bulging jute sack. She jogs up to him and kisses him.

'You're back already,' Lovemore says, smiling. He reaches down, picks her up, continues with Veronica in his arms.

'Did they have everything?' she asks.

He nods to the sack dangling beneath her. 'Pineapples, pocho and Mrs Katumba's hot sauce. I don't know why you want to serve this to our guests, we can get chicken or beef in Jinja—'

'Oh, they'll get a kick out of it,' she reassures him. 'Trust me.'

As Lovemore carries her back towards their home, Veronica looks around at their land, at their school, tries to imagine it through Tom and Judy's eyes, as if she is seeing it for the first time. She is not disappointed.

'I like this,' she says thoughtfully. 'This is a good place. I like it here. I like who I am here. Do you know what I mean?'

He nods.

'Good. Then let's stay for ever.'

Lovemore raises his eyebrows. 'For ever is a long time.'

Veronica smiles. 'We'll see,' she says. 'We'll just see.'

Acknowledgements

As ever, I must begin by thanking my super-agent, Vivienne Schuster of Curtis Brown UK; her compatriots Betsy Robbins and Stephanie Thwaites; and her partner Deborah Schneider of Gelfman Schneider in NYC.

I spent the autumn of 2005 wandering from Nairobi to Cape Town, and the list of those I must thank for their aid in that research expedition is long: Chong & Andrea, and Jorge & Jo, for the crash space and the Lariam; Linda Tom, for the UNICEF connections; Gunnar Hillgartnar and Robert Kihara, in Nairobi; PK & Shirray, in Jinja; Brad and Delphine Mulley, in Goma; and Heather Davis, for connecting us; Jolly Boys, in Livingstone; my aunt and uncle Amalia and George, in Zimbabwe; my guide Lovemore, in Bulawayo; Brenda, Chantal, Courage, George, Grace, Naomi, Prakesh, and everyone else, at Small World Backpackers in Harare – long may you stay an oasis in madness; George Kantsouris, and everyone, at the Ndundu Lodge in the Vumba; Clan Archibald – my cousins in Johannesburg; Gavin Chait, in Cape Town.

The rest of my research consisted of reading far too many books to list here. I would like to particularly praise Redmond O'Hanlon's *Congo Journey* and Ryszard Kapuscinski's *The Shadow of the Sun* as the two finest books ever written about modern Africa. Michela Wrong's *In the Footsteps of Mr. Kurtz* and Lawrence Harte's *Introduction to GSM* were also particularly helpful.

Thanks to my family and friends, for indulging my idiosyncratic lifestyle.

And finally, I am profoundly grateful to my fantastically

wonderful editor Alex Bonham at Hodder & Stoughton, without whose patience and careful guidance this book would most certainly not exist.

Jon Evans
www.rezendi.com